THE WITCH WHO TRADES WITH DEATH

All witches must serve the cruel and immortal Emperor Yamueto. Upon discovery of her powers, Khana was ripped away from her desert home at thirteen years old and enslaved as a concubine. After years in service, her only friend in the palace is brutally murdered for supplying her forbidden birth-control, and Khana must make her escape. But not before accidentally discovering the secret of Yamueto's power and immortality – he has been making deals with Death. And now, thanks to a twist of fate, so is she.

Armed with new magic that she doesn't fully understand, Khana flees to a small mountain town. Although she tries to keep her identity a secret, Khana's powers are soon discovered after rescuing a dying soldier. News of her abilities starts to spread, putting a giant target on her back. And Yamueto is not the forgiving kind.

Khana's magic and courage are put to the ultimate test when she is finally forced to stop running and fight back. But every deal she makes with Death takes another piece of her soul, and there's only so much that Khana can give before turning into the very monster she's trying to destroy.

C. M. Alongi

THE WITCH WHO TRADES WITH DEATH

ANGRY ROBOT
An imprint of Watkins Media Ltd

Unit 11, Shepperton House
89 Shepperton Road
London N1 3DF
UK

angryrobotbooks.com
twitter.com/angryrobotbooks
Even the mighty can fall

An Angry Robot paperback original, 2025

Copyright © C.M. Alongi 2025

Cover by Sarah O'Flaherty
Edited by Gemma Creffield and Shona Kinsella
Map by Catherine Scully
Set in Meridien

All rights reserved. C.M. Alongi asserts the moral right to be identified as the author of this work. A catalogue record for this book is available from the British Library.

This novel is entirely a work of fiction. Names, characters, places, and incidents are the products of the author's imagination or are used fictitiously. Any resemblance to actual events, locales, organizations or persons, living or dead, is entirely coincidental.

Sales of this book without a front cover may be unauthorized. If this book is coverless, it may have been reported to the publisher as "unsold and destroyed" and neither the author nor the publisher may have received payment for it.

Angry Robot and the Angry Robot icon are registered trademarks of Watkins Media Ltd.

ISBN 978 1 91599 853 8
Ebook ISBN 978 1 91599 854 5

Printed and bound in the United Kingdom by CPI Group (UK) Ltd, Croydon CR0 4YY

The contents of this book cannot be used or reproduced for the purposes of training artificial intelligence.

The author and publisher have made every effort to contact copyright holders for material used for the audiobook cover. Any person or organisation that may have been overlooked should contact the publisher.

9 8 7 6 5 4 3 2 1

*To everyone who has lost a part of themselves.
May you also find your happy ending.*

Author's Note

I am a firm believer in trigger warnings, especially with stories like *The Witch Who Trades with Death* that handles a lot of traumatic issues that, unfortunately, are way too common in our day-to-day lives. Look up the stats for rape/sexual assault if you want to get depressed and/or pissed off.

With that cheerful thought, here's a list of trigger warnings. I've noted whether they are explicit or "off-page," the book equivalent of "off-screen" or "fade to black."

- Sexual Assault (off-page)
- Domestic Violence (off-page)
- War and all of its bloody, gory glory (explicit)
- Violent death (explicit)
- Peaceful death (explicit)
- Racism/xenophobia (explicit, but not the focus)
- Consensual sex (explicit)

Make sure you're taking care of your mental health. And if you want to help people like Khana and Haz escape and recover from their traumatic experiences, I whole-heartedly encourage you to volunteer and/or donate to organizations such as RAINN and the National Sexual Violence Resource Center (if you're in the United States), or Rape Crisis English & Wales, Rape Crisis Scotland, and Rape Crisis Network Ireland (if you're in the United Kingdom).

– C

Chapter One

It wasn't yet winter, but it was still colder than anything Khana had experienced in her twenty years. Her breath came out like smoke from a pipe, and the chill breeze cut right through her layers. She wanted to turn around and curl back into bed with all its blankets and furs, but the day waited. Perhaps she ought to have taken the time to get out of her night gown and into actual clothes, rather than simply tossing on a coat and boots and running out the front door.

"I assume someone from your master's family is hurt?" she asked in heavily-accented Ghura to the man leading her through the darkened streets. She'd only recently gotten the hang of the local language.

"The old man's sick again," Sipah answered. He was bearded, gruff, and very large. Or perhaps Khana was just short. "You're going to make him better. Permanently, this time."

Khana sighed. She'd lost track of how many times she'd tried to explain this. "Old people are difficult."

"Figure it out."

She followed Sipah into the blackness, the stars and moon their main source of light. A handful of homes had candles in the windows, and she could see the glow from a few fireplaces, making the dwellings look like spirits in the black, frosty night. Almost every building in Pahuuda was made of stone – the rocks cut out of the mountain range a short walk away and stacked into homes, shops, and taverns with sharply diagonal roofs. Some were built like the tips of spears cutting into the night. Others had their rooftops slide to one side, as if the entire building was one tipsy step away from crumbling.

They walked silently for a while. There was no snow, but frost made the short, tough grass crunchy beneath their boots, like stepping on thin glass. To distract herself from the cold creeping through her flesh, Khana hummed: melodies from her homeland, half-remembered lullabies, part of a Ghuran ballad. Sipah didn't tell her to stop, thankfully. The buildings got larger and spaced farther apart, some even creeping up the mountain, until they reached the boundary of one of the richest families' estates. Little gargoyles and statues peered from the darkness, and they passed by a familiar stone porcupine, its detailed quills puffed up and mouth open in a snarl.

Sipah led her through the Pinnsviris' sprawling estate. Each of the Seven Families had an animal symbol, and the Pinnsviris' were porcupines. Statues of the large rodent, tapestries and even paintings were *everywhere*. One tapestry depicted the major events from the family's last several generations, leading armies and winning battles against invaders trying to attack through the mountain pass. Khana wasn't sure how much of it was true; every rich, important person liked to flatter themselves in history. But they were very pretty.

Sipah took her to the master bedroom. Unlike Khana's cluster of furs and blankets on the floor of the inn, the head of the Pinnsviri family had an actual bed, complete with a mattress thicker than the length of her thigh. It dwarfed the thin, pale man under the blankets, who was barely more than a skeleton.

Khana had once had a bed like that, only a year ago. She pushed the thought from her mind. *You cannot afford to panic over the past right now.*

The last few times Khana had visited, the old man had been surrounded by a dozen family members who had come for a deathbed vigil. Now, there was only his son Veta and granddaughter Bhayana. Through long practice, Khana kept the distaste from her face at the sight of her.

Sipah bowed. "Sir. I brought the witch."

"I didn't realize frogs wore nightgowns to visit their betters," Bhayana said. Her words were barbed, but her tone was light and friendly, as if she and Khana got along. "Is it a new fashion trend?"

If Khana were a braver soul, she'd point out how everyone else in this room – except Sipah – was also in a nightgown under a coat or robe. Even Bhayana herself, who somehow still managed to look glamorous, like a model waiting for the artist to arrive so she could strike the perfect pose.

Khana kept her eyes down. "Sorry," she said, although she wasn't. If she hadn't prioritized speed over appearance, she would have been scolded for that instead.

"Your emperor. Is immortal," Master Pabu Pinnsviri croaked from the bed, wheezing breaths between his words. Every inhale sounded like a battlefield in his skinny, shriveled lungs. "You will. Do that. For me. Now."

"I don't know how," Khana lied.

"You're lying," Veta accused. His silvering hair receded from his forehead, and he was built like a square.

"Emperor Yamueto does not share his secrets," Khana insisted. That part, at least, was true.

"We've summoned you here a dozen times in the last month, dragging my father's life out for a few more days at a time. It's not working."

"It's all I can do." Khana put her hand on Master Pinnsviri's frail chest. Closing her eyes, she could sense his life force, thin and sluggish. Like the light of the candle almost out of wick. "I can... delay. Again."

"Do it," Master Pinnsviri croaked.

"I need a death."

"We have servants," Bhayana pointed out. "They might be a more permanent solution."

Khana's hands turned to fists. "*Animal* death."

Bhayana ignored her, keeping her eyes on her grandfather. They had the same sharp, calculating eyes, like they could see your whole life in a single glance and find you wanting.

Veta sighed. "If we kill anyone under our roof, the chief will have our hides."

"They'd be giving their lives for their master. They should *want* to be sacrificed," the young woman argued. "We can pay their families if they complain."

Khana swallowed. No. She wouldn't do that again. She would not drain the life of a human for selfish old men *ever* again.

"We won't be able to keep it quiet, and the chief *will* punish us for it," Veta insisted. "Sipah, take the witch to our best yak."

Khana relaxed. She hesitated to speak, and when she did it was with a small voice. "It will not keep forever. The first witches tried this. When they got old, they needed more and more life. Every year, then every month, then every day, then..." She glanced down at Master Pabu. "It will come. Someday soon, I think."

"Go kill a yak, death-bringer," Veta spat.

Behind the estate was a field the family used to raise their yaks, big horned beasts that grazed the rough grass. How they could sleep in such cold, Khana didn't know. It probably had something to do with their thick, heavy coats.

She had already killed a handful of the herd in the last couple of months, but the Pinnsviris were one of the richest families in town and had plenty more huddled in their barn, so she didn't feel too guilty about it. After browsing the paddock, she settled on a buck in its prime. It groggily snuffled at being woken, but didn't protest Khana's poking and prodding. She nodded to Sipah. "Keep it still."

Sipah held the yak's side. Khana knelt, the frost crunching beneath her knees, and put her hands on its fur: "Death can be joyful, but it's always a tragedy. I'm sorry."

She reached for the animal's *âji*, the magical element that kept every being's heart pumping and brain working. Their life force. The Ghura – people of Pahuuda – called it *rabala*, similar to their word *rabuul* for "blood." The Reguallian Empire and formerly free kingdom of Tlaphar said *saviza*. Without it, they were called "dead."

She breathed in.

The yak quickly realized something was wrong and tried to shake her off, but Sipah kept it pinned down. Soon, Khana had pulled so much âji that the yak was too weak to fight, and finally, it stopped breathing.

Wisps of glowing smoke curled around Khana's skin, a swirl of yellow and black. Little topazes and onyxes danced around her fingers. It wouldn't be noticeable in the day, but at night she was a torch, enough to illuminate Sipah's bearded face that barely concealed his discomfort.

Khana was not uncomfortable. She felt powerful, far more awake than she'd been a minute ago, thanks to the new life thrumming through her veins. She savored the feeling while she could.

They went back to the master's bedroom. Khana put her hands on him again and breathed out, pushing the yak's âji into the old man. His body resisted it, even more so than the time before, but eventually he absorbed it and the glowing wisps of multi-colored light sank into his wrinkled skin. The temporary energy leeched away from Khana, leaving her exhausted and sleep-deprived once again.

There was almost no change in his appearance, but as soon as Khana stepped back, he sat up without help and stretched. "Ah! Much better."

Bhayana visibly relaxed. Veta hugged his father, muttering, "We really need to find a more permanent solution."

"We will," Master Pabu agreed. He motioned for Khana to leave. "You can go now, witch. Use the back exit."

* * *

Sipah didn't bother returning her to the inn, so Khana walked on her own. The eastern sky had lightened from black to gray, bleaching out the stars, and she gave up all thoughts of going back to bed with a quiet groan.

The mountains to the north loomed in a line of grumpy gods. She passed a pair of hunters heading that way with bows and arrows at their backs, and a trio of fishermen going the other, towards the tundra.

The town gradually resurrected itself. More candles and fireplaces glowed within homes as people prepared their breakfasts; families emptied their chamber pots into stone sewers that then helped farmers fertilize their otherwise near-barren fields; yaks and goats bleated and called to each other at the first signs of light, already demanding food – the music of morning in Pahuuda. Khana tried to focus on enjoying it rather than dwelling on her own fatigue.

She stumbled back into the inn. The only light was from the kitchen in the back, turning all the cushions and walls into dark specters of themselves. Heimili must have woken up. But to her surprise when she rounded the corner, it was not Heimili warming a pot of tea over the fire and readying the dough to cook. It was his son, Haz. "You're awake!" she blurted.

"Good morning to you, too," he yawned, scratching his chin-length hair. It looked like a bundle of black silk turned into a bird's nest.

"Did you get any sleep?" she asked, noticing the bags under his eyes.

"Eh. Sleep is for the weak. Who broke what this time?"

"Master Pabu wanted to cheat death again."

"Ah. That old shit."

"The yaks won't work for much longer," Khana said, sitting on the rickety stool by the warm stone counter. The stool was one of the few pieces of actual furniture in the building –cushions and blankets were so much easier and cheaper. It was made of animal bone and hide, and creaked under her slight weight. "Bhayana suggested using servants."

Haz grunted. "She loves her family. One of her few redeeming qualities – that and her lips. But she often forgets that other people *also* enjoy living. Tea?"

She accepted a cup. Ghuran tea was louder, more bracing than the delicate, subtle teas she had enjoyed in the distant Reguallian Empire. It had caught her off-guard the first time she'd tried it. Now, she gratefully nursed her clay cup, knowing she'd need it to stay awake and alert for the next few hours. Haz downed his like a shot of strong vodka, wincing at the taste or temperature, and poured himself a second.

"Drink that, then get the dining room ready," he instructed. "Baba will chew us both out if customers don't have their breakfast on time, and I'm not nearly awake enough to deal with that."

Before Khana had a chance to sip her tea, they heard the front door slam open.

"I *just* put the bread in the oven!" Haz called out. "Can you be a *little* more patient?"

But they weren't customers. A handful of soldiers ran into the kitchen, blocking the exit. They were armed and armored: thick layers of wool and cloth covered them head to foot, and they held animal-hide shields that probably weighed as much as Khana did.

She instinctively shrank away, flinching when they towered over her. "Come with us."

"Rude!" Haz scolded, swatting the soldier's arm with a bone spoon. The soldier blinked at the flour-stained man. "If you're going to burst into my father's inn and bully our employee, can you at least tell us why?"

"This doesn't concern you, boy. The chief wants to speak with her."

"Why?" Haz demanded. Khana ran through a mental list of everything she'd done in the past few days, wondering which action may have caused offence.

"We found a night creature."

Khana's clay cup slipped from her fingers and shattered on the floor. "What?!"

"Don't talk back, witch," the soldier snapped.

"Where is it?"

"You don't ask the questions here–"

"*Where is it?*" she repeated, jumping from the stool, ready to wring the answer from his neck.

He jerked back at her sudden advance, his comrades tightening their grip on their weapons. "The hunters who found it brought it to the chief. She ordered us to bring you to identify–"

"Let's go." She shoved her cloak and boots on and sprinted outside.

The soldiers quickly caught up with her, with those damn long legs of theirs, grumbling, "We can *walk* there, you soul-sucking bitch."

She ignored them and ran faster. *It's not true. It's just a particularly large or decimated animal. It's not true.*

Despite walking by it a few times, Khana had never been inside the Pahuudan chief's home. The Bvamso family estate was, like other Old

Family homes, on the high ground, built into the mountains. And similar to the Pinnsviris', it was covered with their own family symbol: wolves. Khana ran by two stone canine sentinels that marked the perimeter, and a couple more outside the door that finally slowed her from her sprint.

Khana's breath came out in high-pitched wheezes, but she pushed on. The soldiers led her through a thick wooden door to an audience chamber. Chief Phramanka looked up when they entered. The older woman's dark braid was turning gray; she had a square jaw and thick eyebrows that went up when she saw her. "And I thought you'd need to be dragged here kicking and screaming."

Khana leaned against the stone wall, panting. Phramanka knelt on the floor, over something big covered in a wool blanket. Her son, Sava, stood behind her and gave Khana a grim little wave. Like his mother, his long, black hair was braided over the left shoulder, giving him easier access to the quiver of arrows on his back. That, paired with the wolf pelt over his shoulders and boots still on his feet, told her he had likely been part of the hunting group that found the creature.

On the other side of the room stood another man who looked like an older, wider version of Sava: silvering beard, thicker frame, soft eyes, with a massive, sheathed sword on his back. Sava's father, Thriman.

Phramanka stood with a grunt, brushing hair from her face. "Take a look at this, girl. Tell me what you think."

Trembling, Khana approached the blanket and knelt. Her hands shook as she reached out. *It's not true. It's not true. It's not –*

She pulled back the material.

The creature before her had a mountain goat's twisted horns and hooves, pale fur with black stripes, and long teeth perfect for tearing flesh. Nothing natural about it.

"Well?" Phramanka asked.

Khana's hand fell back in her lap, limp. "It's... it's a night creature. Goat and tiger, by my guess."

Thriman swore. Phramanka sighed.

"Scouts found it dead in the mountains, about halfway between here and Tlaphar," Sava reported. "It was at the bottom of a cliff. We think it slipped and fell, maybe got spooked by something." He turned to Khana. "What do you think?"

Khana swallowed, her eyes never leaving the body. The black stripes looked like knives. "When Emperor Yamueto takes interest in a kingdom, he sends these types of scouts. Experiments. He mixes and matches different animals to find out what the ideal soldier would be in their environment. Once he's done that, he sends an ultimatum: surrender or..."

"But why us?" Sava asked, scratching his square jaw. "We don't have any valuable resources he needs, no strategic position he can use against others, and we haven't done anything to insult his honor."

"We have a witch," Phramanka said, pointedly looking at Khana.

Khana swallowed. "I don't think it's me," she said, not entirely truthful. "I think that conquest is the only thing that truly gives him joy anymore. He's lived for centuries. At this point, I think it's the only reason he's living."

The chief grunted. "Is his entire army made of night creatures? There must be at least one human giving orders."

Khana calmed, just a little. She'd bought the lie. "There are. It depends on the strengths and weaknesses of the defending kingdom, but no more than a fifth of the army will be night creatures. They take up too much time and âji to make a whole army out of them. Yamueto always sends at least one witch to lead them, usually a son or grandson."

Sava knelt next to Khana and re-covered the night creature. She blinked, no longer able to stare at it.

"So. We're at war, then?" Thriman asked cheerfully.

"Technically, no," Phramanka said. "This night creature did not trespass within our borders and did not hurt anyone. So strictly speaking, this is not a declaration of war."

Khana's temper flared, meeting the chief's eyes for the first time that morning. "So you'll do nothing?"

"Easy," Thriman warned.

"I said no such thing, girl," Phramanka replied testily. Khana shrank back.

"The emperor has very poor timing," Sava commented, his deep, soothing voice calming everyone in the room. "He can't get an army across the mountains before the winter snows block the pass, so he's given us ample warning. Five months, at least. That's the earliest he can even get here, unless he's figured out a way to make these things fly?"

He looked at Khana when he asked that. She shook her head. "He's tried. But you can't create something from nothing. Every night creature has at least some of the strengths and weaknesses of the creatures it was before. And there isn't anything with big enough wings to carry a human."

Sava nodded and looked up at his mother. "Are we calling up the militia then?"

Phramanka pointed to him. "That is exactly what we're going to do. I'll send a letter to the king. But first we call a meeting, let the whole town know what's happening, and start training volunteers. By the time the snows melt, and the pass clears, we'll be ready."

ONE YEAR EARLIER

Chapter Two

Balasco, the capital city of the Reguallian Empire, was nothing like the mountain town of Pahuuda. Defensively built in the middle of an impenetrable, tropical jungle, even the coldest days were hot and muggy, like inhaling warm water. The heavens periodically tried to drown this part of the world, the twisted trees and rich soil greedily drinking what they gave. Khana could hear the thunder, feel it vibrate through the polished wood of the palace as if the gods knew what was happening within its walls and didn't like it one bit. Of course, if there were any gods, they would have – or at least *should* have – intervened centuries ago.

Khana stood in the throne room with a hundred other people, almost invisible in her pearls and blue silk dress. Every other known witch in the Empire stood in attendance, some esteemed royals, lords, and ladies, others mere bodyguards born out of wedlock. Most of those around her outshone her in every way, trying to blind each other with their jewels, silks, and furs. They all circled around a dozen condemned men and women in chains, some old and wrinkled, the youngest barely able to toddle.

The prisoners were a sorry sight, dressed in dirty rags when just a week before they'd been in the same kind of finery Khana wore. They were now forced to kneel on the intricately woven rug with a handful of cows, who looked very wary of the tigers, which had also been brought in, albeit drugged. The big cats slept peacefully, unaware of their fate.

Khana couldn't remember the family's name, or their crime. After a while they all began to blend. Had they implied that the emperor would not live forever by suggesting he name an heir? Had they tried to learn the secret to his immortality? An attempted coup?

Standing a few feet in front of the throne – a hideously ornate thing elevated from the rest of the room by a few stairs – was Emperor Yamueto himself. Their immortal ruler. At over three hundred years old, he didn't look a day over thirty. Not one gray hair or wrinkle on his skin. A ceremonial sword hung at his hip, the blood-red ruby on the hilt catching the light. His silks were black or gray, in startling contrast to the rest of his court. He had never been the cutting edge of fashion. He looked down at the condemned prisoners – ah, yes, one of them was his great-grandson – without an ounce of emotion.

"Your house has been confirmed guilty of treason against myself and the empire," Yamueto said, his stern voice filling the massive room. "The punishment is to serve as a night creature for however long your flesh lasts."

The head of the condemned family glared at the emperor. "Don't you have enough of a soul for a merciful death?"

Yamueto's face rarely shifted from a half-bored expression, no matter what he was doing, and it did not do so now. He nodded to the court.

Touching a victim made it easier to drain their âji, but witches didn't technically need to – they just needed to be close enough to breathe.

Together, the court's hundred witches drained the hapless prisoners and the animals of their âji, rapidly absorbing the light of their lives. Glowing with it. Yellow, black, red, blue, all swirling together. Khana hated the magical air in her lungs, the surge of strength in her veins.

They were all dead in seconds, bodies unmoving. As soon as all their life force was absorbed, the witches directed it back.

Logic would dictate that, if someone ran out of âji, then returning it would bring them back to life, but while that was technically true, they weren't *themselves* anymore. Instead, they were mindless slaves to whomever resurrected them, as if death had stolen their very souls. Khana had seen full resurrections where the revived *were* truly themselves again, their minds and souls intact, but she didn't know how to do that. No one did, besides the emperor.

Yamueto stalked to the center of the room, the witches on either side of him smoothly moving to ensure the circle remained unbroken. He began sculpting the bodies like clay, using the magic raging in the room in a way never seen before his reign. The animals' corpses were molded onto the human's and then woven together. He worked in a blur, breathing âji in and out so fast that Khana couldn't follow his movements.

When he was finished, the living, breathing creatures standing around the emperor were nowhere near human. They retained some human features: two legs, two hands, a mostly bipedal form. But some had bull's horns, others had tiger stripes and claws. A handful snarled, baring sharp teeth meant for grinding flesh. Two of them were almost twice as large as the original humans, bulked up with a bull's muscle. And they all had completely white, soulless eyes.

"Excellent," Yamueto said, again with no emotion. "See that our new soldiers find their way to the southern front. Silujo?"

No one answered.

"Where is Prince Silujo?" Yamueto asked.

"Your Excellency, Prince Silujo is dead," someone answered quietly. "He passed away in his sleep two weeks ago."

There'd been a funeral for the eighty-eight-year-old man. Even a feast. Yamueto hadn't spoken one word about his dead grandson.

"Ah, yes. That's right. In that case, is Antallo still alive?"

Prince Antallo, one of Yamueto's sons, with graying hair and hopeful eyes, stood at attention. "Your Excellency?"

"The last time I sent you on a campaign, you failed, and almost cost us a city."

Antallo winced. "Yes, Your Excellency."

"Consider this your second chance. The kingdom of Tlaphar is proving stubborn. You'll be going with these new soldiers to show them why that's a mistake."

The prince brightened. "I'll break their walls down myself."

Yamueto's mouth twitched into the tiniest frown. "Don't get cocky. Conquering the kingdom is more important than your pride."

Antallo bowed. "Of course, Your Excellency. We'll leave at once." He hurried out of the room, ordering the new monstrosities to follow him.

Khana watched him go with pity. Yamueto had dozens of living children, and even more grandchildren, great-grandchildren, great-great-grandchildren, and beyond – the result of having hundreds of wives and concubines over three centuries. They tended to be in one of two camps: those who had accepted the fact that the emperor would never share the secret of immortality and would let them die of old age, and those who hadn't.

Yamueto had already buried hundreds of his own family, Silujo being the latest example. Many, like today's prisoners, had been killed by his own hand. With such apathy and cruelty on display, how could anyone continue to deny his true nature?

"Dismissed," Yamueto said, waving his hand

Khana breathed a quiet sigh of relief and turned to go with everyone else.

"Except you, Khana."

She froze. Some of the other wives and concubines who passed her shared looks of pity. Many looked relieved it wasn't them.

She studied the crimson starburst pattern on the rug and put her hands behind her back, demure and obedient. The last footsteps faded away, until it was just her and the emperor.

Stay still. Don't move, she reminded herself.

"I hardly saw you glowing," Yamueto said. "I hardly *ever* see you glowing."

Her mouth was dry. She'd been found out.

She swallowed, speaking in barely more than a whisper, "I'm sorry, Your Excellency. I'm not much of a witch."

Or a rebel. A brave person would have stabbed Yamueto in the chest at the first opportunity, or died trying. The best Khana could do was perform tiny resistances, like only pulling a fraction of the âji she could take.

"Are you going to let me play with her?"

Khana jumped. She hadn't realized they weren't alone.

Kokaatl, Yamueto's favorite wife, suddenly filled Khana's vision. She was almost thirty, and either hadn't yet realized her husband was never going to give her immortality or didn't care. She was about Khana's size, but seemed to take up so much space, her long sleeves and dress billowing behind her as she moved. She hailed from one of the newest Reguallian conquests, closer to Tlaphar and only subjugated half a generation ago.

Surprisingly, she was not a witch. Yamueto made a point to bed witches or their descendants almost exclusively in an attempt to father magical children. He also arranged for his children to marry other witches or their descendants, and on and on it went. Witches were extremely valuable to the Reguallian Empire as healers and soldiers; many believed them to be touched or descended from gods, a belief that Yamueto actively encouraged.

And yet here Kokaatl was, not one witch in her family for the last five generations. But what she lacked in magic, she made up for in sadism. For that, Yamueto seemed to treat her as... well, not really a *lover*. More like a pet.

She grinned with shark-like teeth, poking Khana's face with cold fingers. "I want to see what's under this skin. It just hangs off her, perfect for flaying! Like peeling a banana."

Khana trembled, but didn't move. Didn't speak. The last person to insult Kokaatl in front of Yamueto had been given to the concubine to "play" with, before being turned into a night creature.

"I'm sure it would be, darling," Yamueto said, sounding almost fond. "But I haven't even gotten a child out of this one yet."

Kokaatl pouted. "It's been *years*."

"Yes, it has." Yamueto stepped up to Khana. She kept her eyes down, tracing the pattern of his lizard skin shoes.

He put a finger under her chin and forced her to look up. There was no emotion in those near-black eyes of his. "So let's try again."

An hour later, Khana stumbled out of Yamueto's chambers. The emperor almost never struck his women, but he was rarely gentle. Her thighs already protested every movement, cords of pain getting tighter with each step. Tomorrow morning she'd have bruises the size of his hands. At least he hadn't made her climax this time. That always made it worse, like her own body was betraying her by finding a sliver of enjoyment out of it.

The servants she passed curtsied and bowed to her. She stopped one to ask for a tub to be sent to her room, "Boiling hot," she said. "And a tea set." She didn't have a permanent bath in her chambers like the more favored members of the imperial family; the servants had to carry the copper tub up and down several flights of stairs, then fill it with buckets of water that had mostly cooled before they reached her room.

She was almost to her room when she ran into one of the last people she wanted to see.

"Prince Antallo." She greeted him with a curtsy.

The old prince was a wider, less handsome version of his father. They had the same sharp nose and near-black eyes, but on Antallo they made him look like an overfed parrot. The insultingly bright clothing didn't help; a robe of violent green and gold over an orange undershirt.

"It's Khana, right?" he asked. "The one from the desert."

"Yes, sir," she said.

He grinned at her, eyes roving over her body, lingering on her disheveled dress and hair. "Enjoying your evening with the emperor?"

She started to walk past him. "Excuse me, sir. I need to wash up."

"You are not excused."

She stopped.

Antallo prowled up to her, a silver-haired tiger. "My father is sending me off to an important battle. Once I win and bring glory to the empire, he'll reward me."

"Yes, sir."

"He might even grant me immortality," he mused. "But if not, I might ask for one of his concubines. I've heard that musicians are particularly good with their hands."

Khana balled her hands into fists to keep from shuddering. "Forgive me, sir, but I do not think that would be wise."

He paused, narrowing his eyes dangerously. "No?"

"The emperor has bedded me for six years, and I haven't borne him a single child. I doubt I could give you one, either."

"I already have children," he snorted. "Too many of them. What I want is a little fun."

He reached out to touch her chin.

Khana jerked away from him.

Antallo's eyes darkened. "Khana. Come here."

Fear turned to panic, and she blurted the first thing that came to mind: "The emperor doesn't like anyone touching his women!"

He hesitated. Khana didn't give him the time to react, and stepped around him to get to her room.

"I'll see you when I return, Khana," Antallo crooned.

She locked the door behind her.

The emperor's descendants often enjoyed taunting the concubines and anyone else they had slivers of control over, even if they couldn't *do* anything without facing Yamueto's wrath. It took a long moment of trembling against the door for Khana to remind herself of the fact.

Despite being the emperor's concubine – and thus technically royalty – Khana's chambers were relatively small and sparse. There were a couple of small windows, four smooth wooden walls, a bed, a wardrobe, a bookshelf, and a writing desk. Originally, she'd tried to liven the place up with plants on the windowsill and woven blankets on the walls, but it did little to alleviate the gloom.

The tub and tea would take a while to arrive. Khana tore out of her silk dress and put on a sleeping robe. She snatched her lute from the corner, a beautifully carved instrument that she'd had for years, and scratched at the strings. Her anger, her grief, her pain poured out of her in bitter, incoherent notes. But eventually, it took the form of a song, a melody of rage and sorrow. She couldn't *say* "damn the emperor," but her music could. The man deserved so much more than that.

A century ago, Yamueto had conquered her homeland, the Naatuun Desert, to secure its trade – and eventual military – route. Like most places with magic, the desert had been ruled by witches. All the males had been put to the sword during and after the conquest. The female witches had been given to Yamueto himself or his princes as trophies, to create a new generation of witches loyal to the empire. Khana's great-great-grandfather had been one of those princes. A century later, Khana was born.

Nobody had known she was a witch. They'd all thought the gift had died with her great-grandmother. It wasn't until she was thirteen, when she accidentally pulled the âji out of a cactus, that she'd realized what she was.

Her handmaiden at the time, Guma, had tried to help her hide it. The sweet old lady had forbidden Khana from showing anyone, even her parents. But eventually, they'd found out.

Khana's father executed Guma and, as was imperial law, sent his witch daughter to the capital. Since she was more than eight generations removed from Yamueto, she'd been given to the emperor himself.

If she thought about the fact that the man bedding her was her great-great-great-great-great-great-great-grandfather, she'd lose her gods-damn mind.

She never considered running away. Other concubines had tried. The public punishments Yamueto had made everyone witness still gave her nightmares.

The servants had to knock twice before she heard them over her lute and called for them to enter. The tub was hauled into the corner, and a whole trail of servants poured steaming water into it. Another brought in a tray with a teapot, cup, and saucer. Someone had thought to add a little bowl of berries, but Khana wouldn't eat. Her stomach churned on nights like this.

"Do you require help bathing, ma'am?" one of them asked.

"No, thank you. You may go."

She waited until they left before pouring herself a cup of tea. Then she went to the spot behind her bed, the one with the loose floorboard. A bit of rummaging produced a small glass vial protected in a silk bag.

Birth control medicine was illegal in the empire. Commoners could expect a public lashing, but royal concubines were put to death. It was one of the rare crimes where the rich were more harshly punished than the poor for violating it. But there were still ways to get the medicine.

Khana poured the concoction in her teacup and slammed it back, grimacing at the bitter taste. That had been good tea, too. But the treatment already had her feeling a bit better before she slipped into her bath and tried to wash the day from her skin.

Chapter Three

The days passed on. Yamueto ordered Khana to his bed almost every night, trying to get a child in her, the iron doors closing behind her with a final *boom*. It was a frequency she hadn't seen since she was first taken to the palace. She hadn't been allowed outside the imperial grounds since, and tried to let her mind drift to wondering what the world was like now as Yamueto forced his way into her. Even when chasing his pleasure, he still looked half-bored, and did little more than grunt when he climaxed.

She drank a lot of tea and played a lot of songs.

While her nights were torture, Khana tried to fill her days with better things. While confined to the walls, it was still a *palace*. There were dozens of gardens to walk through, things to sew, people to mingle with.

The library was one of Khana's favorite places. Sometimes – not often, but sometimes – she'd run into one of the other concubines or their children or even grandchildren, and they'd talk about books, or music, or history, or just gossip. Khana mostly did her best to be a ghost in the palace, but sometimes it was nice to talk to another specter.

When she found Princess Sivusita wandering the shelves of books and scrolls, she almost sprinted to her. The oldest living daughter of Yamueto had been appointed librarian, keeping this part of the palace in order, reading while her hair went gray, and wrinkles carved themselves into her face. She shuffled between the shelves in her slippered feet and indigo robe, never caring for the time of day or night. She and Khana would spend entire afternoons together without saying a word, just reading and sipping tea.

Not today, though. Khana caught up with Sita and presented her with a scroll, bowing over it. "Here, Your Highness. I promised I'd get this back to you." She'd borrowed it a week ago. The last time she'd failed to return something within a month, the librarian had threatened to kick her out.

Sita took the scroll with a smile. "Ah, a history of the Early Kingdoms. Any good?"

"Interesting," Khana admitted. "I was mostly intrigued by the stories of other kings being immortal." Before her reading, she only had half-remembered legends of the first witches trying to trick or cheat death. Even the ones who got away with it had to pay a hefty price.

"Oh, history is littered with people like my father. They get immortality somehow, and then wind up killed in battle, or by envious family, or assassins," Sita said breezily. "I believe the record is eight hundred years, but of course Urdo the Ancient spent almost all of his days hiding in his fortress until someone poisoned him."

"Your brother Antallo seems to think that he'll be the next immortal," Khana mused.

The librarian laughed. "He's an idiot. Urdo's reign was so horrifying and bloody that his killers purged every bit of magical knowledge they could find, hoping that no one would ever become immortal again. It worked for centuries, too. Used to be that witches of a certain rank or skill were taught immortality if they proved themselves worthy through various deeds and whatnot. There was a time when we had hundreds of immortals."

"Were they all... like the emperor?" Sadistic and cruel and uncaring about anything but conquest.

"Some," Sita said. "Urdo was the worst of them, until my father rediscovered the secret."

Khana hummed. She couldn't imagine living in a world with hundreds of Yamuetos. But perhaps the presence of others meant that none could get nearly as powerful.

"What are you doing?" she asked, motioning to the shelves that Sita had emptied, placing the scrolls and books on a rickety cart.

"Antallo is an ass who thinks he's the world's greatest military commander, but he managed to conquer a Tlapharian city – you didn't hear?" Sita asked. "He's sending some of their library to us."

Khana stared at her in surprise. She'd half-expected the prince to get shot full of arrows.

"What comes after Tlaphar?" she asked.

"I don't know. Logic would say 'the next kingdom,' but that's Divaajin, and they're behind a mountain range."

"Has the emperor never gone over mountains?"

"No northern army has ever gotten through *those* mountains. Not ever. Especially not since they posted the Ghura there. They're impassable."

At Khana's tipped head, Sita explained, "Nomadic barbarians. Used to wander around as mercenaries before the kingdom of Divaajin got them under control, some six hundred years ago. Now they guard the mountains in a line of towns and outposts from coast to coast. Pahuuda is the biggest. Those brutes don't even use paper, and send weaklings into the snow to die. No culture whatsoever."

Khana gave a noncommittal hum. Barbarians or not, she hoped they prevailed if – when – Yamueto decided his empire needed even more expansion and tried to push through the mountains.

Sita glanced at the lute on Khana's back, kept in place by a strap. "Would you mind playing for me while I work, dear?"

"Of course, ma'am."

They didn't say another word to each other for hours, Khana playing until her fingers felt fuzzy. She kept the tune quiet – as well as her voice, when she decided to sing along with it – and the songs light and classical as the librarian worked. They went up and down the shelves, organizing the books and scrolls, gently taking down the old ones to be copied onto fresh paper, taking note of anything that was missing or needed more of.

They reached the farthest back corner of the library. "That'll do, dear," Sita said, pulling a medicinal vial from her sleeve. "Thank you."

Khana beamed and took the vial. Like her, Sita and many of her friends had been "barren" for a very long time.

Despite books and gardens and endless wells of gossip, Khana found the best way to pass the time was music. The one true bright spot of the Reguallian Empire was all the different instruments, dances, and types of song that had been collected and created over the last three centuries. Khana spent hours each day perfecting the lute, playing happy tunes to distract herself from her daily horrors, or sad, vengeful ones to safely express the inner torment that threatened to consume her.

The Reguallian court was not a cheerful, festive place, but it still observed the gods and holidays. The Festival of Muobra was fast approaching, a celebration of the god of death. At least, one of them. All gods were welcome in the Reguallian Empire, old and new, homegrown and foreign. But Muobra was one of the oldest and most popular – or so Khana heard.

Yamueto claimed his immortality was descended from Muobra himself, which could be true for all Khana knew.

Whatever the case, this festival was particularly important for the court to observe. Everyone had to prepare, including the concubines. Minstrels were summoned around the clock to help the women learn the year's new dances and songs. Hardly a day passed without dozens of women dancing together in one of the mess halls, slippered feet gliding over thick, colorful rugs. Khana herself volunteered to join the musicians, and the lessons took up so much of her time that she hardly saw Sita during daylight hours. Soon enough, they were rehearsing with the dancers in the ballroom.

Muobra and Vigerion were the only gods Khana had ever seen Yamueto actively pray to. While Muobra was the more popular, raven-headed god that led lost souls to their suitable afterlives, Vigerion was one of the oldest deities, ancient even before Yamueto's reign. The old man with the lantern. He had a small temple in the south wing of the palace that demanded absolute silence from the few allowed to enter. People who broke that rule lost their tongues.

In fact, *no one* was allowed to pray to Muobra and Vigerion, except the emperor. "The gods of death listen not to the trifling concerns of common people," Yamueto had said. "Only the highest rank of witches is permitted to approach them. Anyone else caught doing so will be endangering the empire, and thus sentenced to death."

Khana shook her head to banish such thoughts and focused on a particularly difficult set of notes. The songs praising the death gods were a little bizarre with an air of optimistic melancholy. A celebration of that person's life while still mourning its end.

She hit the last note with the rest of the musicians around her just as the dancers finished their set. All the ladies cheered – it had been the first time they'd rehearsed the full set at once.

"You're quite good at this," a sister-wife said during a break. Khana didn't know her name – was she new? Was she a witch or just descended from one? It was so hard to keep track, especially since Khana preferred to keep to herself. She played the pipes, though, and quite well. "I hope you don't mind me spying on you when I forget the next set of notes."

Khana giggled, feeling her cheeks heat with the compliment. "Thank you. Although your pipe-playing is spectacular. I can never do a song like this on a wind instrument; I'd be gasping for breath after the first set."

"It's all about control."

A young boy in dark gray silk – a courier – scurried into the room, his little body almost swallowed by the great hall. He scanned the crowd until his eyes met Khana's, and he wove his way through the gossiping, drinking women until he was close enough to whisper, "Mistress Kokaatl demands you see her in the dungeons."

Ice poured down Khana's spine. The pipe-player quickly turned away, as if the summons was contagious. Khana carefully wiped the sweat from her brow to buy herself time and adjusted the lute strap on her shoulder, comforted by the instrument's weight on her back. She followed the boy out of the room to a staircase at the end of the hall.

She can't hurt me, she reminded herself. *If the emperor had given her permission, there would be guards to keep me from escaping.*

Still, her stomach clenched, and her hands trembled as they went down, down, down into the dungeons. The city's worst criminals were kept down here, some of them slated for night creatures, others given to Kokaatl for her to "play" with.

"Do you know what this is about?" she asked.

The boy shook his head. "No, Mistress Khana. She just told me to get you."

Khana wrapped her arms around herself, shivering as polished wooden walls turned to cold stone as they went deeper into the belly of the palace. They left the sun behind, the only light coming from torches on the walls spaced so far apart they created pools of darkness between them.

Finally, they reached the correct floor. Kokaatl waited for them in the hall, standing in a gold and black silk dress with sleeves so long they brushed against the floor. She fiddled with something in her hands.

When she looked up and grinned, shark-like, Khana stuttered to a halt. Specks of red blood dotted Kokaatl's otherwise perfectly made-up face.

"Oh, don't be shy. Yamueto still won't let me play with you," Kokaatl said with a little pout. "Boy, you can go. Khana, I want to show you something."

The courier hastily bowed and ran off. Khana forced her numb legs to move and stepped closer. "What do you wish to show me, ma'am?"

Kokaatl opened the door behind her. "My new toy, of course."

The stench of blood almost had Khana running back to the stairs. The coppery tang choked her as it pooled on the floor, reflecting the torchlight from the walls. Kokaatl didn't move, waiting for her to go first with a little smile on her face. Pushed on by her fear of the other woman, Khana breathed through her mouth and went in.

There were two tables. One was covered in tools, red and grimy with fresh use. Knives, hammers, nails – everything a person could possibly need for building a house or tearing someone apart.

It took Khana a moment to recognize what lay on the other table: a corpse, tied by the wrists and ankles. The skin was flayed off, revealing muscle and organs beneath. The fingers and toes were especially bloody, some of them torn to shreds. The only part that wasn't completely destroyed or flayed was the head.

Sita's eyes and mouth were open; she'd died mid-scream.

Khana's whole world collapsed.

"Most people last through the whole flaying," Kokaatl said conversationally. "But this one's heart gave out too soon."

Fear gave way to cold anger. "Why?" she asked in a dead voice.

Kokaatl held up a familiar black vial. "Birth control is illegal in the empire. Especially for the emperor's concubines. You know that, silly kitty."

The cleaners must have found the stash hidden in Khana's room, or maybe Yamueto had suspected something and ordered it searched, or perhaps someone heard of Sita's dealings in the city. Whatever the case...

My fault, Khana realized. *This is my fault.*

"Yamueto decided to give her to me to play with this morning," Kokaatl continued, as if she wasn't ripping Khana's soul to shreds with every word. "He told me to show you after I was done, and to tell you to report to his chambers after. Honestly, I'm not a messenger girl. You should be grateful that I'm even doing this much."

Before Khana knew what she was doing, her hand shot out and grabbed Kokaatl's throat. She breathed in.

Kokaatl, feeling her life force drain away, pushed at Khana's skinny arm. But Khana grabbed her gold-and-black dress with her other hand and slammed her into the wall, breathing in more and more of her âji. She watched, with numbness and rage, as Kokaatl weakly struggled, then tried to scream. Finally, the life completely drained out of her wide, panicked eyes.

Khana let the body drop to the floor. She knew she should feel something about having murdered someone, but felt curiously removed. Yes, there was guilt. But not for this.

She hurried to Sita's body and put her hands on either side of her face. *There must be a way to bring you back,* she thought, trying to probe the body for any clues. *Witches can bring people back without turning them into night creatures. Yamueto's done it. Other witches in history have done it. There must be a way.*

Though the emperor had never shared his secret of immortality, he had, occasionally, brought back to life favored wives or commanders, and they had been themselves. Before the anti-witch purge that followed Urdu the Ancient's reign, plenty of high-ranked witches had done the same. So it was possible. But Khana had never been taught how. Nobody had.

There must be a trick to it, she thought. Her skin glowed with Kokaatl's âji; it was more than she had ever taken at one time, a second skin of yellow, white, purple, pale green, and red. Khana pushed it into Sita's body, aiming specifically for the heart. *It must be the heart. Without a heart, there is no humanity.*

Sita's body twitched. Her heart beat. She took a breath, lungs filling with air. Then she opened her eyes.

All of Khana's hopes crashed. They were completely white, like all night creatures.

Sita's exposed flesh brushed against the shackles, and she screamed. No human could've made that sound; it was entirely bestial, pained, and angry.

Sobbing, Khana pulled the life force back, watching Sita's movements slow, then cease entirely. "I'm sorry," she cried, hugging her friend's weathered face. "I'm so, so sorry."

She couldn't bring Sita back. Even if she did, she didn't have enough âji to heal her injuries. Any existence she could give her would be nothing but suffering.

How long Khana stayed there, hugging the corpse, she didn't know. But eventually, it dawned on her that she had to move. Yamueto had specifically ordered Kokaatl to torture her friend, to show Khana, and send her to his chambers. He knew exactly where she was; as soon as Kokaatl's body was discovered, that would be the end. Khana would be turned into a night creature, or worse.

She had to leave. And she had to leave *now*.

Khana stepped away from the table and wiped her tears. Concubines who had tried escaping before had failed for a variety of reasons: trying to bribe guards who instead turned them in, being spotted while climbing the wall, trusting the wrong people. Those who had managed to escape had been recognized from posters Yamueto ordered hung up all over the empire describing their faces and features, or they were captured after trying to sell distinctive jewelry and clothing, or used their necrotic abilities.

Khana needed to be clever and get as much of a head start as possible. But it took money to travel. It was a shame none of the nobles ever carried rolls of coins or other forms of money – they had no use for it in the palace.

She studied Kokaatl's body. She was covered in silks and jewels, but they would be instantly recognized. She'd have to alter them somehow. She pocketed all the gold rings, earrings, and bracelets, even those she knew she couldn't use. The guards would note that they were missing and specifically search for them, distracting them from her real trail.

She also took her birth control bottle back. No one would be allowed to take that from her ever again.

As she lined her pockets, it occurred to her that Yamueto probably valued Kokaatl enough to want her back. He cared for the woman, as much as he could care about anything. He might go through the effort to revive her.

Well, that wasn't going to happen.

The torturer had stripped Sita of her clothes before working on her, piling them in the corner. Khana threw on the dead princess's oversized dark blue dress to act as a smock and selected the biggest knife the torture table had to offer.

Minutes of sweaty, bloody work later, Kokaatl's head was relieved of its body. Khana removed Sita's dress, wiped her face and arms with the clean spots, and used it as a bag for the head. She would dispose of that on her escape route, and Yamueto wouldn't be able to resurrect his most terrifying wife.

She approached the body a final time and kissed Sita's forehead. "Thank you, dear friend. Please find peace, wherever you are."

Khana dried her eyes and left the torture chamber.

Chapter Four

The next obstacle was Khana's own appearance. She didn't look *that* different from everyone else in the city – certainly shorter than most of her sister-wives, and maybe a little darker thanks to her Naatuun heritage, although her long black hair, almond-shaped eyes, and small nose were distinctly Reguallian – but in her silk dresses, she was clearly a concubine, and thus wouldn't be allowed to leave the palace.

Worse, she still held a faint glow from absorbing Kokaatl's life force; black, green, yellow, and purple flickered over her skin. Thankfully she found a cat strolling down the corridor hunting mice and scooped up the creature to pour Kokaatl's âji into it.

The vibrant life force pooled into the cat. It yowled, leaping from Khana's hands, and bounded down the corridor at lightning speed, literally bouncing off the wall before disappearing around the corner. Khana's own skin was left plain and dark.

Servants' quarters, she thought, hurrying up the stone stairs. The dress-bag with Kokaatl's head swung by her knees. Luckily Sita had always worn dark clothing, so the blood stains weren't obvious.

The servants' quarters were on the first floor, not too far from the dungeons, divided between men and women. Over fifty people shared a single room – the blankets that served as their beds brushed against each other like a massive mis-matched quilt across the entire floor.

Khana poked her head inside and bit her tongue. A servant grumbled as she shuffled through her belongings. Khana hated being mean, especially to someone who didn't deserve it, but...

She straightened her back, set the bag next to the wall, and strode into the room. "You!"

The servant jumped into a bow. "Mistress!"

"Mistress Kokaatl needs assistance."

"Of course, ma'am. Where?"

"The library on the third floor." It was on the other side of the palace. It would take ten minutes to walk there, less if the servant ran. The library was huge though, so it would take a while longer for the servant to wander around and realize Kokaatl was not there. By the time she'd think to return here and ask for clarification, Khana would be long gone.

The servant hesitated, probably wondering why Khana hadn't fetched someone closer to that wing of the palace. But a stern look from Khana had the girl running.

Pushing down guilt, Khana found the shelves hidden behind the sliding paper walls that housed spare uniforms. Some were neatly folded, but most were shoved wherever there was room. She had to rummage for a bit before she found one that wouldn't drown her. Even then, she had to roll up the white sleeves to free her hands, and wrap the cloth belt around the wide black skirt three times before tying it.

She stuffed her silk dress into the back of the shelf, then cast around for something to hide her hair and face. Some of the servants had cloaks – not meant for warmth, since that would roast them like parrots for dinner – but thin rubbery ones to protect their skin against sunlight and heavy rain. She chose the plainest one that fit her, cotton dyed a near muddy brown that covered her and the lute on her back. Then, she scooped up her head-sack and left.

The raised hood made her look a tad suspicious, but Khana had no choice. Not until she got somewhere where people didn't know her face. She stopped by the kitchens, using the chaos of servants, cooks, and chefs prepping dinner as cover. No one noticed her grab a small kitchen knife and hide it under her cloak.

Now just walk out the back gate, she ordered herself. *Nobody checks the servants' gate. Just walk like you do it every day.*

She stepped onto one of the largest courtyards of the palace. The sun was still hours away from setting. Some servants came in through the gate to help with the dinner prep, others walked out on their night off. The guards leaned against the stone walls ahead of her, bored as they watched the staff leave, checking their faces when necessary. Her heart crawled up her throat, but there was no other way. She'd just have to hope they didn't recognize her face without makeup or finery.

She was a hundred steps away. Ninety. Eighty.

The bells atop the roof of the palace rang, echoing across the city.

Khana froze. *They found the body.*

The bells meant an emergency. No one in or out. No exceptions until Yamueto gave the all-clear.

The guards jumped to attention. Some servants groaned as they realized their time off had vanished and cursed whatever had caused the alarm. Others tried to ask the guards what was going on as they closed and locked the gate.

"Everyone return to your rooms," the guards ordered over the cacophony. "We'll let you know what's happening as soon as we're told."

Everyone was supposed to go to their rooms, or other assigned spots, until they were checked and cleared. Their *possessions* checked and cleared. Anyone caught loitering was immediately arrested on suspicion.

I'm dead, Khana thought.

She glanced around the courtyard, looking for solutions. Servants wandered back inside the palace. She needed to move while there were still too many of them to keep track of.

The courtyard led to three different areas: the main palace directly behind her, an extensive garden to her right, and a cobblestone path to the temple of Vigerion on her left.

She'd never been particularly religious. But it was too light outside to effectively hide in the garden, so she went left, following the path around the corner.

As soon as she stepped over the temple's threshold, she was plunged into darkness. While there were windows to help keep the building cool on hotter days, they kept the shutters closed as often as possible, allowing candles to be the only source of light. Khana's eyes slowly adjusted.

There was only one main room beyond the entryway, and it was surprisingly austere for a temple. No grand statues or offerings of gold or anything else to show off the wealth of the building or its architect's ego. Just a single altar at the end of the room, lit by wax candles carefully melted onto the corners. Lanterns lit the edges of the room, flickering light and shadows against the wooden walls, making the small space somehow even more intimate. There were mats and pillows along the floor for meditation, and one silent priest sat in one, dressed all in black.

Khana stood frozen and silent, not daring to breathe, waiting for him to acknowledge her. But he never turned around.

She couldn't imagine Yamueto coming here to pray, yet he must have. This was where he went to revive those he deemed worthy. Supposedly, it was also where he'd learned the secret of immortality, and even the creation of night creatures.

Although the temple was small, Khana knew there was an underground catacomb, where the bodies of Vigerion's priests and most devout followers were laid to rest. Perhaps she could hide there until the gates opened.

She carefully stepped forward, deeper into the room, and found a paper door. Slipping her fingers between the frame and the wall, she silently pushed it open. A storage closet, with more black priest robes, several more candles, and cleaning supplies. Not a catacomb entrance.

Voices raised outside, quieted by a stark command from Yamueto. Panicking, Khana dove into the closet, closing the door behind her. She had to fold herself onto the floor, beneath the lowest shelf, the head-bag on top of her feet. Something wet leaked onto the arch of her foot, but she didn't dare adjust it. She kept the door open a crack so she could see out, just as Yamueto entered the temple, carrying the headless body of Kokaatl.

"Search for her," he ordered, looking back at someone still outside, likely his guards. "Letting her escape will set a poor example for the rest."

"At once, Your Excellency."

The meditating priest finally turned. A mask covered the lower half of his face, as all priests of Vigerion swore an oath of silence. He communicated plenty with the glare he sent to the emperor for speaking in this sacred space.

"Out," Yamueto said.

Huffing, the priest stood, bowed, and left the temple.

The emperor laid Kokaatl on top of the altar, carefully adjusting her dress so it wouldn't catch the candles. Khana couldn't see his face, but his body language was the same as always: commanding and unreadable. She put a hand over her mouth to silence her breathing.

Yamueto put his hands on the corpse and muttered, "Vigerion, I wish to trade."

All the candles, which so far had been still, flickered as one. The air turned cold and somehow heavy. Khana pressed herself deeper into the corner of the closet, her heart thundering in her ears.

It was only a few seconds, but it felt like eternity.

Nothing happened.

Yamueto slammed his fist against the stone altar. Khana jumped. She'd never seen him express any type of anger before. *Did the summons not work? Did Vigerion refuse to answer? Was he even real?*

Yamueto took a deep, meditative breath. He kissed the back of Kokaatl's hand before stalking out of the temple, passing feet away from Khana's hiding place. "Have the priests tend to her body. When you find Khana, keep her alive for me."

Khana swallowed, listening to his footsteps fade away, listening for the guards to leave. The priest didn't come back, probably gathering the others to tend to Kokaatl. They might have to go into her hiding closet to do that. She had to move.

She stepped out, head-bag in hand, then paused, studying the body.

The fact that Yamueto couldn't bring Kokaatl back, while pleasing, meant very little; he'd tried, and he'd tried by directly appealing to Vigerion.

Was it truly that simple?

I don't have time to linger, she scolded herself. Yet it would be a miracle if she got out of the palace while it was in lock-down.

She didn't truly believe in gods. And if they were real, they had ignored her prayers and those of all the other concubines. If they existed; she hated them. And yet, desperate times…

Khana approached the carefully-arranged altar holding the headless corpse, a surreal sight when she'd been alive only an hour ago. Khana set her bag against the stone and mirrored the pose Yamueto had used. She hadn't seen exactly where his hands had gone, but she was fairly sure that one had been on Kokaatl's stomach while the other was near her shoulder.

"Vigerion, I wish to trade."

Chapter Five

One moment, Khana stood over Kokaatl's corpse. The next, she was in a world of shadow.

It looked like the temple. It was, in fact, an exact copy. But the warm glow of candles had been replaced with cold, unearthly light. The altar, the walls, the corpse, all shades of indistinct gray.

Khana held up her hand, and was surprised to see it... *leave* her, for lack of a better term. She stepped to the side, and her spirit glowed with a light that reminded her of âji, flickering between a hundred different colors and intensely bright. The black and dark yellow was similar to Kokaatl's, but there was also a pale blue flickering around her fingers, growing stronger as she grew more curious. Orange tickled her feet. White and bright yellow flared from her chest.

Her gray, shadowy, physical body remained still as she moved. She passed her spirit-hand through her corporeal chest and met no resistance, wiggling her fingers on the other side.

Am I dead? she wondered. She didn't feel dead.

"First time?"

She jumped, whirling around. An old man in tattered robes held up a lantern. Its light didn't even reach the bottom of his beard.

Khana swallowed. "Master Vigerion?"

"That's my name," he said cheerfully. "Well, one of them. One of the older ones, anyway."

"What... what do you mean, sir?"

The lantern vanished, and the old man's body and clothes transformed into a tall woman with reddish-brown skin and a dress made of the night sky. Stars winked at her from the hem, and dark clouds moved across the fabric. Khana didn't recognize her, but it was enchanting.

"Tsermayu, Muobra, White Bone Dog, Hundred-Faced God, sometimes just plain 'Death,'" the figure said. With each name they changed their form: from the goddess of stars to a Reguallian man with a crow's head, to a large hound that was just a skeleton held together with fire, to a man with eight arms each holding a mask that fit on his faceless head, and finally to an androgynous person in a multi-colored robe with all black eyes. Khana cringed at the last; they looked like a night creature.

"They're just names," the deity said. "Names and shapes. I don't have nearly as many powers as everyone says I do. Certainly not as much authority to *act* on those powers. That's why I like talking to nonbelievers, like you. It lets me be a little more authentic." They laughed. "Especially since I span countless worlds and universes. It gets so confusing, playing a role that puts people at ease. What if I choose the wrong one?"

The idea that this wasn't a deity demanding worship made Khana relax a little. "If you're not a god," she asked, "then what are you?"

The being grinned. "Death."

She swallowed.

"Oh, dear. This really *is* your first time," they said, holding their chin. Their multi-colored robe flowed around them as if they stood under water, glowing and sparkling with more shades than Khana had ever seen before. And the colors *moved*, drifting across the fabric like vapor. A bruised purple clashed with deep black that swirled with turquoise across the hem. Blinding white and dull gold just barely missed each other on their left shoulder. A blob of blood red peeled from a larger one and drifted through a sea of sickly green across their chest.

"You didn't do this by accident, did you?" Death asked, sounding concerned.

"No, I needed..." What *did* she need?

Wait. This was Death, the collector of souls.

"I want my friend back," she said. "*Properly* back. I tried to resurrect her in the dungeon, but I just created a night creature. She was little more than a puppet, missing herself entirely."

"Her soul, most likely," they said. "I assume you just poured life force into her?"

Khana nodded, looking down at the dark gray floor. "That's all I knew how to do."

"Full resurrections cannot be done without my intervention," Death said, which made Khana feel marginally less stupid. "Who is your friend?"

"Sita – Sivusita, the princess. She was killed in the dungeons, tortured to death by Kokaatl."

Death prowled around Khana. She stayed very still, feeling like a hare watched by a fox. When Death moved from Khana's back to her front, they'd changed forms again. This time wearing Sita's kind face and silver hair, with a plain blue dress. The only difference was her eyes, still pure black. "This one? Quiet rebel? Smarter than her own good?"

Khana swallowed back tears. "Yes. That's her."

"Great. What are you willing to give?"

"Give…?"

"*I wish to trade*," Death said, using *Khana's* voice before switching back to their own: "I can't just give a soul back, even if I wanted to. You must give something up in return. Therein lies the magic."

"What do you want?" Khana asked cautiously.

"I don't really *want* anything. And before you ask: physical objects do nothing. You can't buy her back with gold or land or animals. You're asking for a soul. You need to give up something just as abstract."

Her throat went dry. "…*My* soul?"

"Not in its entirety," Death soothed. "You're a witch. You have certain privileges. And I prefer to see the unbreakable laws of the universe as loose guidelines. But for this to work, a sacrifice must be made, and it may very well be a *piece* of your soul, the way Yamueto did."

Khana's jaw dropped. "That's how he got immortality, isn't it?"

Death nodded. "Most witches in your world have forgotten how to contact me directly. I like it that way. Immortality does things to humans' heads."

"And his ability to merge bodies together to create night creatures?"

"Another trade, yes."

"What did he give you? If I may ask."

Death tapped a finger to their chin. Which, as they looked like Sita, was very odd, as that was not her habit. "For immortality, he gave me his ability for love and compassion, despite my warnings. He saw them as weaknesses; it didn't matter that they make up almost half of a person's soul. Immortality requires a steeper price than resurrecting one person, which is why most people who *do* know how to trade for it *don't*."

"He actually had compassion at one point?" Khana wondered, trying to picture a younger Yamueto being kind. The closest she'd ever seen was his treatment of Kokaatl.

"Barely. He didn't have a conscience at all, otherwise I'm sure he'd have offered that, too," Death said. "For the night creatures, he offered his passion for everything but conquest. Which means most of his emotions are gone. Hard to get angry about something if you don't care about it in the first place. Honestly, what's the point of immortality if you can't enjoy yourself?"

Khana wondered if one could throw up in the spirit world. Yamueto was a monster who had created himself. And if she wanted Sita back, she'd have to turn herself into the same type of creature. "I don't want to give up any of those things."

"Then you don't get your friend back," Death said, not unkindly. "While the life force required to heal her body would be easy enough, retrieving the soul itself is no small matter. Messing around with reality requires a trade that we can at least *pretend* is fair and equal. And, seeing your current predicament, you would still have to go down to the dungeon to heal her with life force, which would require another trade, and then find a way for you both to sneak out of a palace currently being searched by one of the most intelligent and ruthless people alive, with no plan, no training, and no backup." They spread their hands. "I've seen many things over the course of my existence, but I've never seen anyone manage that."

Khana dropped to her knees, tears running down her cheeks, sobs shaking her chest. She couldn't do it. She couldn't give up such a monumental part of herself to revive her friend, especially not if they were doomed to failure, anyway. How could she revive someone only to have them be tortured again?

"There, now," Death soothed, kneeling in front of her. Their face melted into the androgynous person with the black eyes and multi-colored robe. "There's no shame in this. I am inevitable, even to immortals."

"You don't understand," Khana hiccupped. "She died because of me."

"Perhaps," they agreed. "But if it makes you feel better, she wasn't angry when I collected her. She was mostly worried about you and the other girls she's been smuggling medicine to. I don't think she'd want you to waste any part of yourself over her. Not when she's lived a long, full life, and *you* are still in hot water."

Khana struggled to get herself under control, wiping the tears and snot from her face. Apparently, she could produce the stuff even in the spirit realm. Gross. "I can't linger. The emperor is searching for me–"

"Time is frozen here. Your heart hasn't even gone through a single beat." Death motioned to the shadowy form of Khana's physical body, still standing before the altar.

Khana relaxed. "Oh."

She sniffled, getting her breathing under control. Sita was gone. As much as it pained her to think it, Khana couldn't bring her back. The only thing she could do now was escape. She swallowed. "I need to get out of the city."

Death smiled. "Very good. I do believe I can help you with that."

"How?" she asked warily.

"The palace gates and walls are all heavily guarded. But there's one exit that has almost no guards – the gardens."

Khana frowned. "You mean... the gardens that overlook the *cliff*?"

"The very same!"

A little wall curled around the edge of those gardens to keep people from accidentally plunging to their death twenty stories below. The river had cut a ravine into the land, and the city had built itself around it. It was an impressive view, and she enjoyed walking the trail *well* away from the edge.

"The cliff's walls are unclimbable," Khana protested.

"Jumping is faster, anyway."

"If I do that, I'll die!"

"I'll give you enough life force to survive the fall," Death promised.

Khana studied the being. "At what cost?"

Death smiled again, pleased. "Life force is a much cheaper bargain than a human soul. For enough to survive a fall from that height, I'd only need a memory."

"...Just one?"

"Just one," Death confirmed. "The clearer and more emotional, the better. But it can be any kind of emotion."

Khana thought it over for a long moment. Death patiently waited, not saying anything or moving. They didn't even appear to be breathing, which... they probably didn't need to.

She could see how such a bargain could be twice the blessing. Khana had dozens of memories that she would rather do without. Guma's death. Sita's. The moments the princes had taunted her and the other concubines. All the times Yamueto had taken her to bed.

But who would she be, without her memories? They were still a part of her, unpleasant though they were. She'd spent so long living in the palace that she didn't know who she was outside of it. And if she forgot what she was running from, forgot the horrors that awaited if she were to return, then she'd stop running. She'd fall right back into Yamueto's hands and experience it all over again, if not worse.

With that in mind, she ultimately decided, "The day I was driven away from my homeland."

Death raised an eyebrow. "Really?"

"They fed me into the jaws of the beast, doing nothing to protect me. I want nothing to do with them."

"Fair enough." Death gently touched her forehead with a thin, pale finger. After a moment, they nodded. "Yes, that should be sufficient for what we need."

They held out their hand. After a brief hesitation, Khana took it.

Chapter Six

Khana blinked. Death and the shadowy spirit realm were gone. She was back in her physical body, a hand on Kokaatl's stomach.

A glowing hand.

Khana stepped back and looked down at herself. The servant's uniform covered most of her, but the parts of skin that were revealed – her hands, face, and ankles – glowed like a star. White and orange and indigo. Power surged through her veins, the likes of which she'd never felt before.

She tried to remember her life before the palace. She could recall what the Naatuun Desert looked like with its dunes and cacti and scorching sun. She knew the hazy details of Guma's face and her execution. But she couldn't remember the day she left the desert. Her parents must have packed her away in that carriage, right? Had they said anything to her before they did? Hugged her?

Khana didn't know. She no longer remembered. The last thing she recalled was Guma's blood on her father's sword, and her mother muttering, "You should have told us as soon as you knew. We wouldn't have had to go through this."

Well. That was all she needed to remember.

She pulled the hood of her cloak over her face, knowing it wouldn't do much to hide the glow. She'd be easy to spot until she was over the cliff – gods, was she really going to jump over a *cliff*? This was a terrible idea.

She peeked out the door of the temple. Death had been right: the gates were heavily guarded, as were the walls. And this was just the servants' side; it would be even worse elsewhere. There were at least a dozen guards between her and the garden. She'd have to move fast.

Lute on her back. Head-bag in hand. She sprinted out the door.

There was one factor of the excess âji she hadn't considered: with all that extra strength in her legs, she was much faster than usual. The world blurred around her, a haze of gray sky and wooden buildings. She was halfway across the courtyard before the first guard yelled at her. At the lip of the garden by the time a team of them chased after her.

She ran across the grass. Past the fishpond and its stone art. Past the hedges and jasmines and lilies. Towards the gnarled tree with branches that grew over the hedge perimeter, hiding the edge of the cliff from view.

"She's going to jump!" one of the guards gasped.

"Don't do it!"

Khana squeezed her eyes shut, pumped her legs, and hurled herself forward.

The wind roared in her ears as gravity yanked her down. There was one second of dizzying fall. Two. Three.

She hit the ground with a *thud*.

A bed of grainy mud cradled her. Rough, gritty, and very fatal from such a height.

At least, it should have been.

Khana cracked an eye open and breathed deep. She pressed her fingers to her throat just to be sure she still had a heartbeat. She did, strong and rabbit-quick.

She was alive.

Curled on the ground, she stared at the rock wall above, convincing herself that she was in fact still breathing. Even without looking at her now plain, dark skin, she knew that she no longer had any excess âji. Her *bones* were tired.

The guards' voices drifted down, barely audible over the sound of running water. She couldn't make out what they were saying, but she didn't need to. She stayed perfectly still, too terrified to move, hoping that they believed she was dead and would report that to Yamueto.

The voices soon left. Moving her head just enough to see the top of the cliff, she checked to make certain they were gone before scrambling to her feet. Mud clung to her clothes, and something twanged on her back.

Khana froze. *My lute.*

She scrambled out of her cloak, pulled off the strap keeping the lute to her back, and cried in anguish. It was completely destroyed, nothing but splinters and wires. She pressed the remainder of its neck to her forehead, the last of her tears falling on the shattered wood.

It was just a lute.

But it had gotten her through six years of torment.

Khana looked up, trying to blink the tears from her eyes. She didn't have time to mourn.

She kissed its remaining fragments, set them on the ground and stood. A few feet away, the river lazily sawed through the bottom of the ravine. It was an uninspiring sight, this far down, somewhere between brown and gray, and the beach she'd landed on was just a strip of mud. Rock walls closed in around her.

She found the dress-bag a few paces away, bleeding on the sludge.

"Well, you're not coming back anytime soon," she grumbled. She tossed the whole mess in the water. Giving one last reluctant look at her destroyed lute, she washed the blood from her hands and headed for the docks.

Khana ran until she wheezed, then ran some more. Her body, not used to running or even walking for long distances, held her down. She ignored its cries for rest, for water, for food, and ran harder.

She slowed to a walk only when she reached other people; women washing laundry in the water, children playing as they bathed, a couple of men trying to fish. Khana's breaths came deafeningly loud, and she walked on.

Soon, she reached the city proper. Boats and ships docked, fishermen shouted their wares, whores enticed men into their brothels. Khana let herself be carried by the crowd, into the city's heart. Canals had been dug from the river and nearby lake, allowing small boats to pass through all parts of the city, ensuring that you were never more than a few feet away from an open body of water at any given time. Nobody died of thirst in Balasco, although most refrained from drinking straight out of the canals and river. Khana stopped by one of the numerous pumps and fountains in the city and stayed for so long quenching her thirst that she caused a small line of impatient civilians behind her. She ran off, muttering apologies as she wiped cool water from her chin.

She walked for so long she got dizzy and had to sit against the wall of a building, its wood wet from mud and water. She needed food. Money. A way out.

Once the dizziness subsided, she got back on her feet. There were a handful of beggars nearby with bowls out and eyes down. They probably knew where she could find a free meal, but she'd have to ask and hope they helped her. Hope they didn't sense that something was wrong and turn her in. She couldn't do it.

Her feet carried her away. Already she missed her lute. Her thoughts were much calmer and clearer after plucking the strings.

It took some wandering, but eventually she found what she was looking for: a thin, empty alley, barely big enough to hold a stray cat, but it was clean – throwing one's waste in public was punishable by imprisonment since anything that got in the canals threatened to contaminate the intricate water supply.

Khana settled in the darkest corner and pulled out the jewelry she'd taken from Kokaatl's corpse. Much of it was unusable. Too distinct, too expensive for an average civilian to own. She set those aside to toss into the canals. She used her stolen kitchen knife to pry out the emeralds, rubies, and topazes of the others, bending and warping the gold so it was snarled and unrecognizable, then rubbed dirt into them so they looked older than they were. A dealer might suspect they were stolen, but not from the palace. Khana worked until her back ached and eyes drooped.

Her mind wandered to her homeland. She would have liked to return; stroll around the sand dunes, rock boulders, and oasis that had defined her youth. See if any of her childhood friends were still alive. But she couldn't. The Naatuun Desert was too far and would be the first place Yamueto would think to look. If she went even a mile east, she'd be found and caught.

She could go west, follow the river to the ocean. But if she tried to jump on one of the ships, she'd be caught. Last year a couple of concubines had tried the same, not knowing that ship-searches were one of the first things Yamueto did when hunting runaway wives. She'd have to walk to the ocean first, then proceed on ship.

But the river would be the *second* place Yamueto would look. It led to a walled city that protected the mouth from naval attacks and served as one of the first lines of defense for Balasco, as well as a major trade hub. It was too close, too obvious.

To the north, the empire stretched for over a thousand miles, gobbling up kingdoms like they were appetizers. But if she went south…

The immediate lands to the south had been conquered by Yamueto at least a generation ago. Beyond those borders was the free kingdom of Tlaphar, currently at war with the empire. They'd likely fall within a year.

But beyond Tlaphar lay the Simakhil Mountains, which served as the border between Tlaphar and the kingdom of Divaajin. Northern countries had been trying to conquer Divaajin for centuries and had failed because of those mountains and the country's fierce soldiers – the Ghura, Sita had called them. A group of nomads subdued by the kingdom and put to use protecting the mountains.

Khana shivered. There wasn't much more about Divaajin in the palace library. Just that they were a barbarous people who lived in frigid winters, ate raw meat, and slaughtered anyone who looked at them wrong.

All of that sounded preferable to going back to Yamueto.

If Khana could put them between her and the emperor, she'd be safe.

She looked at her wealth. Everything she owned in the world came down to the clothes she wore, a kitchen knife, and a handful of warped gold jewelry, all of it stolen. The sooner she traded her bounty for coins, the better.

She pulled herself to her feet and got to work.

Chapter Seven
Yamueto

"Tell me exactly what happened," Yamueto ordered. "Leave nothing out."

The four guards who had seen Khana go over the cliff all shifted their feet. They were supposed to look imposing with their metal helmets and thick leather armor, dyed a jungle green, but the action was childlike. Yamueto bit back a huff of impatience. He was immortal. He had all the time in the world. It wouldn't do to be impatient.

The five of them were the only souls in the courtyard, the palace still locked down. The order made the vast courtyard and elegant wooden castle a barren land of ghosts. Yamueto would keep it that way until he knew Khana didn't have an accomplice.

"She came out of the Temple of Vigerion, Your Excellency," the team captain reported, uselessly pointing across the courtyard. "Then ran straight for the gardens and jumped off the cliff."

Yamueto sighed, unable to suppress a flicker of annoyance. She must have been hiding while he tried to revive Kokaatl. They would have passed just a few feet apart from each other. How irritating.

"I've sent a team of guards to fetch her body," the captain continued. "It seemed to be intact, though we couldn't tell from our distance. She landed several feet from the water, so there's low risk of her getting swept downstream."

Excellent. Death may have denied him Kokaatl on account of her not having a head, but they would *not* deny him his justice.

Honestly, what was that girl thinking? He'd been doing this for centuries and had disciplined and achieved total control over *hundreds* of wives, to say nothing of the countries he'd conquered and subdued. He was master over death itself – what chance did any mere mortal have? Some people just didn't learn.

Ah, well. Perhaps she'd make a better night creature than concubine.

"Is that all?" Yamueto asked.

"Ah..." A lieutenant raised his hand. "I don't know if this is important or not, Your Excellency, but she was... glowing."

Yamueto's entire world shrieked to a halt. He stared at the lieutenant. "What?"

He swallowed. "Part of the reason we all saw her so soon was because she glowed. The cloak hid most of it, but I got a good look at her face and hands. They were all sorts of colors."

"The other men say the same," the captain added.

Yamueto looked over the guards' shoulders to the garden and the cliff. "Is she still there?"

"Sir?"

"Is she still at the base of the cliff?"

One of the guards ran to check. It took long moments for him to return, time Yamueto spent calculating if draining Kokaatl's life would have given Khana enough saviza to survive the fall. Or perhaps she had drained more bodies that hadn't yet been discovered?

The guard sprinted back, breathing hard. "She's gone!"

"Did the water get her?" the captain asked.

"No, it's been too slow for that."

Not just survived, but fully mobile then. Kokaatl's death had happened in the dungeons; Khana would've been spotted long before reaching the temple if *that* had been what she'd used.

There was only one answer. She had learned to contact Death.

For the first time in a long time, true worry, the very start of fear, unfurled in Yamueto's belly. He couldn't have anyone uncovering his secrets. As soon as they did, there would be dozens, hundreds of immortals. More architects of night creatures. His entire empire could collapse under the weight of so many powerful witches coming after his throne.

"Send a team down there to follow her trail," he ordered. "Dispatch more into the city. Put checkpoints at every exit. For every day she is at large, I'm executing a guard." He pointed to his captain. "Starting with you."

Chapter Eight

The jeweler she found in the poorest, most crowded part of the city squinted at Khana when she presented her wares, claiming that they were something she found in her late grandmother's house. He gave her a couple strings of coins, a fraction of what the jewelry was actually worth. She didn't try to argue or negotiate, just took the pay and left.

She used the kitchen knife to sheer her hair, the thick black locks sinking to the bottom of the canal. The jungle heat meant that women often just wore a skirt, no top, and half the men wore nothing but loincloths as they went about their daily tasks. Others wore cotton robes or long shirts, sometimes sewn or dyed with intricate patterns and designs.

With no hair, and now enough money to buy a loincloth, plain long shirt, and sandals, Khana became nothing more than a laborer in the city. She bought a threadbare bag and the cheapest, ready-made food she could fill it with: bread made from millet. It had been out all day and was rougher than twigs.

As the final hour of the setting sun cast dark shadows over the buildings, Khana joined the flow of men leaving the city. The farmers and field laborers who had come to sell their wares, or conduct other business, now hurried to make it back to their homes before dark. Khana joined a small group leading donkeys and carrying their loads to one of the gates.

As she suspected, extra guards stood at the entrance. She saw a few imperial horses and sucked in a breath. It was the standard response: Yamueto sent his fastest riders to secure the city when a concubine or other fugitive tried to leave. They always reached the wall and port before anyone else, as hooves are faster than feet. This time tomorrow, there would be posters of Khana's likeness hung all over the city, and everyone would be hunting for her, seeking a reward from the emperor. She had to get beyond those wooden walls by then.

She raised her hood and lowered her face, keeping her gaze on the sandaled feet of the man in front of her. Her loincloth and long shirt felt too big, too awkward, too billowy. Surely everyone around her could see that she was a fraud?

She hardly dared to breathe as she walked past the guards, through the city gate...

And out.

Khana kept walking, not daring to look behind her as the men peeled off one by one, mile after mile, until it was just her walking the southern path that led into the jungle. She kept going until the sky went black, making it impossible to see further than her hand, forcing her to stumble against a large tree and spend the night.

She'd thought she was out of tears, but apparently not. As soon as her bum hit the ground, she wept with relief.

She was out.

The rest of the season passed in a blur of mosquito bites, hunger cramps, and blistered feet. She had to sip âji from the trees around her to heal her feet and keep going, being careful not to take enough to damage the trees and leave a trail. While âji didn't feed her, it did have the benefit of erasing her exhaustion for as long as she glowed, allowing her to travel farther and longer.

While her endurance for the road was non-existent, her navigation skills remained sharp. Every child of the desert knew how to navigate by sun and stars, knew the stories of the constellations and clusters. The palace library had kept a well-stocked supply of land maps and star charts as well, and while the stories were different, the celestial bodies remained the same. There were even songs about them, and she sang them to avoid boredom, missing her lute like a limb. She never got turned around, never had to wonder which way to go, because she could always find south.

She walked quickly through the jungle, wincing at every sound. Slithering snakes, tigers and panthers, falling tree branches – there were a million ways to die out here. She stopped to rest by a stream and refilled her waterskin, breathing hard. Her stomach cramped with hunger, and her limbs shook with exhaustion. Her rations had been eaten the day before.

She glanced up at the nearest tree and froze.

There, on one of the smaller branches by her head, crouched a small, colorful frog. Its yellow and black pattern was almost blinding against the browns and greens around it, and it didn't seem to have a care in the world at how obvious it was to predators. It watched her with big, beady eyes, unflinching.

It took Khana a second to recognize its species. She'd never seen one in real life, but she'd read about poison dart frogs in the library. Some of the earliest people who lived in these jungles had coated their arrows and darts with the frog's poison. The barest touch of its skin could kill a fully-grown man, never mind a small bird.

How can something so tiny be so dangerous? Khana thought. She backed away slowly, choosing a different tree for her âji, curing her fatigue and moving on.

Chapter Nine

Two months after killing Kokaatl saw Khana in Tlaphar, at its southern border with Divaajin. The mountains were the biggest things she'd ever seen, and she'd collected dozens of horror stories during her travels of people falling prey to leopards, avalanches, and the cold air itself. So, with the last of her money, she hired a guide from the village of Pelete at the mountain's feet. The Reguallian forces closed in on Tlaphar's capital, and everyone speculated that it'd be a matter of days before the kingdom fell.

Traveling through the mountains was one of the most stressful experiences of Khana's life. Some of the roads were so narrow that a slight misstep would have sent her careening off the side, with no âji to cushion her fall. The wind cut through her with icy knives, despite her guide assuring her that it was, in fact, late spring.

"In winter, is much worse," he spoke in broken Reguallian. "Big storms, make you not see. Wind blows you off. Snow buries you twenty paces down."

"Snow?" she echoed.

He pointed to the white-covered top of the next mountain over. "White things. Snow. Get warm and turn to water. Get colder, turn to ice."

Huh. Snow. She'd heard of the stuff, vaguely. How did it get there?

The journey took weeks, winding through the maze of stone that made Khana dizzy just to think about. Her guide caught mountain goat, hare, mice, even a fox at one point, cooking them over a fire. Khana shared the last of her bread with him, bought weeks ago in the last town and tasting just as bad as the first batch she had gotten.

They rarely spoke to each other, but about halfway through their journey, the guide said bluntly, "You are girl."

Khana bristled. "What? No, I'm–"

"No hair," he said, patting his own beard that had grown shaggier in the last week. "You go away to pee. No cock."

She stilled, suddenly very afraid. She needed him alive to get out of these mountains. What was he going to –

"Do not worry," he said, grinning. "Me, good man. No sex. Too cold! Unless you want."

"...Thank you," she said, not entirely reassured. Especially since, every night, they had to sleep huddled together against whatever shelter they could find from the wind: caves, stone walls, even an abandoned cougar den. But he kept his word and didn't touch her.

It was a long, harsh journey. Khana usually found herself humming under her breath; if she focused on a tune, she wasn't focusing on how her hands and feet were blocks of ice, how she was miles from anything familiar or how one misstep could spell her death. The guide never asked her to stop, so she kept humming.

Finally, they descended into a town too large to be a village, too small to be a proper city.

"This, Pahuuda," the guide said. "Good town."

Almost all the buildings were made of stone, likely pulled straight from the mountain. When Khana got close enough to touch, she saw that some of them had decorative carvings in the rock: wolves, soldiers, cats, divine beings she didn't recognize. The rooftops were sharply slanted like arrowheads. Even the animals here were strange: rather than herding sheep or cattle, the farmers herded massive woolly beasts with large horns and dark faces. She found out later those were called yaks. Others herded some of the shaggiest goats she'd ever seen.

The oddly-shaped houses were huge, and so were the people. The first few men she passed were almost twice her size, dressed in only a few layers of cotton and wool. Despite it being the start of summer, it was still chilly. How were they not shivering like she was?

Given that the men both held spears and shields, they were likely soldiers, patrolling the streets. They nodded to the guide, who raised a hand in greeting and led Khana past them.

"Most speak no Reguallian," he warned as they passed more people. "Speak Ghura, here."

"I don't know Ghura," she said, trembling. Whether that was from cold, or fear of this land of giants, she didn't know.

"Some refugees here, like you. Go to east of town, you find them."

"Thank you." They were still fairly high up the mountain, enough to look down on most of the town. Beyond that, there was nothing but an empty field of short grass. "What's beyond that?"

"Tundra," he said, using a word she didn't know. "Cold nothing. Big animals. No grass. No trees. Next city, many miles."

"So it's a desert," she muttered. One she didn't know how to navigate. "How do you get through?"

He shrugged. "I never go to tundra."

Great. She needed to hire another guide, after spending all of her money on this one.

"I find inn now," he said. "Sleep in bed. You, go east. Find Reguallians."

"Thank you," she said, sincerely. Though frustrated that he couldn't help her further, she never would have gotten this far without him.

She wandered into the town, clutching her threadbare bag to her chest. Not everyone was as large as those two soldiers; some were merely a head taller than her. Most ignored her. Some people glanced at her, with a frown or sneer of annoyance. She was a dirty, tattered mess after walking through an empire, a kingdom at war, and the mountains. She couldn't imagine she smelled particularly great, either.

Everyone spoke a language she didn't know – Ghura, she supposed. It was almost lyrical, something you'd play a big horned instrument to. She wondered if the rest of the kingdom spoke the language, or just this little piece of it.

A pair of women played a flute and drum on a street intersection, gathering coins in a hat. Khana watched, mesmerized, for far longer than she should have. She didn't recognize the tune at all, something bright but with melancholic dips now and then. Eventually, she forced herself to move on.

As she moved further east, the people felt more familiar, and so did the language. Reguallians, refugees from the very empire Khana had fled, dressed in heavier cotton but with similar patterns that she was used to seeing. She spotted some Tlapharians, too, but they spoke the same language, albeit with a different dialect.

They lived in the same strange buildings as the rest of Pahuuda, though they were smaller and closer together than the others. The people here were still taller than her, but that was true of every adult Khana had ever met. At least they weren't the giants who ran the rest of the town.

She found a small cluster of women hanging laundry between two houses, laughing and chatting. She steeled her nerves and approached. "Excuse me?"

They stopped talking and two of them looked mildly curious, but the third was blatantly suspicious. "Yes?"

"I was wondering if there were any caravans or guides going through the... tundra?"

"Some traders. Why?"

Khana winced. "Tlaphar isn't doing well. It's only a matter of time before it falls."

"Let it. The empire will never cross the mountains."

"That explains why we've been seeing more refugees pass through," another muttered. They spoke fluent Reguallian, but with an accent. Khana wondered if they were refugees like her guide had said, or if they'd been born here.

"Please?" she asked.

The third took pity on her. "If you really want to cross the tundra, you'll need at least a month's worth of food and supplies. And probably some sort of guide. Some of the traders cross to do business in the city, and vice versa, but they don't like taking stowaways, and they already have apprentices to carry their luggage. You'd have to bribe them to get them to agree to take you."

"Sometimes women and boys can do *special* work for them," another added, rolling her eyes. "But... you need to be pretty for *that* job."

Khana's chest tightened.

"Sometimes you can hire the hunters," the first woman continued, like her friend hadn't spoken. "They don't mind taking odd jobs. But again, you have to pay them."

None of this was what Khana wanted to hear. She bowed her head anyway. "Thank you. Where can I start working?"

"The town has a couple of brothels. They might take you; you look exotic, and that's enough for some. Otherwise, Heimili runs an inn. He has a soft spot for refugees."

Khana thanked them again and left. She was beyond the mountains now; that was the important thing. But it was still too close to the empire's borders; as soon as Tlaphar fell, she would be closer still. Khana wouldn't be safe until she had the tundra, a few cities, and maybe an ocean or two between her and Yamueto. She needed money, and she needed to start making it now.

She found one of the brothels first. She'd seen several during her travels, young women draping themselves against the walls to look enticing. This place sported both women and men – a rarity in Khana's experience – all wearing a little bit of pink and flirting with anyone who passed by. A few flirted back, but only a handful actually entered the building. Khana watched them, stalling in the middle of the muddy street.

Maybe letting someone use her body wouldn't be so bad if she was getting paid for it? If she knew for a fact that it was temporary. If she could leave or refuse certain clients. If she actually got something from it...

She crept closer, trying to get a better look at the workers without being obvious. She didn't see any bruises, but those could be hidden with makeup. They seemed happy, but they were whores. Acting was part of the job. Maybe if she could just pull one or two aside to ask...

A man spanked an older whore with a *crack* that made Khana jump. "There's my favorite girl!"

The woman giggled, flipping her black-and-gray braid over her shoulder. "It's been a while! I was worried you'd found someone else."

"Well, worry not, my dear. I just got paid, and I don't intend to leave until morning."

Feeling her face heat as she watched the whore pull the punter into the building, Khana turned and walked away. She would never be able to do that. One of those men would grab her the wrong way or handle her too roughly, and she'd end up crying and begging them to stop. Maybe they would, maybe they wouldn't, but that didn't matter. She didn't have the fortitude for that kind of work; she'd be back on the street in no time.

Selling her witchcraft was too risky. Healing was valuable, even if it meant sacrificing plants or animals to do it. It was also, unfortunately, very noticeable. Talk would spread. Quite possibly beyond the mountains to Yamueto. Best to avoid it if she could.

After asking directions a couple of times, Khana found the inn on the edge of a winding street. It didn't have a name, just *tavenido*, the Reguallian word for *inn*, carved into the stone above the door. Khana stepped inside.

It was her first time indoors in weeks. The warmth made her groan. The ground floor was a restaurant, and there was a massive fireplace in one wall that pulled Khana in like a moth. She almost put her hands in the flames to warm them.

Animal hides hung on the walls, probably for further insulation, as well as colorful blankets woven in intricate patterns. There was no wooden furniture, instead mats and thin cushions marked spots for people to sit and eat. Khana hadn't noticed in her rush to the fireplace, but a handful of people were sat enjoying a midday meal, cross-legged on the floor in trios or pairs, drinking from cups made of animal horns. Most were clearly Reguallian, but there were some native Ghura.

A large man came out of the kitchens, spotted her, and approached with a heavy limp. His leg was missing, replaced by something carved of either pale wood or bone. He clapped his hands when he got closer, filling the air with puffs of flour that stained his wool clothes and bushy beard gray like a ghost. *"Nachu! Imatiya sadat ta?"*

Khana smiled. "I'm sorry, do you speak Reguallian?"

"Some," he replied in a rough baritone. "You want a room?"

"Well, yes, but..." She paused, and he raised a bushy eyebrow, waiting.

Khana took a breath. "I'm a refugee. I have no money. I just arrived today. I'm looking for work."

He hummed but said nothing. Khana bit her lip, waiting. What more could she say? She had nothing to convince him with.

"Too little for kitchen work," he decided. "Clean?"

"Yes!" she blurted. "I can clean. Sweep and mop. Pick up plates. Do bedding and sew up any holes. Do dishes and–"

He held up a hand. She stopped her rambling, feeling her face heat.

"I am Heimili," he said. "My son is Haz. My mother, Amati, she is old. You help her in day. Make beds. Clean rooms. At night, we get people. You help me and Haz. Speak with Reguallians and Tlapharians so we speak to Ghura. Clean kitchen and dining hall."

All the tension Khana had carried since she arrived drained from her shoulders. "I can do that."

"Pay is little. Most money goes to more food, blankets, fire. Your pay is room and food. But customers, they give tips. Extra. They are big in summer, small in winter. You, Haz, Amati, me, we share tips. Understand?"

That would likely not be as much as she wanted, but if she was able to save up...

"I do not have to pay for a room or any food you give me?" she clarified.

"No." He looked down at her. "But do not take too much. Three meals. Maybe a little between. Any more, you pay. You do bad work or steal; I throw you out."

That was fair. She took off the hat she'd bought on the other side of the mountains, running a hand through the inches of tangled black hair that had grown over the last few months. "When do I start?"

"After you eat."

Chapter Ten

Heimili stuffed her so full of food Khana didn't want to move for the next week. He had set her on one of the thin cushions in the corner of the room and fetched her a meal fit for an emperor – noodle soup with bits of meat and roots, served with half a loaf of chuta, a type of bread that had an almost grainy taste that Khana couldn't identify, but cinnamon, ginger, cloves, and seeds came through strongly. There was no silverware, but that didn't stop her from inhaling the soup, using the chuta to mop up the dregs.

All of this was washed down with a pot of tea, which was the most familiar part of her meal, and yet still foreign. Reguallian teas were subtle, delicate, made from fruits, flowers and other sweet things. Ghuran tea was sharp and bitter to the point of needing a few spoonfuls of cream, which Heimili also, thankfully, had on hand, even if it came from an animal she couldn't identify.

Khana couldn't remember the last time she'd had a proper meal, never mind one she actually *enjoyed*, free from fresh horrors and immediate worries. She snatched up another half of bread that Heimili wordlessly placed in front of her in between tending to customers and gobbled that down as well.

"If I didn't know any better, I'd say Baba just hired a wolf in girl's clothing."

Khana startled. The young man kneeling on the opposite cushion was not Heimili, though they shared the same wide nose, reddish-brown skin common in this town, and dark eyes. When he grinned at her, it showed the gap between his two front teeth, and his brown wool shirt was almost dark enough to hide the food stains of various age and size.

She swallowed her last mouthful, considering denying that she was a girl. But she knew she wouldn't be able to keep that lie going for very long. Best to start this employment off with some level of honesty. "Sorry. It's really good!"

"Oh, I know. Best chuta in town. Don't let those liars in the restaurant down the street tell you otherwise. I'm Hasyamin. Call me Haz."

"Khana." She tipped her head in a bow. "Good to meet you, Master Haz."

"Blech. Baba might be all right with you calling him 'master' since he's employing you, but not me. I'm too young and pretty to be ordering anyone around." He made a face. "And now, of course, he's asked me to order you around once you're done eating, or at least show you your room and what you'll be doing here."

Khana finished her tea and got to her feet, fighting back a yawn. Being in a warm building with a belly full of hot food made her tired. But she refused to show her fatigue as Haz took her dishes to the kitchen, then brought her upstairs, leading her through the narrow stone halls.

"Why is only the front door made of wood, and the rest here are curtains?" she asked. Most of the curtains blocking off rooms were blankets of woven wool, or animal skins.

"Because wood is horribly expensive," Haz explained. "To get to a forest, you have to either cross the mountains or the tundra. Baba was ridiculously proud when he was able to install that wooden door out front. The Old Families, though, they have wooden doors for every room *and* a bunch of furniture in each room, too."

"Old Family?"

"They run the mountains and tundra. Seven families, and one person from each is elected chief every seven years. Most are from here – like Chief Phramanka, her family's always been in Pahuuda – but a few are from other Ghuran towns. The Cila family's all the way by the ocean but sent someone here to help Phramanka run things. This is you."

He showed her a room that had the skin of a very furry animal as a door – perhaps it had been one of those creatures she'd seen grazing the tough grass out in the fields. More pelts on the floor served as her bed. There was a fireplace in the corner, a metal lantern and a handful of candles she could use for extra light, and a small window with a stone grate over it. A bit of wool served as a curtain, which she figured she could use to "close" her window.

"Animal bones burn hotter and longer than wood," Haz said. "You ever burn bone?"

"No."

"We can show you how to do that. It takes a while, but it's worth it."

"Thank you," she said. "Your Reguallian is very good."

She'd guessed that Haz and Heimili were mostly, if not entirely, Ghuran given the skin, height, and facial features. But that fluency came with years of experience, and Haz didn't seem much older than her. He'd grown up with it.

"Well, Baba's never been that good at it, which annoyed Mimi enough that she made sure I was fluent," Haz explained. "Speaking of, I should probably introduce you to her. She gets cranky if we forget about her."

Khana left her meager belongings in the room and followed Haz to the back of the inn, where an old woman washed a bedsheet. A Reguallian, with wrinkled tan skin and a delicate, bird-like build.

"Mimi, meet your new employee," Haz cheered. "At least until dinner. Khana, this is my grandmother, Amati."

Amati studied Khana with cold, sharp eyes. Khana dipped into a small bow. Amati sighed. "Your father needs to stop picking up strays."

"You know he can't resist a pretty face."

Khana stiffened. Was that why Heimili had taken her on? Maybe she should've kept pretending to be a boy.

"Do you know how to sew, girl?" Amati asked.

"Yes," she said. She'd mended all her clothes at the palace. And before that, she and her mother would work on various sewing and weaving projects together.

Amati motioned to a pile of folded pelts and linens in the corner. "Those each have at least one hole or tear in them. Get a kit and sew them up."

With that, Khana's first day of work officially started. It had been years since she'd had to sew pelts, and they were far tougher than the silks and cottons she was used to. But she made sure every tear was meticulously mended, difficult to re-break, and as invisible as she could make them. Amati grunted over her work, and when she said only, "Help me fold these sheets," Khana took her lack of complaint as a compliment.

Amati coughed into her sleeve, so hard and harsh that Khana worried she'd break. "Are you all right?"

Amati waved her off. "Old lungs kicking up a fuss."

"I'll get some water–"

"I'm fine. Hand me the black thread."

Khana silently obeyed, keeping a worried eye on the old woman. "Will I be meeting Haz's mother?"

"Only if you die," Amati said. "Sickness got her after the birth."

"I'm sorry."

"Bah. None of us survive this life."

Haz came to fetch Khana as the sun set and the dinner rush began. It was far more stressful than sewing. Heimili spent most of the time in the kitchen, leaving her and Haz to handle the dining room while he heated soup in a giant cauldron and pulled chuta from the stone oven.

The dining hall filled with customers: a couple of happy farmers in the corner celebrating a birthday, a harried mother looking for someone else to feed her children by the fireplace, an exhausted-looking hunter who drooped against the wall. Khana fetched bowls of soup and bread, and poured an endless amount of tea, vodka, and mead. When someone left, she took their dishes to the kitchen and, following Haz's lead, beat the dirtier cushions outside or over the fire to get the crumbs out.

Most of the customers spoke Reguallian, which was a relief, and the ones that weren't fluent knew enough to communicate what type of food they wanted. Only one person came to the inn looking for a room to sleep in – a trader from the east who only spoke Ghura. Haz handled that one.

"You're new. Refugee?" several asked. She smiled and nodded.

"Just tell Heimili I want my usual. He'll know," a few said.

"Pretty face. No wonder Heimili hired you," someone else said with a wink. Khana's polite smile became forced as she buried that particular worry further down and asked for their order.

"At least we're not packed," Haz commented, handing her a new kettle of tea. "Some nights, we have more customers than cushions. Just don't dump this in someone's lap."

"I'll try," Khana replied dryly.

One unexpected joy came from the fact that the more drunk some customers became, the more they sang. No instruments, no audience, just bursting into random song. Some of them were Reguallian ballads that she'd heard performed in court. Others had lyrics better suited to a brothel. It made her face heat and Haz laugh. Others still were in Ghura that she didn't recognize, but she nodded along to the beat as she refilled their cups. The songs raised everyone's spirits, including her own. They made her a little more confident, especially when she knew one enough to sing along.

One thing that Khana noticed was Pahuudans were a lot more tactile than other people she'd seen. Certainly more so than imperial culture permitted, which taught from birth that you didn't touch anyone unless they were family. She saw a bit of that familiar hesitancy in a few of the Reguallians here, but many still clapped their friends on the back, squeezed each other in hugs, or ruffled each other's hair. In the Naatuun Desert, she'd had no siblings, but one of her friends had had six brothers. The people in the inn reminded her of them.

About halfway through the night, a new face entered, alone. Khana almost bumped into him on her way to the kitchen, swerving at the last second so hard she almost tripped.

He grabbed her arms to steady her. *"Thitchu nalahami ta?"* he chuckled.

"I'm so sorry," she blurted, quickly regaining her balance. Thank goodness she hadn't been carrying any food.

He let her go as soon as it was clear she wouldn't fall, palms up in a soothing manner. Like everyone else here, he towered over her by almost two hand-lengths. He had a short, well-trimmed black beard on his square jaw, and hair the same shade. He wore it long and braided over his left shoulder, probably to make it easier to reach the quiver of arrows on his back.

"It is all right," he said in a thick Ghuran accent, his voice soft and kind. He reminded her of the hunting dogs her father raised that would cuddle up to her by the fire, hoping for treats or scratches.

She fixed the pale gray and white cloak on his shoulders that had almost been pulled off in their collision, the soft wolf fur swallowing her hand. She wondered if his beard was just as soft. "Oh good, you speak Reguallian."

"Some. I am still learning."

"That's all right," she said. "Better than my Ghura."

"Khana, we need you in the back!" Haz called over.

She jolted. Here she was standing in front of this man like an idiot when she had a job to do.

"Oh, hey Sava!" Haz greeted.

"Good evening, Haz." Sava grinned, which – unfairly – made him more handsome.

His name was magic. The place had been lively before, but as soon as everyone realized Sava was here, they all shouted greetings. He politely moved around Khana to sit with a group of men playing dice, patting people on the shoulder and smiling.

Khana joined Haz. "Who is he?"

"Sava? He's Chief Phramanka's son, part of the Bvamso family."

She couldn't hide her shock. "He's... royalty?"

Haz laughed. "We don't have royalty here. But the Bvamsos are one of the Old Families. See the wolf pelt? They're the only people allowed to wear those, just like the Pinnsviris are the only people allowed to wear porcupines, Cituvas wear leopards... you get it."

"What's he doing here? Shouldn't he be in the... richer part of town?"

"Is that your polite way of saying, 'What's he doing in a dump like this?'"

"It's not a dump!" She rather liked this little inn. It was warm, homey, and seemed safe. So far.

Haz snickered. "I'm just teasing you. Sava likes going out into the town. He asked me to teach him Reguallian so he could actually talk to everyone. He comes here every few days to practice. Fast learner, that one. Help me get these loaves to that woman in the yellow hat; Heimili made her extra for her parents."

Khana did as asked, stealing glances at Sava as she went about her duties. He quickly shed his cloak, revealing long, muscled arms and a brown vest cinched at the waist by a surprisingly bright blue belt. She didn't see any trace of fear, disgust, or apprehension on anyone's faces, not even when Sava lost all his coins to the night's gambling. He just knocked the winner's shoulder with a laugh and let them buy him another drink. Khana was right there to refill their cups and bowls.

Yamueto and most of his princely children ruled with fear. Servants and nobles alike crept in their shadow, never daring such levity to their superiors. The fact that these people were so open and relaxed around the chief's son put Khana further at ease.

Sava's group was the last to leave. The sun had set two hours ago, and Khana's legs and back screamed at her while her stomach grumbled once more. But at least she was warm.

She carried the last of the dishes into the kitchen, where Heimili and Amati washed them in a basin of water that she'd seen them toss and refill half a dozen times. It was already murky brown again.

Heimili jerked his chin toward a pair of steaming bowls. "For you and Haz. Go eat."

Part of her jumped at the chance, but the kitchen was still a mess, and she didn't want him to think she was lazy. "Do you need help?"

He shook his head. "Your first day. Good work. Go eat."

Beaming with the praise, she took the two bowls of soup and looked for Haz. He was sitting on the cushion next to Sava. Half of the gambling group had left, leaving plenty of room. Khana hesitated. She should give Haz his bowl and then retreat to her room. Looking at Sava made her stomach flutter in ways she didn't understand and filled her with a nervousness she would much rather leave alone. The excitement from earlier was replaced by the dread and fear of reality.

"Khana! Over here." Haz waved her over.

The decision had been made for her. Khana quietly joined them, handing him his bowl. The gambling continued without missing a beat. Sava, Haz, and the others lost and gained small piles of coins while Khana sipped her soup and wondered if the money on the floor in front of her was enough to hire that guide over the tundra.

"Oh! Almost forgot." Haz handed her a pouch that jingled. "Your share of the tips."

Payment already? This job kept getting better and better. Khana did a quick count. "Will this get me a thicker coat?"

"Pfft. Just use one of mine. I've outgrown half a dozen, and they're all shoved in the back of my closet for Amati to tear apart." He looked her up and down. "Maybe trim them a little, so you don't drown."

"That's... thank you, Haz."

The boys quickly finished their game. Khana couldn't quite follow it, being unfamiliar with the rules, but she knew that Haz had lost, given his grumbling and Sava's snickering. The other two men were deep in their cups, and one of them started singing. Badly.

His friend – who wore a scarf and had been silent all night – clamped a hand over his mouth before he could get past another stanza in cracked, out of tune lyrics.

"*Thank* you," Haz said empathetically, covering his ears.

The drunk man – a Ghuran – said something. Haz snorted, then translated for Khana: "He says that a beautiful night needs a beautiful song. But that requires someone to *sing in tune*."

"What are good Reguallian songs?" Sava asked.

"You will pray for death if I sing them," Haz promised. "Khana? Know any good ones?"

She almost choked on the last mouthful of soup. "Um..."

The drunks stared at her with wide-eyed curiosity. Sava put his square chin on his hand and gave a patient smile.

Khana straightened her back and sang the first thing that came to mind:

"There once was a frog
With little green toes
Who wanted to jump
The mountain..."

It was a children's tale, sometimes sung as a lullaby, about an ambitious little frog. The impossible task of jumping the mountain took a year and involved him almost getting eaten by every type of animal there was, until he finally did it.

When she was done, the drunk bellowed his approval, and the others clapped.

"You have a great song," Sava said warmly, making Khana's cheeks heat even as he frowned. "No, not song. Haz, what is...from the neck..."

"Voice," he chuckled. "Singing voice."

"Yes!"

The drunk begged for another, and Khana kept them entertained until her voice got scratchy and Haz finally kicked them all out. Gods, it felt good to make music again, even if her audience probably wouldn't remember it.

Sava finished his drink, counted his winnings, then split it between Khana and Haz. "Tips."

"What?" she gasped, staring at the pile of coins in front of her.

"Ooh, more money," Haz cheered.

"This is yours," Khana argued, pushing the coins back to Sava. "You won them."

"And now I tip," Sava replied, getting to his feet and donning his wolfskin cloak.

She opened her mouth to argue further, when Haz shook his head. "He won't take them back. Baba *and* Mimi have tried." He gave a dramatic sigh. "Best to resign yourself to it."

Sava snorted, flicking Haz in the head. "Good night."

"'Night!"

Sava left, and the inn was bereft of customers. Khana hadn't realized that the singing and gambling had relaxed her so well until it sank in that she was alone with her employers.

"That's enough to get you three pairs of boots with holes in them, or one that will actually keep your feet warm," Haz said, motioning to her share of Sava's winnings.

"What about a tundra guide?" she asked.

"Hmm. We had a refugee work for us a while ago who was good with his money, collected big tips, and was a decent gambler. It took him two years."

Khana's hopes fell. She bagged her coin. "Well. We'd better head to bed."

She looked over her shoulder to the kitchen. It was dark, all the candles and oven fires out. "Where's your father?"

"Bed, by now. He goes down like a rock after a long night."
She relaxed. She was safe. For now.
Unless *Haz* pressured her.
He didn't. He yawned and stood. "I'm going to bed. Good night."
"G-Good night."

Chapter Eleven

The next day, Haz announced his desire to take her on a tour of the town. "Baba likes to send me to do his dirty work down the street," he explained over an early lunch, during those odd hours between rushes. Although "rush" wasn't the right word; it seemed the evening gush of customers watered down to a trickle in the morning.

"If I show you around, that means we get to send *you* out there to fetch his ingredients and argue with farmers over prices," he cheered.

"I can't imagine his leg makes it easy," Khana said. "What happened?"

"Childhood accident. Apparently, he got cocky trying to climb the mountain when he was a few years younger than me and took a bad fall. It got infected, and the healer had to amputate. Good thing that break wasn't any higher, or the world would've been deprived of my marvelous presence."

Khana chuckled and sipped her tea. Haz had woken her that morning by tossing his old cloak at her head, and she wrapped it around herself now. It trailed at her heels, but it was thick wool, dyed almost black, and when she tucked herself in not even the wind could cut through it. She walked out of the inn beaming.

Haz pointed to various stone buildings and told her who lived there or what business it was. Most people dressed like him: plain wool or cotton clothes, maybe a cloak, hardly any shivering or bundling. These people were accustomed to the cold. Some women wore dresses or skirts, some men wore robes, but it seemed most people wore trousers, including the women, sometimes with a short decorative skirt over them. Khana wondered if that was warmer.

"What's the Ghuran word for house?" Khana asked. Might as well pick up the language while she was here.

By the time they'd drifted to a statue in the town square, Haz had given Khana basic Ghuran vocabulary for house, street, left, right, man, woman, child, and a handful of other words. She studied the statue as they approached. It was a bearded man with a walking stick in one hand and a sword in the other. Haz pointed to it. "That's Chief Pahileed. Before settling the mountains, our people used to be nomads."

Khana remembered that bit of history from the palace library. "Really?"

"Traveled all around. Sometimes trading, but mostly we made money with mercenary work." His buck-tooth grin went crooked. "It got to the point where if two kingdoms were at war and one of them hired us, the other would immediately surrender."

"Did Divaajin beat you in a war?"

"No! Is that what they teach you over the mountains?" he laughed. "We would've been nomads forever, but kingdoms got bigger. More powerful. It got too dangerous to cross their borders, and too much of a pain to beat them in a fight. Lucky for us, we'd done a lot of work for Divaajin. They were our favorite client. So when Chief Pahileed decided it was time to lead his people to settle down, he asked the King for a spot."

"And he sent you *here*? That doesn't seem very nice."

"Khana, think about it. You're king of a land that's as flat as frozen piss on a plate. Most of your kingdom is near the ocean, with all your trade and farmland and everything else a country needs, and you've got a tundra and these big mountains in the north blocking most enemies from getting through. Except there are paths through the mountains that armies can get through and attack from behind. So, when a tribe of the fiercest, toughest warrior mercenaries pledges their allegiance to you and asks for a place to build, do you put them with the rest of your army, or put them where everyone else is too much of a pussy to spend more than a few summer months?"

"I'd give them the choice," she said.

"Oh, he did. If we lived in the southern cities, we would've had to lick the boots of some fat lord or other who'd make us work his land until we died. Up here, we're still the King's subjects with all of the taxes and trade that comes with it, but we run things *our* way."

"You have a kingdom's protection, but also relative freedom," Khana realized. The best of both worlds.

Haz nodded. "That's worth a few blizzards, don't you think?"

"I was born in a hot desert and raised in a jungle, so, no."

"Ew. No wonder you left…"

"Haz!"

His open, happy face shuttered into complete neutrality when he saw the girl who called him coming around the statue. "Bhayana," he growled.

Bhayana was a beautiful girl – well, woman, seeing as she was likely a year or so older than Khana herself. Porcupine quills stuck out of the shoulders of her cloak like wings, her eyes as dark as a raven's beak. Despite being slimmer and shorter than Haz, she was still a Pahuudan giant. She stalked up to them and said something to Haz in Ghura.

He replied shortly, curtly. Khana frowned at the sudden change of tone and body language. The casual, friendly, joking demeanor was completely gone, replaced by something cold and distant.

Bhayana said something else, dark eyes piercing as she reached out with a finger to touch Haz's cheek. He jerked back, just out of reach.

And Khana knew that look. She *knew* that look. Worn by countless concubines and her own self whenever Yamueto got too close.

She loudly cleared her throat, drawing both of their attention, and gripped Haz's arm. "Weren't you going to take me to the farmers? Your father will want us to finish that business as soon as possible, and I don't want to upset him."

She tugged him away. Bhayana glared at her, snapping something in Ghura.

Khana cheerfully cut her off, "I'm sorry! I don't speak Ghura. But you have a splendid day, ma'am!"

She and Haz left Bhayana fuming at the foot of the statue. Khana had no idea where she was leading Haz, just as long as it was away from that woman.

When they had turned a few corners and were well out of sight and hearing, she cleared her throat. "Porcupine quills. An Old Family?"

"The Pinnsviris," Haz confirmed, still tense. "Spoiled fuckers, every one of them. She and I… were lovers, for a time. It did not end well."

Khana glanced nervously behind her, but all she saw was a throng of people walking the streets, haggling with each other and hollering after their children. "Are we going to get in trouble for that?"

"Probably not. There's no law against being rude." He gave a shadow of a smile. "And you, poor thing, are new. You don't even speak Ghura. How can we possibly expect you to know our basic manners?"

"Woe is me, I'm so ignorant and helpless," Khana deadpanned.

He snickered, knocking his fist against her shoulder. "Thank you. I would've been stammering like an idiot for much longer without your rescue."

"Any time."

* * *

Wandering the town became a near-daily habit. On particularly slow days when Heimili didn't need her, and Sava wasn't gambling with them – or at night when she was woken from nightmares and couldn't get back to sleep – Khana would explore Pahuuda. Haz usually acted as a guide, teaching her the local language as they went, but not always. Heimili often needed him for more physically taxing or complicated tasks than Khana could handle, leaving her to her own devices. She had grown so used to traveling alone through war-torn kingdoms that one little town was nothing.

She still managed to get lost a week into her stay, however, finding herself on the edge of the empty tundra, the town and mountains at her back. There were a handful of farms and huts this far out, but the space was largely dominated by an open field of short, tough grass and stone. The tundra. The local military used it for drills, amid a handful of goats hunting for grass.

Khana watched archers fire shots, spearmen practice formations, and a couple of squads run laps in full gear. Surprisingly, while most of the spears and arrows were of bone, some were carved from wood. They must have been bought from the forests of Tlaphar over the mountains, or perhaps gifted by the Divaajinian king to better protect his mountains. She recognized Sava's wolf cloak among the archers and considered going to him, striking up a conversation with the new Ghura she'd learned. But he was busy hollering drill orders. It was such a change from his calm attitude at the inn. Here, he was every inch the chief's son, his back straight and his face stern. Khana stayed away, frightened, reminding herself that she didn't really know this man.

She continued observing the small army. Heimili didn't need her back right away, so she had time. It seemed the squads were largely divided by cultural origin. All the large, tall, native-born Ghura were separated from the shorter, slimmer Reguallian refugees and descendants, and then further subdivided into spearmen and archers. She noticed that the little wooden spears and arrows were exclusive to the Ghura while the Reguallian refugees had the cheaper, less valuable bone weapons. She couldn't get an accurate count of their numbers, but there had to be a few hundred men out here at least. Men *and* women.

A group of runners sprinted past her, and she noticed at least a third of them were women. She wasn't sure how she felt about that; not even the empire liked putting spears in the hands of their girls.

One of the closer Reguallian squads practiced throwing their spears at cloth targets. One spear went off-target, striking a stone instead. Even from a distance, Khana could hear the metal spearhead break. She winced.

The leader of the squad – a captain, perhaps? – berated the soldier, who looked properly abashed. She wondered if the unlucky soldier had some Ghuran blood; he was certainly tall enough, with the darker skin of a farmhand. The captain dismissed the soldier, and he picked up his broken spear and jogged away from the group, toward the town.

Maybe I can ask him directions, Khana thought. She did need to get back to the inn. And while the temperature was better than a few days before, the wind still nipped at her nose. She needed a hot cup of tea.

The soldier moved quickly, almost reaching the closest farm. Khana was just starting to follow when she noticed a couple of the Ghuran runners – whose group had stopped for a water break – peel away from the others to follow him, sharing dark looks with each other.

A bad feeling settled in her gut. She made sure the runners couldn't see her, following at a distance.

The Reguallian soldier disappeared behind a barn. So did the two Ghura.

Khana broke into a run, slowing only when she neared the farm. She was being paranoid. Not everyone lived a life of danger and fear. They had crossed an open field and no one else had stopped them. She was making something of nothing, she was...

...hearing the sound of flesh beating flesh.

Holding her ragged breath, Khana pressed herself against the stone wall and peeked around the corner.

The three were locked in a fistfight, the Reguallian managing to hold his own before one of his attackers pulled a knife. Khana took a breath to scream, to shout a warning, but it froze in her chest. *Don't move. Don't speak. Don't speak don't speak don't –*

The Ghuran runner stabbed the Reguallian in the back once. Twice. Three times. The Reguallian gasped, all the air leaving him in a rush so he couldn't even shout. He fell to the ground. Khana clasped a hand over her mouth, stifling a scream that came too late.

The other runner yelled at his friend. The knife-wielder looked at his red blade, panicked. They both ran.

Khana waited as long as she dared, counting to ten before emerging from her hiding place. She knelt next to the Reguallian and put a hand on his back. Still alive, but blood and life force spilled out. This close, she could see the bean-shaped birthmark on his left cheek, see the fear in his wide brown eyes.

He coughed, tried to brush her off. She pushed him down. "Don't move."

He stilled. "Who...?"

"I'm Khana. What's your name?"

"X... Xopil."

He wasn't dead yet. There was still time to save him. She just needed to find a source of life.

"I'm... my wife..." he panted. "Can you... tell her..."

"You'll be fine. Just hold on a moment."

She could make a new deal with Death. Sacrifice another memory. Unless...

There! A goat. Khana stood and carefully approached. The goat studied her as it chewed on a bit of grass, unimpressed. It was getting on in years, thoroughly domesticated and didn't pull away when she put a gentle hand on its head. "Sorry about this."

She inhaled, taking its âji as quickly as possible. The goat jerked, pulling away, but not far or fast enough. She drained it completely, knowing she would need every ounce to fix the damage under Xopil's red-stained clothes. The goat collapsed onto the ground.

Faintly glowing with orange, yellow and black magic, Khana ran back to Xopil, relieved to see him still breathing. "I'll need you to keep this a secret."

"Wha–"

She pressed the goat's life force into him, watching the magic sink into the three stab wounds and stitch up the damage. The massive bleeding slowed to a trickle, then stopped.

Khana breathed easier, gently prodding at the still-wet flesh. "You still have the wounds, but they're shallow now. Make sure to clean and bandage them."

Xopil gingerly sat upright, poking the holes in his wool uniform. He stared at her in wonder. "You..."

"Are nobody. Certainly not a witch. Do you understand me?"

Someone cleared their throat.

Both Khana and Xopil cringed. Khana looked over her shoulder.

A Reguallian soldier glared at them. Her hair was pulled back in a tight braid, and she wore a gray leopard skin cloak around her shoulders. Xopil's two attackers stood behind her, gaping. Khana's stomach sank to her feet.

"I do believe that we need to speak with the chief," the soldier said.

Chapter Twelve

The town hall was a large stone building with guardian gargoyles. Khana counted foxes, bears, wolves, leopards, and several others as the soldier escorted her, Xopil, and the attackers into the building.

A handful of other soldiers had been assembled to assist, and they all gave Khana wary, disgusted looks. She kept her eyes on her boots as they led her down halls and around corners.

They left her in a small room with a yak-skin door; a couple of guards stood watch, separating her from Xopil and the others. She sat on a square cushion and studied a tapestry hanging opposite her. The creator must have spent a fortune on dyes: whites, silvers, and blues colored the robes of a winter god who created blizzards with the moon by his head; a goddess of the sun and summer was sewn from reds, oranges, and gold, a pair of antlers springing from her temples. The two held each other in an embrace, and from their union Khana counted a war god, a love god, and a goddess of some sort of art or music. Separate from the family was an elderly woman whose dress made up the mountains and beneath everything and everyone was a black ocean – or maybe it was the night sky? – with a corpse-pale goddess sitting on a throne, overseeing a parade of ghosts. It was one of the forms Death had taken when they'd spoken. She'd rather hoped not to see them again for a while, but now...

What will it be? she wondered. *Enslavement? Exile? Back to Regualli?* She'd kill herself before she let that happen.

They kept her waiting for what felt like hours, long enough for her to memorize every detail of that tapestry while the two soldiers stared at her, not moving a muscle, not saying a word.

Finally, someone came to fetch her. The guards led her through a stone hall decorated with even more tapestries. She saw ancient Pahuudan soldiers battling kingdom after kingdom for money, then the chief from the statue in the town square – with staff and sword – negotiating with a king, then people building towns. She tried to slow her steps to get a closer look, but the guards pushed her forward.

Legal matters of Pahuuda were dealt with in some form of throne/courtroom. It was big enough to hold half the town, with torches and two fireplaces on opposite walls warming the room. The space was decorated with relics of war: shields, armor, weapons, pieces of art and jewels taken from a dozen kingdoms throughout history. Seven stone chairs sat on a dais in a half-circle facing the room with the central chair being the biggest and most ornate. They each held a person, most of them elderly. Each person was adorned with some part of an animal: one wore a headdress made of eagle feathers, another curled bharal horns, fox fur, bear skin, and several teeth and claws. All of them were Ghura. One very old, very frail man with dark eyes and a sharp nose wore a cloak adorned in porcupine quills, reminding Khana of Bhayana. The woman in the center throne had a necklace of wolf's teeth and claws. *Sava's mother*, Khana realized. She recognized the square jawline and archer's braid, though the chief's was going gray. She held a staff, the same one depicted in the town square statue. It was a surprisingly simple thing for a scepter, though carved from ivory or bone. Short cords hung from the top, dangling animal teeth and bones that gave an old woman's cackle every time they moved. The bottom had been coated in iron, perfect for acting as a gavel on the stone floor.

Standing before the members of the Seven Families was Sava, who had completely lost his friendly, safe aura. He looked at Khana with the same stern, authoritarian look his mother gave her. Like she was a stranger. A threat. It hurt. She turned away to the rest of the room.

The soldier who caught her also stood before the thrones, still in her leopard cloak. It was then Khana realized she must belong to an Old Family, despite her obvious Reguallian blood. She even looked a little like the man with leopard teeth pierced through his ears.

The rest of the room was filled with people, held back by a stone, waist-high railing. They watched her get marched through the room in silence. She spotted Haz and Heimili on the edges of the crowd and couldn't meet their faces.

The guards positioned Khana in the center of the room, between the thrones and the mob. She bowed to the chief.

The chief said something. Khana swallowed, not understanding.

"Neta, please speak for her," Sava ordered.

"Chief Phramanka is asking for your name," said the woman with the leopard cloak. She was all height and muscle, holding a spear in one hand and a knife and axe at her hip like she'd been born with them.

"Khana," she said.

"And you're a witch," Neta translated for the chief.

She swallowed. Whispered, "Yes."

"You should stand up straight. We don't bow here." A direct request from Neta herself.

Khana stood but kept her eyes down.

"We have two issues to muddle through today," Neta continued for the chief. "First, you will tell us what happened between these three soldiers before I found you."

Khana glanced at the furious soldiers and Xopil. Easy enough. She told the truth.

Sava, oddly, turned to the woman with the bharal horn headdress and made a series of motions with his hands as Neta spoke for Khana. Chief Phramanka's face, and several others', hardened when she got to the end.

When she was done, one of the attackers shouted something. Neta, thankfully, approached Khana's side and whispered a translation: "You're trusting the word of a cowardly soul-stealer?"

"Midya Grahanu has received several reports against Damani and Rathara," Sava reported to his mother, as if they weren't there. Neta kept Khana informed, though she didn't explain what a "midya" was, whether that was part of the name or a title. "Almost all from Reguallians and Tlapharians accusing them of harassment, ill treatment, and physical attacks."

"And they were allowed to stay?" the chief asked.

"Apparently, they've never taken it this far. Usually they pick on Neta, but she always wins."

Chief Phramanka huffed. "We'll work on prevention later. For now..."

She pointed to Xopil's attackers, Damani and Rathara. "These two are discharged from the militia, stripped of all rank, titles, and pay. They are banned from re-enlistment for seven years unless otherwise decreed."

The two men shouted obscenities. The chief's glare silenced them.

"What about the farmer who lost his goat?" the head of the bear family asked, a massive man with a thick fur around his shoulders.

Chief Phramanka thought for a moment, then decided, "You two and the witch will all *each* pay him its worth for his trouble."

"How much is that, Mistress Neta?" Khana whispered.

"About fifty coppers," she answered. "And I'm just a soldier, not a mistress."

That was going to blow up Khana's savings. She wondered if Heimili would even keep her around to earn it back.

"If you can't pay it, the usual solution is military service," Neta added, perhaps seeing the dismay on her face. "That's the traditional way debts are paid if money isn't an option."

Chief Phramanka waved the two ex-soldiers off, and they were escorted out of the room. Xopil was also dismissed, but he was allowed to merge with the crowd, hugged by a plump Reguallian woman. Probably his wife.

"Now, on to the witch herself," Phramanka said.

"We should banish her," said the woman in the eagle headdress. "Witches are bad luck."

"She could be a spy for the empire," agreed the fox.

Khana stiffened with every word Neta translated. Phramanka silenced them all, and asked, "Tell us why you are here, girl."

This was tricky. These people wouldn't take kindly to hearing that Khana had warmed the emperor's bed, even against her will, or worse, that she was related to him. And if they knew that she'd found the secret to reviving the dead, they'd tear her apart for it.

She licked her dry lips and said, "I'm a refugee. I was hoping to put as much land between myself and the empire as possible, but I ran out of coin and cannot cross the tundra on my own. Once I reach the coast, I'll get on a ship and go further, if I can."

"Why leave?" croaked Bhayana's elderly relative, the porcupine quills on his shoulders twitching with every breath. "I hear witches are revered in the empire."

Khana chuckled. "Revered? You're sure that's the correct translation, Neta?"

"Quite," she said dryly.

"We are not revered, sir. Respected, yes. And perhaps some cults believe we're descended from or chosen by gods. But every witch is ordered to attend the emperor, regardless of our opinions of him. We have to help him create his night creatures or be turned ourselves. We're kept under constant guard, every movement watched, forced into breeding for more–" She cut herself off, breathing hard, unable to say more.

Neta studied her for a moment before finishing the translation. A couple of the Old Family members began to look sympathetic. Sava winced, still signing to the bharal woman.

Phramanka waited a long moment, long enough for Khana to calm herself, before asking, "And how did you escape?"

"I disguised myself as a servant and jumped off a cliff."

Neta didn't immediately translate. "Come again?"

Khana decided on a white lie: "First I killed a woman in self-defense by absorbing her âji – life force, Reguallians call it saviza – and that apparently absorbed the damage? I think? I was never able to finish my necromancy training, but if you hold enough saviza it gives you extra strength and heals your wounds…"

Finally, some people began to look approvingly at her, once Neta passed her words along. But not everyone.

Someone shouted something from the mob behind her, angry. Other voices joined them. Phramanka had to bang her staff on the floor to gain order.

"What are they saying?" Khana whispered.

"Half of them think you're a spy, the other half think you'll bring a curse or bad luck," Neta said. Her tone was blank enough that Khana couldn't guess what she thought on the matter.

"I agree with the people," the fox said. "We should return her."

"Please don't!" Khana begged.

"It's the smartest decision."

Khana stepped forward. The guards pointed their spears, and Neta snatched her shoulder, an iron weight stopping her in her tracks.

Khana knelt, the stone bruising her knees. "Chief Phramanka, if you are seriously considering exiling me back to the empire, I ask that instead you execute me and burn my body."

The room went quiet after Neta's startled translation, the only noise the flickering of the torches and fireplaces. Khana didn't dare look up, her eyes on Phramanka's boots.

The chief stood from her throne and approached Khana, forcing her chin up with a calloused finger. Khana met the old woman's shrewd, cold gaze. She spoke accented, but perfect Reguallian: "So if I ordered my son to shoot you through the heart with an arrow, we wouldn't have to tie you to a post?"

Neta continued her translation duties, her quiet voice in Ghura the only other sound in the room.

Khana swallowed. She thought of Yamueto's rough hands on her, hands she had seen shape corpses into abominations that lived only to serve his cruel will. A quick, clean death was worlds better than that, but she still trembled. And she knew Phramanka could feel it; she hadn't let go of her chin.

"Would the first shot be immediately fatal, or would it just wound me?" Khana asked.

"My son is the best archer this side of the mountains. It would only take one arrow."

"Ma..." Sava warned. Khana wanted to scream at him to not interrupt his ruler.

"Then no, you would not have to tie me up," she said. "I would only ask that you first take my cloak and return it to Hasyamin, son of Heimili. He loaned it to me."

Phramanka let go of her chin. She stood, leaning on her ivory staff, and switched back to Ghura: "Being a witch is not a crime in this town or kingdom. The girl is free to go as she wishes, so long as she limits the use of her powers to extreme circumstances and doesn't take the rabala of any person or their animals without that person's explicit permission."

As soon as Neta finished translating, Khana went weak, almost faint. She dropped her forehead to the cold stone, trying to wrap her mind around the order. She wasn't going to be executed? Or forced to use her powers?

Half of the mob hissed or booed at Khana's back. It sent ice down her spine.

"My decision is final," Phramanka snapped over the noise. "We're done here."

Khana watched the Old Families leave, dread settling in her bones. The chief might not want to hurt her, but it was clear that she didn't speak for the rest of the town.

Chapter Thirteen
Neta

Though Neta couldn't say she and Xopil were friends, she sought him out immediately after the witch's trial. He was one of the first to leave the building, and she caught him with his plump, bronze-skinned wife, Tlastisti, just off the road, visibly shaken.

"You said she healed you most of the way," Neta said to him. "But those wounds can still get infected. Are you able to get the salves needed to prevent that?"

"We'll find a way," Xopil promised.

Neta snorted, dug into her pocket, and tossed him a small coinpurse. "Consider it an apology for not getting to you sooner."

She'd *known* Damani and Rathara were up to no good. They'd spent the last several days glaring at both her and Xopil, making snide comments but not having an opportunity to touch them. Not since the last time they tried to fight Neta; she'd broken Damani's arm and Rathara's nose.

She had noted their absence almost immediately after Xopil broke his spear, just not soon enough. Part of her was relieved that Khana had been there, though she was annoyed the witch hadn't actually stopped the attack.

Perhaps Neta should have found some private method of dealing with it, rather than immediately dragging the problem to the chief. Her frustration over Damani and Rathara had gotten the best of her, and it wouldn't have been the first time her superior officers had let their behavior slide. If every soldier was dismissed for bullying those with Reguallian and Tlapharian blood, there would be no army.

Neta had been certain she'd done the right thing, right up until Khana had begged to be executed rather than returned to the Reguallian empire. That would be bad enough, but now most of the town wanted her dead or gone anyway, despite Phramanka's ruling.

Well. What was done was done. Now they had to live with the consequences, whatever those were.

Xopil stared at the pouch of money in his hands. "Are you sure? You're not an officer; you get paid just as little as me."

She gave him a droll look. "My mother is one of the town's wealthiest landlords and store owners. I can spare a few coins."

She didn't bring up her father's Old Family status. That man had never given her any sort of help.

He tucked the bag away, under his bloody armor. "Thank you, Neta."

She waited outside, letting the town hall empty before going back in. Despite overlooking militia companies (which each consisted of about fifty soldiers), midyas were not assigned their own offices per se. Not like maverstis, who overlooked battalions (typically seven or more companies). But midyas had access to financial and personal records of soldiers, which were stored in the back rooms of town hall.

As Neta suspected, Ghrahanu was there, shuffling through records hanging from shelves made of elk and yak bone, his hair the same dark gray as the stone walls. Paper was a rarity in these parts, so the records were kept through a complicated series of knots and beads on strings. It was how the town kept track of harvests, trade agreements, legal disputes, and soldiers.

"Midya," she greeted.

"Don't," he ordered.

She frowned. "Don't what?"

"If you're coming to say, 'I told you so,' I don't want to hear it."

She had warned him about Damani and Rathara multiple times. He'd always brushed her off.

Being right left a sour taste in her mouth. It shouldn't have taken a man almost dying to get this handled. "I merely wanted to ask you something, sir."

"Yes?" he asked, tired.

"What's the plan for preventing the next attack?"

"The next attack?"

"This will happen again."

He snorted. "Did you miss the trial? The chief stripped them of all honor and dignity. Others will know not to make the same mistakes."

"No, they won't."

He frowned.

She considered her words carefully, knowing they might be her last as a soldier. "I've served in this military for five years. I have had to deal with Damanis and Ratharas through that whole time, and even when a commander punished them, there were always more. And frankly, most commanders let them go with a slap on the wrist, if anything. Usually, those aggressors would beat whoever reported them, and the cycle began anew. So there *will* be another attack, and the next victim might not be lucky enough to have a witch nearby."

Ghrahanu sighed. "What should I say, Neta? Soldiers are supposed to trust each other. If you can't do that, maybe this isn't the career for you."

"I disagree. I think I can help fix a glaring problem in our militia. Reguallians and Tlapharians make up a third of our forces, yet only a handful of them are serjis, and none of them are midya, never mind maversti."

He scoffed. "Are you suggesting I promote you?"

"I suggest you promote someone with Reguallian blood who has seen combat, was commended by the chief herself for said combat, and has proven resilient to the anti-foreigner nonsense that plagues this whole town," Neta countered.

"No."

She gritted her teeth. "Why?"

"Are you questioning your commander?" he snapped.

"Yes. Why?"

He glared at her. She didn't budge. The line between a Ghuran soldier's right to speak up over an unjust order and insubordination was thin.

Thankfully, it seemed she hadn't crossed it.

Ghrahanu huffed. "This whole thing started because so many people hate Reguallians. They fear your empire. I don't want to know what consequences will come if I promote one to serji, even if she is Old Family."

"It's not my empire, and I can handle those consequences."

"Not happening."

"Sir–"

"No."

Frustration bubbled in the back of her throat. She should've been promoted to serji two years ago. Half of her company had been killed in that battle, so some rank shuffling had happened, anyway. Yet here she was, still stuck in place.

Others with Old Family blood could just bat their eyes, and they'd have titles and honors thrown at them. But Neta, born not of her father's wife but a "Reguallian whore" did not have that privilege.

Briefly, she considered taking the matter to Chief Phramanka, but immediately dismissed it. The chief was an ally to use sparingly, especially since the two of them weren't particularly close. She was barely friends with Sava. She couldn't use that type of political leverage for her own advancement without wearing thin what goodwill she had with them. She'd spent almost a year teaching Sava sign language, and that hadn't gotten her any advancement or favors, either. They clearly weren't going to give it to her.

And they shouldn't. Neta wanted to earn her promotion. If she got it because she whined to the chief or taught a few signs, that would undermine her for the rest of her life.

Ghrahanu turned away, clearly done with the conversation. "Let things settle down a bit, first, and we'll discuss the topic again. Who knows – war is usually the best time to get promoted, and we might be in one soon."

Serji Athicha waited for her in the hall. Though they had been in the military for as long as Neta, they were leaner and trimmer, and had studied archery rather than the far more common and easily-accessible spear and axe. Athicha was never seen without a wool scarf wrapped securely around their neck, even in summer. The fancy one – which they brought out for special events – even had painted bone and stone beads knitted into it, matching the ones braided in their shoulder-length hair.

All right? Athicha signed.

Annoyed, she sighed back. A handful of her Cituva relatives were deaf. In fact, about one in twenty Ghura went deaf in their twilight years, and one in thirty were born without hearing at all, making sign language a fairly common second language in the town.

Athicha wasn't deaf, only mute. But Neta still preferred to sign with them. It made their conversations feel special, more intimate.

I say raising me can help. Midya say no, she explained. There was no sign for "promotion."

The serji gave an annoyed look. *Your midya idiot.*

She chuckled. Athicha was so vocal about their annoyance with some of the officers, and she'd always found that deeply amusing. Attractive, even. So, she tugged on their scarf and kissed them. Athicha backed her into the wall to deepen the kiss until they both paused for breath. Unfortunately, they couldn't linger.

Should go back, she signed, reluctantly prying herself from her lover. Being caught kissing in public wouldn't improve her chances of promotion.

Athicha stole one more kiss before letting her go. *Be safe,* they signed. *If no safe, then destroy.*

Chapter Fourteen

The next several days saw Khana withdrawing from the town. She didn't go out exploring anymore, not leaving the inn, or even her room if she could manage it. Children pointed and screamed at her when they saw her on the street, like she was a nightmare made flesh. Adults stared and whispered to each other. Many made holy or religious signs when she passed them. When she tried to work, the customers didn't even look at her, turning away or spitting at her feet, calling her death-bringer and soul-sucker. Heimili had to relegate her to kitchen duty, limping through the dining hall himself.

Khana considered that a blessing. She'd been shocked when she'd left the town hall, fully expecting to be kicked out of the inn. But Haz dropped an arm around her thin shoulders and said, "Thank you for thinking of my lovely cloak before your life. I doubt it's worth enough coins for that, but I appreciate the sentiment!"

The touch, friendly though it was, made her freeze, and her mind went blank for a moment. "Oh… you're welcome."

He immediately let her go, blinding her with a gap-toothed grin. "Can magic make you wash dishes faster?"

The question completely threw her off-guard. "Uh, not to my knowledge?"

"What about bread? Can it make bread cook faster?"

"No."

"Then what even is the point?" he grumbled. "I'm glad you're not dead."

"…Me too?"

Heimili limped up behind them. "You. Next time, tell us this thing, yes?"

"Er, yes," Khana said. "I'm sorry, I didn't mean for any of this…"

He waved her away. "Bah. Some secrets, good. Others, hurt. You, help Amati with rooms."

And that was it. Khana continued working, handing over the fifty coins demanded by the chief when she sent men to collect. She kept her eyes down so she wouldn't have to see the people shy away from her or curse her. Even her fellow Reguallian refugees avoided her. She hadn't seen Xopil since the trial, and Amati barely tolerated her.

"Death-bringers are signs of bad luck," she said as she and Khana changed the blankets in one of the rooms. "They either carry misfortune or are a sign that it will follow. So, which are you, girl?"

"I don't know," Khana admitted.

Sava didn't return to the inn. She refused to analyze why that hurt as much as the rest.

Three weeks after the trial, Khana worked alone in the dining room, replacing the old floor cushions with new, clean ones. Heimili started on the day's stew in the kitchen, letting it cook over the fire for hours. Amati and Haz were both out shopping, bargaining with farmers.

The front door creaked open. Footsteps on the stone. Khana swapped the next cushion, keeping her eyes on her task. She stumbled through her Ghura: "I get Heimili."

"I would rather talk to you."

She jumped, looking up. "Sava?"

He gave a sheepish smile, rubbing the back of his neck. His black beard had grown out a little thicker, but he'd continued to keep it short and trim, framing his face in a way that made him look older and sophisticated, even when his expression reminded her of a puppy. "May I come in?"

He spoke Reguallian, so she did the same: "Of – of course. This is an inn."

Khana wiped non-existent dust from her dress, a shapeless piece of wool she'd spent her meager funds on. Heimili still gave her tips, but they'd taken a hit since her trial. She almost wished for her old Reguallian silks. They made her look less like a lost little girl. "Tea?"

"I would like that."

She fetched a pot, almost running over Heimili in the kitchen. He raised an eyebrow at her but didn't argue as she gathered what she needed and returned to the dining room. Sava had sat on a cushion near the fireplace and removed his quiver, bow, and wolfskin cloak, revealing his thick, muscled arms. She had only brought the one cup with the pot, and he frowned as he watched her pour. "You, too?"

"Oh, you want me to… of course. Hold on." She hurried back to the kitchen to get another cup, ignoring Heimili's odd look, and returned. Sava took the pot before she could grab it, pouring her drink himself. She sat on the cushion across from him, back ramrod straight.

"How are you, Khana?" he asked.

"I'm all right. Your Reguallian has gotten better."

He gave a small smile. "I kept my lessons. My mother does not like me coming here now. She thinks it says our family 'favors' you."

"Then why are you here? You could get in trouble, Sava!"

He made a face. "I waited long enough. Haz is my friend, I don't like politics, and I don't think you're evil. An evil Khana lets Xopil die."

"A better Khana would have stopped him from getting stabbed in the first place," she muttered into her cup.

Sava shrugged, not arguing, but not agreeing. "Maybe you join militia? Soldiers are respected around here."

"Like how Xopil got respect?" she dared to ask.

He nodded to her. "Truth. But that's still better than if he wasn't enlisted."

"I've seen enough armies, soldiers, and blood. I don't need to join in. But thank you. I'm sure your army is quite good."

He chuckled. "Not *my* army."

"You lead the men, don't you?"

"Only the archers."

Khana briefly considered learning archery. Maybe Sava could teach her himself. She banished the thought. She was too scared to leave this building; she'd be eaten alive on the field.

"Do you like it? Leading the archers?" she asked.

"Sometimes, the soldiers are great." He gave her a deadpan look. "Other times, they are children."

She giggled. "Really?"

"One time, my friend Athicha decided to put a quiver on a goat..."

Khana could've sat in front of that fireplace forever, listening to Sava share his stories of the militia, of hunting, of his first struggles learning Reguallian from random refugees. Heimili limped in at one point to replace their teapot, and when Khana reluctantly offered to go back to her duties, he shook his head. "We have a guest. You *are* doing your duties."

"What about you?" Sava asked, after Heimili went back to the kitchen. "How did you know you were a witch?"

"It's a boring story," she admitted.

"So are mine."

Khana huffed, but it was with a smile. "When I was thirteen, I was walking with my friend Guma by the river. There's very little water in the desert. You have to be very careful when you're out of sight of a river or lake, because you can die of thirst so easily. Even the plants know this. Here, in Pahuuda, animals can eat grass and plants without worry. But in the desert, many of them have little spears. Spikes. One is called a cactus: a round, ugly thing that is *covered* in spikes, so animals cannot eat it and steal its water. I was talking to Guma and wasn't watching where I was looking, so I stepped on one. Barefoot."

Sava hissed. Khana pointed at him. "Yes, that is exactly what I did. After my initial shout, I breathed in sharply, and that's how I first absorbed âji – er, saviza. Life force?"

"Rabala," he said.

"Rabala." She tested the new word, storing it in her growing dictionary of Ghura. "The cactus turned brown and died, and the wounds on my feet healed."

"Were you happy?"

Khana's bright nostalgia faded to melancholy. "No. All witches must report to Emperor Yamueto. No exceptions. Guma and I hid it for as long as we could, over a year. But when my parents found out, they killed her for treason and sent me to the capital."

Sava blinked. "Your parents killed your friend?"

"It's the law."

He blew out a breath, looking down at his tea. "Wow."

She'd never told anyone that story. Sava's reaction made something settle within her.

A woman burst into the dining room, almost ripping the door from its hinges. Khana stiffened as she frantically looked around, then pointed at her. "You! You're the witch?"

"Yes…"

"I'm from the brothel. One of the girls gave birth last night, but she's dying now. The physician says she doesn't have long."

"Oh," Khana said, confused. Then, "Oh!" when she realized why this woman was here. She jumped to her feet, almost spilling her tea on Sava. "I need my boots!"

That was how early autumn went for Khana. As Tlaphar desperately tried to fight off the Empire, she became Pahuuda's unofficial witch. People still ignored her, but they stopped spitting at her feet as she was called to heal more and more frequently. A hunter breaking her leg on the mountain. A man getting stabbed in a bar fight. The Pinnsviri patriarch dying of old age, again and again.

There were no nearby plants with enough life force to be useful, not unless she drained an entire field of barley or potatoes, so she always had to use an animal. Sometimes, especially near the farms, one was ready and waiting for her. Other times, she had to send someone out to fetch one and hope her patient didn't die in the interim. Once or twice the people offered their own life force, which she took, but never fatally. A very, very few times, the illness or injury was serious enough that she conjured the âji herself, giving memories to Death to heal ruptured organs or – in the case of an archery accident – an arrow through the lung. She made sure to make those deals away from the patient and any witnesses, pretending to go out looking for an animal. If the town realized she could conjure life force out of thin air, they'd demand she do it more and more often. She didn't know how much of herself she could lose.

She hadn't seen it the first time she returned to the spirit realm, or the second. But the third time, she noticed that her colorful spirit body was just the tiniest bit duller than last time, the light not quite as bright. Death gave her a grim smile and explained, "You're selling pieces of your soul. Sell too much, and it takes its toll."

She no longer remembered the color of the dress she'd worn when she'd first arrived at Yamueto's palace, or that time a kind-hearted concubine had taught her the names of the empire's northern provinces. Losing those memories did not affect her, but she was still scared of the deals she made. Terrified that one day, she'd have to trade something that truly mattered, like the way Guma would mutter nonsensical curses over the littlest things when all other adults were gone, just to make Khana and the other children giggle. Or Sita's favorite music to listen to while she worked in the library. Or just how terrifying Yamueto could be. The second she lost sight of that, she would grow stagnant. She'd stop running. And he'd catch her.

Not once did Khana demand payment for her services, especially not from people who struggled to get so much as a sickly goat for her to use. It didn't feel right. She may not believe in gods, but she did believe that some things, like witchcraft, were gifts. Not something to be monetized.

It also didn't feel safe, her position in this town too precarious for her to rattle it further. They already hated and resented her for her powers;

demanding money to use them when they were needed most would be putting salt on the wound.

So, most people sent her off with nothing. A few pressed a casserole or loaf of bread or dried fish in her hands. When she saved a farmer's son from illness, the farmer said that he'd sell Heimili anything he wanted for half its value. One woman gave her a nice dress that no longer fit her daughter.

More refugees came in from the mountains as autumn loomed and Pahuuda celebrated a harvest festival with singing, dancing, and one last massive hunt across the tundra for elk and moose.

Those refugees brought the news Khana had dreaded to hear: the once free kingdom of Tlaphar had fallen to Yamueto. Now, only the mountains separated her from the Reguallian Empire, and a tundra guide was still well outside her price range. They were now all charging her double. She was stuck.

"No one who's tried to get through those mountains to conquer us has ever succeeded," Haz assured her. "And that emperor is an idiot if he thinks he can beat Jadok and Dhunhada."

Jadok was the Ghuran god of winter, wind, and the moon, lover of the sun goddess. Dhunhada was sometimes called "Mother Mountains," as she was their goddess of stone, the harvest, and the earth itself. Khana didn't have faith in either of them.

The only true bright spots in all of this were Sava and Haz. Haz continued to make her feel welcome, telling silly jokes and teasing her and the customers in turn. Being around Sava made Khana feel almost safe, even as her stomach fluttered and her face heated whenever he smiled at her. The quiet times were best, as Khana could set aside her other duties and play host to him, even if it was just for a few minutes at a time. But a close second was when it was busy, and the other patrons got Sava to play his flute. He was shockingly good, and Khana would whistle the tunes for the next couple of days to keep her spirits up.

The good feelings never lasted though. Khana always knew, deep down, that it was only a matter of time before it all came crashing down. And as the first chill winds of winter began to blow, it crashed *hard*. For, after once again visiting the Pinnsviri patriarch to extend his life a little longer, the town discovered its first night creature.

Chapter Fifteen
Yamueto

Yamueto studied the map of the world while his advisors bickered around him. He had his usual team: his masters of ships, swords, coin, spies, hammers, and current high priest, as well as his graying son Antallo, fresh from his victory over Tlaphar. He leaned back in his chair with bloated arrogance.

"Did you have to kill the entire royal family?" the master of coin groaned. He was new. Yamueto couldn't remember his name. Was he a grandson or great-grandson?

"I didn't," Antallo defended. His obnoxiously-orange armor was polished to a near-blinding shine. "I kept the daughter for myself, as is my right as conqueror."

"You should have given the daughter to the emperor."

"She's not a witch, nor is she descended from one," Yamueto cut in, not lifting his eyes from the map that spread out across the entire table, focusing on the kingdom of Divaajin, its coastline, and it's so-far impenetrable mountain border. "Antallo can do whatever he likes with her, so long as whoever he left in charge of the kingdom does their duty."

"I placed my own son on Tlaphar's throne," Antallo said proudly. "He's more than happy to keep the peace in your name."

Yamueto nodded. Antallo almost glowed with it. Then the boy went and ruined it: "We should continue to press our advantage further south."

"We've barely managed to get Tlaphar under control," the master of swords argued. "We need to solidify our claim on it before moving further."

"The mountains will prove a sizeable obstacle as well," Coin added. He glanced at Yamueto. "While I'm certain we *could* expand our borders further, I do not believe now is the right time."

"It's the perfect time!" Antallo snapped.

Yamueto cleared his throat. Antallo gulped and shrank in his seat.

"Divaajin has held the land south of the mountains since my grandfather's day," Yamueto said. "A land assault is impossible in winter, difficult in summer. Navy would be best, but I hear they have quite the fleet."

"They do, Your Excellency," said the master of ships. His white hair was see-through around his spotted scalp. Yamueto idly wondered if he had barnacles on his aged skin. "While their numbers aren't as great as ours, their ships are smaller, faster, and more advanced. If we were to throw our entire forces at them now onto the open sea, we could win, but it would be of great cost. And that's before the land battles and harsh winters."

"They don't even have witches," Antallo argued. "They see us as 'bad luck' or some other such nonsense."

"Tlaphar did the same thing. Yet they lasted a good long while and took a toll on our resources," Ships countered.

Yamueto hummed. Divaajin was an incredible prize. Not for its resources, but its status. Nobody from the north had ever conquered that land. Yamueto intended to be the first. He had sacrificed so much in the name of conquest. It was the only thing that truly gave him joy anymore. He would have the entire world under his control.

One day.

He was immortal. He had all the time in the world to make that happen.

He was just about to order his men to focus on securing Tlaphar, to save Divaajin for another generation, when his master of spies spoke: "Not necessarily. Divaajin does have a witch guarding its borders."

"Just the one?" Antallo scoffed.

"There are a few in the major cities along the coast," Spies elaborated. He smirked at Yamueto. "But I was thinking of the one in Pahuuda, a town tasked with guarding the mountains. She's a foreigner, apparently a Reguallian refugee."

Yamueto straightened in his seat. "Physical description?"

"Small. Dark skin. Black hair. Arrived just a few months ago."

Khana.

He'd kept his promise to the captain of the guard and had executed a soldier every day since she'd escaped, ending it only after reaching a hundred to avoid the hassle of re-hiring an entire staff. Their bodies decorated his walls until the stench got too bad. The master of spies had promised to keep an eye out, but at that point they'd agreed that she was probably dead, killed by something in the jungle.

Apparently not.

"I want war strategies for conquering Divaajin within a month," Yamueto said. "The sooner the better."

PRESENT

Chapter Sixteen

News of the night creature spread through the town even before Phramanka made her announcement. Suddenly, everyone regarded Khana with even more suspicion and wariness. A customer even walked right back out the door when he spotted her setting up the dining room cushions. He hadn't even taken off his boots.

Heimili pulled her into the back. "They think you brought the night creature," he explained. "Or summoned it, somehow."

"I didn't," she insisted, scrubbing a dirty pot.

"I know. You've been running yourself ragged helping with this place and healing their ungrateful asses."

Khana rinsed the pot with already-murky water. "I didn't realize Pahuuda doesn't have a standing army."

"Not really. There are some career soldiers, and most of the Old Families have household guards, but the bulk of the force is militia. Almost anyone can volunteer, if they're physically fit," Heimili grumbled, limping across the kitchen to pull some chuta out of the oven.

"Will you be enlisting then?" he asked.

Khana stared at him. "Why would I do that?"

"It's how most refugees make a living here. They even get bonuses, like voting for a chief after three years. Normally you need to have lived here for seven."

Khana tried to picture herself in the wool and pelt armor of the Ghuran soldiers, spear in one hand, animal skin shield in the other. She tried to imagine what it would be like facing down an army of night creatures. Facing Yamueto.

Her hands began to shake. She covered it with vigorous scrubbing. "I've healed dozens of weapon injuries. I don't need to inflict them."

"They're looking for medics, too."

"So are the civilians," she countered.

Heimili hummed and didn't say anything further.

It was a slow day, the type where there were hardly more than two customers in the dining room at a time. Khana couldn't tell if that was her fault or not. Haz barely had anything to do, leaning against the spot on the kitchen counter that let him see the dining room.

"I'm going to enlist," he said out of nowhere.

Khana's heart sank. Heimili nodded and limped over to give his son a half-hug. "Good. I wish I was right there with you."

Haz smiled. "Someone has to help Mimi with the inn."

"Don't worry. We'll save plenty of work for you when you're done."

"Aw, Baba!"

Heimili snickered. Then he looked past Haz at the dining room and smiled. "Hey, you! I haven't seen you in forever!"

He limped over to the fresh customer who greeted him just as cheerfully. Khana cleaned another dish. Haz crossed his arms and joined her. "What about you? Are you signing up?"

"No."

He frowned. "Why not?"

"This isn't my home," she snapped. Why did they both want her to fight Yamueto? Didn't they realize how terrifying he was? Everyone needed to start packing and evacuate, not ready their swords.

"Maybe not, but being a soldier is one of the most honorable things a person can do. I'd have enlisted years ago if Baba and Mimi didn't need me around here."

"You think hurting and killing people is honorable?" she demanded. "That leaving your family to die on the battlefield, and have them mourn you for the rest of their days, *that's* honorable?"

"Defending your home and the people you love is honorable," he corrected. Another customer came in, cheering at Heimili. Haz sidestepped Khana. "You'd better finish those dishes. We'll have a rush soon."

Khana and Haz avoided each other the next day, which was easy as Haz joined the long line trailing from the town hall to go to war. Khana poured tea for herself as she sat alone in the dining room, eating her midday meal. Sava hadn't been by since finding the night creature, too busy preparing the town and getting ready to train thousands of new recruits. Khana knew that. Understood that. She still wished he was here.

Instead, it was Amati who walked up to her, taking those small, deliberate steps women do when they reached the age of fragility, and carefully sat herself on the cushion across from her. She held up an empty teacup, and Khana filled it.

"Slow days are good now," Amati said. "Lets us save our strength."

"True," Khana agreed.

Amati sipped her tea, savoring the taste before swallowing. "Heimili told me you don't intend to enlist."

Khana sighed. "I wasn't aware that was a requirement for living here."

"It isn't. If everyone was a soldier, who would farm the fields? Build the houses? It just seems a shame that a woman of your talent isn't going where it'll be most needed."

"I thought my only talent was bringing bad luck."

Amati gave her a stern look. "I was thinking of my grandson."

Khana looked into her cup, ashamed. She hadn't considered that joining the troops would mean she could look after Haz. After all he and his family had done for her, she owed it to them.

But that would require going toward Yamueto and his undead army, not away.

Amati coughed. She'd been doing that a lot. Khana held out her hand. "Do you want me to…"

The old woman shook her head. "It's old age. You can't cure that. *Shouldn't* cure that."

Khana withdrew her hand.

Amati sipped her tea again, taking the time for her throat to recover. "When I first got here, decades ago, we had a border skirmish with Tlaphar. One of many. They had always nipped at our lands until Regualli drew their attention. Anyway. Enlistment started. I thought it was dumb. Especially recruiting women. Women shouldn't fight. And besides, I had just got here. Had only been here a few months. Why should I fight for them?

"It wasn't until I'd had the chance to get to know these people, especially Heimili's father, that I realized that this is a place I wanted to fight for. That these were *people* I wanted to fight for. So, I enlisted."

Khana blinked, staring at the frail old woman before her. "You were a soldier?"

"Combat medic. I still don't like the idea of women fighting, but it is what it is. The pay was quite good, too. Certainly more than tips from a shabby inn. Probably enough to cross the tundra and the rest of the continent, too."

"Now you're just goading me," Khana grumbled.

"A little," Amati agreed with a toothless grin.

Khana sighed, looking at her dark reflection in the teacup. "You don't know the emperor like I do. We should be running, not fighting."

Amati set her cup down. "You're afraid."

"I'm terrified!" she burst. "Do you know what will happen to me if they find me?"

"The same things that'll happen to all of us if they take the town," Amati countered. "We're all afraid, Khana. Some are just better at controlling it. Fear is natural. Useful, even. But if you think running away will get rid of it, you're wrong. It'll fester, like a wound. And you'll never be free."

"But I'll be alive," Khana argued. That was all that mattered, the only true victory she could claim.

"Will you?" Amati challenged. "What happens after the empire takes us? Takes the kingdom? Even hundreds of miles away, will you be safe? I lived in the same empire you did for decades. They conquered my homeland when I was a baby and treated my people like filth, so I left. I thought I was safe. Now…"

Khana didn't say anything. Yamueto had several flaws, but impatience and lack of endurance weren't among them. He'd waited over a century for the perfect moment to strike at a target kingdom. Some of his conquests required generations of strategizing and fighting. The first year she'd been in his palace, his guards captured and dragged in one of his daughters who'd escaped decades previously. He'd looked for her all that time, finding her as a weathered old woman with a husband, children, and grandchildren. Yamueto killed all of them, starting with the youngest, and turned them into his night creatures.

Amati was right; Khana would never be safe. Never be free.

"You still think you're alone," Amati commented. "But I assure you, you're not. When you face this fear, you'll have an entire army with you."

Amati's words rang in Khana's head for over an hour as she cleaned guests' rooms and prepped the kitchen for Heimili. Haz came back with his official enlistment paper – the only piece of real paper Khana had seen in this town – signed with a wax seal imprinted with a wolf. He proudly showed it to his family.

Amati tutted. "If you were a few hands shorter, I'd give you my uniform."

"Aw, you'd let me look better than you did in your own clothes?" he teased. Amati tugged at his ear and sent him to his chores.

Khana hurried after him, catching him on top of the stairs. "You're really doing this?"

Haz shrugged. "Everyone is. We can't just let this happen to our home."

"Have you thought about what it'll do to your father and grandmother if you die?"

Haz's smile was surprisingly kind. "We all die, Khana. At least this way I'm going out in dashing armor."

He walked away. Khana stood numb. He was going to war.

Haz was her friend – or at least the closest thing she had to one – and he was going to war. With creatures she had helped create. And if they successfully cut through him and the other soldiers, they would come for Heimili and Amati. They'd do worse to the leaders of the resistance: the Bvamsos. Sava.

Khana grabbed her cloak and ran outside.

The town hall was packed so tight with recruits that they lined up outside in the cold, the frost crunching under their boots and the northern mountain wind cutting through them. The atmosphere was surprisingly amicable: people laughed and told jokes, an old man told war stories to his adult grandchildren, a trio of musicians sang righteous war songs to collect tips in their hats, and one clever woman sold butter tea mixed with flour, which created a sort of stew excellent for eating on the go.

Khana noticed several people standing together: a father half-hugged his adult son as they waited, a young woman grumbled to her friend about how she wasn't going to fit into her uncle's armor, and a married couple held hands.

Eventually, she made it inside. The courtroom had been converted into a recruitment station. Four desks – made of wood, no less – were placed where the mob had been at her trial. Official-looking people knelt behind each of them, taking down names and handing out the enlistment papers. One of them was Sava.

His Reguallian lessons had certainly paid off, since almost everyone he took was a refugee who didn't speak much Ghura. He'd come far since she'd first met him over three months ago, barely stumbling over his words. His eyes met hers as she reached the front of the line, and he stood. "Khana! Are you all right?"

"I'm fine," she muttered, trudging to his desk.

"You look like you're going to be sick."

"I might be," she admitted. "I need to enlist."

He opened and closed his mouth. He glanced at the lines of curious onlookers, mumbled, "I'm taking a break," and gestured for Khana to follow him.

Curious, Khana obeyed, and they walked out of the room into a back hall.

"You don't have to enlist," Sava said. "You plan to leave, anyway."

"I know," she said faintly. "But that's going to take a while."

"If someone's pressuring you to do this because of your powers or lineage or–"

"Sava," she said, warmed by his concern. "I have to do this."

He studied her, mouth thinning into a frown. "I really don't like the idea of you fighting."

Frustration bubbled within her. First everyone wanted her to fight, and now that she had decided to, they'd changed their minds?

"Well, that's not your decision," she said, the words slipping out before she could stop them.

Sava huffed. "I know. But in Pahuuda, we're all taught the basics as children. Almost everyone serves for a few years, even in peacetime. You've never even touched a spear."

"No, I don't know how to fight. But Amati said something about being a medic?"

He gave a tired sigh. "We take medics. But we also put them through the same basic training as the rest of the soldiers, in case they find themselves attacked. You'll be in a training unit, probably with Reguallians, and then transferred to a healing unit when training is over."

She nodded. "Can you put me in the same unit as Haz?"

He started to loosen. "All right. I can do that."

Chapter Seventeen
Sava

Sava had no need to enlist since he was already commander, midya in fact, of one of the archer divisions. The chief was also automatically enlisted by default and had to publicly opt out if they couldn't fight a war that they themselves had declared. His father, Thriman, on the other hand, had to fill out the paperwork.

"I don't suppose I can convince you not to do that," Phramanka said as she worked on her tapestry in the sitting room. It was a family portrait of the three of them that she'd been chipping away at, off and on, for the last five years. With the sun going down, the room was lit by the warm glow of the fireplace and a handful of lanterns.

Thriman snorted, sharpening his sword. "Like I'm going to let the two of you fight without me."

"Fine, then. Sava?"

He paused in cleaning his flute. "Ye-es?"

"Since your father's being stubborn, perhaps you should stay behind so the Bvamso family doesn't completely die out in one war."

Sava froze. Swallowed. She might as well have carved open his chest and removed every vital organ within. "Ma, please don't ask me to stay behind again."

She cursed and abandoned her tapestry, putting her hands on his shoulders, leaning down as he sat cross-legged on a cushion. "I'm sorry. But as much as we don't want you to be miserable, we do want you to live. You're strong enough to heal from a wound like that."

He highly doubted that. Two years ago, he'd lost Myrta, the woman he'd been making wedding plans with, and it'd felt like losing a limb. He was only now starting to truly look ahead, to perhaps find a new love.

"Is that an order, chief?" he asked coldly.

Phramanka's mouth thinned. "No. You're not a poor enough soldier to justify such an order."

"We could keep some extra archers behind to look after the town..." Thriman suggested.

"Baba," Sava hissed.

Thriman shrugged. "I'm just saying. Your mother and I are old. If we don't die in this war, we get to look forward to rotting away in our beds, pissing ourselves, and forgetting our own names."

"You're barely fifty."

"Point still stands."

"You're not allowed to die in this war, dear," Phramanka said tiredly.

"Aw."

The tension broke, as it always did. Thriman shot Sava a sneaky wink, and he relaxed.

Napha, one of the family's servants, cleared her throat at the doorway. "The Pinnsviri family is at the door."

"All of them?" Phramanka asked incredulously.

"Master Pabu, his son Veta, and Veta's daughter Bhayana."

The chief's face soured.

"Perhaps you're sick or busy?" Sava suggested. He didn't want to deal with these people, either.

She gave an annoyed huff, blowing gray bangs away from her face. "No. Whatever they're about to complain about, I'd rather deal with it now before it festers. Send them in."

Napha quickly obeyed, going back to the front door and leading the three Pinnsviris into the sitting room. She did not offer them refreshments, nor did Phramanka demand it.

Sava watched the elderly Master Pabu carefully as he limped in on his cane. His health had fluctuated wildly the last few months, some days so frail it was a wonder he still breathed, other days he barely needed the cane at all. Haz had told Sava that Pabu regularly summoned Khana to replenish his health, for free no less.

Pabu slowly, delicately, sat himself on a cushion across from Phramanka. Veta, who was around Thriman's age, sat on his right, and a scowling Bhayana on his left. They all had the signature Pinnsviri dark eyes and sharp noses, though Veta was more box-shaped than his bone-thin father and slender daughter.

"I hear we've recruited enough people to fill all seven battalions," Pabu said in his rasping, weathered voice.

The Blue and Yellow battalions were the only two that were in use full-time, in peace and in war, mostly patrolling the mountains and protecting all Ghuran settlements. But in times of active war, Red, Black, Purple, Orange, and Green battalions were filled, almost always made up of temporary recruits. Battalions were then broken into companies, and those were broken even further into units. Sava was a midya of a Blue company, in part due to experience, but largely because of his family. Since a chief could only be elected from an Old Family, it was preferable to give members as much leadership experience as possible.

"We have," Phramanka confirmed. "Almost every family has enlisted at least one person to fight, most two or three."

"We heard that *you* were assigning midyas their companies."

"I am not. I keep that decision to the maverstis," Phramanka corrected.

"Do you?" Bhayana challenged. "I'm told I'm to lead one of the Red companies."

"And that's a problem?"

"Red battalion is full of Reguallians!" Bhayana spat. "They're literally naming one of the companies the Frog Company. It's an insult."

Sava stiffened. It was true that Red and Orange were almost exclusively Reguallian, a decision made on purpose to minimize any remaining language barriers (but also because Blue and Yellow simply refused to have "empire scum" within their ranks). The Red battalion's maversti was Thulu Bhalu, one of the Seven Family Masters, and Sava had asked him to keep Khana and Haz together as a favor, at least through training.

Now it seemed there was a chance that Bhayana was going to be their commanding officer.

"Well then, this should be an excellent learning experience for you," Phramanka said. "Perhaps you'll discover more about them and become more empathetic."

"Phramanka, please," Veta said smoothly. "Surely you realize what an affront this is to our family."

"There is no insult except that which you've made up in your own heads. The Reguallian refugees know what we're fighting better than any of us. I daresay they'll fight harder than our full-time soldiers."

"Do you get joy out of belittling my family?" Pabu asked.

"Haz enlisted a few days ago and will almost certainly be in Red," Sava cut in. "Placing Bhayana as his superior officer is a clear conflict of interest."

Phramanka grunted.

"I think you were right about exposing her to Reguallians though," Thriman mused. "So long as it's not the same company as Hasyamin."

Bhayana glared at him, but Pabu quelled her with a hand on her leg. "My granddaughter is trying to make a fresh start. It's very difficult when she keeps getting dragged down by her past."

"Besides, the Cila boy flaunted a potential courtship with her, and then started courting a Bhalu," Veta grumbled. "All because of those... nasty rumors."

Sava hadn't heard anything about that, but he couldn't say he was surprised. Before Haz, Bhayana bounced between courtships like a stone skipping water. Since her trial, she hadn't been able to win anyone's affections.

"Probably for the best. We can't always marry within the Old Families, or we'd be inbred lumps," Phramanka said. "I will ensure that Bhayana's company does not include Hasyamin, but you will remain within the Red battalion. If not to learn humility, then at least to learn respect."

Bhayana sputtered.

"Chief, please reconsider..." Veta tried.

"My decision is final. If there's nothing else, get out of my house."

Veta huffed and helped his father stand. The three of them, slowly, left.

Thriman waited until they were gone to smirk at Sava. "You know, if you're looking for a new relationship, I hear Bhayana's available."

Sava kicked him, sending him laughing to the floor.

"Where are you going?" Phramanka asked the next day.

"Into town," Sava replied smoothly from the doorstep. The morning was crisp and clear, and he wanted tea and conversation before diving back into work.

"Where in town?"

Damn.

"...the inn," he confessed.

"I told you to stay away from the witch."

"You said nothing about Haz," Sava weakly defended. Phramanka glared at him. He sighed. "All right, yes, you did say so. But I disagreed with that order. I just wanted to make sure my friend was all right, and that no abuse was happening to Khana."

"I thought you trusted Hasyamin."

"I do. And his father and grandmother. But the rest of the town... You know Pabu's only alive because he summons Khana to heal him, and half the town has asked her to do the same. She's either too nice or too scared to say no, or to charge them."

Phramanka huffed and motioned for Sava to come closer. Confused, he obliged and let her fix the wolf cloak that had gone askew on his shoulders. "You," she said, "are a disobedient little twit."

He smiled. "Only sometimes."

"Bring me back some of that good chuta."

He kissed her cheek and practically skipped down the mountain. The whole town was abuzz. Military training would begin next week, once all the details of who was going to what unit, company, and battalion were finalized. There'd be a lot of gossip, vying, and favors.

"Neta!" he cheered, spotting her pale gray, black-dotted snow leopard cloak and joining her side of the road.

"Sava," she greeted. Despite having known each other since childhood, and teaching him sign language as she courted Athicha, she had always intimidated him. There was an intensity there that made him think of an approaching avalanche, unstoppable and burying everything in its path.

"How's the unit?" He tried to keep his voice purely curious. Any time he had expressed true concern, she'd always brushed it off.

"Boring," she said. "No one's tried to punch or stab anyone yet."

"Well, maybe you'll get promoted to serji. It's about time for that, anyway."

She snorted. "My midya turned me down when I asked for it."

Sava frowned. It'd taken him less than a week to learn the incalculable value of good under-officers. Maybe his view was simply colored by knowing her for so long, but he'd have killed to have a serji like Neta in his ranks. Unfortunately, she wasn't an archer.

"I'll just have to wait until a few officers start dropping in battle," she finished with a grim smirk.

Ah, yes. There was that intensity. There was nothing malicious to it; Neta would rather chop off her own hand than kill her way to the top. But Sava had no doubt that she would have a battalion under her command by the time she was done with this life, if not the entire mountain range. Why nobody would help her with this was beyond him.

"Neta, if you don't get promoted soon, then it'll mean everyone in the militia has collectively lost their brains," he said seriously.

She blinked.

"You seem surprised," he teased.

"Only by hearing someone else say it out loud." She motioned to the bag she carried. "I need to get this to my mother."

"Right. And Neta? If you run into any more issues, you can always come to me. I know you can handle yourself, but you don't have to."

She smiled, punching him in the shoulder. "Worry about your own company and unit, Sava. I can handle mine."

He frowned, watching her go. That woman was confusing. The only reason he hesitated in calling her a true friend was because she would always do things like that: pulling away whenever he tried to be sincere.

He shook the thoughts from his mind. Neta could handle herself. He had other friends in need of him.

The inn was rarely busy in the early afternoon. At most there'd be a couple of regulars sipping tea and talking to each other while the staff cleaned and prepared for the next rush.

As Sava took off his boots, Khana sewed a dull green dress by the light of the fire, worrying her lower lip between her teeth. Across from her, Athicha worked on a bone carving, beaded hair falling over their face.

Sava grinned, clapping his best friend on the shoulder. "Oh, good, you two have met."

Khana looked up and gave a sheepish smile. "Oh, they're your friend? Sorry, I can't say we've *met*. They don't talk much. But Haz said your name was Athicha?"

Athicha nodded. Then reached up and tugged down their scarf. Khana's eyes popped at the long, thick scar across their neck.

Sava cleared his throat. At Athicha's nod, he explained, "The Tlapharians over the mountains have never liked us. Their hunters often clashed with ours, which would usually escalate into a skirmish or minor war. At least, until the Reguallians drew their attention."

Khana's hands twitched. "Maybe I can–"

Athicha shook their head and signed, *Scar. No heal.* Sava translated.

She gave an annoyed frown. "Magic ignores many rules, you know."

Athicha laughed, which was a hoarse, almost whispered sound. Khana smiled, obviously pleased. They signed, and Sava translated, "Save the energy for something more life-or-death."

She huffed, making a final stitch on her dress. "Fine."

"That's new," he commented.

"One of the farmers asked me to heal her daughter from fever last week. She gave me this in return. I just have to make a few adjustments."

That made Sava breathe a little easier. His people were stubborn, he knew that, so it was nice to see them slowly come around to their witch neighbor.

"Did you want your tea?" she offered.

"Please. And Haz, if he's in."

Khana quickly disappeared and came back with tea set in hand and Haz in tow. His friend grinned. "I'm not calling you midya until I get my armor, at least."

"Fortunately for both of our sanities, you and I are in completely different battalions," Sava retorted.

"Aw, I'm going to get a grump, aren't I?"

"Possibly. You almost got Bhayana."

Khana sucked in a breath, studying Haz, who went eerily calm. Athicha narrowed their eyes.

"She's going to be in Red Battalion, same as you, and holds the midya rank," Sava said apologetically. "But we've made sure that she's not going to be your direct commander. You'll be in different companies."

"Well… small mercies," Haz said, pouring the tea.

Khana frowned. "You don't have to tell me, but what, exactly, did Bhayana–"

"Khana!" Amati called from upstairs. "Help me with this bedding!"

"Never mind," she murmured, once again setting aside her sewing and carefully stepping around them to reach the stairs.

Sava bit his lip, watching her hurry away. Her hair almost reached her shoulders; he wondered how it would look braided with Ghuran beads. "I was surprised you both enlisted. You haven't shown much interest in the military, and Khana looked terrified when she came to town hall."

Haz winced. "Yeah… I think that was my fault."

Sava frowned.

"I like the inn and all," Haz explained. "But I can't sit still while everyone goes to war. I enlisted so my life would at least have some meaning." He said it with a self-deprecating chuckle, but it made Sava frown.

Athicha signed, *Good tea, good meaning.*

"Yeah, because that's going to keep us safe and prosperous. Oversteeped tea."

Before either of them could argue further, Haz continued, "I think Khana enlisted to keep an eye on me. Mimi mentioned talking to her and… yeah."

"Ah." Sava studied the dark surface of his cup. "Most soldiers I know don't enlist because of 'higher meaning.' Most do it for money, plain and simple. But a lot of them signed up because of their friends or family. They didn't like the thought of them being in danger alone."

"That's supposed to make me feel better?" Haz asked.

Athicha snapped their fingers, drawing attention, and signed, *Witch always scared. Jumpy. She calm with you. Every time.*

"Exactly. You're Khana's closest friend here," Sava stressed. "She doesn't strike me as the type of person to take that lightly."

Haz scratched the back of his neck. "No, she isn't. That's part of what makes her so adorable."

Sava almost choked. "Adorable?!"

"Like a baby bear. One of these days she's going to be deadly, but until then she's just… cute." Haz grinned. "I can't wait."

Sava tried not to let his heart drop. "I… didn't know you felt that way about her."

Haz gave him a confused look, then quickly stifled a laugh as his eyes bugged out of his skull. "No, not like that! Not my type! She's my friend. I see her almost as a sister. No naked shenanigans are ever going to happen."

Sava huffed. "Well, it wouldn't have surprised me. She's about the furthest thing from Bhayana."

"Very different from Myrta, too."

Ah, shit.

Sava drank some tea to buy himself time. Athicha grinned.

"Not in a bad way," Haz continued. "I just can't see Khana getting drunk and throwing snowballs at Old Family members who annoy her. And I've tried to get her to laugh at my impeccable humor, but, apparently, she doesn't share Myrta's good tastes."

Both fighters, Athicha pointed out. *Just different ways.*

Sava sighed, now out of tea. "Myrta was… we fell together quickly. She enjoyed life to the fullest, and everything seemed… more, around her. I liked that. I liked how she never held back. That came from confidence. Inner strength. Khana has that too, it's just… quieter. I didn't really notice her at first, but the more she's here, the more I see it."

Haz tipped his head in agreement. "I'm happy for you. Every time I think about getting back into courting, I always shy away from it."

Fine, Athicha stressed. *No race. You grieve.*

He made a face. "Did you get some rotten tea, Athi? Because I'm not the one whose lover died."

"You can grieve yourself," Sava said quietly. "The person you were before Bhayana got her claws into you. That's worth crying over."

Haz looked away. "How did we get from me teasing you about your obvious crush to you both making me feel feelings? I'm outnumbered. This is unfair."

We have many talents, Athicha quipped.

Sava chuckled. "Honestly, Haz, I don't know if *I'm* ready for another courtship, either. So, if you could refrain from telling Khana anything…"

"Lips are sealed." Haz nudged him. "But try to survive this war so you have the option."

"An attempt will be made," he promised. "Want to tease Athicha over their relationship with Neta, instead?"

The archer squawked and smacked Sava with a cushion. Haz burst out laughing.

Athicha sobered. *Regualli Leopard serji now?*

"I don't know," Sava admitted. "We've filled out all the battalions, so there's going to be a round of promotions in the coming days."

He didn't have to worry about that because Blue Battalion was always fully stocked. He pitied the newly appointed Red, Green, Orange, Purple, and Black midyas, though. That was a lot of decision-making and arguing.

"If they have any sense, they'll promote her," he said.

Athicha nodded, but Haz snorted. "Sure. That'll be the day."

"You haven't seen her fight."

"Don't have to. She's Reguallian. They won't promote her."

Athicha scowled as Sava frowned. "What do you mean?"

Haz rolled his eyes. "I mean that only a handful of Reguallians and Tlapharians have been promoted to serji since my grandmother came here, and that number goes down every time we fight because people are idiots and think we'll betray our home to the empire. Also, the Old Families tend to hoard all the powerful positions for themselves. *You* might be willing to share, but a lot of people get overlooked because a bear or eagle or porcupine wants to play soldier instead."

Sava's frown deepened. "But Neta is Cituva."

"Not really. That family hates her. Everyone knows that. So, anyone who promotes her is going to get the entire Cituva family pissed at them. Who's going to risk that?"

Fuck.

He dropped his head in his hands. "Ugh. I'm an idiot."

"They might let her be serji later in the war," Haz offered. "Or after, if she fights really well and there aren't any other options. But after that?

No Reguallian has ever become midya or above. A lot of us didn't even want to become soldiers. I overheard a dozen customers the other day talking about how they weren't going to enlist because that one man – Soril? Xopil? The one who Khana healed– got stabbed. For what? Not being Ghuran."

Sava never truly *forgot* that his friend was a quarter Reguallian, even if Haz looked Ghuran. But it was easy to forget that Haz's life was so much more difficult because of his bloodline, the way Sava's was easier for the same reason.

Athicha snapped their fingers, getting their attention. *Singing Wolf Old Family. You ask favor?*

He sighed. "I already did that to get Haz and Khana in the same unit."

"Really?" Haz asked, delighted.

"She asked."

He should've called the favor to make Neta serji two years ago, but he'd been so clouded with grief that everything else faded away.

"If Neta's Reguallian, her best bet would be Red," he mused. "Thulu Bhalu's the maversti…"

Bear Master like Regualli? Athicha asked.

Haz shrugged. "Eh… I haven't heard that he *dislikes* us."

"My mother likes him," Sava added. "Says he's pragmatic, practical, and not easily swayed."

That last one might cause problems, but Sava was growing more confident.

He downed his tea and stood. "Excuse me, friends. I need to run an errand."

Chapter Eighteen
Neta

It was not every day one received a summons to an Old Family. Curious, worried, and perhaps a bit hopeful, Neta hurried to the Bhalu estate as soon as the messenger finished speaking, leaving her mother Varisa calling after her, "Be careful! And don't let them disrespect you!"

The road took her past the Pinnsviri estate, where Pabu's granddaughter Bhayana leaned against a stone porcupine as she talked to Chaku, a former serji recently promoted to midya – in Red Battalion, if Neta recalled correctly.

Bhayana saw the movement, glanced at Neta, and dismissed her, smiling bright and coy at Chaku. Neta rolled her eyes. She'd watched Bhayana's trial for abusing the innkeeper's son during their courtship. Sava and Athicha had been furious for weeks afterward at her light sentence. Everyone knew the only reason Bhayana hadn't been banished to the tundra for at least a year was because of her family.

The Bhalu family did not have their seat of power in Pahuuda, but another Ghuran town several miles west. Thulu's sister held command out there, while Thulu, his husband, and their adopted children moved to Pahuuda to take the Master's seat beside the chief. Thulu's home was guarded by stone bears and was carved deeper into the mountain than the other estates, meaning there were fewer windows and a lot more candles and torches. But the walls themselves were carved with animals, soldiers, gods, and their nomadic ancestors, and they echoed with the sound of little feet and bickering from a dozen different directions.

As Neta stepped inside Thulu's cavernous home and removed her boots, shouts echoed down the stone halls.

She stiffened. She knew that voice.

Her uncle, Athor Cituva, stormed into the hall, thunder on his face. He stopped when he saw her, and their eyes met. He wore the leopard family symbol as teeth pierced through his ears and claws around his neck. With the exception of skin tone, the two of them looked incredibly similar, likely because Neta's father was Athor's twin – same button nose, broad shoulders, and dimpled chin.

As Thulu stepped into the hall, Athor looked back. "You're making a mistake."

"I think I can survive rankling your pride, Athor. This meeting was a courtesy. Keep yelling at me in my own home, and I'll toss you into the street face-first."

Thulu dwarfed even the tallest of soldiers, and Athor hadn't served in the militia a day in his life – rare for a Master. He turned to pick up his boots, but as he put them on, he hissed under his breath, "Reject his offer, Neta. If you know what's good for you."

Now beyond curious, Neta replied, "I didn't follow your last order, uncle. What makes you think I'll follow this one?"

His glare sharpened when she called him uncle, a forbidden word. "If you want to *earn* that cloak you insist on wearing, you'll learn to obey."

She chuckled without mirth. "I tried that, remember? All it got me were tears and a broken hand."

She'd been a dumb thirteen-year-old, living with a mother who refused to have anything to do with her ex-paramour's family. Neta had offered to help tend to her sick, dying grandmother, thinking it would endear her to the rest of the family that had rejected her for her Reguallian blood. But all she'd received was humiliation. Her cousins bullied and pranked her while Athor had only used her to clean his estate. Her father Aravi – who had only visited Pahuuda to see to his dying mother – hadn't even looked at her and had left town to go back to his current wife and children a hundred miles away.

The final break had been when her cousins called her mother "the Reguallian whore." She'd gone home that day with two broken knuckles and a painful lesson: if she had to "earn" love and respect, it had never been there in the first place.

The next month, she'd hunted a snow leopard, tended to the pelt herself, and worn it in defiance. She was a Cituva by blood, and nothing Athor, Aravi, or anyone else said was going to change that.

Athor had still tried to order her to give up the cloak. She'd refused. The matter had gone all the way to the chief, who had backed her up.

Her uncle sneered at her as he finished putting on his boots and left.

"I see why you live away from them," Thulu drawled.

"My mother's house is closer to the training field anyway," Neta agreed. "You asked to see me, Master Thulu?"

He led her into one of the smaller rooms, lit by candles and the hearth, as there were no windows, and handed her a slip of paper. Neta savored the feeling in her hands, so rarely did she ever get to touch the stuff.

"That's a transfer order," he explained as she unfolded it. "You're going to be part of my battalion. As a serji."

Neta's head shot up. "Sir?"

He shrugged. "I need officers, and Sava called in a favor."

Annoyance soured her joy. Of course it wasn't because of her own merit. That was how it worked in Pahuuda.

Still. She knew Sava didn't use those favors lightly.

"I also talked to Ghrahanu," Thulu continued, "who said that you'd be an all right officer, if you could stay out of fights."

"I don't start fights," Neta assured him. "I finish them."

He grinned. "Then you'll do fine. I'm also giving you the witch and her friend. Another favor for that wolf pup; those two wanted to stay together. At least for training. There's talk of her joining the medics after."

Neta paused. "That tiny wisp enlisted?"

"She did."

"Can she even carry a shield?"

"No idea."

"And you want me to turn her into a soldier?"

"Yes. One who can kill and defend herself without cheating with magic."

Neta tried to keep the smirk from her face, but knew she failed. She'd never been afraid of a challenge.

Chapter Nineteen

Heimili went to wake both Khana and Haz before dawn, but she was already awake. Plagued by nightmares about undead creatures and Yamueto's hands.

This was a mistake, she thought, picking at the breakfast Heimili made for them. She didn't understand how Haz could wolf his down; it tasted like ash. "What happens if someone deserts?" she asked, quietly enough that only Haz heard.

"It depends. Sometimes it's tundra banishment for a week or a fortnight. But sometimes they just execute you," he said. "Abandoning your comrades puts everyone at risk."

She gulped, stomach churning around what little she'd managed to eat.

Amati trudged into the dining room, carrying a shield, spear, and heavy-looking bundle in a blanket. It was very odd seeing such a frail woman carrying weapons of war, but she held them with confidence.

"I think the spear and shield are big enough for Haz," she grunted, dropping the blanketed bundle. "But the armor is definitely not."

She handed Haz the spear. It eclipsed him in height by at least an arm's length. He whistled, testing the edge. "Did you sharpen this last night?"

"No, I'm sending you to war with dull weapons," she said, rolling her eyes. She unwrapped the bundle, passing him a handaxe and sheathed knife. "You get the shield and weapons. It's best if they stay in the family. Khana, take this and try it on."

She pressed a folded piece of clothing in Khana's hands. She swallowed, her throat dry, and went up to her room.

When Khana heard the word "armor," she thought of the Reguallian suits of metal and leather carefully folded on top of each other, or the ancient bone armor preserved in one of Princess Sita's library books. She did not think of cloth, but that's what Ghuran armor was, at least for foot soldiers. Multiple layers of linen, pelt, and wool had been sewn to form a tough hide, which Khana had no doubt would keep her warm, though she worried about its ability to protect her from spears and claws.

The armor wrapped around her arms, chest, and stopped at her shins; it was supposed to go only to the knees. It came with underclothes, too: a long shirt and trousers. The belt cinched in at her waist and would probably be used to hold weapons. Bulky leather gloves went on last. Everything fit well enough, but still felt wrong. Like she was a cheap actor about to put on a laughable performance.

She went back downstairs to find Haz hiding behind his new shield as Amati threw seat cushions at him. "Your baba spent far too long cleaning the dishes this morning! All the debris was hard and crusty."

"Sorry, sorry!" he laughed. "I surrender! Baba, I swear, I just forgot."

"I'm aware," Heimili grumbled, but he couldn't quite hide his amusement. He looked up, spotting Khana first. "Well, gods damn. You look like a soldier."

I look like a child playing dress-up, Khana thought, but didn't say.

Amati pinched the armor, testing how it fit. With a satisfied nod, she handed Khana one last piece: her helmet. The metal was dulled with age, but she trusted it to protect her a lot more than cloth. The inside was covered in leather, not that that made it particularly comfortable when she put it on.

Haz rapped his knuckles on the helmet. "Great! Now we just need to get me some armor, so *I* don't die."

"You're not going to die," Khana grumbled, adjusting the helmet from where it'd tilted at Haz's touch. "That's half the reason I'm doing this."

The line to town hall was almost as long as last time. Despite the cold pre-dawn air, Khana was completely warm, almost cozy, in her armor and cloak. She took the helmet off, tucking it under her arm. It made her feel a little less ridiculous.

Almost everyone around her had a similar conundrum as she and Haz. She saw several spears, but their owners were missing helmets or armor or shields. Some shields needed a spear. Some people were in full armor, but still needed directions.

"Move," someone ordered, roughly pushing her aside. Khana stumbled to her knees and dropped her helmet.

"Hey," Haz barked. His eyes widened. "Sipah? That you?"

Khana pushed herself to her feet with her helmet, brushing the snow from her legs. The burly, bearded guard from the Pinnsviri household was indeed there, crossing his arms as he waited impatiently for the line to move forward.

"Why, good morning, my dear friend Hasyamin," Haz said, lowering his voice to sound like Sipah. "Would you mind terribly if I join you in line? I'm in a great hurry and it would mean so much if I–"

"Shut your mouth," Sipah ordered. "I don't have time for you militia brats."

"You're militia, too, aren't you?"

"No, I'm a Pinnsviri guard, employed directly by an Old Family. They loan us out to the chief in units so we can fight with the other full-time soldiers, separate from you goat farmers. But the town still makes us get supplies with the rest of the rabble."

"Gods, it's almost like we're all soldiers in this mess together," Haz taunted.

Sipah pushed him back with a single hand. "First rule of the military: just because you carry a spear doesn't make you a soldier. You're still a nobody." He gave Khana a side-eyed glare. "Or a filthy soul-sucker."

She shrank back, wishing her armor would swallow her.

Haz whistled. "Bhayana always said you were a jackass before your morning tea. I see she underplayed it."

Sipah rounded on him. "What did you call me?"

Haz did not back down. "I merely repeated what your master's granddaughter told me."

The guard smirked, brown beard twisting with the movement. "Tell me: when you showed such disrespect, did she slap you, punch you, or go for your non-existent balls?"

The two glared at each other. Khana and everyone else stayed back, wondering who would throw the first punch.

"The line's moving!" someone shouted behind them. "Get out of the way if you're going to fight."

"Haz, let's go," Khana whispered, pulling him into town hall. "Can you try to avoid getting hurt until we're in an actual battle?" she hissed, once Sipah was safely behind them.

"When he stops being a jackass."

"I'm serious, Haz."

"So am I," he said.

Beneath the main hall was the armory. Tired-looking soldiers – those full-timers Sipah mentioned, perhaps – helped fetch weapons and told people where to go. "Where do they get all of this?" Khana asked, gaping at the rows of spears and shields. Most were made of bone, but at least a quarter of them were wood. She hadn't seen this much wood in Pahuuda ever. Not even in the Pinnsviri house.

"If a soldier outgrows their armor, or dies without heirs, it ends up here," Haz said. "But most of it is made by workers. Not everyone can make a good suit of armor or a spear that won't break the first time you use it. The ones who are good at it are hired by the chief. She even buys wood from the rest of the kingdom – and Tlaphar, once upon a time – because it's easier than metal."

"How much will it cost us?"

"Nothing. They're technically free, paid for with those good ol' taxes."

"How do you know all of this?"

"Bhayana told me." He grimaced. "Gods, every time I say her name, I feel I need to wash my mouth and ears out with soap."

The soldiers found some armor for Haz and weapons for Khana. The shield was multiple layers of animal pelts and hard leather, surprisingly heavy, and big enough to cover most of her body. They gave her the shortest spear they could find, which was still two heads taller than her, as well as a knife and axe that both went on her belt. All of it felt too heavy, bulky, and unreal.

"Try to look a little less terrified, girl," the soldier grumbled, helping her slip the axe into her belt.

"We'll have more luck with that if you can tell us where to go," Haz cheered. He actually managed to look confident and almost dashing in his armor, as if he was wearing any other outfit.

When they handed over their enlistment forms, the soldier checked them against a slate slab covered in numbers and glyphs Khana couldn't read. He said, "Well, you're both in the same squad: the Red Frogs Nine." He made a face at that. "What's a frog?"

"It's like a lizard, from the Reguallian jungles," Khana explained. "It hops."

"That strikes fear in the heart," Haz snorted. "Why are they giving us names like that?"

"The color is the battalion, the animal is the company, and the number is the unit," the veteran explained. "Most companies only have seven units, but we've got so many recruits that some have as many as eleven. Most Reguallians are in Red and Orange Battalions, so that's where all the weird names are. You'll find your unit on the field. They'll have a banner. Now get going."

Finding their unit turned out to be more difficult than anticipated, as half the town was doing the exact same thing. They made a sea of gray and black on the tundra, trying to gather under bright-colored fabrics clinging to bone poles.

"Who do you think our serji will be?" Khana asked, straining her eyes against the ocean of banners.

"Hopefully not a rotten bastard," Haz said. "We should probably go toward the red flags."

The soldier had spoken true: all the dozens of flags were divided into seven colors. A closer look revealed that they each had an animal sewn on in a contrasting color under a number. Despite being able to speak Ghura, Khana couldn't read it, though she quickly picked up the symbols used for numbers as Haz counted them for her.

They walked past red panthers, monkeys, and snakes before finding the frogs. Or at least, blobs that looked vaguely like the silhouette of a frog. The anatomy was warped: the back legs too long, the front ones too small. But at least it was recognizable, and there was a symbol for nine under it.

"This should be it," he said.

Most of the squad was already there, and Khana blinked at a familiar face. "Xopil!"

The tall man's wide face brightened. "Mistress Khana! Good to see you here."

"I haven't seen you since you got stabbed. How are your injuries?"

"Healed. My wife took good care of me." He hesitated, then bowed his head so far he bent in half. "I need to apologize. I should have thanked you properly for saving my life, long before this."

Khana squirmed, uncomfortable in the face of so much unwarranted gratitude and regret. Especially in public. "It's... it's all right. It may have been best to avoid me, given how bad my reputation is."

"That's what my wife said," he replied, straightening. "She didn't want me attacked again, and I thought I'd lose what little respect I had by being with the witch. But I was stabbed; I already had none. I was just afraid." He brightened. "But, now you're in our unit!"

"Hurray," said a new face in a deadpan voice. He was older than Khana by at least a decade, his face scarred by an old pox sickness. He leaned against his spear and didn't hold his shield, letting it rest against his leg instead.

There were two other new faces. One was a wiry old woman who had grown her hair out to her waist and wrangled it into a single braid. The ends were so old they were still black while the top of her head was gray. The sixth person was the youngest of the unit, if not the field: a lanky teen with a big nose and yellow wool cap who looked just as awkward in his armor and shield as Khana did.

Everyone under the flag had undeniable Reguallian blood – or possibly Tlapharian; she couldn't quite tell at a glance. She wondered how many of them had been born in Pahuuda; they were all speaking fluent Reguallian.

"I count six. Who's the seventh?" Haz asked.

"Our serji," Xopil said. "I don't know who it is, yet."

"Who cares? They all treat you like shit, especially in training," said the one with pox scars.

"Only if you're rude, Itehua."

"Or try to start an illegal drug trade," grumbled the older woman.

Itehua scoffed. "I performed a valuable service that the chief refuses to acknowledge. Which is a shame for her, because it's a gold mine."

Xopil nudged Khana's shoulder and pointed to the old woman. "That's Lueti. The young one is Yxe."

"I'm Haz."

"Khana."

"We know," Itehua sneered. "The witch. Just our luck."

"Nine is an unlucky number," Lueti mused.

They might be onto something there. So far, Khana counted a criminal, an old woman, a boy, and herself. That didn't make for a particularly fearsome unit, even with Xopil. Looking at the other units around them, they had a lot more grown men and muscled women. What were the chances that all the bad apples ended up in the same group?

"Well, if it makes you feel better, I'm only with you for training," Khana said. "I'm joining the medics after this."

"How do you plan to get the life force necessary to heal others if you're not in the front with access to the enemy?" Yxe asked.

Khana hadn't considered that. In her mind, animal sacrifices were always an option. But if they were fighting in or beyond the mountains, it wouldn't be practical. Not to mention she'd burn through the entire town's food supply after the first battle. She would have to sacrifice more memories, more of herself, to secure the âji.

"I... don't know," she stammered. "I suppose the commanders will have to figure that out."

"We'll make a strategy for that later."

Khana jumped at the new voice. She hadn't heard her approach. But as soon as she saw the face, she calmed. "Mist – er, Serji Neta!"

Neta was just as large and intimidating as she'd been in the trial, with the same snowy leopard cloak on her shoulders. She had the same shield, spear, axe, and knife as they did, but had an additional one on her belt, almost long enough to be a sword.

"Oh, thank the *gods*, someone with a spoonful of sense!" Haz cried.

Xopil saluted with a fist over his chest. "Serji."

"You're the one who's supposed to be in charge of us?" Itehua demanded. Khana winced at his tone.

Neta raised an eyebrow. "And?"

"You've got a leopard cloak. You're a Cituva, aren't you? What's an Old Family bitch doing here?"

"I'm a bastard, as I'm sure you know," she said. "And you are going to follow my orders without question."

"Yeah?" He stepped up to her, letting his shield fall to the ground. "Or what, bastard bitch?"

Khana put a hand over her mouth. Lueti hissed. Yxe subtly stepped behind Xopil for protection.

Neta smirked. "Spears and shields on the ground. If you can take my cloak from my shoulders, I'll call you serji."

Itehua grinned, his pox scar twisting, and dropped his spear. Neta set hers on the ground.

"I can't look," Khana whispered.

"Ten coppers on Itehua," Haz said.

"Haz!"

Neta had barely put her weapons down before Itehua struck. Rather than block or dodge, Neta grabbed his arm and swung him over her shoulder. He hit the ground with a thud. The other nearby units froze to watch as Neta twisted his arm, making him howl.

Keeping Itehua pinned, Neta turned to the rest of the unit. "This is the way to bloodlessly put down an opponent. Of course, when you're in battle, your goal is to kill. So be sure to keep them secure enough that you can free a hand." She unsheathed her knife and pressed the point to Itehua's throat.

He froze, swallowing.

"You want the neck, but you can also hit them under the armpit." She pointed to that with the knife. "This is usually the weakest part of the armor. Invaders' armor often doesn't even cover it, as they're made of metal, and it leads to friction. Unfortunately for them, there's a big vein right there. They'll bleed out in seconds."

Neta dropped Itehua and sheathed her knife. "Any other objections?"

Nobody said a word.

"Excellent. Let's begin."

Chapter Twenty

The next week was nothing short of grueling. Khana, Haz, and every other recruit were run into the ground from sunup to sundown. The Red Frog Company midya was not Bhayana, but a man named Chaku, and he was the one in charge of determining the company's schedule for the day. Running laps in the morning, learning weapons in the afternoon, etc.

Serji Neta was responsible for the hands-on training of their unit. She adjusted Khana's grip on her knife, axe, and spear, which was unbearably long and awkward. She barked at Khana – and Yxe – to hold their horribly heavy shields a few inches higher to properly fit in a phalanx. She ordered them to do extra push-ups if they didn't succeed in a proper task or fall in line quickly enough. Itehua was usually on the receiving end of that punishment, but Khana found herself on the ground with him for trailing behind the others during their mile-long runs, wheezing and struggling just to keep up the pace. Most of the time, Neta ordered the entire unit to do push-ups right alongside the offender.

"Is this what it's like having siblings?" Haz grunted, doing his push-ups much more easily than Khana, whose arms felt like they would catch fire. She'd only done her first ten and had twenty more to go. "Getting punished for something I didn't do?"

"A unit lives and dies by the strength of its weakest link," Neta said sweetly. To her credit, she was also on the ground, doing the push-ups she had ordered the unit to do. Not all the serjis did that. "That's how we'll be treated during graduation. If we don't *all* nail our weapon sets and finish the runs in time, none of us become soldiers, and you only get half the payment you were promised."

Khana cringed. It was obvious to her, and probably everyone else, that she was their weakest link. Their success or failure depended on her.

"Don't you know any magic to help with this, witch?" Itehua growled, pushing himself up and down easily enough, though he still breathed hard. In fact, the only members of the squad who seemed to have no issue with the exercise were Neta herself and Xopil, who did everything without complaint.

"No," Khana gasped, lowering herself closer to the ground on shaking limbs, trying to forget about the power she felt when full of âji.

It didn't help that Heimili and Amati still needed them to work the inn. They'd gotten a couple of neighborhood children to assist, but there were still busy nights. Every now and then Khana and Haz would stumble back to the inn, leaning on their spears and dreaming of baths and sleep, only to find the dining room full of customers. Haz would groan, then plaster on a smile and start waiting tables while Khana went to get a head start on dishes. When she finally did get to bed, she was greeted by nightmares. She woke up gasping, her pelts and wool blankets soaked in sweat as she tried to wipe away her tears and the memories. Heimili would feed her and Haz breakfast, and they'd start a new day.

"What did I say the punishment was for deserting?" Haz yawned, after a couple of weeks of this.

"Execution or tundra exile, which is just as good as," Khana replied, trudging alongside him to the field. The black sky gradually turned pale gray in the east, but the sun had been offering less and less warmth lately. She'd started wearing an extra layer under her wool armor.

"Would you like to be my exile buddy?"

She shrugged. "It'd be useful to have something to eat out there."

Haz blinked. "What?"

"Nothing!" Khana cheered.

He pressed a piece of chuta against her. "Eat this before you start eating me, please. It's the perfect appetizer."

By the time they'd met up with the rest of the army, they found all of Frog Company getting ready to move out, Neta packing several yards of rope into a bag.

"Serji?" Haz asked.

"We're going into the mountains," she said. "Get ready to move."

Khana looked at the black and gray towers of stone and gulped. She'd crossed those once already; she had no desire to repeat the experience.

"What are we going to do up there?" Haz asked.

"Glass diving," Neta answered.

Itehua and Xopil groaned while Haz whooped. "Yes! I've always wanted to try that!"

"What's glass diving?" Khana asked.

"When the town was first settled, explorers found stores of black glass in certain caves and crevices in the mountains," Yxe explained, adjusting the yellow wool hat on his head that tried and failed to make him look older. "Scholars call it obsidian. It's most common around volcanic islands, which lends credence to the theory that these mountains were once volcanoes. They're very difficult to get to, unless you have a team. As such, it's been a traditional military exercise for every new unit to fetch a piece of black glass."

"It builds trust. You're supposed to decorate your helmet or armor with it," Xopil said, motioning to a string of leather hanging off of his shoulder. A bit of black glass was tied on the end of it. "My son always tries to pull on this. Thinks it's one of his toys."

"It's a pain in the ass is what it is," Itehua growled.

"Is that why you don't have one?"

"I would've gotten it if an avalanche hadn't started. Mother Mountain herself tried to kill us."

Xopil's face fell. "I was there with my unit that day. I lost a friend."

Itehua's mouth thinned, but he didn't say anything degrading.

"How come you aren't with one of the other companies, the ones with permanent soldiers? Blue or Yellow?" Yxe asked. "You have the experience for it, don't you?"

"My unit was dismantled after two of the men stabbed me," Xopil said. "I think they moved me here to avoid bullies."

"Those units are made entirely of spoiled, rotten bastards," Itehua grumbled. "All they do is kiss Old Family asses."

"I'll try not to take that personally, recruit," Neta said, tossing her pack on her back. "We march in less than two minutes."

"How do you know all this about the glass diving?" Khana quietly asked Yxe.

"My mother's a governess for Master Thulu's children," he said. "She tutors his youngest son, and then tutors me. There's a lot of fascinating history that gets left off the tapestries. Did you know that one of our first chiefs was a potter?"

He said it with such enthusiasm and excitement that Khana couldn't help but smile, even as they heard the order to move. She stayed next to Yxe as they were marched toward the mountains. "I didn't know that."

"It's rather fascinating. Potters were incredibly important in our original homeland, which we think is a forest about a three-month-march away with a river that had a large clay deposit. But as our people traveled wider and ceramics became less useful than things like cloth bags and reed baskets, potters had to find other means of…"

"Gods, boy, shut *up*. No one cares," Itehua snapped.

Yxe shut his mouth, a beaten look on his face that reminded Khana a little too much of the concubines and their children that had the wills whipped out of them. She nudged his arm. "You can tell me later."

They climbed up the mountain, starting down the wide path that Khana had used to get to town, but then turned at a narrower trail she didn't know. It was impossible to find unless you knew to look for it and disappeared in some areas. They had to climb up a sheer rock wall at one point, which made Khana tremble. Luckily more experienced climbers, including Neta, went first.

"Well, that explains why you brought the rope," Khana said as Neta pulled her over the edge.

The young serji chuckled, winding the rope around her arm. "Oh, we're not done with this yet."

Confused, Khana continued to follow the company until they came upon a long crevice in the mountain. A black scar in the gray stone and white snow. The first few units had already got there and looked down, egging each other on. Khana crept to the edge.

The first several feet were regular gray stone. But farther down – far, *far* down – was some sort of black glass, like the teeth of a giant monster.

She shook her head, stepping back. "This is insane."

"This is *amazing*," Haz said, grinning. "Can I go first?"

"I'll go first," Neta said. "Serjis must go first. That's the tradition. Let's find a good spot."

The crevice was plenty long enough for all eleven Frog units to spread out. To Khana's growing horror, one of them tied a man's feet together.

They found a spot that looked just as terrifying as the rest of the crevice. Neta sat on the ground and tied the rope around her ankles.

"You're really doing this?" Khana asked, her voice cracking.

"Of course. It wouldn't even be the first time." Neta pulled a necklace out from under her armor, strung with a few animal teeth, a couple arrowheads, and a polished piece of natural black glass.

"What happens if you fall?"

"Then the six of you get punished for *letting* me fall," Neta said cheerfully. "So don't get any ideas."

"Damn," Itehua muttered.

That tundra exile looked better by the minute.

"After I'm done, Haz can go next," the serji continued. "Be sure to take your axe; you use the back of it to break off a good piece. But don't bring anything else unless you want to lose it."

She removed her own leopard cloak and necklace. It was the first time Khana had ever seen the woman without it; she might as well have shed her skin. Sitting down to hide her height and bulk, she looked like almost every other Reguallian, with tan skin, black hair, and almond-shaped eyes. The only clue of her Ghuran blood was the button nose.

Once Neta had tightened the knot around her ankles to her satisfaction, she ordered the six of them from weakest to strongest, which meant Khana was closest to the edge – even Yxe could lift more weight than her. The other units did the same around them. Already Red Frogs Three had lowered someone down.

"Got the rope?" Neta asked, sitting near the edge of the crevice as casually as if she was in a kitchen.

Khana tightened her gloved grip, grateful her sweat wouldn't interfere. "Are we sure this won't break, serji?"

"I knew a man who died on one of these because the rope broke," Itehua offered, second from the back.

Khana gulped.

"We got the rope, serji!" Haz cheered. "Don't you worry about a thing."

"Good." Neta fell sideways, right off the edge. Khana yelped as the rope went taut, pulling her forward. The rest of the unit held tight, keeping her from going over the edge, too.

"Lower me down!" Neta ordered.

"Easy and steady," Itehua said. "A little bit at a time."

They slowly lowered Neta further. Khana dared to look over the edge. She could only see the bottom of Neta's boots as they got smaller and smaller.

"That's good! Stop!" Neta ordered. They did.

After a bit of hacking and cursing, she called again, "All right! Bring me up!"

They pulled her up a lot faster than they'd lowered her down. Khana and Yxe grabbed her legs as soon as they were in reach and hauled her over the edge.

Neta held up a palm-sized chunk of obsidian. "Got it!"

Xopil whistled. "Good job, serji!"

"Very good job," Lueti said, kneeling to get a closer look. "If you break it up, you can make earrings that match your necklace."

"I just might." Neta untied herself. "Haz, I believe you wanted to go next?"

Khana hissed as she watched her friend's ankles get tied up. "Please be careful, Haz."

"You be careful. You're the one holding the rope," he snarked, pulling his axe out of his belt. Khana studied the rope. It was a little frayed, but not enough to worry about.

When he was ready, he practically jumped, whooping. Khana gritted her teeth and lowered him inch by inch with the others. She didn't relax until they'd pulled him up again, waving a piece of black glass. "I got it!"

"I'll go next," Itehua sighed. "Let's get this over with."

"There's not enough snow yet for an avalanche. You'll be all right," Xopil said.

After Itehua went Xopil, then Lueti – who cursed like a crew of sailors as she hacked at the glass with her axe – then Yxe. Finally, it came down to Khana.

"It's a lot easier than it looks, darling," Lueti assured her, holding her small piece of obsidian between two wrinkled fingers. "Believe me: if *I* can do it, anyone can."

"The last time I was dangling this far over a cliff, I fell," Khana replied. "It would've been fatal if I didn't have life force."

"Khana, you crossed half an empire, a foreign kingdom, and these very mountains to get to Pahuuda," Neta said, rolling up the rope. "You can fetch a piece of glass. Now sit down so I can tie your legs."

Gulping, Khana did as she was told, hugging her thighs to her chest as Neta worked. The rope felt like a chain. Her heart pounded so hard she felt it in her toes.

"I don't like heights," she said weakly.

"No one likes heights," Neta grumbled.

"I don't like speaking in front of crowds," Yxe offered.

"I don't like wolves," Lueti said.

"I don't like standing around in the cold," Itehua snapped. "Can we move along?"

"Oh, shush. She's obviously terrified," the old woman retorted. "That was me the first time I took a man to bed."

"*You* shush. You're a whore. That's the easiest job in the world. You just lie back and let him do the work."

"If that was all I did, I wouldn't charge nearly as much."

"Enough," Neta ordered. "Khana, let's go. The sooner we're done with this, the sooner we're back for lunch."

Khana looked over the edge and swallowed back bile. Had it gotten deeper in the last five minutes?

She looked up at her unit. They all gripped the rope, Yxe in front and Xopil in the back. Haz gave her an encouraging smile.

"Before my balls freeze off, please," Itehua called.

"I hate to agree with him, but yes," Neta said.

All right. Just get to the highest point so you don't have to go that far. Gripping her axe, Khana crawled over the edge of the ravine. Gravity tugged her into its grasp, gently at first, then all at once. The rope held firm, forcing her upside-down. The bottom of the ravine yawned at her, looking like the bottom was miles away when really it was only a fatal few hundred feet. Just like the top of the palace wall back in Balasco. *Don't think about that Khana.*

"We're going to lower you down," Neta called.

Khana whimpered, and the rope took her deeper into the pit. She stayed close to the wall, pressing herself against the stone with her free hand as she went. A worm dangling on a hook, waiting to drown or be swallowed whole. After an eternity, the gray stone turned to black glass.

"Stop!" she shouted. "I'm here!"

They thankfully stopped lowering her. By now the blood had pooled to her head, making her dizzy. Or maybe that was her nausea and fear. She took the back of her axe and smashed it into the obsidian. A piece broke off, but she couldn't grab it. She had to let go of the wall with her other hand but grabbed it again as soon as she started to swing, terrified at the feeling of free-fall. The piece of obsidian she'd knocked free fell into the darkness below.

"You still alive down there, Khana?" Haz called.

"J-Just a moment!" She'd have to let go of the wall to get the obsidian. She couldn't; the wall was the only thing keeping her tethered.

She needed the glass.

Holding the wall isn't doing you much good. If they drop you, it won't help. But they won't drop you. They can't. They'll all be hanged for it.

It still took a long moment to let go of the wall, gently enough that she didn't swing or even move in the air.

There was a spot of obsidian naturally jutting out. Khana took hold of it with one hand and struck it with the back of her axe. It took a couple of tries, but the piece finally dislodged.

Khana grinned, looking at the light reflecting off the dark glass. "I got it," she whispered.

The rope jolted, sending her lower a few inches. "Hey!" she shouted. "Don't lower me! I got it!"

"We didn't," Yxe called.

Something snapped. She dropped again, farther. Khana yelped, her stomach dropping to her neck.

"Shit! The rope's frayed!"

"Pull her up!"

They yanked, hauling Khana up. She couldn't grab onto the wall; that'd just slow them down. She couldn't climb up herself; she was upside down. She couldn't do anything except clutch her axe and piece of obsidian as she was pulled higher and higher.

The rope frayed again, and another piece snapped, the sound echoing off the glass walls. She screamed as she dropped, but only a few inches.

"You're almost there, darling. Just a little more," Lueti called.

A hand grabbed her ankle. Yxe hauled her over the edge.

Khana rolled and scrambled back, as far away from the ledge as she could get, with her legs still tied together until Haz snatched her shoulders and stopped her. "You're all right! You're all right! You're fine. All clear."

Khana put a hand over her mouth to hold back a sob, her vision blurred by tears. The entire unit panted. Yxe trembled, either from cold or fear, she couldn't tell.

Some women from the closest other unit jogged up to them. "Everything all right?"

Neta held up the rope. It had been frayed to its last strand. "We'll have to borrow some rope for the trip back to town, but everyone's out."

"Thank the gods," Xopil said, wiping sweat from his forehead. "Nine really is a bad number."

"Tell me you at least got the glass," Itehua said.

It took Khana a moment to realize he was talking to her, and longer to move her limbs. When she held up the finger-sized piece of black glass she'd freed from the wall, Haz pulled her into a half-hug. "I told you we wouldn't let you fall."

Khana wiped her face, surprising herself by leaning into Haz, away from the feeling of free-fall. It grounded her. The rest of the unit sat down around her, catching their breath, while the other unit that'd come to help left them alone. Lueti undid Khana's ropes with deft fingers, and she was finally free.

"Got a lot of experience with ropes, Lueti?" Itehua asked, waggling his eyebrows.

"Plenty. You should try it, once you learn to get a woman to completion."

"I see we should've dropped *you* in that crevice."

"You don't want an old woman's ghost haunting you. The nagging alone will make you commit suicide."

"My aunt said she was haunted by an old ghost," Xopil commented. "She always said it was responsible for stealing her sandals."

"My aunt said trousers make women infertile and that the mountains were made of the gods' dung," Ixe said.

Itehua, Lueti, and Haz all laughed. "God Shit Mountains!"

"That's their new name," Haz snickered. He still hadn't let go of Khana, and she wasn't inclined to move. Sitting on that mountain, listening to the unit talk about nothing, she realized that Amati might have had a point. For the first time in a long time, she had people looking after her.

Chapter Twenty-One

Things were a bit looser among Red Frogs Nine after glass diving. Itehua barely insulted anyone on the way back to town, except to rib Khana for how long she took. "No wonder the rope frayed. She was there for half the day!"

"That's definitely what it felt like," she muttered.

"My father's squad had a woman who took over an hour," Yxe said. "Every time she'd get a piece of glass, she'd drop it. She took so long she had to be pulled back up twice to rest before going down again."

"I had to train for my first dive for months," Neta admitted. "I was terrified."

"Really?" Khana gasped. At Neta's raised eyebrows, her face heated, and she sputtered, "Sorry, I'm just… you don't strike me as the type of person who's afraid of anything."

"Everyone's afraid of something. If you're not, then you're not alive," she said. "But in my case, my cousins dangled me over a well when I was five. A single slip would've killed me, and I was terrified of being upside-down and of darkness for years after."

Everyone stared at her. Itehua blew out a breath, muttering, "Shit."

"So, in the lead-up to enlisting, when I was about Yxe's age, I trained myself out of it. I dangled myself from the ceiling of my room for a few seconds at a time, then minutes, first during the day, then at night with only a couple of candles, then in pitch darkness. It worked."

"Are those the same cousins who got promoted to serji and midya over in Green?" Lueti asked.

"The very same," Neta said. "I won't say there were *no* consequences. Their father Athor was forced to pay my mother enough money that she was finally able to live on her own and grow her own business, and my father Aravi left town in shame. He lives on the other side of the tundra with his new wife and children."

Khana watched the broad shoulders of their serji – more specifically, the snow leopard cloak that covered them. She wondered why Neta so stubbornly associated herself with such horrible people.

Lueti offered to have their obsidian trophies fashioned into jewelry. "I know a boy who does excellent work for cheap. He made me this bracelet." She showed off a woven bracelet with bits of painted glass sewn in. It wasn't the jewels and gold from a dozen conquered kingdoms that Khana was used to seeing, but it was pretty, so they all agreed.

The casual attitude continued for the next couple of days as focus shifted from strength building to learning how to properly use their weapons. Neta led them through forms that were similar to Khana's dance routines, except far more forceful. Xopil and Itehua, having already learned them, took on roles of co-instructors.

"Wider legs give you a strong stance, brings you closer to the ground, and also makes you a smaller target for enemy spears," Xopil said, pushing Haz and Khana's bent knees wider. "So you'll be almost invisible!"

"You want to be as immovable as the Shit Pile Mountains over there," Neta agreed, pushing against Khana's back. She moved, but didn't fall, her feet holding firm.

"Better," Neta said. In the weeks since they'd started training, she'd given out praise only a handful of times, and each time Khana felt like the sun had risen in her chest. "Hold your spear higher. Just because you're tiny doesn't mean the other soldier will be."

That day of training started with the sky covered in clouds lit from the inside. Halfway through, as Khana thrust her spear at an invisible enemy, something white and cold drifted down from above and landed on her gloved hand.

Confused, Khana stared at it, until another one fell. And another. And another. It was like rain, but it was that snowy stuff from the mountaintops. Why was it falling from the sky?

"Khana!" Neta barked. "We're restarting."

"But…" She pointed up, confused as to how nobody else had even noticed. It fell more frequently, drifting down like little dancers. "Is that normal?"

"The snow?" Neta asked, sounding dubious.

"Have you never seen falling snow before?" Yxe asked, sounding bewildered.

Khana shook her head, her face feeling hot. She'd thought snow just appeared on the mountains, caused by a reaction with the stones. Apparently, it just... fell from the sky. Haz tried to catch one on his tongue.

Xopil chuckled. "I remember the first time my wife and I saw falling snow. We thought the world was ending. She sacrificed an entire goat to the gods to appease them. Just wait until we get the first few inches. It makes the town look so beautiful, like a magical otherworld."

"You'll get sick of it the first time you have to shovel it," Itehua promised.

"That's probably going to be tonight. Baba always makes me shovel," Haz groaned.

"All right, that's enough," Neta said, snapping her fingers. "Everyone take it from the start."

Khana got back into position as the snow fell on everyone's hair and shoulders, giving them white halos. It was frightfully cold, but oddly beautiful.

Khana had just gotten a handle on basic spear forms – namely, how to hold it so it didn't drop on her own head, and how to maybe stab someone – when Midya Chaku ordered them to do the line game.

"The what?" she asked, her confusion echoed by Yxe and Lueti.

"Do you have tug-of-war where you're from?" Neta asked.

"Yes."

"It's the opposite of that." She pointed to a couple of full-time soldiers setting up two lines of rocks in the field running parallel to each other, leaving only a few feet between them. Snow had continued to fall in the last few days, on and off. But the field was in so much use that what should have been at least ankle-deep was trampled to a crusty white skin.

"That strip represents some of our narrowest mountain paths," Neta explained. "Two squads face each other and try to push each other off or get to the other end of the strip. If you get pushed over the line, you 'die.' Your squad wins if you 'kill' the other or push them all the way back."

"I played this when I was a boy," Haz cheered. "It's fun."

"They'll be pulling squad numbers from a helmet soon. Bring your shields, no spears."

Two other squads – Red Frogs Three and Red Frogs Eight – began the first game. The squads organized themselves into pairs to fit on the narrow strip with the biggest and strongest in the front, shortest and smallest in the back.

"We're playing clean games here," Chaku said, his clear voice carrying over the tundra. His silver-streaked beard waved with the wind. "No punching, kicking, or hair-pulling. Just pushing. We clear?"

"Clear, Midya!" the two squads answered.

On Midya Chaku's count, they rushed each other, shields slamming with a crack that made Khana cringe. They pushed, shoved, and jostled each other. There were two referees, one on each side of the line, and they called out whenever anyone had at least one foot over the line. Both teams lost half of their squad before a winner was declared.

The ones still standing helped the others up as two more numbers were pulled from Chaku's helmet. "Lucky Seven and Unlucky Nine!" he called.

"That's us," Neta said.

She arranged the seven of them to her liking: Xopil and herself at the front, Itehua and Haz behind them, Yxe and Lueti behind them, and Khana in the back. Khana had gotten stronger in the past few weeks, able to run farther and do more push-ups than when she'd first enlisted, but she was still the weakest.

"Put your shield on your back," Neta ordered her. "Your job is to push against both of them at the same time to add to their energy. Go low, not high."

"All right." Khana put her shield at her back – a turtle with a shell too big for its body. Everyone got ready. She put one hand on Lueti's back and one on Yxe's, their armor giving little ground against her gloved hands. The bottom of Lueti's braid brushed against the back of her wrist.

Chaku counted down, and at "Go!" they ran.

Khana knew they'd be stopped by the other squad, but she still ran into Yxe's back face-first, squishing him against Haz. She regained her footing and pushed both him and Lueti with all her might, focusing on their lower backs, right above their tailbones. But no matter how much she dug her boots into the slippery tundra grass, she couldn't get any traction. Couldn't move forward. She even slid back a few inches.

Then Haz slipped, which caused Xopil to do the same, and he was roughly shoved off the line. Haz quickly followed.

Itehua rushed to fill the gap while Neta slammed her shield against a moving opponent, getting him over the line and out. Khana slipped back another few inches.

One of the other squad members reached over his shield and punched Neta in the face.

"Hey!" Haz barked from the sidelines. "He hit my serji!"

Chaku shrugged. "I didn't see anything."

Khana gritted her teeth. *You lying little –*

Neta spat a mouthful of blood into the face of the man who punched her. He stumbled back in disgust, and Red Frogs Nine pressed their advantage. Khana thought at least two of their opponents would step or stumble out during their retreat, but while they came close to the rocks, they didn't take that fatal step.

One of the unit Seven soldiers managed to get under Itehua, lifting him off the ground and over the line. Before Yxe or Neta could fill in the gap, Neta was roughly shoved aside, over the rocks and onto the ground.

Uh-oh, Khana thought, just before Seven was on them. Yxe and Lueti gave it their best, and Khana dug in her heels continually pushing them forward, but the three of them didn't have enough muscle to push back six beefy recruits. One of them broke through, cutting between Yxe and Lueti, and pushed Khana herself.

As she stumbled, trying to regain her footing, he bashed her cheek with the edge of his shield. Pain bloomed across her face. Copper filled her mouth, and her teeth clacked together as she fell to the ground, eyes watering.

The man spat on the ground. "Necrotic filth."

A shrill whistle brought everyone's attention to Chaku. "That's enough," he scolded. "If I see that again you're getting a week of latrine duty."

Unit Seven groaned as Nine picked themselves up. Khana pushed herself to her feet, wiping the blood from her mouth. Neta, face also bloodied, made right for her. "Let me see."

"I just bit the inside of my cheek," Khana said, allowing the serji to move her face this way and that. She'd been so focused on the inside of her mouth that she hadn't noticed the cut on her cheekbone until Neta wiped it with her thumb. Her other hand was used to pinch her own nose, stopping the blood flowing down her chin. "Why did they punch you?" Khana asked.

"Being a bastard is one thing. No one really cares so long as the parents are working to raise you," Neta explained, her voice watery, congested from blood. "But being half Old Family and half 'refugee scum' is more than some people can swallow. Doesn't help that my father blames me for his mistakes – he left my mother and tried to get out of financially supporting us, and because of that, nobody wanted to court him. Not until he left town and found someone who hadn't heard about it. So the Families don't offer me nearly as much protection, and the refugees see me as a spoiled brat. You get damned by both sides."

"I'm sorry," Khana said, because she couldn't think of anything else. She and Neta weren't friends; the woman was her commander. But she deserved far better than that.

Neta shrugged. "It's the way it is. Do you know how to handle this without using life force? I can't justify killing a goat for a scratch."

"I'll be fine." The bleeding was already slowing down. She dug a kerchief out of her pocket.

The company played for the rest of the afternoon, shuffling units so nobody had a repeat, but Khana's head wasn't in it. Everyone was distracted and downtrodden, their unit winning only two of a total of ten rounds. They were all grumpy and glum when Chaku dismissed them.

"Tomorrow's a rest day, so you can all screw your heads on straight," Neta said, waving them off. At least nobody else got punched.

Chapter Twenty-Two

Rest days were only restful in theory. No drills, no training exercises, a day for them to spend time with families and relax. But, in Haz and Khana's case, it was a day to get caught up on chores at the inn. Khana spent all morning repairing torn sheets and dining room cushions and was grateful for something to do that let her sit down by the fire in the empty room. The warmth did little to sooth her sore muscles, but it was still nice.

It would have been far nicer without Bhayana.

She strolled into the inn like she owned the place, fine black cloak wrapped around her slender frame. With Haz upstairs, Amati resting, and Heimili busy elsewhere, she went up to Khana. "Death-bringer. Where's Haz?"

"I don't know," Khana lied, concentrating on her work.

"*Recruit*. Where is Hasyamin?"

Khana paused in her sewing but kept her eyes on Bhayana's boots. They were a very nice black leather. "I don't know, midya."

She huffed. "In that case, get me some tea."

Khana hesitated. She knew what Bhayana was doing: she was going to stay here until Haz showed himself and then use whatever power she had over him to make herself feel better, and him feel weak. Serving her would make Khana complicit.

On the other hand, she was Khana's commanding officer.

Bhayana snatched her sewing away before Khana could make up her mind. "Are you deaf, recruit? I said I wanted tea."

Khana swallowed, heart hammering. "Yes, ma'am."

"You're not commander of our house, Bhayana," Haz said, coming down the stairs, his face cold.

Bhayana smiled sweetly at him. "Shouldn't you be calling me midya?"

"Not here. Officers have no legal right to order their recruits around in their own homes, especially on rest days. I checked."

"Well," she huffed, sitting down on the nearest cushion. "Be that as it may, I would like a cup of the finest tea in town, if you please."

"It doesn't please me. Get out."

"Haz, really. I'm a paying customer."

"Baba and Mimi banned you. And the chief ordered you to stay away."

"Because of lies you told them," Bhayana said, pouting prettily. "Honestly, I know break-ups aren't always pretty, but did you have to spin such stories?"

"Spin such stories?" he echoed. "You broke three of my ribs."

"You fell down some stairs."

"Because you *pushed* me."

"No, you tripped. I do believe you also hit your head, which is why you don't remember it correctly."

Khana stood silently and joined Haz. She couldn't fight this battle for him – didn't even know where to begin – but she could at least give her friend some support.

His back straightened, just a little. "Why are you here, Bhayana?"

She glanced at Khana. "May we speak alone?"

"No," Khana and Haz said at the same time. She squeezed his shoulder.

Bhayana sighed. "Fine. I'm here because I regret how our relationship ended. Since we're going to be working together for the foreseeable future, I wanted to clear the air."

"Really," Haz deadpanned.

Khana tightened her grip. She'd seen this type of behavior before. Yamueto never did it, as he didn't have to. But his princely sons, grandsons, and great-grandsons would often try to re-write their own history with their wives, mistresses, and children. They would insist that they had never been cruel or abusive, that their families were lying or misremembering. Then they'd act sweet and adoring, often showering their loved ones with gifts to lure them back. A little while later, the bruises re-appeared.

Bhayana gently smiled. "Come now, Haz. We had fun, didn't we? And we *did* love each other."

He hesitated.

The front door swung open. Sava stomped the snow from his boots, stepped inside, and froze, taking in the scene.

His eyes hardened on Bhayana. "What are you doing here?"

She shifted, ever so slightly. "Trying to enjoy a cup of tea. Not that the service is particularly great today."

"You need to leave. Now. That was part of the agreement."

"Oh, Sava. That was *ages* ago—"

"Now."

She gave a dramatic sigh but stood and made her way out of the inn before calling, "See you tomorrow, Haz," over her shoulder.

Sava slammed the door behind her.

Haz sagged. Khana led him to a cushion and set him down. "I'll get you some tea."

"Thank you," he mumbled.

She busied herself in the kitchen, grabbing a pot and three cups. When she returned, Sava was sitting across from Haz. "...hoped that more exposure to Reguallians and Tlapharians would inspire a bit more respect for them, if not compassion. Clearly that's not happening."

"I just want to know why she's bothering me at all," Haz grumbled, accepting his cup when Khana poured and handed it to him. "I'm not Old Family. I'm connected to the town witch, but they already have Khana coming over to heal her grandfather whenever they want."

"Since the exact details of your relationship came to light, Bhayana has been unable to find another suitor." Sava's face got caught somewhere between smug and apologetic as he accepted his own cup of tea. "Not even from other Old Families. And, more importantly, the scandal is why she's leading a Red Company rather than one of the more 'respectable' ones, like Blue or Yellow."

Khana paused. Obviously she didn't know all the details, but it was clear that Haz's relationship with Bhayana was similar to Khana's relationship with Yamueto. That wasn't a shock; people in power had done far worse. But they always got away with it.

"She... actually faced consequences?" she asked.

Sava choked on his tea. "Do they not in the Empire?"

Haz tipped his hand in a so-so gesture. "It's usually husbands beating their wives, because they have the added bonus of patriarchy. But if it's a high-ranked person beating another? That never gets punished, or even reported."

"It might even be encouraged," Khana added darkly. "You have to put such unruly people in their place, after all."

Sava swore. Haz smirked. "It's not like that here. Not really. I only hesitated to report Bhayana for so long because she got in my head, even threatened to go after Baba and Mimi. And sometimes, yes, Old Family members can get away with things that the rest of us can't. But this idiot"

–he nudged Sava with his foot– "realized that something was wrong and kept bugging me about it, so I told him and practically dared him to do something."

"She has a permanent strike on her record, she's banned from visiting Haz's home and is unable to vote in any election or take advantage of any Old Family privileges for seven years," Sava told Khana. "That means she can't inherit, she can't order the family guards around, and she cannot take any rank above midya for another four, almost five years. The military also barred her from serving in the full-time, more 'respectable' battalions, which is why she's stuck in Red. If you retracted your statement, that would be grounds to reverse her punishment, which is probably another reason why she bothered you. Sorry."

Haz shrugged. "Not your fault. You wanted her banished."

"To the tundra?" Khana gasped.

"Ma and I both fought for at least a one-year exile, preferably seven," Sava confirmed. "But we couldn't get enough of the Old Families to sign off on it. So here we are."

That was leagues better than what would've happened in Regualli. And the fact that Sava had fought so hard for harsher justice made her want to kiss his cheek. She drank her tea instead.

Haz drained his cup, stood and yawned. Encounters with Bhayana always seemed to drain him. "I'm going to take a nap. Don't burn the place down."

"Very well," Khana replied dryly with a smile.

"I'd better report this nonsense to my mother," Sava said with a sigh, getting to his feet.

Khana hid her disappointment. Damn porcupine.

Chapter Twenty-Three

When Khana was fifteen, she had believed she was safe. Yes, Yamueto had taken her to his bed when she'd first arrived at his palace, forcing himself on and in her almost every day for a month, despite her pleas and screams.

But then mercifully, he'd left her alone for a year. He had so many wives and concubines – almost two hundred – that it was easy to get lost in a sea of pretty faces. Sita had helped ensure that the first month did not leave her pregnant, and Khana had dedicated her time to losing herself to music and dance. Ribbon dancing was probably her favorite thing about palace life: the dancer used one or two brightly colored lengths of cloth and twirled them around her body in an elaborate series of spins. More advanced versions even included flips and acrobatics.

One of the older concubines, a lovely woman named Marianya, had taken it upon herself to teach Khana one of Regualli's oldest and most beloved dances. She was a witch herself and had passed away during Khana's third year. But before that, Khana had counted her as one of her best friends and allies in this strange, cruel place.

The imperial palace had dozens of rooms suitable for dance lessons: studios and chambers and musical halls. Marianya and Khana had been in one of them with a couple of musicians, going through the next set, when Emperor Yamueto entered the room. The two bowed to him, but he waved it away, saying, "Get back to it," in that bored tone of his.

Noticeably more tense, Marianya resumed her instruction. Khana focused on the pretty silk in her hands and the proper wrist-flick to get it to flare and spin the way she needed it to. The two of them went through the series of movements slowly, then more rapidly, then to actual music provided by the drummers and flutists in the corner. She'd almost forgotten Yamueto was there. Dressed in his customary black and gray robes, he melted into the shadows.

"Stop," he ordered.

The musicians stopped, the only sound Khana and Marianya's labored breathing. The two of them stood at attention as Yamueto ignored his older concubine and approached Khana. Her heart thundered in her chest. Had she done something wrong? How had she caught his attention again?

She wasn't wearing a fancy silk dress with multiple, intricate layers like she would at court. For a casual workout session, the standard wear was essentially a robe with one knot tied over her shoulder and another at her side. It was simple and made it easy to move.

Yamueto used his thick fingers to tug at the knot at her shoulder, while Khana didn't dare move. Her dress crumpled to the floor, leaving her completely naked.

"Go again," he said, stepping back against the wall. He pointed to Marianya. "You, older woman, you rest."

Khana swallowed salt. Marianya turned away, trying to respect her privacy. Despite the heartbreak in her eyes, she scooped up Khana's dress, folding it neatly, and ordered the musicians to start again.

Khana danced alone on the studio floor with the silk banner, completely naked. She didn't dare break routine to wipe the tears on her face.

When the music ended and she finished, Yamueto ordered everyone else out of the room.

Khana woke in a cold sweat, her heartbeat in her ears.

No, that wasn't her heart. Those were footsteps, thundering down the hall.

Haz burst into her room. "Khana! We need you."

She shot upright. The fire in the hearth was down to embers, keeping him in darkness, but she heard the panic in his voice. "What is it?"

"Mimi."

She ignored her boots and cloak, rushing after him out of the room and down the hall, cursing herself. Amati's cough had gotten worse. She'd been more tired recently, sleeping in later and going to bed sooner. She hardly had the energy for more than sewing. Now Khana didn't have time to wipe the tears from her nightmare before she was thrust into another.

The old woman lay in bed, her breath raspy. The windows were sealed up tight with animal pelt curtains, and someone had tossed multiple bones in the fire to bring the room to a sweltering heat. Heimili sat next to her, holding her hand, looking anguished.

Khana put a hand on Amati's heaving chest and winced. There was hardly any âji left in her, and there was something – a couple of somethings – in her lungs.

"Can you heal her?" Heimili asked.

"It'll take a lot."

Amati shook her head. "No."

"Ma..." Heimili insisted.

"We can't afford..." She coughed, almost hacking up a lung. Heimili and Khana helped sit her upright while Haz poured a cup of water. She drank it down before continuing. "Can't afford livestock."

"Maybe Khana can take some of ours?" Haz suggested, glancing at Khana. "Not enough to kill us, obviously, but..."

Amati shook her head. "No. I won't accept that."

"And I won't accept you leaving," Heimili said, eyes wet. "I'm not ready to say good-bye, Ma."

She huffed a weak laugh. "I'm eighty-seven. That's longer than more deserving people get."

Khana bit her cheek so hard she tasted copper. Amati lay back down. Heimili tried not to cry, and Haz trembled beside her.

Fuck it.

"Death, I wish to trade."

The world plunged into darkness and shadow. Death stood across from her, multi-colored robe blinding her for a moment. They glanced down at the scene before them. "Ah. I was wondering when I'd have to collect her."

"Not today," Khana challenged.

Death grinned at her, their teeth as pasty white as their skin. "What are you giving up?"

She'd planned this ahead of time. It was easier making these deals when she'd already decided which memory to lose, even though the memory of her nightmare was certainly tempting. She couldn't forget the monster she was running from. She'd thought she was safe then, and he proved she wasn't.

"The first time Sita gave me birth control," she said.

The princess had given her dozens of vials over the years. But the first time stood out stronger than the rest, the realization that she had an ally in that cursed place, and the sheer relief of having some control back in her life.

Death held out their hand. Khana took it.

Back in the room. Haz cursed, jumping away from her as she glowed white-red-purple-blue. She knelt next to Amati and poured the âji into her. The tumors in her lungs evaporated. Her heart beat stronger.

When she was done, everyone stared at her. Amati slowly sat up, pressing her frail hand against her chest. "...huh."

"Are you all right?" Heimili asked, grinning because he already knew the answer.

"I think so," Amati said. Her voice was stronger, not nearly as raspy as it used to be. She gave Khana a wry look. "How long will it last?"

"I don't know," Khana admitted. "You had a couple of tumors in your lungs. They're gone now, but I think you still have some heart issues that I couldn't get to."

She huffed. "You ruined a perfectly good deathbed."

"Ma, she saved your life," Heimili chuckled.

"How, exactly, did you do that?" Haz asked.

Khana winced. "Luck?"

All three gave her flat looks.

"You said something about trading with Death," Haz said.

She sighed. "Yes... that's what I do. I can make deals with Death to secure âji."

"What type of deal?" Amati demanded.

"Nothing major!" she promised.

Haz sputtered. "So, you could've been producing life force this whole time? Why the fuck have you been draining our livestock, then?"

Khana winced. Heimili scolded, "Haz!"

"No, I want to know. If she can just produce it out of thin air, why force anyone else to lose a part of their livelihood? That's just selfish!"

She shrank back from his anger. Haz buzzed with it, glaring at her with a sudden mistrust that hurt. That terrified her.

She left the room.

Chapter Twenty-Four

Khana wandered the town without aim or direction, humming to herself to fill the empty air, wishing for her lute. The winter air was a vice grip around her, scratching at every bit of exposed skin it could find. With the rush of adrenaline and âji fading away, her body felt her lack of sleep, making her movements slow and tired. Her eyes drooped. Yet her mind worked too furiously for sleep to be an option. Every time she closed her eyes it was Haz's anger, Yamueto's hands, Death's grin.

Her thoughts plagued her. Haz, Heimili, Amati, they would tell everyone what she'd done. The Pinnsviris would be on her like a hawk, forcing her to give up pieces of herself to keep their patriarch alive. Phramanka would demand it be used in the war effort, keeping her troops healthy while Khana forgot her homeland, her reasons for hating Yamueto, her very self…

"Khana?"

She jumped. She had walked toward the mountains, to the Old Family part of town. Sava carefully approached her, snow softly crunching under his boots. "What are you doing up? Is someone hurt?"

"No, I…" His black hair looked unfairly pretty in the moonlight. She shook her head. "I couldn't sleep."

He hummed. "Me, neither."

She peeked at him through her bangs. He was dressed for a midnight stroll, too. But no bow or quiver.

"Nightmares?"

He grimaced. "Paperwork. It takes a lot to keep a military running, and someone made a mistake when calculating everyone's pay, so we've spent the last several hours redoing it and going over it again so it's accurate. At this point, it's just easier not to go to bed."

"That sounds terrible," she said, for lack of anything else.

"It is what it is. Let me walk you–"

"Death-bringer!"

Khana groaned as Sipah emerged from the darkness, jogging toward them. "Not now," she said.

"The old man's sick again," he huffed. "Come on."

Sava frowned. Heat flushed to Khana's face, humiliated that this was happening in front of him.

"Let's *go*!" Sipah ordered, moving to grab her arm.

She slapped his hand away. "Don't touch me," she snapped, her nerves frayed.

He glared at her. Sava stepped closer, putting himself between the two of them. "She doesn't have to offer her services if she doesn't want to."

For a moment, nobody moved. Everything seemed to hover as the snow sprinkled down. Khana wondered if this was the last time she'd have a say in the matter.

"They'll pay you," Sipah offered.

"They haven't already?" Sava drawled.

"She never insisted."

Sava glanced at her, questioning. Khana straightened. "I insist now."

"Fine. Let's go. The old man's fading fast."

She briefly met Sava's eyes before turning her face down to his boots. "Would you mind coming with me and perhaps–"

"I'll help you negotiate a fair deal," he agreed.

Khana relaxed. The familiar route to the Pinnsviri estate was silent. They went straight to the yaks this time, draining one and arriving in Master Pabu Pinnsviri's bedroom already glowing.

Once again, Veta and Bhayana were at his side. They were both visibly surprised to see Sava there.

"Come for an early breakfast?" Bhayana asked, subtly adjusting her legs to show off her hips and hourglass figure.

"No. I'm here to help Khana negotiate a price for her services," he said.

Bhayana turned her dark gaze to the witch. "That's just cruel."

"You haven't charged anyone else," Veta agreed.

Khana shrank back, just a bit. "No one else is an Old Family."

From the bed, a skeletal Pabu gave a frail chuckle. "How much... for immortality?"

"I told you, I don't know how to do that," she lied. "And you should know this is unsustainable. You're going to need me back here any day."

Bhayana played with her hair. "I still don't see why you have to charge us. We're already killing a yak for this."

Sava again put himself in front of Khana, physically blocking her from the Pinnsviris before muttering to her, "You know you can walk away at any time, right?"

It was that knowledge – the fact that she *did* have a way out – and that someone was guarding her retreat, which made Khana straighten. "No. I'm fine. What's the standard rate of a physician?"

"Ten coppers?" Sava guessed. "A skilled specialist could charge as much as twenty."

Khana studied the dying man in the bed, then met Bhayana's eyes. "Forty."

She sputtered. "You extorting little–"

"For bullying Haz the other day."

That shut her up. Veta sighed. "Bhayana, I told you to stay away from that boy."

"I just wanted to talk," she grumbled, crossing her arms.

"Forty coppers seems more than reasonable," Sava said. "Right now. Or we walk."

Grumbling, Veta left the room. The only sound was Pabu's rasping breathing before his son came back with a jiggling bag. Sava counted the coins while Khana gave up the âji, having to force Pabu's body to accept it. When he sat up, he wasn't quite as lively as normal.

"It's getting more difficult," she warned. "I don't think I'll be able to pull it off again."

"Not for another forty coppers, anyway," Bhayana muttered.

Pabu waved her off. "You've been paid. Now get off my property."

Sava handed Khana the bag, and they quickly went back outside. When she sucked in the cold night air, she smiled, feeling much better than she usually did after visiting the porcupines.

"Can I walk you home?" Sava asked.

"That's halfway across town," she protested.

He shrugged. "I'm not going back to bed."

The knowledge of what was waiting for her at the inn dampened her spirits, but she nodded. They walked side-by-side, snow crunching beneath their boots.

Sava frowned. "You all right?"

"What's the difference between being selfish and self-preservation?"

His frown deepened. "What do you mean?"

"Just answer the question."

He took a deep breath, thinking it over as it misted out from his lips. "We are nothing without our friends and family. Our community. The reason I joined the military, risked my life, is to protect them. But boundaries are important," he stressed. "Everyone has lines that others don't get to cross. And only we get to decide where those lines are. After all, if you give up too much, you'll eventually destroy yourself. Then you'll be of no help to anybody. Some people, like the Pinnsviris, they don't respect any boundaries unless they're met with force, and then they try to make you feel guilty for enforcing them because they want to keep taking advantage of you."

Her chest loosened, just a little bit.

"Sometimes, people struggle with drawing those lines, like you do. I knew someone who was… well, I guess you could call her an enforcer. Whenever her friends got uncomfortable with something or wanted to say no but couldn't, they'd call Myrta and have her do it for them. She could be polite about it, but normally, if they were calling her, it was because the polite method had already failed. Myrta would call the interlopers out on their nonsense; they would respond by saying she was being rude. Her usual response was, 'You wish I was merely rude. Today, I'm a bitch.'"

His smile was tinged with sadness. Khana noted the past tense but didn't press, especially since they were approaching the inn.

She still didn't quite know where she fell on the scale, whether she was right to keep her Death-deals a secret to prevent anyone from abusing the power. She supposed she was about to find out.

"Thank you, Sava. Good night," she said, stepping into the inn.

The smell of baking bread reached her before anything else. While Heimili tended the oven, Amati made tea, which was a shock. Khana didn't think she'd ever seen the woman up and about so early. She still had that stiff, delicate walk, but she was moving.

Haz sat on one of the cushions, looking into the fire. He jumped up when he noticed Khana. She flinched back at the sudden movement.

"Go get dressed, Khana," Amati said firmly. "Haz has something to say to you, and then you can both have breakfast."

The two of them walked upstairs. Khana felt like a child who'd just been scolded.

"I'm sorry," both she and Haz blurted when they reached the top of the stairs.

"You're sorry?" Haz asked.

She hugged herself. "I don't make everyone give up livestock. If they can't afford it, or if there's no time, I'll give them the pretense that I'm searching for an animal, when, really, I'm making a deal. But I shouldn't have lied to you."

Haz huffed, muttering, "Shit, I should've gone first."

"What?"

"It wasn't any of my business!" he said, louder. "I was just surprised, and still thinking of Mimi's near-death. And then I found out you were keeping this from me – again, *none of my business* – but it was still a shock. I'm sorry."

Khana's throat closed up with something salty. This had not been what she'd expected.

Haz glanced back downstairs. "You should get dressed. Neta's going to kick our asses today."

He hurried back down. Khana went into her room, slipping into her armor and trying to ignore her fatigue. She contemplated the bag of money, then took half of the forty coins she'd earned and went back down into the dining room. All three of them sat on cushions near the fireplace, eating stew and chuta. Khana accepted her bowl with a quiet thank-you and set the coin in front of Haz.

"What the…?" He poked the money.

"Pabu Pinnsviri needed healing again," she explained. "I made them pay double because of Bhayana, so that's technically your half."

"Did you finally start charging them?" he said gleefully.

She shrugged. "Well, I bumped into Sava on the way…"

"Yeah, hard to argue with a wolf at your doorstep." He took the money.

"So," Amati said. "What did you trade for me?"

Khana slurped down some of her soup. "One of my memories. That's the cheapest price for âji."

Haz paused. "You're kidding."

She shook her head.

Amati sighed. "Not worth it."

"It wasn't a *serious* memory," Khana insisted. "It was the first time a friend helped me." She could still remember the other dealings with Sita. Just not the first.

"You have to give up a memory every time you do that?" Heimili asked, horrified.

"For âji, yes." Bolstered by everyone's reaction so far, she swallowed her fear and took the plunge: "Other trades are much more expensive. Revivals take a much larger chunk of your soul. And immortality? Even worse."

Haz choked on his food. "Immortality. Like, the emperor?"

Khana told them what Death had said about their deals with Yamueto, everything he had given up to get to this point. Haz set down his half-eaten stew, looking very lost. "What... is the point?"

"I'm sorry?"

"Giving up your passions and your hobbies for power I can understand. I don't *agree* with it, but I understand it," he said. "But giving up the ability to care about people? That's the whole point of living! Make it make sense!"

Khana gave a helpless shrug.

"Perhaps he sacrificed such compassion so he wouldn't feel anything when he outlived his family," Amati mused.

Heimili shook his head, flour already caught in his beard. "No. If he truly cared about them, he'd have given *them* immortality instead."

"True."

"Can we not tell anyone about this?" Khana pleaded.

"And let the Pinnsviris walk all over you?" Haz snorted. "No fucking way. We're keeping this a secret."

Heimili nodded in agreement. The last tension in Khana's chest evaporated.

Amati sipped her tea. "You're not to revive me when I die."

Heimili swallowed. "Ma–"

"No. I've lived my life, and I have no fear of death." She pointed a bony finger at Khana. "No more of these deals for my sake. Understand?"

Khana nodded. "Yes, ma'am."

"Good."

Chapter Twenty-Five
Sava

The mountains were impassable in winter, but there were ways around them. They just took weeks, if not months, and involved braving both tundra and ocean. The Kingdom of Divaajin had one of the best navies in the known world, so the Ghura weren't worried about the empire winning by sea. This also meant that messengers, scouts, and spies could go from Divaajin to the Reguallian Empire and back again by hopping on ships, passing critical information as they went.

The Bvamso family welcomed one such messenger that stumbled onto their porch one chilly afternoon with news. He gratefully curled around a steaming cup of tea while he thawed in their sitting room.

The messenger introduced himself as Haka. He was too dark-skinned to not stand out, stout, and missing an ear.

"My first winter," he said, motioning to it. "I wasn't prepared for the cold."

"Happens to the best of us," Phramanka said. Sava refilled his tea while the family servant Napha came in with a big bowl of stew.

Myrta would've been all over Haka, Sava thought, demanding questions about life outside of Pahuuda and stories of far-away lands. She'd always wanted to travel. *Had* traveled, going with hunters and escorting traders through the tundra and over the mountains. She'd always dreamed of more, of seeing the ocean and big cities and forests.

Sava shook his head to rid himself of the thoughts. They didn't hurt as much as they used to but were still distracting.

"What news?" Phramanka asked, getting to the point now that Haka was warmed and filling his belly.

Haka swallowed a mouthful of yak meat. "Mm! Sorry – it's really good. Reguallian ships have been spotted in Divaajinian waters, but our fleet pushed them back. We've noticed a few night creatures in the water, but so far, they haven't been able to bring down any ships."

"Yet," Phramanka muttered.

"It looks like the majority of the emperor's forces are coming for Pahuuda," Haka said. "While his navy is nipping at our borders, most, if not all, of his land troops are gathering on the other side of the mountains, ready to punch through in summer. I hope you're ready."

Phramanka and Sava shared wolf-like smirks. "The mountain passes are narrow and treacherous. Numbers mean very little."

Haka shrugged. "Very well. My superiors think the emperor is being unusually rash. We all expected him to wait at least a few more years before striking. At first, they weren't sure why the rush. But then they received news that one of his concubines ran off."

"Concubine?" Phramanka echoed. That word hadn't been said in Ghura; it was Reguallian. She glanced at Sava, but he shrugged. He'd never heard it before, either.

"Ah… wife, I suppose is the best translation? Or mistress," Haka explained. "Emperor Yamueto has dozens. Hundreds, even."

Sava blinked. "Where does he find the time? The energy?"

"He's immortal," the messenger said with a shrug. "Anyway, one of them ran off, and he's been trying to find her ever since. He must've found her in Divaajin."

"Name? Description?" Phramanka asked. "Maybe we can capture her first, see if she knows anything."

"She's a witch," Haka said between more bites of stew. "They all are. That, or descended from them."

Sava's stomach dropped.

"This one's a desert girl. Short." He snorted. "She killed another one of the emperor's wives. Probably argued over his affections. Or jewelry. My wife's always on me about jewelry…"

Phramanka's face was unmoved, even as she side-eyed Sava. He swallowed.

"Thank you, Haka," she said at last. "How long will you stay?"

"The night, if you don't mind. I'll be gone in the morning."

They got Haka settled in one of the guest rooms. By then, Thriman had come home from his own military training, and they told him what they'd learned.

Thriman whistled. "So. She's either running from him or spying for him."

"Most likely, yes," Phramanka said. "And since she didn't tell us…"

They both looked at Sava. He bristled. "What?"

"You know her best. Do you think she has an ulterior motive?"

He shook his head. "I don't know. She's kept so many secrets… But if she was on the emperor's side, why enlist?"

"Better cover story," Thriman said, without missing a beat. "Not to mention, it gives her better access to the juicier information. Troop sizes, movements, supplies, plans, strategies…"

Sava felt ill. He'd encouraged that woman to stay here, had vouched for her. Helped her. And all this time she'd been married to the emperor?

"Let's not jump to conclusions," Phramanka said, holding up a hand. "She's been doing this town a great service with her witchcraft, at little to no cost to us. There might be another explanation. Sava's told us how cruelly the empire has treated its people."

That gave Sava some hope, but he didn't chase it. If the emperor had a hundred wives, surely they'd be vying for attention. For power. One way to do that would be to sneak into enemy territory. Haka had mentioned that the bulk of the Reguallian forces were on the other side of the mountains. Perhaps they had a plan to use Khana to cripple them, leaving the passes undefended.

What's the difference between being selfish and self-preservation?

And yet, she'd looked so scared since she arrived. More so when she'd enlisted…

"How do you want to handle this?" Thriman asked.

Phramanka thought for a moment, then said, "Bring her to me."

Chapter Twenty-Six

The days, somehow, got even colder. Snow fell hard. Children ran around flinging snowballs and building lopsided masterpieces, and even some adults joined the fun. After one particularly heavy snowfall, Khana found Athicha carefully crafting a series of startlingly lifelike animals: a wolf, a leopard, a bharal, all symbols of the Seven Families. When night fell, more than one person was tricked into thinking their shadows were the real thing.

Hardly a day passed without someone having to shovel the front steps of the inn, and several soldiers were recruited to keep the roads clear for wagons and animals. Red Frogs Nine often found themselves on shovel duty.

"I thought these were randomly assigned," Itehua grunted as he tossed another shovelful against a wall.

"Sometimes," Neta huffed, doing the same. "And sometimes, we get a reminder that Midya Chaku is a friend of the Pinnsviris."

Khana gasped. "He is?"

"'Friend' may be a strong word. But I've seen him visiting their house multiple times over the past month. They'll invite him to dinners, and he's often seen talking to Bhayana, supposedly about training strategies. It's not that surprising; most midyas try to cozy up to the Old Families to make connections. And it goes both ways, favors for favors. My uncle's been hosting a different officer every week since recruitment started."

"Can you tell him to cozy up to Chaku?" Itehua asked.

Neta snorted. "He'll just say that Chaku knows what he's doing, that these hardships make me a better soldier, and that I shouldn't look for the easy way out. And then he'll make sure my cousins never have to shovel a day in their lives."

Itehua jammed his shovel into a bit of ice. "Your family's fucked up."

Khana understood the importance of the work, but she was sweating in her armor. And the snow was already coming down *again*, which meant this time tomorrow all their hard work would be gone.

"I like the shoveling," Yxe said quietly, a few snowflakes gathering on the tip of his big nose. "We don't get teased or hit as much."

"We're training for war. We're supposed to get hit so we learn how to dodge when it counts," Neta grumbled. "Poorly trained soldiers are the first to die in war."

"Great motivational speech, serji," Lueti muttered, flipping her black-and-gray braid over her shoulder.

Neta set the metal edge of her shovel on the ground. "After this, we're doing a short training session. I want to see everyone's spear and fist forms. Itehua, Xopil, you'll help me with the others."

Itehua groaned. "Dammit, woman, at this rate you're going to kill us long before the Empire."

"Deal with it. People are assholes who prey on weakness. So shut up and at least act tough."

"Excuse me?"

They looked up. They'd come to Heimili's inn, and Amati looked down on them from the second story window. She'd already grown frailer since Khana had healed her, having to sit for longer periods of time, voice getting weaker. "Sounds like the serji is keeping my grandson and ward late tonight?"

"Baba was complaining that the new hires didn't have much experience," Haz called back up. "They'll get *plenty* tonight."

"We're sorry, Amati," Khana said. "We'll be in as soon as we can."

She waved them off. "Bah, stay as long as you need. My son will make you butter tea right now, to keep you warm. And when you're all done with that extra training tonight, you come here for dinner. Best chuta and stew in town. Haz and Khana have it free, and you five get a unit discount."

Neta glanced at the others. Xopil was already drooling. "Thank you, ma'am," she said.

Thus began the Red Frogs Nine tradition. Midya Chaku gave them the drudge jobs: shoveling the streets, digging latrines, and whatever else he could think of. The other units did their best to avoid them, as if their status was contagious, and war games were just as brutal as before. Then when the day was considered done, and the rest of the units went home, Red Frogs Nine stayed on the tundra to train. They went through their weapon drills again and again, until Khana dreamed of them almost as much as her nightmares. But then, when the sun finally went down, they'd go to the inn and be treated to a big dinner, their frozen skin warmed by the fire as they shared stories and poked fun at each other.

The night Yxe finally managed to disarm Itehua called for a round of cheers and a kiss on the cheek from Lueti, which turned the boy red for an hour. When Lueti landed her first solid hit on Neta in hand-to-hand – and apologized profusely for bloodying her nose – the serji grinned all the next day. And when Haz beat Xopil, their best fighter besides Neta, in a fight with sheathed spears, he bragged about it to everyone at the inn.

During another spar, after teaching a few misdirection maneuvers, Xopil knocked Khana's spear out of her hands. When he tried to rush her, she let him run into her shield and used his own momentum to carry him up and over her. He crashed to the ground, snow and frost flying.

Khana's knife and axe were on her belt, but she didn't go for either of them. Didn't even think of it. Instead, she acted on instinct, putting a hand on Xopil's chest and breathing in. His âji pooled out of him, into her hand, and she held it there. A glowing mass of yellow and orange and pink around her fingers as Xopil went weak and wide-eyed on the ground.

Khana smirked, wiggling her glowing fingers. "I win."

She put the life force back in Xopil, and he coughed.

Haz whooped and knocked into Khana. "There's the terrifying witch I know and love! I was wondering when she'd come out."

Face heating, Khana helped Xopil to his feet. He rubbed the top of her head with a grin. "That's a good move. But I think the glowing will make you a target for archers. Maybe use the knife next time?"

"If I got hit, the âji would heal me," Khana pointed out. "We have stories of witches getting shot through the brain, but they were carrying so much force that they just walked it off."

"Did you ever see that for yourself?" Neta asked dubiously.

"No, but I fell down a cliff twenty stories high. And I'm still here."

She blinked. "Right. Take all the life force you want. In fact, is it possible to do what you just did to Xopil, but to *several* targets?"

"Uh..." In combat? She'd never tried. But creating multiple night creatures involved draining many people's life force at once. Granted, she'd always been with a group, but perhaps she could. "Probably."

"We'll have to try that," Neta mused.

"Our goal in battle will be watching Khana's back, then?" Itehua asked, sitting on top of his shield so the snow wouldn't cling to his bottom. The setting sun across the empty tundra turned the snow-covered ground lavender and made his pox scars look huge. "Seems like a good idea to keep the healer alive."

"She's going on to the medics," Neta said. "After training, she'll be in a completely different unit."

Khana had forgotten all about the upcoming medic training, and, for the first time, felt glum about it. She'd be safer with the healers, yes, and wouldn't have to face nearly as many night creatures. But that also meant leaving the soldiers who had become her friends.

Before she could dwell any further on that, someone whistled. Khana's dim mood immediately vanished when she recognized Sava's wolfskin cloak.

"Squeezing in some extra training?" he asked.

"Midya Chaku's barely keeping us in regular training," Neta said. "At this point, we're just going to be fodder."

Sava's face hardened. "I'll talk to him. Khana, the chief wants to see you."

Khana's stomach dropped. She scooped up her spear and rushed after him. "Is she hurt? What happened?"

"No one's hurt," he said, his square jaw clenched. "She got some new information about the Empire and needs to talk to you about it."

Khana frowned but didn't question further. Sava's shoulders were tenser than his bowstring. Whatever this information was, it couldn't be good. But why was Phramanka demanding to see her? She was hardly a high-ranked official or advisor, and far from the only Reguallian in town.

Inside, Sava led her to an audience chamber. Chief Phramanka sat on a plush cushion, pouring tea. She was dressed the most casual Khana had ever seen her, without any wolf fur or tooth jewelry. Instead, she had a thick cotton robe and slippers, like she was about to go to bed, her silvering hair tumbling around her shoulders.

Conversely, on the other side of the room, Thriman wore a wolf cloak and sharpened his massive broadsword. The sight made Khana uneasy. Sava motioned for her to sit across from Phramanka, putting her back to Thriman. She could still hear the whetstone against the blade.

"Do you take milk with your tea?" Phramanka asked. Sava sat on the other cushion, a little bit behind his mother.

"If you have some," Khana said, keeping herself still. "We tend to save it at the inn for stews and other meals."

"We have plenty." Phramanka added the milk and handed Khana the cup. She poured her own. "So. You lied to us."

Khana blinked. "I did?"

"By omission. You said witches had to attend to the emperor. You didn't say that you were married to him."

Oh, no.

"What makes you think I was?" she asked, trying to feign ignorance.

Phramanka looked decidedly unimpressed. "Just because we can't pass the mountains this time of year doesn't mean we're completely blind to our enemy's ways. Ships travel year-round. They heard talk of one of Yamueto's wives, on the run after killing another. A young desert girl."

All the confidence Khana had felt from beating Xopil fled. She sipped her tea, buying time. Thriman gave the sword another lick of the whetstone. Sava refused to look at her.

"Being a concubine is not the same as being a wife," she said at last. There was no use denying it. "There were no marriage vows. I was little more than a servant."

Phramanka's eyes hardened. "You said nothing about this during your trial."

Fear transformed into anger in the blink of an eye. As if a sleeping beast within Khana had just had a bucket of ice dumped on its head.

"What was there to say?" Khana snapped, slamming her teacup down. "I'm sorry, oh great chief, that I was taken from my home against my will and raped by my ancestor for *six* fucking *years*! Please forgive me for not wanting to bring it up!"

The room went completely silent, save for Khana's hard breathing. Sava's wide eyes looked between her and his mother, who remained stone-faced.

"So, you were unwilling?" she said at last. "You had no options at all?"

"Disobedience means death. At best," Khana said. "He transforms most traitors into night creatures. Occasionally he gave them to Kokaatl to 'play' with."

"Kokaatl?"

Khana's face heated. "One of his other concubines. She *was* willing. And her favorite hobby was torturing anyone the emperor gave to her. She was also the woman... the woman I killed when I escaped."

"In self-defense, was it?"

Khana looked down. "Not exactly. I had a friend named Sita..."

It all spilled out of her. Her parents trading her into the empire, the birth control, Kokaatl's murder and dismemberment... She probably shared a little too much. By the time she was done, she felt nothing. Like all her emotions had been drained out.

Thriman sat next to his wife. His sword was gone. "We thought you were a spy when we heard this," he said, unapologetically. Phramanka glared at him, but he kept going: "No one is forced into marriage or bed in Pahuuda. Not without getting their asses kicked. So, when we heard that you and Yamueto shared a bed…" He shrugged.

"A cultural misunderstanding," Sava said, shifting his legs so he could put his bearded chin on his knee. He was much more relaxed than earlier. "I think it's one of the reasons some Ghura don't like the Reguallians who live here. Your ways are strange, and they never bother to learn how or why."

"You're getting there," Khana said, willing to forgive them.

"It would have saved us all a heart attack if you'd come forward earlier, publicly or privately," Phramanka said, a slight scolding edge to her voice. "Is this why he's attacking our kingdom? To get you back?"

"I don't know," she admitted. "He's wanted to conquer this land for a long time. No northern army has managed to hold anything south of the mountains."

"What happens when he learns you're here?"

She gulped. "He'll demand you return me, and if you don't, he'll destroy Pahuuda."

Thriman snorted. "And I'm sure he'll be so kind to us if we obey."

"Even if he spared us, he's going to conquer the rest of the kingdom," Sava pointed out, voice hardening with his passion. "Kill our soldiers, pin down our women, enslave any other witches taking refuge. We can't let that happen. The reason we settled in these mountains is to ensure that doesn't happen!"

Phramanka finished her tea. "And if he should get through us, I doubt that anywhere on this continent will be safe."

She looked at Khana, and Khana understood. Protecting Pahuuda was her best chance at protecting herself, no matter how much the upcoming war terrified her.

"I'm not going anywhere," she said, barely above a whisper.

Phramanka nodded. "Good. Sava, why don't you escort our guest home? You both have a long day tomorrow."

Chapter Twenty-Seven
Sava

The night air had turned crisp and sharp in the short time the sun had been down. Sava was grateful for the extra layers he'd thought to wear. Next to him, even in her wool armor and cloak, Khana shivered.

Guilt was an inky stain in his chest. He was no expert in trauma, but he knew that forcing people to relive it did more harm than good. Haz could only talk about his when he felt safe and comfortable. Same with Athicha. The opposite of what his family had just done to Khana.

"I'm sorry about your friend," he said, breaking the silence that had stretched as they reached the street. "And for ambushing you like that. That wasn't right."

"No, it wasn't," she agreed, finally looking up at him. Snowflakes fell on her ebony hair; it'd grown since she'd first arrived, the longest strands brushing her shoulders. "But thank you."

He relaxed, the weight in the air lifting. "I'm glad you made it here. Some of us like you, at least."

She snorted. "Yes, I can tell your mother adores me."

Sometimes Sava forgot that his mother was not *just* his mother; she was an intimidating leader who was harder to read than stone – to anyone outside of her family.

He shrugged, smiling. "She's coming around. She was willing to talk to you rather than arrest you right away. She has a soft spot for courageous types."

Khana burst out laughing. He gave her an odd look, not seeing the joke.

"Oh, you're serious," she realized, her mirth tapering off. "I'm not courageous. I've been terrified since... well, childhood."

"Courage can only exist in fear," Sava said, his heart twisting with her admission. "We're going to war. If you're not scared of that, then you're not brave. You're a fool. And *you* know what we're fighting better than any of us."

She looked down at the snow crunching beneath their boots. "Sava, if I had the means, I would be running to the other side of this tundra as we speak. And I'd keep running."

With anyone else, he'd put his arm around them in a half-hug. But he'd noticed Khana often shied away from being touched, and he didn't think it'd be welcome right now. So he asked, "Why did you enlist?"

"I wasn't going to let Haz go off without me. He's the closest thing I have to – well, I suppose we *are* friends now," she said. "Besides, the night creatures that Yamueto's going to throw at us… I helped make those."

Sava raised his eyebrows. It was funny, especially considering the conversation they'd just had in his house, but he sometimes forgot that Khana was a witch, and what that meant. Even when she stood next to him in a soldier's armor, she didn't look particularly dangerous. She looked *good*. Really good. But he could never claim to be afraid of her.

Watching her heal Pabu had been an experience. He'd never seen a person glow before. She'd sucked the life from a yak with two breaths, killing it without a touch, and used its strengths for her own ends, defying death itself.

And yet she was terrified of everything, especially the empire. That did not bode well.

"How?" Sava asked, forcing his mind to the present.

"When Yamueto executes multiple people at once, he has all of the witches in court attend him. We all drain their âji, and then push it back into him, and he uses it to create the night creatures. If you refuse, you're next." Again, she looked down, a slice of black hair shielding her eyes. "I always took as little as I could get away with. Just enough to start a glow. But I still did it. And I can't… I can't run from that. It just seems wrong, to flee while the creatures I made are going to attack the people who have helped me."

Sava's chest warmed. He wanted to reach out to touch her shoulder but pulled back at the last second.

"You may not think you have courage, but never doubt that you're a good person," he said.

Khana looked at him, heartbrokenly confused and maybe a little hopeful.

And then her stomach grumbled.

Sava inwardly cursed. "We should've offered you some food instead of just tea! I'm sorry."

"I don't think I could've stomached it," she muttered. "I hope the inn isn't busy."

"If it is, I'll insist on you serving me," he said. "It's rude to not eat with a guest, you know."

"Thank you, Sava. But you should get some rest, too."

"Bah. I'm usually up far later, gambling my money away." He considered her for a moment, wondering if they should talk further about what she'd been through. Any other secrets she might be keeping.

But that atmosphere was gone. And Sava decided that the best way to get her to open up would be to show her some trust. A bit of friendship.

"Do you know any games from your desert land?" he asked.

She huffed a laugh. "My mother *hated* gambling, so no."

"What about music?"

Her face turned wistful. "Yes, actually. A lot of the instruments were unique to the desert, made of the animals and plants there. But I was able to replicate some of the music on Reguallian lutes and flutes."

"I thought you didn't play the flute."

"Not well. I'm far better with strings." She held up her gloved hands. "Skinny fingers."

"You should perform," he encouraged. "The inn could use a bard."

"Shouldn't that be you, Mister 'I have an entire collection of flutes?'" she teased.

"Ugh. With what time?"

"Excuse me, I have *two* jobs! You only have one!"

She said it teasingly, but he still felt the contrition. "Fair. Here." He pulled his bone flute out of his jacket and handed it to her. "Show me a desert tune."

She blinked, then carefully took the flute. Music, in Sava's opinion, was a universal language, and one of the best ways to introduce someone to a new place or people. It had been what first drew him in to the Reguallian refugees: their songs of hardship, of endurance and prosperity and happier times. Of joy and rebuilding and defiance of a tyrant.

He'd tried to get Athicha to learn after they'd lost their voice. But they were tone-deaf and couldn't carry a beat to save their life. At least the disastrous flute lesson had gotten them to laugh for the first time since Myrta died.

Khana bit off her gloves and gave the flute a few gentle blows, getting a feel for the notes it could make. It was a simple instrument, short and high-pitched, so it didn't take her long. Sava found himself distracted by the shape of her lips against the mouthpiece, the way her thin fingers skillfully danced across the holes. So distracted that he didn't realize she was playing a song until it was almost halfway over.

He turned away, focusing his ears as they continued down the mostly empty, darkened streets. The tune was eerily beautiful, reminding Sava of the rare flowers he would find growing stubbornly out of the frozen tundra, the only green thing for miles. It was simple and soothing, something that could lull children to sleep.

His guess was confirmed when the song ended, the last note fading into the starry sky, and Khana wiped the mouthpiece. "That's called 'Oasis Lullaby.' It sounds better on a lower octave, and I probably missed a few notes."

"It was beautiful," Sava said, taking the flute back. Even through the gloves, he could feel the warmth that Khana had breathed into it. "Is that something that you'd play for those ribbon dances?"

Khana gave him a kind smile. "No. That's just a children's lullaby. Ribbon dance songs tend to be a bit more complicated and much more fast-paced."

"You dance?" That was something Sava would love to see. That, and her with a lute.

"Quite a bit," she said, a note of pride curling around her voice. "I had ten of the twelve sub-sets mastered by the time I left the empire."

"Really? You need to show me before the Feast of Garmiva."

"Feast of what?"

"Garmiva. She's the summer goddess. We celebrate her return when the ground turns green, and the elk migrate back to this side of the tundra. Lots of singing and dancing. There's even a music competition. I got third place once. Spent all the money on drinks for me and my friends."

That had been a bittersweet night. Myrta's loss had still been a fresh wound barely scabbed over. But Haz had gotten out of his relationship with Bhayana, and it had been good to hear him laugh while Athicha dragged them from dance to dance and ate way too much food.

"That sounds lovely," she said, rubbing her wrist with a wistful look on her face.

"Khana?" he prodded.

"Sorry. I just miss my lute. I tried to take it with me, but it didn't even make it out of the palace."

"That must have been precious to you," he said. If he had to leave Pahuuda immediately to escape an evil, immortal emperor, he would want to bring only the essentials. Food, money, clothing... and yes, one of his flutes. That would, at the very least, make the travels more bearable.

She smiled, as she visibly blinked back tears. "You have no idea. I don't think I would have survived there without it."

Sava silently let her pull herself back together as they reached the inn. Lutes were expensive, but gifts were expected at the festival. Maybe...

She cleared her throat just as a man staggered out of the inn, cutting between the two of them and reeking of vodka. He saluted Sava. "Sir chief-son. Ma'am witch ma'am."

Sava bit back a snort. Khana watched him go and huffed. "I should get in there."

"Is it busy?" Sava asked, opening the door to get a peek.

To his surprise, the dining hall was mostly empty. The bulk of the customers were the rest of Khana's unit, eating dinner in the corner.

"I don't think I'll need to do more than wash dishes after I eat," Khana said cheerfully.

Which meant there was no reason for Sava to linger. Well, it was a public inn. He could stay for as long as he pleased. But he'd already pushed Khana enough today.

"Right," he said, stepping back. "I should probably..."

"Would you like to stay?" she blurted.

Sava paused. *What?*

"Just for a quick bite," she added in a rush. "Unless your parents really need you, then you should go. Or if you just don't want to, of course."

She's nervous, he realized. But not in the cornered, scared of her own shadow way that he typically saw from her. No, *this* nervousness was... lighter? More innocent. As if she genuinely wanted him to stay. Like a friend.

Maybe more.

He smiled. "I'd love to."

Chapter Twenty-Eight
Neta

Neta dared to think that things were going well. Graduation was less than a month away, and her unit was on track to succeed. Even Yxe and Khana were comfortable with their forms and winning a few spars against the more experienced members of the unit.

They went to the inn together on days Chaku gave them too much drudge work, forcing them to stay out an extra few hours so they could actually train. That was twice or thrice a week, but Neta might have to thank the midya, because these nights were some of the most content she'd felt in a long time. If they were lucky, Athicha and sometimes Sava were able to join them.

She left the inn alone one night, full of Heimili's good cooking and slightly tipsy. Snow sprinkled down from the black heavens, creating a brand-new sky of stars in constant movement. One of the last snowfalls of the season. Already the air had warmed. Soon, the mountains would be clear.

This part of town was almost all Reguallians, and Neta passed a few of her neighbors, some of whom greeted her with a cheerful, "Good night, serji!" She waved back.

"Well, you're popular."

Neta paused. That was not a voice she expected to hear in this part of town, never mind in the shadow of her mother's shop.

"Midya Bhayana," she greeted cautiously. "What brings you out here so late?"

The tall Pinnsviri melted out of the darkness, into the moonlight. "Graduation's getting close. I thought I'd check on the serjis, see how their units are progressing."

"I'm not part of your company."

Bhayana shrugged, then shivered. "Ugh. I know we want those

mountains blocked off as long as possible, but I miss summer. Do you have any tea?"

It was an obvious change in subject, a way for her to wiggle her foot in the door. Neta could say no. Bhayana might be her superior, but they were off-duty, and she had no legal right to command Neta.

Perhaps it was curiosity that made her lead Bhayana inside. Or perhaps some strategic corner of her mind determined that it was best to let her say whatever she wanted to say, so Neta could make the most tactful decision. Or maybe she'd had too much mead.

Neta lived with her mother, Varisa. The bottom floor was the hearth and seamstress's shop, the top floor private bedrooms. Varisa was likely upstairs, already in bed as Neta lit a couple of candles and re-started a small fire in the hearth to get a kettle going.

Bhayana trailed her long fingers around the weaving equipment, spindles, baskets of yak and goat hair, and the half-finished tent on Varisa's workstation. "Your mother's making your tent?"

"Made," Neta corrected, getting the tea leaves and goat milk ready. "She's making more for the war. Phramanka already paid her."

Varisa had set one aside for Neta, and another for Athicha, grumbling that yes, she knew the mute archer could afford their own, but frankly hers were better and that money should go toward their family. Athicha had known better than to argue, in part because Varisa was right; her work was some of the best in town. It was how she had clawed her way from penniless refugee to one of the wealthiest Regualians in town.

"Remarkable," Bhayana muttered. "I thought they didn't have yaks in Regualli."

"They don't. Ma learned."

"Smart woman."

Neta studied her. Haz never talked about his courtship with Bhayana, and Neta never probed. She wondered how much of Bhayana's interest here was genuine, and how much was faked in an effort to soften her up.

Neta said nothing, watching Bhayana and waiting for the water to heat. She wasn't going to give the woman anything to work with.

Bhayana didn't let it get awkward. After a beat, she said, "My father had Chaku over for dinner the other day."

"So I've heard."

"The topic of your unit came up. He is, and this is a quote, 'grudgingly impressed' with your work so far."

She said it like it was a compliment. Neta checked the temperature of the kettle and poured the tea, letting it steep.

"Frankly, I'm impressed, too," Bhayana continued. "I know how stubborn fresh soldiers can be, and your unit certainly didn't look the most promising."

Neta grunted.

"Honestly, though, I don't know why you're pursuing a career as a public soldier. Private work is so much more lucrative."

"Rather closed-off, though."

"I can change that."

Neta raised her eyebrows. "You almost sound like you're getting to the point."

Bhayana smiled, a warm, bright thing. *Ah, this is why Haz fell for her*, she thought.

"How would you like a career as a private guard?" she asked. "The pay is better, and so is the respect. You'll have a much better chance at climbing the ranks with an Old Family properly backing you."

Now that was interesting.

Positions in the Old Family guard were hard to come by. They hired only the best and they were very cushy outside of wartime. They often resulted in lifetime connections, friendships, even romances. Thriman had been a Bvamso family guard for two years before he and Phramanka properly courted.

But nothing ever came free.

"In exchange for what?" Neta asked, keeping her voice level and devoid of interest.

Bhayana visibly considered her next words. "The whole point of training is not only to gain an army, but to weed out the weak. Those unfit to be soldiers."

"And who among my unit do you believe is unfit?" she asked, already guessing two possible names.

"Hasyamin."

"Why?" she asked.

"That doesn't matter," Bhayana insisted.

"Yes, it does. If you're going to bribe me, I need to have some justification if I'm caught for it."

The Pinnsviri sighed, looking into the fire. "You're not like the other Reguallians, Neta, so I think I can be frank with you. I liked Haz. Maybe even loved him. He was exciting. New. Exotic. All I'd ever courted before him were the same old Seven Family snobs. But Haz was... dorky. Funny. Genuine. Didn't really seem to care about the money or power. But that also meant he had no respect, not for my name or its history. He didn't understand the struggle. And he certainly didn't understand that if *he* – a Reguallian brat, the grandson of a nobody immigrant – broke things off with *me*, that would be an embarrassment I could never live with. You saw the damage that type of thing did to your own family. So, I had to make him stay, and oddly enough, that made me want him more. All he had to do was play along, but he defied and fought back at every turn. And that would've been fine. I could have made that work. But then he decided to go public. Turned my friends, the whole mountain range against me. And that *cannot* go unpunished."

Neta studied her. "Your idea of punishing him is to get him excluded from the militia? That's not going to do much. He'll just go right back to the inn."

"He needs to know that actions have consequences," Bhayana said. "I'll save the inn for after the war."

The tea had steeped. Neta handed Bhayana her cup and took a sip, hating herself for seriously considering the offer. The Pinnsviris were not a popular Family. But they were influential and could help her make serious strides toward her ultimate goal of chiefdom. There would be consequences, but not necessarily fatal ones.

Is that the type of chief you want to be? asked a little voice in her head. *One who sacrifices a person – possibly his whole family – for her own gain after he'd welcomed her into his home? And for what? To be a lapdog to someone who will never view you as an equal?*

Neta swallowed her tea and set aside her cup. "You've made three mistakes. The first is forgetting that our job as serji and midya is to not only command and train soldiers, but also protect them. Second: gaining you and your family as an ally would cost me Sava and the Bvamsos –" *And Athicha.* "– which is not a price I'm willing to pay."

"Phramanka's term ends in three years. She has no guarantee of re-election, of even surviving the war," Bhayana argued.

"Neither do you. And your third, and most egregious mistake, was insulting my mother in her own home."

"I did no such thing!"

"You insulted the Reguallians, which includes me and my mother. Let me know if you're willing to make an offer with a better price."

The Pinnsviri laughed. "You're not getting another offer. It's this or nothing."

Neta smirked. "My mother came here with nothing. Now you're standing in her shop, one of the wealthiest in town if not all of northern Divaajin. We are *experts* at weaving gold from nothing."

Chapter Twenty-Nine

It was a rest day, and a quiet evening. No training, no unit, and barely any guests visiting the inn. Khana beat out a cushion over the hearth as a new customer came in. Haz gave an over-exaggerated groan. "Ah, shit. Even on days off we can't escape you."

Serji Neta brushed the snow from her leopard cloak, like a giantess swatting at flies. "Fuck you," she said evenly. "Is our usual spot open?"

"It is. Did your mother burn the dinner?"

"She's visiting a friend, and I'd rather not try my father's side of the family."

"No Athicha?"

"Their unit needed a little extra training tonight. Do you have any of that spiced mead?"

Khana and Haz shared a look. "I'll get you a horn, serji," she said. "Warm your cloak by the fire."

The soldier nodded her thanks. "We're off-duty. No need for the serji nonsense."

"As you say, serji."

Neta glared at her while Khana giggled, going into the kitchen. As she got Neta's drink ready, she heard Haz cheer, and echoing cries from Lueti. When she popped back out, horn in hand, Lueti, Yxe, and Itehua had made their way to Neta.

"We ran into each other during errands," Lueti explained, taking her customary seat in the back corner. She wore a faded pink cloak over form-fitting clothes. Khana had learned that pink was a whore's color, almost like a uniform. "We all thought to have dinner here, take a break from cooking our own food."

"And because our boy here hasn't ever been drunk," Itehua said, squeezing Yxe around the skinny shoulders.

"Whaaat?" Haz asked. "You whose mother works for an Old Family? You must have access to the best alcohol in town."

The boy shrugged, wiping his large nose. "My parents don't approve of heavy drinking. I had to promise them I'd only have half a cup of ale."

"We won't tell if you won't," Neta promised.

"And you don't have to if you don't want to," Khana stressed, handing the officer her horn. "I've never been drunk either."

"Oh, I want to," Yxe quickly assured. "I just don't want to get caught. Or pass out on the streets and freeze to death."

"It's best for a person to drink under a safe roof," Lueti said wisely.

Khana shrugged. "More mead, then?"

"Now we're talking," Itehua said, his grin stretching the pox scars on his face. "But I'll take a tea. I'm the responsible one tonight."

"*You*?" Neta laughed.

"We're off-duty, so I can freely tell you to shut your mouth."

She rolled her eyes. "Get yourself a horn, too, Khana. If you can."

"Maybe," Khana said, surveying what few customers there were in the rest of the room. It wasn't that she was opposed to drunkenness. Plenty of other concubines had used that to deal with Yamueto, or opium, or other substances. But some of them had made terrible, fatal mistakes while under the influence, or drank so much they died, and had their corpses turned into night creatures, which was why Khana had abstained.

But Lueti had a point: she was safe here. Why not indulge a little?

"Do you need me and Haz?" she asked Heimili in the kitchen. "The rest of the unit's here and…"

He waved her off. "It's a slow night. You two have fun."

Haz cheered and gathered the drinks. The younger hires went into the dining hall to wait on customers while he and Khana took their seats. They'd just asked for their food when the final member of the unit strolled in.

"Xopil!" Haz cheered. "Who's the beauty?"

Xopil's thick arm was wrapped around the shoulders of a heavy-set Reguallian woman with a toddler bundled in furs. The big man beamed. "This is my wife, Tlastisti, and our son Ponti."

"I refuse to cook tonight," Tlastisti said, settling herself next to Haz like she'd known the group for years. "And Xopil says nothing but good things about this place."

"Best spot in town," Haz promised, and then promptly started making faces at the toddler, who giggled at him.

Food and drinks poured freely for the next hour. With every horn of mead, Khana felt herself get a little looser, a little more relaxed, a little freer. Why hadn't she done this before? Tlastisti shared the story of how Xopil – then a tongue-tied pig farmer – had tried to initially catch her eye by training a piglet to deliver her flowers, and it was *hilarious*.

Lueti shared some bawdier stories from her job, making Xopil cover his son's ears and turning even Itehua red. Haz and Yxe held an eating contest to see who could consume the most chuta in five minutes, with Neta amusedly keeping time. Yxe won at three whole loaves. Where he put them in his skinny frame, Khana had no idea.

Haz switched between making faces at Ponti and flirting outrageously with Tlastisti, calling her "the reason we're fighting" and "clearly descended from the goddess of beauty." Every name was answered with a friendly swat to his shoulder and a laugh.

At one point, Khana got to chase after little Ponti while Tlastisti ate some soup, keeping him away from the fire and out of Heimili's way. "He has your nose," she said.

"Hopefully he'll have my good sense too, instead of his father's," she teased.

Xopil pouted at her. "I bring home *one* wolf cub to raise–"

"And a turtle. And a baby alligator. More birds than I can count. One time he tried to bring an *adult* tiger home because it was injured!"

"And I nursed her back to health, despite her trying to claw me!" he declared.

Tlastisti gave a good-natured sigh. Her amusement faded when she turned back to Khana. "Anyway. I need to apologize."

Khana blinked. She looked at the toddler, wondering if he'd have any answers, but Ponti just batted at the hem of her dress.

"You saved my husband's life, when he got stabbed, and I told him not to have anything to do with you," Tlastisti said. "I worried that if he was seen with the witch, he'd get hurt again. That wasn't fair."

Khana shook her head. "You were protecting your husband. I don't blame either of you. Besides, it all worked out."

Tlastisti's mouth thinned, but she didn't argue. Just took her baby back and resumed the dinner conversation. Khana refilled her horn, warm with both company and alcohol. She was having what was probably the best night of her life, until Haz turned to the door and went *white*.

Even in her state of hazy drunkenness, that didn't seem right. She followed his eye and found Bhayana, Sipah, and a handful of soldiers standing at the door.

Bhayana's black eyes gleamed. "Service, please!"

"No," Heimili growled. He'd gone to clean one of the spots across the room, and the clay teacups fell from his hands with a clatter. "Get out."

She pouted. "Oh, don't be that way, Baba Heimili."

"I am not your baba. Get out. Now."

"I wouldn't talk that way to a Pinnsviri," Sipah threatened.

Heimili pointed to them all, limping closer. "None of you have any right to come to my inn after what you did to my family. Now. Get. Out."

"Mmm... no," Bhayana said. "Hi, Haz!"

Haz's hand was shaking so much his mead looked like an ocean in a storm. He was too afraid to move.

But Khana wasn't. For the first time in a long time, she felt strong. She felt *brave*.

So, she took her own horn of mead, and threw it at Bhayana's smug face. Her aim was off, and the horn arched toward one of the Pinnsviri men. He ducked, and it smashed into the wall, spraying mead everywhere.

"She attacked me!" Bhayana shrieked.

"Oh, shut your face!" Itehua said, getting to his feet. The rest of the unit followed, Neta and Lueti standing in front of Haz. "What did you expect coming here?"

"Some respect for your betters," Sipah said, leading his group further into the room. "We're Pinnsviri men. You obey *us*. That's why we're the predators, and you're the frogs."

Khana grinned, alcohol flushing her head. "Did you know that poison dart frogs can kill a fully-grown man just by touching them?"

"P-Please leave," Yxe stammered.

"No one's talking to you," Sipah snapped, "Reguallian brat."

"Actually, I'm Tlapharian," he muttered.

"Shut up!"

Even though Yxe had drunk more than Khana, the mead hadn't given him the same bravery. He shrank into himself, hiding under his cap. Out of the corner of her eye, Khana saw Xopil gently push his family toward the back kitchen before joining the unit. "You aren't getting service here," he then said. "So please leave."

"Absolutely not," Bhayana snapped from behind Sipah. "Haz, do you have any idea what I've been through since you spread those lies about me?"

"I said shut your face," Itehua snapped. "We're not buying that yak shit here."

"You're only making it worse for yourself," Neta warned. Her short sleeves revealed powerful muscles, and with her back straight and eyes flashing, she looked more assured than most royals Khana had met. "There might be eight of you against seven of us. But you're all unarmed and we have a witch. Do you expect this to go easily for you?"

"No one threatens Mistress Bhayana in the presence of her guard," Sipah growled.

"Oh, that's not a threat," Khana jeered, blood and alcohol roaring in her ears as she got right up to Bhayana's face. "I would *love* just five minutes alone with you."

"That's it!" Sipah punched her.

The exploding pain in her nose shocked sense back into Khana. Itehua retaliated and kicked Sipah in the chest, sending him into his men. Bhayana shrieked and went after Neta, and it all descended into chaos.

A Pinnsviri guard swung at Khana, but she managed to dodge, if a little sloppily. She kneed the woman in the gut, then grabbed her ear and twisted, making her yelp. A guard got Yxe into a chokehold, which the drunk boy escaped by biting into his arm like a feral rat. Lueti armed herself with a horn of mead, splashed it into a man's face, and then beat him over the head with it. Itehua and Xopil both grappled with multiple opponents; the ex-criminal drove one into a wall only to be punched in the ribs by another, while Xopil bodily picked up and threw a man into two others with a roar.

Bhayana and Neta traded blows, and it was only an even fight because Neta had a few horns of mead in her. Haz toppled the scales by throwing his plate like a disc, and unlike Khana, hit his mark. The plate slammed into Bhayana's temple and sent her reeling back. Sipah avenged his lady by tackling Haz and punching him in the face.

The few other customers in the inn gave them a wide berth, even cheering them on. But Heimili, prosthetic or not, had no intention of being a spectator. He came out of nowhere and attempted to drag Sipah off his son, but the soldier shoved him away, pushing him onto the floor, and resumed hitting Haz.

Khana's vision turned red. She abandoned her own opponent, ran up and jumped on Sipah's back, winding her elbow around his throat and squeezing. Sipah wheezed, stepping away from Haz as he tried to shake Khana off. She stubbornly held on and breathed in.

He fell to his knees as she drank his life force, then dropped to his hands. Her bleeding nose healed and the drunken fog in her head lifted as her skin glowed.

"Khana, don't! Give it back!"

She blinked at Neta's order.

"Please..." Sipah begged. "Please don't kill me."

"I should make you crawl back to your hole like this," she growled.

"Khana," Neta ordered.

She looked up. The rest of the fight had stopped, and everyone stared at her. The Red Frogs Nine unit looked at her with fear.

She pushed the âji back into Sipah. Not all of it; she reserved a small amount as she climbed off his back.

Lueti helped Haz sit up, wincing at what she saw. Blood covered his whole face, at least one black eye already forming. Khana pushed the âji into him, clearing it right up. "Anyone else badly injured?"

"We don't need your help, witch," Bhayana spat.

"I wasn't talking to *you*."

"In that case, get the fuck out of my inn," Heimili huffed from his spot on the floor.

The Pinnsviris helped each other up, Sipah needing to lean on another soldier, despite not being injured and Bhayana tried feebly to stem the bleeding from her temple. She glared at them on their way out. "You're all going to regret this."

When they finally left, there was only silence. Lueti turned to Xopil. "Where's your wife?"

"She went to get help," Amati said, coming out of the kitchen and leading Ponti by the hand.

Neta hissed. "Even disgraced, Bhayana has supporters. Are you sure that was wise?"

Xopil made the noise of an insulted elephant. "She knows better than to get more porcupine men."

As if on cue, Tlastisti ran back into the inn, breathing hard. To Khana's embarrassment, it was Sava Bvamso on her heels, looking around the room with naked concern. "What's going on?"

Yxe threw up on the floor.

Heimili sighed. "What's going on is you're all helping me clean up."

"Sorry about this," Haz said as they finished cleaning up Yxe's mess and replacing torn or stained floor cushions with clean ones. Since no one was in need of âji, Khana tended to people's injuries with bandages and ointment. The other guests who had not been involved in the fight were sent away with Heimili's apologies and promises of a discounted meal next time – although most had shrugged it off and said it'd been fun to watch.

Itehua laughed. "No one gets through life without at least one drunken brawl. That was fun!"

"Yeah. Fun," Yxe hiccupped. Tlastisti tended to him while Ponti slept on a cushion, giving Yxe tea and a bucket as needed. Khana was thankful that the âji had cured her own drunkenness, saving her from the same fate.

"If you get it all out now, you won't have to deal with it tomorrow morning," Neta sagely said to Yxe, sitting still so Khana could wrap her bleeding knuckles.

Sava helped Heimili gather up and divide the dishes into salvageable and non-salvageable piles, even though his presence was no longer necessary. He'd already interviewed everyone, participants and witnesses alike, his normally cheerful face growing more and more grim.

He tossed another broken horn into the trash pile. "I'm just amazed Bhayana had the gall to do this."

"It's what she does," Haz said. "She'll never admit defeat, never go away, she's like a wound that just festers and gets worse and…" He drifted off, turning red as everyone else stared at him. Even Itehua looked sympathetic. Heimili limped over and gave his son a hug.

"I'll talk to my mother," Sava promised. "Bhayana was specifically ordered to stay away from you."

"The first infringement is only a fine, though," Itehua pointed out. "She's rich, so what does she care?"

"She came here once before," Sava said. "I had to kick her out. The second infringement can get up to a month of unpaid community service. The third is imprisonment or exile. She's not getting away with this again."

Haz's smile was tight. "Thank you, Sava."

Itehua nudged Neta. "Maybe next time don't order Khana to show mercy?"

"A corpse would've made this a hundred times worse," the serji defended. "I don't want to get us kicked out of the army a week before training ends."

Khana choked on her spit. "We're done in a *week*?"

Neta nodded. "That's when the weather turns, and the snow starts to melt. The mountains become passable for invaders."

The blood drained from Khana's face. "Have we heard from…"

Sava shifted his feet, hesitating before saying, "The king just sent word: Emperor Yamueto sent an ultimatum. Join the empire or face utter destruction."

The inn was completely silent. Haz's snort broke the tension. "With charms like that, it's a wonder he's not married."

Khana ducked her head, hoping to hide whatever was on her face. Sava very carefully did not look at her.

"We're telling him to fuck off, right?" Itehua asked.

Sava's smirk was a feral thing. "Of course. After all this training, it'd be a shame not to fight."

"Damn right!" Itehua cheered.

Khana wished she could share their enthusiasm, but all she felt was dread.

Chapter Thirty
Sava

The Iron Scepter was the most sacred object of the Ghura. The great Chief Pahileed had carved it himself before settling his mercenary people in the mountains. Cords hung from the top, from which animal teeth and bones were tied and cackled with every movement. Every seventy years, another was added to symbolize the greatest event of the last two to three generations so that when the chief held it, they literally held the weight of the entire people's ancestry.

Chief Phramanka looked like she very much wanted to shove the entire Scepter down Bhayana's throat.

"They attacked me!" she insisted, her watery voice filling the throne room of the town hall. Only two of the thrones were occupied: Chief Phramanka's and Master Pabu Pinnsviri's. While the trial was technically public, it had taken place quickly enough that most of the town wasn't aware of it. Sava had ensured that, reporting the bar fight to his mother and pushing for a quick trial before the Pinnsviris could try to adjust public opinion.

Besides the soldiers assigned to keep the peace within the town hall, the only other people in the room were Sava, Bhayana, a handful of the witnesses Sava had interviewed at the inn, and Serji Neta. Though Neta wasn't there was a witness, instead standing against the wall, half in shadows, simply watching the proceedings. Sava was surprised to see her; graduation was days away. She should've been training her unit.

"I came to the inn to get some food, and they all attacked me," Bhayana repeated. "Unprovoked!"

"You trespassed," Sava growled. "That inn is off-limits to you for another five years."

"That doesn't give them the right–" Master Pabu Pinnsviri cut himself off with a long, painful cough. Bhayana rushed to his side, patting his back and handing him a kerchief to wipe the spittle and blood from his lips.

"That doesn't give them the right to escalate it to violence," he said. "The witch almost killed one of my men."

"The one that was trying to beat Hasyamin to death?" Phramanka asked drolly. The witnesses all nodded.

"So, to rephrase," the chief said, "you went to an inn – the one inn in this town that you are expressly forbidden from entering – with half a dozen soldiers, taunted the man you had abused for months–"

"He lied!"

"*Taunted the man you had abused for months*," Phramanka repeated, barreling over Bhayana's protests. "They told you to leave. And when you refused – thus officially trespassing on their property – Khana threw her horn at you and missed. After some more yelling, *your* man threw the first punch and drew first blood. The fight devolved from there until Khana almost killed your man, who was punching Hasyamin's face, but stopped at Serji Neta's orders."

"With witchcraft! Which you told her not to use!" Bhayana pointed out.

"Self-defense is exempt. That is common sense, which you seem to lack." Phramanka twisted the Iron Scepter in her hands, swishing the cords of bones and teeth to rattle. "What damage was done to the inn?"

"Minor," Sava said grudgingly. "Broken horns and plates, ripped cushions and the like."

"Physical injuries?"

"Several."

"And I assume the girl healed them?"

Sava gritted his teeth. "Yes."

"Then what's the harm?" Pabu croaked. "It was a drunken brawl. Nothing more."

"The brawl never would have happened if your granddaughter obeyed the laws I set before her," Phramanka retorted. "Graduation is in less than a week, and we'll be marching as soon as the snow clears. My soldiers need to trust each other, not play these ridiculous mind games!"

"That's obviously what my granddaughter was trying to do," he argued. "Making an overture of friendship, to put the past behind them. This Reguallian boy is the one holding the grudge."

Sava barked a laugh.

"I don't care who's holding a grudge. Bhayana is banned from that inn and from all contact with Hasyamin and his family," Phramanka said, glaring at the defendant. "I ought to strip you of your rank and all military service. Your behavior has been appalling for that of a midya."

Bhayana stiffened but managed to remain calm.

"Then I suppose you don't need *any* Pinnsviris in your military," Pabu mused. "Nor our financial support."

Phramanka glared at him. Sava balked and said, "You would let the emperor invade without defending your homeland? For a petty grudge?"

Pabu shrugged. "Obviously, the chief feels confident that she doesn't need our help. Who are we to deny her will?"

Sava looked between him and his mother. The old man *had* to be bluffing, right?

But when he saw Bhayana smirk, he knew Pabu wasn't. The Pinnsviris were some of the richest people in the mountains. They even had properties beyond the tundra. A tenth of the militia's armor, weapons, food, and supplies were funded by them.

Pahuuda could do without them. But it would hurt.

After a moment of charged silence, Phramanka looked down at Bhayana. "This is your second offense. As such, you will pay a fine of seven yaks or their equivalent."

Bhayana balked at such a high price, but a tiny shake of Pabu's head silenced her.

"Your third offense will, by law, result in exile at the minimum," Phramanka warned. "Not even a member of an Old Family can avoid that. Do I make myself clear?"

Bhayana nodded.

"Good. Now get out of my sight. Pabu, you, too. If I have to hear another smug word, I'm tossing you in a snowbank."

Bhayana helped her frail grandfather stand and slowly leave. The witnesses were all gone before they even reached the door.

When they were finally gone, Sava huffed. "They can't legally withdraw military support."

"Sure they can," Phramanka said. "All war efforts are voluntary. If you must force people to participate, then there should not be a war."

He growled. He knew that. Understood that. There had been plenty of times in Ghuran history where such protections of civilian freedom had curbed an overly aggressive or would-be tyrannical chief. But sometimes, he wished his mother had more power.

"Serji Neta, you're still lurking," Phramanka said, standing from her throne and stretching. "Shouldn't you be training your unit?"

The soldier pushed off the wall. "I put Itehua in charge for the morning. I was hoping to speak with your son."

"What about?" Sava asked.

"Midya Chaku has been seen visiting the Pinnsviris several times the last few weeks. They've been hosting him for dinner."

He immediately understood. "You think they want him to interfere with your unit's graduation?"

Neta gave an imperious shrug. "Would you put it past the Pinnsviris to ask for such a favor? Bhayana already tried to bribe me to expel Haz."

"What?!"

"Why didn't you report this?" Phramanka asked.

"No evidence," Neta replied. "We were alone. It would've been she-said-she-said, if it made it to trial at all. We have better things to do."

Sava. Really. Hated. Politics.

He turned to his mother, but Phramanka was already shaking her head. "I have no grounds to transfer or demote Chaku."

"I'm not asking you to," Neta said smoothly. "I was hoping Midya Sava or someone similar would be there in attendance for our graduation. Act as witness. Chaku will be less likely to pull such a stunt if you're there."

Sava paused, considering that against the needs of his own Blue Owl Company, whose graduation he would be overseeing. "What's the date of your test?"

"Five days from now."

The Blue Owl Company's was in six. "I'll be there."

Her whole body relaxed. "Thank you. One more thing: Khana said she initially enlisted to become a combat medic. When we graduate, she'll be transferred to a medical unit."

"That is how that works, yes," Phramanka snarked.

"I would like to put in a formal request to keep her in mine," Neta said.

Sava sucked in a breath. The combat medics were in a dangerous enough position, but at least they were held behind the front line and given a certain amount of protection. Most other armies also avoided hitting them out of respect. In the event of their capture, they were kept as valuable prisoners of war and returned home unharmed more often than not.

The idea of sweet, scared Khana being in the front lines made his gut twist.

"We cannot force such a decision without due cause," Phramanka said. "And neither can your commanders. Khana's proven her worth as a medic time and time again, so there will be no reason to deny her if she chooses to transfer."

"I understand that," Neta said. "I simply wanted to make a second choice possible."

Sava gritted his teeth. Neta wasn't the first serji to do this type of thing. Many made such formal requests, even knowing that there was nothing that the chief could actually do about them. They were simply declarations of intent, a way for serjis to show their subordinates their desire to keep them in their units.

He'd have to make sure Khana understood that. If she felt pressured to stay with Neta, to fight on the front lines, that would be another careless cruelty inflicted under his watch.

"Your request has been noted," Phramanka said. "It will mean nothing if your unit doesn't graduate."

Neta smirked. "I wouldn't worry about that, chief."

Chapter Thirty-One

The last week of training was a blur of jogging on the tundra in full armor, smashing shields in the line game, and endless combat drills. Neta warned them that soldiers passed and failed as a unit, and that Midya Chaku analyzed each individual to see if they were combat ready.

"He's going to have each unit show him their sets for spear, axe, knife, and empty hand," she said for about the twentieth time in as many days. "And we're all going to participate in the line game. If we *all* don't nail those sets and secure at least three wins, we're out. You'll get paid for your time in training, but only half."

Khana gulped. Other than her powers – which she couldn't use without cost – she was the weakest link in the unit. If they failed, it would be on her. Part of her wondered if that would really be a bad thing. After all, soldiers went to war. They could die. Failing the whole unit meant that her friend Haz, young Yxe, and kind Lueti wouldn't be subjected to that. They'd be safe and sound in town.

But Neta was so driven, so clearly ready to go to war, that Khana didn't dare oppose her. Not out of fear – at this point Khana knew that Neta would never hurt her – she just didn't want to disappoint her.

Failing the unit meant depriving the Ghuran militia of seven capable warriors it desperately needed. She wouldn't be able to use her necromancy skills to heal injured soldiers and keep them in the fight, lowering the town's chances of success even further.

And it meant depriving herself – and Xopil's family, Haz's family, and the others – of the money they all needed.

"What, exactly, is stopping Chaku from failing us even if we do everything perfectly?" Itehua asked.

"The fact that I asked Sava to be present," Neta replied.

"Ah."

Khana dropped her face in her hands. Somehow, that made it worse.

She continued to work on drills, kept up Neta's extra late-night training sessions on shovel days, and worked out with the rest of the company without complaint.

She continued to wake from nightmare-memories long before the sun rose. Sometimes she could get back to sleep. Sometimes she had to wander the town to exhaust herself first. And sometimes she just made herself tea and waited for sunrise.

On graduation day, Khana and Haz arrived on the field to find Lueti handing a small cloth bag to Neta. The serji waited for everyone to assemble before opening it. "Lueti's friend is finally finished with our obsidian."

Khana had almost forgotten about the glass diving. Neta handed out their hard-earned prizes, and Khana cooed when she realized the jeweler had shaped the black glass to look like a frog, just a little fatter and rounder than the real thing.

"Sorry it took so long," Lueti said, analyzing her own obsidian with a critical eye. "But you can't rush quality."

"I like it," Xopil said, adding it to his shoulder next to his other piece. "My wife will be so jealous."

Each of the little frogs had a string of leather wrapped around a hole in their backs to tie into place. Itehua put his on his spear, Lueti fastened hers as a bracelet, and Khana positioned hers as a necklace, like Neta.

"Regardless of what happens today, you are Red Frogs Nine," Neta declared. "You are warriors, and some of the bravest, most *infuriating* people I've had the privilege of training."

Khana's chest warmed at the sentiment. Haz grinned. "Aw, serji, we love you, too."

"Everyone says we're going to fail, partly because nine is an unlucky number," Lueti mused. "Khana, what did you say about the poison frogs?"

"They live in the Reguallian jungles. Predators don't dare go near them because their skins are coated in venom. One touch will kill you. And they're surprisingly adorable."

Haz grinned. "Adorable and deadly? That sounds like us."

"None of the commanders will call us anything besides Red Frogs Nine," Neta said. "But between us, the Poison Dart Frogs sounds more fitting."

Midya Chaku whistled for the company's attention, scowling as the spring breeze toyed with his long beard. Sava stood next to him, arms crossed.

"All right, you dumb frogs. Let's get this over with," Chaku snapped. "Five laps around the field. Go."

One lap was just under half a mile. They'd never gone more than four in a day. Khana kept pace with Haz on one side and Yxe on the other, Xopil, Lueti, and Itehua in front of them, and Neta in the lead. Red Frog units One through Eight were ahead of them, and Ten and Eleven were behind.

As they jogged, Khana noticed Yxe getting more and more pensive. The Tlapharian boy was always quiet, but this was new even for him. "You all right?" she huffed, her breath puffing in white clouds before her.

"I'm worried," he admitted quietly. "If we fail, it's going to be because of me. I'm the weakest one here."

Khana blinked. Then laughed, a big-bellied laugh that almost made her lose her place in line. "I was thinking the same about myself!"

"Oh, that's a relief," Lueti called from up ahead, braid swishing back and forth as she ran. "I thought the weakest member of the unit was the old whore."

"You shouldn't talk about yourselves like that," Xopil scolded. "You'll all do great."

"Yeah, we busted our asses making you halfway decent fighters," Itehua added. "You're saying you don't believe in us?"

"I believe you're only in this unit to make the rest of us look prettier by comparison," Haz goaded, showing the gap between his front teeth.

"Fuck you and your little glass frog."

Khana and, to her relief, Yxe both giggled as Haz and Itehua verbally poked each other for the rest of the run.

They all quickly sobered when, after they stopped and were allowed to catch their breath, they realized they'd already lost a unit. Someone from Red Frogs Ten had stumbled off the trail and refused to get back up. Not unable, as they were perfectly fine, just unwilling. Chaku immediately failed them, and the rest of the company watched the unit walk away with bowed heads and slumped shoulders.

"Now that playtime is over, let's get back to it," Chaku called. "Red Frogs One, let's see your spear form."

He went through each unit, watching them go through all their forms, Sava a silent specter beside him. Red Frogs Three was sent home when one of their men fumbled the spear, dropping it in the snow. They almost lost Five, but the woman who nearly dropped her axe caught it again in the last second. The midyas let it slide.

"Unit Nine," Chaku snapped. "You're up."

They lined up and got in their starting positions. Khana's back was to Sava, and she could only hope she didn't make a fool of herself.

They went through the spear form first. Khana retreated into her mind, just a little, falling into a quasi-meditative state. She focused on the feeling of the bone in her gloved hands, the sound of the blade cutting through the wind, the cold air in her lungs. They replaced spears with axe, then knife, then fists, attacking imaginary foes.

When they finished, Sava glanced at Chaku – his mouth flattened into a thin line.

"Unit Eleven, you're up."

Yxe almost collapsed in audible relief. Lueti scooped him in a hug and half-carried him off. "Well done!"

"Thank you," he said weakly.

"Two tests down, one to go," Haz said, stretching his arms. "We've gotten better at the line game."

Neta hummed. She seemed perfectly calm, but Khana was nervous, and so were the others. The line game was their weakest point. It's not that the team was weak, but they had old Lueti, lanky Yxe, and tiny Khana. The weakest members of most other units were built more like Haz and Itehua. Not for the first time, Khana wondered if that was on purpose.

"I don't think a double line is going to work, serji," Itehua said, studying the remaining nine units. "Maybe we should try one of the new ones."

"I think you're right," Neta replied.

Khana's stomach twisted. In the last week, they'd been experimenting with different strategies. Sometimes they did a single line rather than two, trying to cut through the opponent's middle and push them apart. Other times they tried a tiny phalanx, a reverse of the usual formation: instead of one person (Khana) in the back, one person (Neta or Xopil, usually) was at the front. The physical constraint of the lines made a proper phalanx impossible, which was probably why Neta said, "We'll go with the single-file line. The usual order."

"Maybe we should switch it up a little," Xopil mused.

"Now isn't the time to experiment."

"Hear me out," he implored. "Before Pahuuda, I was a rebel soldier in my town. They conquered us in my grandfather's day, so we never liked them. We fought against imperial soldiers, and won a couple of skirmishes, too."

Khana's jaw dropped, matching the timeline in her head. "You were part of the Namari Belt Rebellion? You caused such a headache messing with those supply lines that Emperor Yamueto wanted to skin all of you and feed you to his night creatures!"

He grinned, the pea-shaped birthmark on his cheek wrinkling. "That was us, though only the conquerors call it Namari. It's called the Kostikli Belt. Anyway, we once had a fight over a stream. It was autumn, and half-frozen and treacherous. So we decided it was best to jump over it to get to the enemy archers. Our smallest fighters were in the front with the shields. They stopped just short of the water, and while the archers got new arrows, the rest of us jumped onto their backs and over the water, right into the archers."

"We're not fighting archers," Itehua complained. "And there's no stream to serve as a buffer."

"No, but it serves as an element of surprise," Neta said. "All right, we'll try this for the first one…"

She quietly explained the strategy. Khana was almost as dubious as Itehua, but it couldn't hurt to try. The worst that could happen was they made utter fools of themselves and had seven more attempts.

They were called first for the line game, the two rows of stones neatly laid out. Chaku assigned them to fight Red Frogs One, one of the best units in the company.

Mumbling started from the others as soon as they saw the lineup: Xopil was in the back, not the front. Not a good position for their strongest to be.

Other than that, they were in double rows: Neta and Itehua in front, Haz and Yxe behind them, then Khana and Lueti. Everyone had their shields out and up front as Chaku counted them down.

At "Go!" the six of them jogged, leaving Xopil behind, to their spectators' growing confusion. Though they moved fast, they didn't sprint, instead letting the enemy unit pass the halfway point. Right before they ran into One, Neta ordered, "Down!" They stopped running and took a knee, bracing themselves like a rock before the crash of waves.

And crash they did.

Red Frogs One slammed right into their shields. The forerunners of the unit almost tripped over them, not expecting them to be so low. Not a single member of the Poison Dart Frogs budged, taking the brunt with only a few grunts.

Before they could recover and figure out what happened, Khana heard Xopil's hurried footsteps in the snow.

This was the part she was skeptical about, even though Xopil had assured all of them that he'd done this before across slippery river stones covered in ice.

The four behind Neta and Itehua moved their shields up, covering the top of their heads. Khana tilted hers a little behind, making it easier for Xopil to get on top.

His weight hit her shield, enough to feel like she was being crushed, then it was gone in a flash as he stepped on Haz and Yxe's, using the boys as a launching point to jump over Neta and Itehua, straight into Red Frogs One.

It was like dropping a massive stone into a puddle, rippling the water. Khana couldn't see much at the back and behind her shield, but she saw two unit One soldiers tossed out by the force of Xopil shoving his way into their ranks. Another was pushed over the line before she could properly brace herself. The pressure unit One had put on them was practically gone, having almost forgotten them in the shock and confusion.

"Up!" Neta ordered.

The rest of the unit got to their feet and charged, Xopil now at the head as they shoved Red Frogs One down the row.

Haz whooped when they won, half-tackling Xopil in a hug. Khana grinned.

The celebrations were cut off when Chaku whistled. "Unit Nine is disqualified. That is an illegal–"

"No it's not," Sava interrupted.

Chaku glared at him. "That strategy would get their man shot full of arrows."

"Probably," he admitted. "But it's not an illegal move in the line game. Merely unorthodox. They pushed the other team to the end of the lines without drawing blood. That's the rule."

Chaku glared at him. Khana bit the inside of her cheek, waiting.

"Winner," Chaku said through gritted teeth. "Unit Nine."

The Poison Dart Frogs cheered in victory. Sava did a bad job of not looking smug.

"Not bad, rebel," Itehua said, rubbing the top of Xopil's head. "I don't know if we'll be able to pull that off a second time."

"No, the element of surprise is what did it," Neta agreed. "And we shouldn't push our luck with Chaku. But it's given us a good start…"

They strategized for the rest of the round, coming up with plans for each possible opponent. Khana couldn't contribute much, as this was not her area of expertise by any means, but the excitement was contagious, and she found that she was looking forward to the next match.

Looking back, she realized it was the team's enthusiasm that carried them. Out of the eight matches, they won six and tied a seventh, a shocking reversal of their usual ratio.

By the end of the day, a grand total of four units out of eleven – twenty-eight recruits – were sent home with rejections. The Poison Dart Frogs, on the other hand, stood tall and proud when Midya Chaku said, "Congratulations. From this point on, you are all soldiers of the Ghuran militia."

Chapter Thirty-Two

That night, the unit celebrated their victory at the inn. Heimili cooked them a special roast chicken, a rare import in this part of the world, and refused to charge them for it, brimming with pride as he ruffled Haz's hair every chance he got, tangling it worse than usual. "My son the soldier. I knew you had it in you!"

Xopil's wife Tlastisti was probably more excited than any of them. "I don't have to cook for this big lug, *and* I get expensive food for free? I should sign up for the militia myself!"

"Don't even joke about that," Xopil grumbled, feeding his squirming toddler.

Neta was a latecomer. But she made up for the tardiness with a bottle of wine from a country Khana had never heard of that made Haz choke. "How did you get your hands on this? It's worth more than every house on this street!"

"My mother's made good friends among the traders."

Everyone helped themselves to a horn of the wine, except for Itehua, who stayed with tea. "To the Poison Dart Frogs!" Neta toasted.

"Poison Darts!" They clanked their cups together.

They stayed up late, taking tiny sips from the wine bottle and talking even after Heimili and Amati closed and went to bed. Haz and Khana promised to clean up any lingering mess. Tlastisti went home with her son and refused her husband's offer to go with them. "You stay and celebrate. The army's giving you the next few days off, so don't think I won't work you like a dog."

With that cheering sentiment, she left the unit to its own devices. Itehua passed the wine without drinking from it. "Incredible woman you've got there."

"The best," Xopil said, his wide face beaming like the sun.

"Was she part of this rebel thing, too?"

He nodded, sobering. "We were just a small village, one of many in the Kostikli Belt – that's the river basin around the Kostikli River," he explained. "The emperor renamed it to Namari after conquering it. Anyway, all of us were hit with a drought, our crops withering in the fields, livestock dying. The empire had never been kind to us – our grandfathers had fought back hard against the invasion, and they made sure to punish us for it – but during the drought they refused to give us any food, and worse, taxed us so bad that we had to give them what little rice we stored away for emergencies. All the town elders across the Belt got together and decided to revolt. I agreed to join, but I got worried on my way home to tell Tlastisti. We had just gotten married, and she had never liked violence, preferring to talk things over. I had prepared a speech and practiced it all the way home, but when I got there, I found her sitting on the mat carving spears out of cypress.

"'What are you doing?' I asked.

"'We're revolting, aren't we?' she said. 'All the women in town agree: if we can't talk you into fighting, we'll do it ourselves. But we don't have any steel, and I wouldn't know how to make a sword if we did, so I'm making do with this.'"

Haz laughed. "Did you use the cypress spears to fight?"

"Some of us. Others used their farming tools."

"You had no training, no real soldiers, and no weapons, and you still went against the empire?" Neta clarified, clearly impressed.

Xopil nodded, his smile dropping. "It didn't work. We knew it wouldn't. But we had to try. By the end, when it was clear we'd lose, some of us wanted to surrender, others wanted to make a final stand and die fighting, but…"

"It didn't matter either way," Khana said. "All their bodies were turned to night creatures for Yamueto's army."

He nodded. "Tlastisti was pregnant. We knew it was cowardly, but I couldn't endanger her life. And I couldn't let her try to raise that child without me, so we ran. Came to the mountains, thinking we'd be safe. Now the empire's come again."

He sniffed, wiping a tear. Haz rubbed his shoulder.

"That was the right thing to do," Khana stressed. "You were never going to win, but this way you're alive, and so is your son."

"There's no shame in retreating from a losing battle," Neta agreed.

"Yeah, and now you have much better odds at winning," Itehua said. "The empire's going to regret picking a fight with you again."

Xopil snorted.

"At least you managed to kill a handful of imperial bastards," Lueti grumbled, taking her sip of wine. She didn't wear pink today, going off-duty. "Me, I just smashed the head in of a rough client with a tea kettle. That's all it took for the empire to come after me."

"You're a whore," Itehua said at length. "How rough was he?"

"Oh, he wasn't getting rough with *me*," she clarified. "I worked at a brothel that employed all kinds of folk, and some of my work-sisters had children. They helped with cleaning, cooking, some of the older boys stayed on as enforcers, that type of thing. And *only* that type of thing. Some houses sell children's bodies, but not us."

Khana's chest tightened as she realized where this was going.

"But this man..." Lueti shook her head. "He was some petty lord or whatnot. Never learned to take 'no' for an answer. And he decided he wanted the nine-year-old girl cleaning the dishes in the back. I was the first to hear her scream."

Licking her dry lips, Khana asked, "What happened to her?"

"She was fine," she assured. "Scared, of course, and her mother was furious. But he didn't do more than tear at her clothes before I hit him on the head with a teapot. Spilled his brains all over the floor. Of course, the house couldn't protect me, and it was only a matter of time before imperial brats started sniffing around, so they smuggled me out of town and lied about where I was going. Wound up here."

"Shit, Lueti," Haz whistled. "Remind me not to piss you off around tea sets."

Her grin was all teeth. "What about you, Itehua? I imagine you left an impressive reputation behind."

He snorted. "Probably not beyond my hometown. I ran a ring, smuggling some less than legal goods in and out."

"Drugs?"

"Opium, mostly, but also birth control."

"Birth control?" Neta echoed.

"It's illegal in the empire," Itehua and Khana said at the same time. She wondered if they would've done business together if he'd been in the capital.

"Barbarians," Neta growled.

"You have no idea," Lueti agreed, flipping her braid over her shoulder. "Girls like me relied on boys like Itehua if we wanted to avoid anything from crotch-rot to pregnancy."

"Thank you," he cheered. "And Xopil, you said your village starved from drought? That never would've happened in my town. We kept a steady supply of food and medicine. Anytime anyone needed anything, they knew to come to me."

"For a price," Neta guessed.

He shrugged. "Nothing more than they could pay. Sometimes it was coin, other times, a small favor here and there. But I'll say this now, because Lueti's making that face, that I never sold people or bargained with sex, and I never beat or killed someone. Unless they deserved it."

The serji snorted. "I'll be nice and not ask what constitutes 'deserved.'"

"Shush."

"You always talk back to Neta, I can't imagine you working for a crime lord," Yxe said.

Itehua gave him a look. "I *was* the crime lord."

"Really?!"

"That's not hard to believe," Neta muttered. "How'd you end up here?"

"The empire disapproved of my business," Itehua said imperiously. He deflated. "It didn't matter that we didn't cause them trouble. I barely had to bribe the imperials to look the other way because I made sure to stay out of their way every chance I could. Then suddenly they came for our necks."

"They can't afford to have the people rely on anyone but them," Khana said. "Methods aside, you provided an essential service to your community, outside of imperial control. That's Yamueto's worst nightmare."

"Yes, well, we paid for that," he grumbled. "Half of my men and women – good people – were executed, the others scattered with only the clothes on their backs. And I couldn't do anything. I went into the business to look after them, and…"

"And you lost a war," Neta finished kindly. "Don't feel bad because you fought for what you believe in. You and Xopil, and Lueti, too. We've all been there."

He nodded, still looking grim.

"Feel bad because you should've realized that Pahuuda doesn't need that specific business of yours," she teased.

"A common businessman's mistake," he defended. "I don't see why I should be facing years of military service for it."

"Because now you have us!" Haz cheered.

"Hurray," he deadpanned. "I get to be on the dredge unit."

"We're soldiers now," Xopil defended. "Just as strong as the others."

"No, this unit was fixed," Neta admitted, looking into the empty wine bottle. "As soon as I got promoted to serji, my uncle assured me that I would never go farther. He made sure all the 'weaklings,' as he saw them, got to me. The old whore, the bad-luck witch, the troublesome criminal, the cowardly rebel, the Tlapharian boy – he saw all of you as worthless in some way. He even made sure I had unit *nine*, for that extra bit of bad luck."

"I figured as such," Khana said.

"You're uncle's the Cituva *Master*, right? On the council?" Itehua clarified, refilling his teacup. "What an ass."

"We proved him wrong, though," Haz said with a smirk.

Neta smiled back. "We sure did."

"Gods, your family sounds awful," Lueti said.

"Eh, they don't see me as one of them," Neta explained.

"But there's nothing wrong with a child born out of wedlock," Yxe protested. "Every Old Family has them in their family tree. The Cilas' Master is one. There's no shame in it."

"No, but according to my Cituva relatives, there *is* shame in having a lowly outsider refugee in your family tree. So, I go out of my way to show them that I'm a Cituva whether they like it or not." She patted her snow leopard cloak.

"Bet that pisses them off," Itehua said with a smirk.

She laughed, the wine turning her cheeks pink. "So much, you have no idea! I can't wait until I become midya, then maversti, and finally chief. Rub *that* in their faces."

"That'll be a day," Lueti cheered.

"Keep us alive in the upcoming war and I'll even vote for you," Itehua teased.

"Deal," Neta said.

"There has to be better ways to become chief than fighting," Khana insisted. "It's not just warriors here."

"True, but it's the surest route," she said. "This war has perfect timing. There will be plenty of opportunity for glory and promotions."

"That's a terrible thing to say!"

Neta gave her a deadpan look. "The war is going to happen. People are going to die. Quite possibly some of my friends and family. I don't like that, nor do I want it, but it will happen no matter what we do. But fuck me for trying to find a bright side."

Khana looked at her lap, embarrassed.

"I just enlisted because I didn't want to be called a coward," Yxe admitted quietly. "Everyone was doing it, mocking the ones who didn't or couldn't, and I wanted to make my parents proud so... I wish I had your bravery, serji."

"You and me both," Khana muttered.

"You are not a coward," Haz said tiredly. "Neither of you. You've made it this far. Yxe, you feral rat, you *bit* a man twice your size right there by the fireplace."

The boy blushed and giggled as Itehua gently punched his shoulder.

Haz continued, "And Khana, I don't even want to know what horror you dealt with in the imperial court."

The alcohol loosened her lips, tinging her voice with bitterness: "I was a concubine. I was his quiet little mouse who did as she was told and never fought back. I didn't leave until he was going to kill me."

"You survived," he insisted. "Just like I did."

"Wait a minute," Yxe said, tipping his head in confusion. "Didn't you say that witches attend directly to the emperor? To help with the night creatures?"

Xopil nodded. "We had a witch born in our town. He was taken straight to the capital. Had to be a bodyguard for one of the princes, I think. One who had eight concubines?"

"Every royal man gets those?" Haz asked.

Itehua snorted. "If you're rich enough, and can handle the drama, you can have as many women as you want. Most of the royals have at least three. The emperor has...what, two, three hundred? Who were you stuck with Khana?"

She winced, giving them a guilty look.

Lueti realized it first: "Oh my gods. You were *Emperor Yamueto's* concubine!"

Khana shrank into her cushion. "...yes. Unwillingly, I should point out. And I made sure I never got pregnant, no matter what he did."

"Why would he do that?" Neta asked. "It must take a massive amount of time and energy to keep you all in line, to say nothing of food, clothes, and shelter. What's the purpose beyond showing off?"

"It's to create more witches," Khana explained. "He takes the women for himself and if they're too closely related to him, he marries them off. Male witches also get arranged marriages. All of them are forced to serve and help him create night creatures. The more witches he has, the more night creatures he has, the more kingdoms he can conquer, and since they usually have a few witches themselves..."

"An endless cycle," Yxe said. "Like planting wheat: one sprout can give you multiple seeds. Plant those and you get even more."

"How long were you there?" Neta asked quietly.

"I was fourteen when I arrived and left last year, so six years," she answered. "Oh, I'm twenty-one now, aren't I?"

"Happy birthday," Xopil offered.

"Wait, wait, wait," Haz said, holding up his hands. "You said you didn't let yourself get pregnant. You smuggled illegal birth control into the palace, didn't you?"

Khana nodded. "It's the one thing I could do to him."

"And you have the gall to call yourself a coward?"

She blanched, never really considering that before. "Plenty of others did more," she said dismissively.

"And I'm sure they had a very happy ending," Neta pointed out.

Khana shuddered, thinking of the women whose bodies were twisted into night creatures, or hung from the palace walls, or even those who were locked in their rooms for months on end, receiving nightly visits from Yamueto.

"Fear keeps us alive," Xopil said. "That's what my wife said when we were deciding whether to flee or fight. Bravery is good, but too much makes a man stupid. That's why the gods gave us fear."

"Agreed." Lueti took Khana's hand. "Darling, you weren't even a soldier. I know dozens of girls just like you who suffered that kind of abuse for far longer than six years, and many of them blame themselves for not being able to get away, even when they were only children!"

A weight Khana hadn't been aware of lifted from her shoulders. She realized she had been carrying an invisible fear: what her unit would think of her when they found out about the truth of her past.

None of them condemned her. They didn't scold, berate, or hate her. They were all looking at her with variations of compassion, understanding, and even admiration.

Khana's eyes watered. Lueti pulled her into a hug, letting her sniffle into her shoulder.

After a few heartbeats, Haz asked, "So… is the emperor compensating for something?"

"Hasyamin!" Lueti scolded as Khana pulled back in confusion.

He held up his hands. "I'm just saying! Someone who so aggressively wages war and rapes women to prove what a big man he is… He's probably a little smaller than average, no?"

"This is not something we should talk about," Neta growled, glancing at Khana.

Khana wiped her face. Talking about this, surprisingly, did not result in panic or dread. Haz's smirk invited her to make fun of her tormentor. To strip away a little bit of the power he still held over her. "Well... what's average?"

"Or maybe we should," the serji muttered.

"Ah, the age-old question," Itehua said with a smirk.

Yxe raised his hand, though his face was beet red. "I've read books where some physicians say that a flaccid penis is averaged at a finger's length, and erect is two."

"They wrote that down?" Xopil wondered.

"Whose fingers?" Haz asked.

"You can't trust a book to *that*," Itehua scolded. "Besides, I know men with plenty bigger. Myself included."

"Oh, sure," Neta drawled.

"Would you like a demonstration?"

"Only if you want to lose it."

"Did the book mention girth?" Haz asked. "Because I heard that's what's important."

"Scholars disagree, depending on location," Yxe said, pulling his hat down over his red face. "That's all I read."

"Boys, boys!" Lueti called, raising her hands. "As the resident expert, I believe my word is law."

They all backed down. Lueti drew her knife, tested her hand against the handle and blade like she was about to wrap her fingers around it, then nodded. "A limp cock is just long enough to wrap a hand around, maybe more. A hard one is about the size of this blade."

Khana looked at the knife. *He's average, then,* she thought. But that's not what they wanted to hear, and they could all use a laugh.

"Well, he's definitely compensating," she said.

Itehua howled. Xopil and Yxe both chuckled while Haz called, "I knew it! I *knew* it!" Neta buried her face in her hand, likely regretting her decision to rise the military ranks. Lueti snickered, giving Khana a knowing look. She'd likely told similar lies to get the same results.

For the first time in a long time, when Khana went to bed that night, she didn't have nightmares.

Khana clicked the coins together again and again. She'd worn jewels and silks, but this was the most amount of *money* she'd ever held. And she'd earned it all herself.

"What are you going to do with your pay?" Haz asked. The unit had gone to the town hall together to collect their first payment as soldiers, a nice stipend to make up for the winter months, with more promised next year. The seven of them clustered around each other in the corner of the throne room, reluctant to go back into the freezing cold. The midyas sitting at tables had marked their names on tablets and sent runners to get the promised coin from the vault, the seven stone thrones looming behind them. Other units stood in line, waiting to get theirs, jostling and teasing each other. Neta's coin purse was a little larger than theirs, but that was to be expected of officers.

"I'm getting myself a massage," Lueti cheered. "The type with hot stones."

"A regular massage, or are you going to a co-worker?" Itehua asked, waggling his eyebrows.

"Oh, shush. I don't like sex."

They all blinked at her.

"Uh, aren't you in the wrong line of work, then?" Yxe asked, turning red as always.

Lueti snorted. "Let me rephrase: I'm *good* at sex, and I do enjoy it. But it's not something I seek out or crave. Frankly, I don't understand how anyone can look at someone and think, 'Ah, yes, I'll put my genitals in their mouth.'"

Khana choked, also spotting Sava walking down the hall with Midya Chaku. Sava waved and she gave a little one back. Lueti raised a knowing eyebrow but didn't comment.

"I'm getting my wife a present with this," Xopil said proudly. "She's been wanting to make Ponti a new outfit."

"Save that for the Festival of Garmiva," Itehua advised.

"You give gifts for that?" Khana asked, jolted back into the conversation.

"Oh, yes. Big ones. Especially to people you're married to."

Haz shrugged. "Mimi, Baba, and I usually hand-make our presents. Cheaper that way." He held up his purse. "This is probably going straight to the inn."

Khana looked down at her purse. Her first instinct was to save it toward her continued travels; this alone was about half of what she'd need to comfortably move on. But… "How expensive are lutes?"

Haz gaped. "You play?"

"Lutes, lyres, most anything with a string."

"When were you going to tell us this?"

"I'm telling you now."

"Good ones are expensive," Yxe said. "Even my family has trouble getting the money for a lute that'll last more than a few years. When I did music lessons, it was with a hand-me-down."

"Oh, you play, too?" Haz bemoaned. "We could've had two bards in the inn this whole time?"

Yxe shrugged apologetically. "I'm only good at drums. And I'm horrible with a crowd. All those eyes make me choke."

"And I can't play if I can't pay," Khana sighed, tucking her purse away. It wasn't worth it.

"Khana!" Sava called. "A moment?"

"Ooooooh, you're in trou-ble..." Haz sang.

Face heating, Khana excused herself and joined him and Midya Chaku. "Sirs?"

Chaku huffed, his beard twitching with his breath. "Since you managed to get through basic training, you'll be transferred to one of my medic units so they can get you caught up."

It was like a bucket of cold water. Khana blinked. "Transferred?"

"Medic units get extra training in the healing arts and are held back during combat until needed," he said. "They also get a pay raise. Though why they get more money for *not* fighting is beyond me..."

Khana opened her mouth. Closed it. Looked back at the Poison Dart Frogs. Itehua must have said something insulting, because Lueti shoved his shoulder while Haz laughed. Neta was the only one facing Khana's direction, a knowing look in her eyes.

Your choice, they seemed to say.

Khana touched the little glass frog hanging from her neck. She turned back to Chaku, straightened her back, and said, "Thank you for the opportunity, midya, but I'd rather stay with my unit."

Chaku blinked. "Come again?"

Sava studied her intently but didn't say anything.

"Forgive me for saying so, midyas, but lot of people in this town don't like me," she admitted. "Outright hate me, in fact. And they don't like the rest of Unit Nine, either. Xopil was stabbed by his fellow soldiers the day we met. Haz was abused by another midya who keeps trying to torment him. And Neta's hated by her own family just because of her mother's origins. Most of your militia and people of your own company would love to see us ripped apart by night creatures. But we love and look after each other. I can't leave that. I can't leave them."

"That's not your choice," Chaku scolded. "It's mine, or the maversti's."

"Actually, no," Sava cut in. "If two units lay claim to a soldier, and the soldier is qualified for both, then it's the *soldier*'s choice. And Neta formally requested that Khana stay with her unit."

Neta did what? Khana thought, bewildered.

"Neta is a frog's brat who doesn't know anything about war or strategy," Chaku insisted.

"She knows enough to get one of the most neglected units to pass basic with flying colors," Sava said, a dangerous edge in his voice. "Despite their midya denying them the proper time to train and occupying them with busywork."

Chaku's face turned red. "Are you accusing me of neglecting my soldiers?"

"Officially? Not yet."

Khana looked between the two men staring each other down. Sava spoke again. "Witches can heal, yes. But they can also take down perfectly healthy, armed enemies with only a touch."

Chaku gave a heavy sigh and turned back to Khana. "Fine. You can stay with Unit Nine. But I'll not hear a word of complaint."

Khana beamed. "Thank you so much!"

Grumbling, Chaku walked away. Sava smiled, and Khana's stomach immediately turned to butterflies. "Thank you," she repeated. "You didn't have to do that."

"No, but Chaku deserved it," he said. "He's a selfish brat who only cares for his own pockets, rather than the needs of the army. If it were up to me, he and Bhayana would both be discharged, and I'd have you, Neta, and the rest in *my* company. But we're all archers, so…"

"That wouldn't be good," she said, thinking about how long it took her to handle a spear and axe. A projectile weapon like the bow and arrow? "I'd probably shoot you by accident."

"I'm good at dodging. Just ask some of the newer recruits." His smile faded, and he lowered his voice. "Are you sure about this? You don't have to stay. Plenty of people transfer. It's not a mark of shame."

"Did Neta really make that request?"

"Lots of serjis do that. The whole point of the unit is to learn to trust each other."

She looked down at the stone floor. Her hands shook, just a little. "I'm… not looking forward to fighting. But I feel happier and safer with my unit than I have in… in a very long time."

Sava swallowed and nodded. "All right then. Your choice."

They stood there, a little awkward, as Khana thought of something to say in response. She wanted to hug him, but he was technically her officer. In the end, she took his hand, giving herself a moment to feel the callouses on his skin, and said again, "Thank you," before rejoining the others.

Neta feigned ignorance. "What did the midya want?"

"I'm not transferring. I'm staying with you."

"Seriously?" Haz gasped.

"We're going to be in the middle of the fighting," Neta warned.

Khana's stomach twisted, but she nodded. "I know."

Then, because it was Neta and not Sava, she didn't hold back. She wrapped her arms around her neck and hugged her tight. "Thank you for fighting for me," she whispered.

Neta rested her big arms around her. "For my unit? Any time."

Chapter Thirty-Three

The snows went from heavy storms to sprinkles of white dust, melting before they hit the ground. What was already on the ground didn't melt away completely, but turned to muddy sludge from which green things began to grow. The air warmed enough that Khana could go out with a thinner cloak and got the news she dreaded to hear: the mountain pass had opened. Already scouts reported Reguallian troops moving in.

Which meant the new Ghuran militia was ordered to march.

Khana's armor felt ten times heavier as she put it on, and she took extra care making sure everything was tied to its proper place. Her weapons no longer felt foreign, but she still hated carrying them.

Haz met her in the dining room, also dressed for battle, along with Heimili and Amati.

"I've made you both some extra chuta," Heimili said, stuffing their bags full of the round loaves. "No mead or vodka; you need your wits about you. But there's plenty of tea in the kettle."

"And a medical kit," Amati added, seated on one of the cushions. "You might not need it, but I made one just in case."

"Thank you," Khana said gratefully, taking her bag.

"Now listen here both of you," she instructed. "It's going to be very boring outside of battle. Lots of free time. Time the other soldiers are probably going to fill with gambling. So don't bet more money than you have and come back broke."

Haz gave his gap-toothed grin. "Aw, Mimi, you have no faith in me, do you?"

"Not in your ability to count," Khana said, remembering how he miscounted his dice while gambling with Sava a few weeks ago, losing the game.

"Right then," Heimili declared. He straightened Haz's wool armor. "Right."

Haz set his bag back down and hugged him. "I'll be fine, Baba. Khana's keeping me out of trouble, remember?"

Heimili gripped him tight. "I remember."

Amati tugged Khana down to her level so she could tuck a stray lock of black hair behind her ear. "If any of the other soldiers mock you, then asks you to heal them, let them bleed out."

Khana shook her head, smiling. "I'm not going to do that, Amati."

"Then at least sic that scary serji on them."

"I will."

Heimili finally let go of Haz, then hugged Khana, who tensed at the sudden contact and was relieved when he let go. The two soldiers left with their packs loaded with tea and bread, shields and spears in hand.

"I hate this," Itehua grumbled, helping Khana set up a tent. It was two or three soldiers to each tent, made of animal pelts to keep out the cold. "The day before a fight is always the worst."

She hummed, focusing on the task at hand and tune in her throat. It was the only way she'd been able to maintain her sanity for the last week of mountain travel: focus on not falling into ravines, on setting up and taking down tents, on cooking the meals, on the music that the soldiers sang as they marched.

Don't focus on how her stomach dropped with every step she took.

Don't focus on her nightmares, growing more and more vivid every night.

Don't focus on the fact that her unit might not come back alive.

She tightened the tent's knot and let out a breath, watching the wind whisk the white smoke away. Around them, other units got their tents and fires started up and down the mountain ledge, glowing like lanterns as the sun set. A few firepits down, someone played a flute. Neta started a fire from the same charred animal bones they'd been using for the last week while Lueti and Haz readied their meal: dried rabbit meat and Heimili's chuta. Yxe read a book – the first Khana had seen in town – while Xopil sat apart, quietly praying, though she didn't know to which deity. She wished she believed in some sort of god; it seemed to calm him. But the only entity she believed in was Death and praying to them would do no good. They could only affect the world through trade.

She found that she wasn't nearly as afraid of the endless chasms and pits that dogged their steps as she used to be. She wasn't sure if it was because she'd already conquered them twice now, or because she was too terrified of what lay ahead to spend the energy. Because to the north, just over the farthest ridge, she could see another set of fires. The Reguallian imperial army.

They'd be fighting tomorrow.

"You ever fight in battle, serji?" Itehua asked, sitting at the fire.

Neta added a few more bones. "More skirmishes than battles. Tlaphar tried to bully our hunters a few years ago and it escalated."

"You ever shit your pants?"

Haz looked up, startled. "That's a real problem?"

Itehua nodded knowingly. Neta smirked. "I was given fair warning and ample time to relieve myself beforehand, so no."

"I was *not* given fair warning my first fight," Itehua grumbled, making Lueti laugh. "Even the bravest men lose control when they see the enemy lined up, and then they're good to go."

"Xopil?" Haz asked.

"We learned to wear brown or black trousers before fighting," he said.

A few birds landed in the snow nearby, chirping at each other, looking for food. Khana had no idea what type they were, but they were small enough that two could fit into the palm of her hand. Xopil crumpled up a bit of his chuta and tossed it to them, coaxing the little birds closer. To Khana's surprise, he got one to hop into his hand.

"You are not holding a wild bird," Haz said dumbly.

Xopil gave a careful, one-shouldered shrug. "I have a way with animals."

"You have witchcraft is what you have."

If Khana didn't feel so sick to her stomach, she'd have giggled. She managed a fleeting smile.

"Yxe, can we start those lessons?" Lueti asked.

The boy looked up and nodded vigorously. "Absolutely."

"Lessons?" Haz asked.

"Yxe's teaching me to read and keep records," Lueti explained. "I'm going to run my own brothel one day, and it's a lot easier to do that when you know your numbers and letters."

"Isn't paper almost impossible to get around here?" Khana asked.

"It is," Yxe said. "Most small business owners use knotted cords on belts to keep financial records, or chalk tablets, or bone."

"I didn't know you wanted to be a matron," Itehua said.

"I already have a few girls and boys willing to work for me. I just need the money and the building," Lueti replied. "Yxe?"

"Right." The boy sat next to her, pulling out a string of loose cords. "We'll start with the alphabet. Enough to get you to spell your name so you can sign things."

"I like it."

Khana edged closer so she could see the distinctive knots Yxe made. She'd seen some of this odd method of Ghuran record-keeping – Heimili used it to record the inn's profits. She didn't know that the knots could also be used to denote letters, that a cord could be tied in such a way that it could communicate an entire sentence, never mind a legally binding contract. Khana considered asking to join the tutoring when she heard snow crunch beneath a pair of boots.

She reached for her spear before recognizing the familiar silhouette. "Sava?"

"Khana," he greeted. He glanced at Neta, who stopped sharpening her knife. "May I borrow your soldier for a moment, serji?"

"Don't break her," Neta warned, giving her blade another lick of the whetstone.

"Wouldn't dream of it. Khana, if you please?"

Wondering if this was Sava her friend, or Sava her superior officer, Khana obeyed, following him just out of reach of the fire's light. His black hair and dark gray uniform blended into the darkness, making him a guardian spirit of the night. "Is everything all right?"

"Of course," he said. His face softened. "I just wanted to check on you. I thought, with you and the emperor..." He shifted. "I don't know. I wanted to make sure you were okay."

Khana couldn't stop the smile. "I'm... as well as can be expected, I suppose. As much as I would *like* to hide, I–" She looked back at her campsite. Itehua was sensibly going to bed, shaking a dozing Haz awake so he could do the same; Xopil fed the birds some more before following suit; Yxe and Lueti bent over their work, talking quietly, while Neta moved on from her knife to her spear. "I can't let them fight this alone. Or you."

She studied him critically. There were bags under his eyes. "You look almost as bad as I do."

He shrugged. "Just tired."

Khana frowned. "You don't have to pretend with me, Sava. You can't possibly be more scared than I am."

His broad shoulders slumped. "I'm a leader, Khana. I have to put on a brave face for my people."

"Not with me," she promised. "Besides, Itehua says soiling our pants is a real concern, so…"

He gave a strangled laugh. "Oh, yes, I found that out the hard way. My father hasn't let me live it down."

Her smile wasn't so hard to force. "You're allowed to be scared, Sava. I won't ask you to pretend. Just you being here helps."

He softened. "Thank you, Khana. I needed that."

He moved to hug her. Khana jolted and stepped back.

Sava dropped his arms, looking embarrassed.

Khana pinched the bridge of her nose. "Ack. I… Some days, *most* days, especially when the emperor is on my mind, I don't like to be touched. Even when I actually want to. It reminds me of… I just don't like being touched. It's not you, I swear."

"Ah," Sava said.

"I'm sorry, I know that it's important to Ghura. I see you people hug each other and slap each other's backs all the time, but I just can't…"

"Khana. Look at me."

She peeked up. Sava gave her a warm look. "It's all right. I don't understand it, but if you don't want me or anyone else touching you, then I won't."

She relaxed. "Sorry. Thank you."

"No apologies, but you're welcome. And" —he held up a finger— "if you ever need a hug from me, just ask. My arms are always open."

Khana's face heated. "I will. Thank you."

"Get some sleep." He smiled, nodded and left.

She still had nightmares that night, but they weren't as terrible.

Chapter Thirty-Four

The mountains weren't all narrow paths and sheer cliffs. There were plenty of valleys and sloped fields that the militia had used to set up their camps during their march, the lower ones still blanketed in snow that hadn't yet melted.

But if they fought the Reguallians in a wider space, the smaller Ghuran force would be slaughtered. Easily overcome by the hundreds of thousands of imperial troops swarming over the snowy rocks.

Instead, the Ghura set up their forces in a natural chokepoint: a skinny ravine that cut through the mountain walls like a knife, essentially a narrow canyon. Yxe muttered how an ancient river used to run through the mountains, before eventually drying up. The result was a path that looked a bit like a fat-bottomed vase – skinny at the top, wider on the bottom – but still too narrow for the Reguallian forces to use their numbers to any advantage. The militia could only stand seven soldiers abreast. Beyond the ravine, one of the rock walls dropped away entirely, creating a sheer cliff to a valley below. The other wall continued, offering cover and a height advantage for their archers.

Blue Battalion, all full-time, professional soldiers, made up the vanguard, taking up all the front row seats and scheduled to do most of the work in the fight. Red Battalion was right behind them, meaning Khana was faced with a thousand Ghuran backs. Red Frogs stood next to Red Panthers, Gorillas, and Snakes. She'd seen Bhayana near the front for a moment before the commander vanished in the sea of bodies.

"At least we'll get to play a proper round of the line game," Haz quipped, standing beside Khana. She pretended not to notice the way his spear trembled.

He was technically right. All the units were lined up to support each other, all their strength going to the very first unit, Chief Phramanka's. It would be exactly like the line game, but on a much greater scale.

For a fleeting moment, Khana wished she was up there with the chief, just to see the continuing rock wall that stretched over the deadly cliffs. Blue Owl – Sava's company – was hidden there, their wool and fur armor colored gray to blend in with the stone. She always felt a little braver when Sava was around.

Not brave enough to face down an invading army, though. For the thousandth time, she wondered what could have possibly possessed her to sign up for this.

Xopil muttered a prayer to one of the Ghuran gods: Mother Mountain herself.

"The scouts say over a hundred thousand soldiers are coming at us," Lueti admitted quietly. She looked as awful as Khana felt. Haz and Yxe, too.

"They're exaggerating," Itehua scoffed.

Khana shook her head. "They're not. Yamueto has millions of soldiers at his disposal."

He huffed. "I was trying to downplay it so she wouldn't shit herself."

"Their numbers mean nothing," Neta declared, adjusting the snow leopard cloak on her shoulders. "Pahuudans have used this exact spot to turn away armies a hundred times our size for centuries. Yxe can probably give a whole lecture on it."

He hiccupped. "In front of all these people? Do I have to?"

"Kid, you're about to fight a battle where you could die," Itehua said. "Don't tell me you're scared of public speaking."

There was a beat. Then Yxe said: "I'd rather be fighting that army by myself than addressing a crowd."

Itehua barked a laugh. It echoed in the ravine, making a few other soldiers look their way. Yxe blushed while Lueti shook her head and gave him a half-hug. "Well, at least you're only dealing with your second biggest fear today."

Their mirth died as the smaller stones at their feet shuddered. Several Ghura shouted in alarm. Haz snorted. "An earthquake? Now? Why not?"

"Mother Mountain, you bitch," Itehua growled.

"That's not the earth," Khana said quietly. "It's *them*. All those marching feet."

From somewhere upfront, Midya Chaku whistled. "Stay in position, you frogs! The mountain's not coming down, the imperials are just causing a racket. Stand firm."

Khana swallowed, watching the little stones tremble. It was hard to tell what was shaking more: them or herself.

Haz nudged her, catching her attention. He motioned to the Blue Battalion in front of them. "They're such proud snobs, they're probably not even going to let us do any fighting today. All we have to do is sit still and look pretty."

"Way ahead of you," Lueti said, flipping her gray-and-black braid, Yxe's little hiccup bringing some swagger back into her.

Khana managed a weak smile before noting a shadow pass over Haz's face. And another one.

She looked up, a few other Ghura having noticed. A flock of something flew over the top of their ravine, shadows flickering over the narrow crack. Birds?

But they weren't flying by. They circled. The glaring sunlight obscured their bellies in shadow, and the top of the ravine was almost too skinny for a man to crawl through, so Khana couldn't determine their species. But they were *big*. Eagles, maybe?

"Khana," Neta said coolly, "didn't you say night creatures couldn't fly?"

"Yamueto hadn't found a way to get them airborne before I left, no," she replied, dread filling her stomach.

"That was over a year ago."

Khana gulped as one of the things that was definitely *not* a bird flew down. The ravine was so narrow up top that it had to stop flying and squeeze its way through the rocks, claws scraping against stone directly over Red Battalion's head.

Soldiers swore and at least one screamed when they got a good look at the creature struggling to get to them. It was easily the size of a man, its arms melted into four membranous wings of a bat, ending in claws. The head resembled something closer to a dolphin or wolf, with a long, sleek snout full of sharp teeth. It shrieked at them, wiggling through the crevice.

Neta regained her senses first and threw her spear. It hit its mark, the metal head cutting through the creature's chest just as it got through, sending it crashing to the ground with an almost human-sounding scream.

A dozen more following behind, just as someone far ahead yelled, "Brace for impact!"

"Shields up!" Chaku ordered.

Red Battalion obeyed, shields over their heads, just as the first night creatures squeezed through and attacked.

Chapter Thirty-Five

Flying nightmares raked Khana's shield as shouts and grunts from Blue Battalion indicated the imperial forces had smashed into them. The back of Blue Battalion crowded her and the others as they were pushed back by imperials. The rear units of Red Battalion – far enough back that they hadn't even seen the nightmares come in – pushed them forward, effectively trapping the Poison Dart Frogs in the middle. A man screamed as he was plucked into the air by a night creature and torn to pieces by another, raining blood and entrails onto the soldiers below. Something wet and red smacked against Khana's helmet but she didn't dare look.

Soldiers threw spears and axes, some of them hitting the creatures, others missing. At least one soldier died of friendly fire. Blue Battalion was pushed back into the ravine, forcing Red Battalion further. The shuffle made Khana lose her footing, and she ended up on her back; a couple of soldiers stepped on her legs.

A flying nightmare landed on top of her, snapping at her face, its weight pressing her against the stone, shoving the other soldiers away. She dropped her spear. Only her shield protected her, and she screamed as it tried to punch through with its snout.

Then it gurgled, jerked, and stumbled away from her. Khana peeked over the rim of her shield to see Haz had stuck it with his spear. Yxe, on her other side, followed suit, stabbing with surprising force for his lanky build.

They were so focused on the night creature in front of them that they didn't notice the one flying toward them from above. As soon as Khana registered the threat, she jumped to her feet and pushed Haz aside, shield ready. The creature slammed into her, pushing her into Haz and Yxe. No matter. She breathed in.

The âji went straight into her lungs. The boys pushed her forward as the nightmare's thrashing attacks weakened. Khana drank its life in a matter of seconds before it twitched and died.

With life force in her, she felt much better. Stronger. Angrier.

"You all right?" Haz asked, shouting over the chaos.

Khana nodded. She noticed something had changed; there weren't as many people crowding them. "The Blues are advancing."

They were. No longer being pushed back, they now pushed *forward*. Sava's Blue Owl Company on top of the cliff must have started shooting the imperials, causing enough death and chaos in their ranks to distract and weaken them, allowing the foot soldiers to press the advantage.

It gave Red Battalion more room to fight. Neta called her name and pointed to a nightmare feasting on the corpse of a man against the rock wall. "Get more force! You'll need it! Poison Darts, we're helping her."

"How?" Xopil asked, brushing aside a few jostling soldiers.

"I need to get close enough to breath it in," Khana instructed. "Distract it. Pin it down, if you can. *Do not* kill it."

The unit marched off to their target, the nightmare oblivious in its feasting until Xopil stabbed it through the wing with his spear. It shrieked and snapped at him, its snout ramming into his shield. Neta found a new spear from somewhere and used it to poke its other side, making it bat a wing at her. Itehua taunted it from behind. Khana, hiding behind her shield, got as close as she could and breathed.

It took a little longer than the other because it wasn't on top of her, but she still managed to drain it. Her skin glowed with red, black, and yellow light.

Neta smirked. "Let's find another one."

They didn't have to go far. Most of the Ghura had grouped together into half a dozen herds with their shields over their heads, spears slashing, creating leather and metal porcupines that the nightmares tried to claw and bite their way into.

"Incoming!" Xopil warned as a nightmare swooped down from the wall.

Khana gritted her teeth and breathed in, focusing on the creature on the other side of her shield so she wouldn't accidentally take from her unit. It tried to fly away, but Xopil grabbed its leg and threw it to the ground like the behemoth he was. Khana finished it off, wondering if she had enough âji to do the same trick.

"Witch!" someone shouted. "Khana!"

They followed the call, finding a soldier standing over another with his head bashed in, but still alive. Khana immediately healed him by breathing out some life force, then got distracted by another nightmare trying to take a chunk out of her unit. Her supply was quickly replenished.

"I think I'm getting the hang of this," Lueti panted, poking her spear at their latest target. They were down to the last four or five night creatures. The winged monsters had killed a solid handful of people, but their own numbers hadn't been more than a couple dozen.

"Blue Battalion needs support!" Chaku shouted. "Let's clean up and get ready to go!"

Khana, distracted by the order, didn't notice the nightmare behind her.

Claws pierced her shoulders and pulled. The creature yanked her into the air, and she screamed as her feet dangled over the heads of the other soldiers. None of them were able to help her as it flew her up and out of the ravine.

Chapter Thirty-Six

The nightmare's claws sank into her armor, piercing the thick wool and drawing blood as it flew into the open air, over the heads of Blue Battalion and the imperial troops. Khana had no time to observe the raging battle as she tried to wiggle free, but only caused more damage to her shoulders which her excess âji had to heal.

She stopped, calling herself an idiot. She'd survived a much higher fall with magic.

She inhaled the nightmare's life force in a single gulp. It died mid-air, and gravity claimed them both. They plummeted to the ground.

Khana coughed. She pushed the creature's corpse off her and pulled herself to her knees. No bones broken. Even the scratches on her shoulders were healed. And she still had a lot of glow left. Somewhere along the way she'd lost her helmet.

The relief died quickly when she looked up and realized where, exactly, the nightmare had dropped her. Behind her, she could hear spears on shields as Blue Battalion clashed with imperial soldiers. But in front, she faced a sea of boiled leather and pointy Reguallian helmets.

"...hi?" she said.

They sprang into action. One man tried to gut her with his spear, but she blocked with her shield just in time. Pain bloomed in her side as the man behind her got her under her ribcage, setting a fire in her chest and pushing all the air out of her lungs in a pained gasp.

She gritted her teeth and forced a breath in, the longest draw she'd ever taken.

The three men closest to her dropped dead. Khana pulled the spear out of her side, letting it heal, and stood. A reckless swordsman came at her. She held up her shield and let him push her back toward the high mountain wall, where no one could sneak up on her. She breathed in, and he dropped to the ground.

That's how I survive this, she realized, backing up until the rock wall brushed against her armored shoulder. *Take the life force of anyone who attacks and make your way back to the Ghura.*

That plan immediately failed when the soldiers, wise to her tricks, resorted instead to throwing their spears at her. Luckily Ghuran shields were so big, and she was so tiny, that when she crouched and hid behind her wall of layered animal hide, almost every part of her was covered. Spears and knives clanged against the shield, a couple of metal tips poking through.

Khana hoped to wait them out; for them to disarm themselves fully and then attack. But all hopes were dashed when they picked up rocks and continued their assault. Their projectiles pounded against the shield. One of them grazed her temple, drawing blood before the wound healed. But the âji wouldn't last forever.

She desperately wished Neta was here. Or Sava. Haz. Anyone. They'd know what to do. They'd give her strength, bravery, a plan. She was just a scared girl.

The assault grew as more and more soldiers realized what was happening. More rocks dented her shield and bloodied the bits of her arms and legs she couldn't protect.

"Just keep throwing until she stops glowing!" one shouted. "We'll give her to the emperor as a prize!"

Rage, fear, and panic spiked through her at the thought.

The rage won.

With a blood-curdling scream, Khana charged the Reguallian soldiers, shield-first. Someone scored a hit on the back of her head with a rock, but she barely noticed the injury. She breathed in.

Bodies dropped like flies around her as she absorbed the âji of everyone she could get close to. Within minutes she'd cleared the area of soldiers who had seen her fall from the sky. Her next victims only knew that a witch had somehow gotten behind their lines, and they reacted by throwing spears. Khana once again ducked behind her shield and breathed in.

Her skin glowed brighter than she'd ever seen it. She was washed in vibrant red, yellow, black, and orange. Her blood vibrated. She could see the Ghuran soldiers behind her now, cutting down the Reguallians with axe and spear. From the mountain wall on her right, archers rained death from above. To the left, Ghuran units threw Reguallians over the sheer cliffs.

Where's the imperial witch? Khana wondered. Yamueto never sent an assault without at least one witch to heal and lead. So where were they?

An arrow slammed into the back of her shoulder, pushing out those thoughts and bringing her to her knees. With a sigh, Khana grabbed the bloody arrowhead and ripped it out. The enhanced necrotic strength made it as easy as plucking a flower. A very painful flower. The agony blinded her for a moment before the injury healed itself. She turned around.

Reguallian archers, who had previously been firing at the Ghuran archers on the rock wall, now aimed at her. With her skin glowing brighter than the moon on a clear night, she was the obvious target.

Imperial foot soldiers stayed away from her, their commanders holding them back until the archers took care of the problem. But she had no interest in punching further through their lines. She turned and ran to safety toward the Ghura.

The enemy was so close to the front lines they hadn't noticed her, too busy fighting to stay alive. She came up behind them and inhaled, hoping Sava and his archers wouldn't mistake her for a Reguallian. At least she could make things a little easier for Phramanka and the other Ghura before hiding behind them.

She lost count of the number of soldiers she killed, but she'd created a void of dead soldiers that the Blue Battalion surged to fill. Chief Phramanka slapped her on the back with a "Tend the wounded!" before disappearing into the fight, leaving Khana safely behind friendly lines again.

Khana quickly located some of the most injured and got to work. A man with a spear in his gut got back up and joined his comrades to fight. A woman with a bloodied head blinked up at her, poking at the spot where her brain had previously been visible. A woman who'd lost an arm… did not regrow the arm; that was impossible, as far as Khana knew. But she did stop the bleeding and ensure her survival.

The Ghura suddenly stopped advancing and cheered. Khana looked up and saw the Reguallians run over snowy rock, risking a slip off the cliff rather than onto a sword.

By now Khana was almost down to her own âji, her skin's glow barely visible in the sunlight. She was exhausted, like she'd run ten miles in a single afternoon. She skipped over a few minor injuries, ignoring their calls to heal broken arms or skinned knees, and found one with an arrow in his chest. She pulled it out, wincing at the very loud screaming directly in her ear, and healed it.

As soon as that extra âji was gone, every remaining thread of strength left. Nausea and dizziness took over, worse than when she was a child spinning around in circles watching the sky twirl until collapsing. She turned away from her patient and threw up her breakfast – well, what little she'd been able to eat that morning.

Boots appeared in her vision as she retched again. She spat and looked up, meeting the raised eyebrows of Chief Phramanka.

"You look like you had a bit of an adventure," she commented. "I thought we ordered Red Battalion to the back."

Khana looked down at herself. The chief was splattered with blood and gore, her spear covered in the stuff. It felt like Khana should be, too, but she wasn't. She'd killed, what, two dozen? Fifty? A hundred? But the only red on her armor was her own.

"Night creature got me," she murmured. "Plucked me up and dropped me out here. I got back as soon as I could."

"If you had lingered and punched a larger hole in their ranks, we'd have been done an hour sooner." Phramanka handed her a waterskin. Khana took it gratefully and savored a few mouthfuls, washing out her mouth and spitting. "But thank you for handling the wounded. Their families will be very grateful."

Khana nodded, taking a proper drink. "Why wasn't there a witch? Yamueto always sends one."

"Same reason he sent a fraction of what he could have," the chief explained. "He's testing our defenses. Seeing what tricks we have up our sleeve." She pointed to the distance, to a ridge behind the Reguallian lines. Khana had to squint, but she could just make out a tent and some human figures.

"I can't tell if it's smart or cowardly," Phramanka mused. "Staying all the way back there while your soldiers suffer and die. Eventually, they'll come down to play."

Khana held the waterskin in limp hands. "If Yamueto didn't know I was here before, he will now."

Phramanka nodded. "A perfect chance to get revenge, don't you think?"

"I don't want revenge," Khana said numbly. "I just want him to leave me alone."

The chief made a face. "Do you really think he'll do that?"

She looked at the field of snow and bodies, and knew it was only a fraction of what was to come. "No."

Chapter Thirty-Seven

"We thought you were dead," Haz said as they all finished their meal. The militia was back at the campsite, away from the body-filled battlefield. Each unit sat around a fire, filling up after a very eventful morning. "That nightmare just plucked you right up like a fish and pulled you away."

"That would've been a disappointing end," Itehua teased, his smile pulling at his pox scars. "Worst war story ever."

"Boys, shush," Lueti scolded. She patted Khana's shoulder. "We're just glad you're all right, darling. Eat up."

Khana had, surprisingly, already eaten one bowl of stew and was halfway through a second. The battle had famished her, but she hadn't noticed until now, sick with worry over what had happened to her unit.

Turned out, they were fine. Worried sick about *her*, but completely unharmed. Neta had even scolded her for getting surprised like that, and for losing her spear and helmet, which she'd pressed back into Khana's hands.

"Do you think we'll be pushing on?" Xopil asked, finishing his second bowl. "Kick the Reguallians out of the mountains?"

"We won't have to. Look." Neta pointed to some distant storm clouds. "That's coming right at us. The snow will bury anyone still here by the end of the week."

"I thought winter was done," Khana complained.

Neta laughed. "You're sweet. We get spring snows all the time, especially in the mountains. Summer is the only season where there's never any snow."

Haz snorted. "Here we were getting all worried that we'd have to do a lot of fighting, only to find out the weather does it for us."

"It does," Yxe chirped. "Most wars we've fought have ended by the enemy losing so many soldiers and supplies trying to cross these mountains."

Neta's prediction turned out to be true. Chief Phramanka made the announcement that they were to retreat back to Pahuuda. "Let those imperial brats fight Mother Mountain and Snowy Jadok if they're begging for another beating," she said to a round of cheers.

So, after only one battle, they gladly marched toward home. Some units sang war songs, others were more glum. The units who had lost soldiers carried their dead back, wrapping them in blankets with their weapons.

"Hey, witch!" a man called. He motioned to the dead body his unit carried. "Can't you do something about this?"

Khana winced, doing some quick calculations. Over two dozen dead. She'd have to lose two dozen pieces of herself – *significant* pieces – to bring them back, to say nothing of the life force needed to heal their fatal injuries. Her conscience would revive one, maybe two. How much would she get for her compassion? All of her memories? Would there be anything left by the time they were done? "I never learned how to raise the dead."

"Can't be that hard, can it?" the soldier called. "You just put that glow in them."

"No, that's how you get night creatures. If I tried to revive your friend in that way, they'd be a monster, with no memory or sense of self. No soul. Trust me, I tried."

The man caught up to her. "How much do you want?"

Khana blinked. "What?"

"How much do you want us to pay you to bring him back, death-bringer?" he asked, annoyance flavoring his tone.

"It's not a matter of money. That's the reality. A person cannot be revived with a simple transference of life force. I don't know what they need; I never got that training. No one does. I'm sorry."

The soldier sighed but didn't protest further. He lumbered off, re-joining his unit. Haz brushed his shoulder against Khana's and gave her a nod of silent support.

"We only lost a couple dozen soldiers," Neta commented. "The Reguallians lost almost a thousand, thanks to ill training, no magical healer, and no impressive commanders. Overall, this is probably one of the most successful battles in Ghuran history. Well done, Poison Darts."

"Ill training?" Lueti echoed.

Khana grimaced. "Most Reguallian soldiers are farm boys, or even slaves. Yamueto can rely on sheer numbers to overtake a battlefield now, rather than using his more elite fighters."

Lueti looked behind them as if she could see the bloody field they'd left behind. "Poor boys."

Neta pulled Khana away. "Here. We took trophies from the night creatures we killed. This is yours."

Khana took the tooth. It was pitch black, longer than her middle finger and just a little skinnier.

"I cleaned it for you," Neta continued. Her face twisted in annoyance. "Phramanka should have publicly lauded you. You took out more of those things than the rest of us, and healed what would have been the most fatal injuries. But…"

"Ire toward witches is still too strong?" Khana guessed.

"It's stupid. She worries more about her public image than doing the right thing."

She bumped Neta's shoulder. "Thank you, serji."

There was a little hole naturally formed in the base of the tooth. Khana used it to string the tooth onto her necklace, right next to her obsidian frog.

Everyone brightened considerably when they reached Pahuuda. Khana didn't think she'd ever be more relieved to see the snow-speckled stone houses. Scouts must have run ahead to tell everyone that the battle was successful, because a whole crowd waited for them, cheering and ready to embrace loved ones.

"Baba!" Haz called, dashing off to Heimili, who sat on the lip of one of the wells with Amati. Khana watched them hug with a smile that quickly slid off her face. Part of her yearned for that type of community – dare she even say, family – but the thought of being touched right now made her shudder.

Khana stayed apart from it all, watching everyone happily reunite but feeling unable to join them, even though she knew Heimili and Amati, at least, would be moderately happy to see her. Instead, she stood near a building, halfway in an alley.

"Are you all right?"

She jumped, so deep in her thoughts she hadn't heard Sava coming to stand next to her. The two weeks in the mountains had made his normally well-trimmed beard a bit scruffy, but she found she didn't mind.

"Just thinking," she said.

"Doesn't look like happy thoughts."

She grimaced. He wasn't going to let her sulk on her own. "This won't last," she said. "The empire will be back."

Sava leaned against the building. "Of course it will. We know that. They know it, too. But the way to win a war is to keep morale up. Celebrate the little victories. Remind everyone what they're fighting for."

She hummed in response. She didn't need any reminders. She was fighting for survival, or at least not to be dragged back to Yamueto.

Sava moved to nudge her arm, then visibly remembered what she'd said about touch. He moved just a tiny bit closer. "The first battle's always the roughest. You'll get used to it."

"Should you?" Khana asked, thinking of all the men she'd killed. Men who probably had families and villages just like this one.

He shrugged. "That's a question for the philosophers. We're a town of warriors."

"Here I thought there was at least one bard."

"Aspiring, not practicing." He gave a quick grin. "My archers are already singing your praises. We saw you on the field, tearing a hole through the other side like they were snowmen."

She looked away, face heating up. "I got lucky."

"Probably. But they feel a lot better with you fighting on our side."

"Yamueto has witches, too. Hundreds of them. With far more training than me. It's only a matter of time before they join the fight."

"I doubt he'll be able to send them all," Sava mused. "You know what happens to empires who stretch themselves too thin?"

She did. She'd spent a fair amount of time reading up on histories and talking about them with Princess Sita. Most of the historians blamed ancient civilizations' collapse on their barbaric ways or turning away from the gods, but most of them expanded beyond their means, taking more land than they could actually govern. In short order, usually after a plague or civil war or other disaster, it all came crumbling down.

"Besides, those witches are all used to fighting against mere mortals like myself," he continued. "I'll bet good money they haven't had to fight someone as powerful as them."

"Yamueto has," she said quietly. "He's fought and killed dozens."

Sava scooted closer. "We won't let that happen to you."

He said it so intently, dark eyes boring into her, that she almost believed him. She wanted to fall forward, bury herself in his chest, and let him handle all the darkness in the world for a little while so she could forget it existed and just... be.

She resisted the urge and pulled away. "I should... go take a bath. I can't imagine any of us smell good."

"The soap-makers are going to have a fantastic couple of days," he agreed, pushing off the wall. "I'll see you around, Khana."

Khana breathed out, unable to shake the feeling that she'd missed some sort of opportunity there.

Chapter Thirty-Eight

He kissed along her neck and collarbone, soft beard tickling her skin. She wrapped her legs around his waist, wanting him closer, wanting the clothes that separated them gone, not wanting his lips to leave her.

He came up and devoured her mouth, moving against her as he caressed her thighs, hips, breasts, every inch of her that he could reach. Her muscles felt weak, and she whimpered, wanting more, more, Sava…

Well, at least it wasn't a nightmare, Khana thought, replacing the blankets and furs that made up her bed. She'd never had a dream like *that* before. Not that she was complaining! It was the kind of thing that she thought only existed in songs and plays, one character flirting with another by saying, "I dreamed of you."

She was on laundry duty and carried the blankets downstairs to the back room, where she would wash them before hanging them outside to dry. Then she went back up the stairs to collect more blankets from other rooms, going up and down, up and down, not nearly as winded as she'd been when she first started working at the inn. She didn't know if Heimili or Neta were to thank for that.

The last room was Amati's. She hadn't been out of it recently, growing frailer by the day. Khana's bargains with Death had always had an expiration date, but she'd hoped to put the grandmother's passing off for a little while longer.

Amati's room was full of neatened clutter. Unspun wool and finished yarn poked out of boxes and baskets. A few shelves made from bone and stone hung from the walls, holding candles, decades-old sloppy clay bowls made from inexpert children's hands, old dolls, and other keepsakes from a family all grown up. There was even a short tapestry hanging from the wall, depicting Tsermayu and her dress of stars.

Amati sat upright in her bed, gnarled fingers sewing up a hole in Heimili's shirt. She moved slowly, pausing to squint at her work before making another stitch.

"Did you want me to change your bedding?" Khana asked.

Amati sighed, looking down at herself. "I suppose that would be the smart thing to do."

Khana fetched the fresh bedding first, making sure to grab a spare cushion. Then she helped Amati stand, take delicate steps to the cushion, and set her down before going about her actual task, humming as she did.

"You should be a bard," Amati said, cutting her off. "I swear, most of this town is deaf. Can barely carry a children's lullaby."

"I need an instrument for that," Khana replied sadly.

"That'd be easy to buy, if you charged for your magic."

"I'm not charging anyone for healing unless I must. It's just cruel." She paused, re-considering. "Unless they're Bhayana."

Amati held up her wrinkled hands, letting Khana stand her back up and bring her to bed. "People take advantage of those who let them. It's not cruelty to want something for yourself, even if you think you don't deserve it." Amati studied her. "*Especially* if you think you don't deserve it. You have the worst sense of self-worth out of everyone I've ever met."

"Sorry?" Khana asked, confused and embarrassed.

Amati waved her off. "I suppose time will be the best healer. Just don't let the Old Families use your healing anymore without charging them. *They* can afford it."

Khana nodded in agreement.

"Before you start on laundry, ask Heimili for a bit of money and go into town. My favorite soap-maker only comes once a year. If I'm to be trapped in this bed, it's going to be on the best-smelling blankets we can afford."

"Any specific scent?"

"Anything with flowers. I'm a terrible sucker for them. He charges me an arm and a leg. Don't tell him I'm dying, or he'll charge even more, the shameless bastard."

"Yes, Amati."

The soap-maker was easy to find. The marketplace had sprouted a half dozen brand new wagons from across the tundra since the first sign of spring. A couple of them specializing in weapons and metalwork were almost sold out already. Another carried tobacco leaf, coffee beans, spices, beer, mead, and ale. One sold jugs and barrels of wine, while another had fabrics: silks, laces, wools, and linens. Neta haggled with the trader of a wagon full of tea while a line stretched behind her. Khana had to squeeze through half a mob and wait in a very long queue before she got to the right one.

In line, everyone gossiped.

"Heard that night creatures have been hitting the Divaajinian ships all along the coast," someone reported. "Apparently the emperor's been playing with sharks, whales, and squids."

"I heard he's got an entire armada sailing for the capital."

"It takes a lot longer to get an armada."

"How do you know? You an armada expert?"

It *did* take longer to get an entire armada together, especially to a magnitude that Yamueto would need to first break through Divaajin's navy, then besiege their coastal cities, *then* push into the heartland. And he hated using ships because of the unpredictability of ocean storms. Not to mention Divaajin apparently had a reputation for an excellent navy, having built the kingdom on naval trade. Yamueto would want an overland army, and the only way to do that was through these mountains.

How long until he created flying night creatures big enough to carry troops?

Khana pushed the thoughts aside as she reached the front of the line.

"Ah, I see the tundra has a beautiful desert flower!" the trader cried when he saw her. "Come, come, my dear! Not every day I meet a lady of the Naatuun Desert, no, no!"

Khana giggled, a little flustered by the attention even though she knew that it was only to smooth her over for a sale. He was twice her age, and thankfully managed to make the compliments sound paternal rather than creepy. "I haven't been 'from the desert' in a long time. What floral soaps do you have?"

"The lady knows what she wants! I appreciate that. I have many. Roses, tulips, lavender, a whole garden! If you're hoping to catch the eyes and nose of a handsome gentleman, then may I recommend the lilies. That's how my wife caught me."

Khana's face heated, briefly wondering what Sava's favorite flower was. "Well, this is actually... for my grandmother. I'm sure you know we have a festival coming up."

"The Festival of Garmiva! Yes, the lovely summer goddess. A fine gift, a fine gift!"

"I already have a gift made for her," Khana said, and it was true. She'd spent the last several evenings sewing her presents after cleaning up the dinner rush. "But I have a little extra coin today, so I thought I might as well see if I could get her a second. Do you have red clover? I've heard that's good for breathing problems."

He pointed at her, grinning. "You're a medic, aren't you? Or a midwife?"

"Best in town," a familiar, deep voice said behind her.

Khana jumped, face heating when she saw Sava had come up behind her. "What are you doing here?"

"Getting away from Haz." He pointed over his shoulder, to one of the metalwork wagons. Its trader was a handsome man in his late twenties, perhaps early thirties, with red hair curling around his ears. Haz leaned against his wagon as the two talked, sly smiles and heat in their eyes.

Khana gaped. "Is he *flirting*?"

"*Actual* flirting," Sava confirmed. "Not teasing. And I'm not going to discourage that."

"Ah, I see Loy has found another bed companion," the soap-seller mused.

"Is he gentle with his companions?" Sava asked seriously.

"Very much so. I just hope your friend isn't looking for anything long-term."

Both Sava and Khana relaxed. Khana even grinned. "No, he is not. He just got out of a nasty relationship, so this is good. *Really* good. Oh, is that the red clover soap?"

"It is! Take a sniff." The trader held up a thick, milky white bar with flecks of dried clover in it. It smelled phenomenal, which meant, of course, the asking price was quite high. Khana managed to haggle him down a little bit further, but she still left the wagon with a much lighter coinpurse than before. Sava, too, as he purchased a small vial of sunflower lotion.

Haz caught her and Sava's eyes as they left and smirked before going back to his conversation.

"I'm happy for him," Khana said, downright giddy. This was an excellent sign of healing.

"Me, too. I haven't been this pleased since Neta and Athicha started courting."

"Oh, they're so cute together. Is it true she taught them sign language?"

"She taught both of us," Sava admitted. "I was shocked. She and I always got along fine, but before the ambush, she and Athicha *hated* each other."

Khana gaped. Whenever she saw Neta and Athicha together, they were always so comfortable and cozy. It was hard to picture them as anything other than adorable. "Was it because she's Reguallian?"

"It had more to do with her 'flaunting' her Old Family status despite very clearly not being welcomed in that family, so they got off on the wrong foot and it spiralled from there. Then the two of them lost half of their companies in the span of an hour, and Athicha lost their voice. They were bedridden for weeks. I was... not in a good place, either. I lost someone in that fight. And then also lost my best friend's voice?" He gave a fond smile. "Then suddenly Neta barges into my room, telling me she's done watching me sulk. She dragged me out by the collar all the way to Athicha's, who was just as surprised. Sat us both down and started going over the basic signs. We met almost every day for months, learning from her, and I think that is when Athicha's views on her started to change. They started teasing each other in a *good* way. Finally, I came in for one of our last lessons and found the two of them kissing against the wall, already half naked."

Khana laughed. The story reminded her a bit of Itehua, how he used to be so acerbic.

Sava shook his head. "Is that for the inn?"

She held up the bagged soap in her hand. "Oh. Not quite. It's for Amati."

Sava winced. "Ah. Haz told me she wasn't doing too well."

She shook her head. "I offered to help, but..."

"She's lived a long, happy life," Sava concluded. "This is, honestly, what we all hope to achieve."

Khana hadn't thought about it that way. She spent so long focusing on surviving the month – if not the day – that she didn't give much consideration to growing old. But she supposed that was the ultimate objective.

"Not Yamueto," she murmured.

"Well, I don't think any of us are looking up to him as an example."

"Master Pinnsviri is."

He grimaced. "All right, most *sensible* people aren't."

She hummed, then decided to change subjects again. "Sunflower lotion?"

He looked around conspiratorially, then lowered his voice: "Don't tell anyone, but it's a favorite of both my mother and father's."

"The *chief*?" Khana gasped. Phramanka had always seemed too scary to have something as human as delicate tastes. Thriman, too, though not as much.

"Mm-hm. And if those traders knew, they'd charge even more."

"I think this may blow your cover." She poked his soft wolf fur.

"They only visit for a week or so before leaving. They haven't quite figured out what an Old Family is or how to spot us. So, don't go telling."

"I am forever silent," Khana promised.

It was a lovely day, the air warm and the ground muddy, the snow almost completely gone. Sometimes she missed the tropical heat of Regualli, but she couldn't deny that the cool summer days were growing on her. Especially since it meant Sava wore short sleeves under his cloak, showing off his arms.

She thought about her dream. Her eyes went to his mouth as she wondered if his trim beard was soft or coarse. The thought of finding out sent a little thrill through her, washed with a sense of panic. The old, familiar fear of what would happen if they did get close…

Which was ridiculous. Sava was *nothing* like Yamueto, and she was furious with herself for even thinking such a thing. And yet, that fear was rooted in the core of her being, its tendrils wrapped around her spine.

"Khana?" Sava asked, jolting her into the present.

"Sorry," she said. "I got lost in thought. I… have far too much laundry waiting for me."

"And I have more shopping to do," he agreed with a secret little smile.

"All right." She braced herself, then went in for a quick hug. It was too fast for Sava to properly get his arms around her before she fled, calling, "See you later!" over her shoulder as she was certain her face caught fire.

She did not go to the inn. Instead, she went to one of the three local brothels in town.

Lueti was not among the (mostly young Reguallian) men and women, dressed in dusky pink and hanging against the walls of the skinny stone building, calling out to potential clients. Khana braced herself and approached one of the women, who smiled at her sweetly. "What type of fun are you looking for, little witch?"

"I'm sorry, I'm not here to pay for… service. I need to speak with Lueti. Is she busy?"

"Probably not. Hold on." The prostitute turned to go inside before being knocked aside when a man was thrown out the doorway, the moose fur door almost tearing off the frame.

"He *said* 'no gags'!" Lueti snarled, storming out of the building. "What part of that did you not understand?"

"Found her," the young prostitute snickered, leaning against the wall she'd been pushed against.

The man sat up from the ground, spitting out a mouthful of blood that ran down his nose. His pants were half-off, and he struggled to pull them up as everyone on the street stared at him. "I paid for pleasure. He owes it to me! And it's not as if I hurt him!"

"If you wanted to use a gag, we would've found someone happy to do that with you," Lueti snapped.

Khana silently stepped away from her. Not because she was afraid of Lueti, but to get behind the man now getting to his feet. Built thick like a soldier, he was probably a part of their militia.

"All right, fine, I won't do it again," he grumbled.

"I don't care. You're banned from this establishment."

"But I already paid him!"

"Don't care. Go."

"I want my money back!" he shouted, stepping forward.

Lueti got into a ready position, the same one Neta had spent hours teaching them. But it was unnecessary.

Khana touched the man's back and sucked in a breath. Âji flowed from him to her, making him stumble and her glow. Several onlookers gasped, one even screamed. She didn't care.

The man turned, almost falling back down. "You... you *witch*."

"Take one more step, and I take the last of your life," Khana promised him.

He stayed still, wide-eyed and fuming.

"Is your friend injured?" Khana asked Lueti, not taking her eyes off their enemy.

"No, darling. Just shaken."

"Are we bringing this to the chief?"

Lueti glanced into the building. Khana chanced a quick look, seeing the silhouette of a young man before glaring back at his attacker.

Lueti and the boy whispered before she said, "No. We just want him gone."

Khana shrugged and gave the man back his life force.

He jumped, scrambling away from her and the brothel. He hesitated, squaring his jaw. "I want my money back."

Lueti barked a laugh. "You're lucky you're getting your *life* back. If we see you again, we're breaking bones. I don't care how much you pay."

Still grumbling, the man left. Lueti whispered a few words to her friend before strolling up to Khana, beaming. "Thank you for the back-up."

"Of course. And sorry, I know you have to work. I can come back later...?"

"Oh, please." Lueti slipped her wiry arm through Khana's and walked her down the street. "At my age, I don't get nearly as many clients. Most of my time these days is spent training and... well, matchmaking, for lack of a better term. Matching the client's desires to the workers' so we don't have to deal with the mess you just helped me clean up. Anyway, you didn't come all the way over here to listen to me prattle. What's on your mind?"

"Uh, well..." Khana's face flushed. "I wanted to ask, since you're the expert, or at least the closest thing to it. What does it mean when you have a – an *explicit* dream about someone?"

Lueti raised her eyebrows. "That can mean any number of things. It could mean absolutely nothing. But in your case... This is the first time?"

She flushed. "Ever."

"Then it may perhaps be a sign of healing. Was it about someone specific?"

Khana looked down.

Lueti leaned closer. "Someone a bit *wolf-like*, perhaps?"

"Shush."

She cackled. "I tease because I love, darling."

"But that's part of the problem," Khana vented. "I was talking to him just before coming to you, and I wanted to... I thought about... but then I got scared. Like I always do. All I could do was hug him. And that's the first time I've even done *that* much."

Lueti gently took her hand. "You must be patient with yourself. This dream? It's a good sign, but only a single step. If you push yourself too hard, you could damage your mind and soul further."

Khana huffed with impatience, biting back tears. "I just want to be better *now*. What if he gets impatient?"

"Then kick him in the balls. It won't be a big loss."

"Lueti!"

"I'm serious! Would it be all right for *you* to push him into something he's not comfortable doing?"

She paused. "No."

"How about Haz? What if someone pressured him into bed before he was good and ready?"

Her vision went red at just the thought. "No!"

"Then there you go." Lueti squeezed her hand. "Give yourself the kindness of healing on your own terms. Everyone will be much happier for it."

Khana sighed but nodded in agreement.

"Now, in the meantime, there are ways that you can guage yourself," Lueti said. "Have you tried touching yourself between the legs?"

She said it so matter-of-factly. Khana's face heated. "Um... no. People do that?"

"Sometimes. It's a good way to figure out what you like or don't like in a safe environment. Try it, the next time you have one of these dreams. But again, don't push yourself too hard. Go at your own pace."

That wasn't the advice she had expected to hear, but she was grateful for it. "Thank you, Lueti. Stay safe, all right?"

The old woman's smile was a sharp, vicious thing. "Don't worry about me, darling. There are plenty of knives and teapots where I work."

Chapter Thirty-Nine

Despite the recent battle, the festival of the spring and summer goddess Garmiva went on as planned. Khana expected the inn to be packed all day and was all for hiding behind the stone walls. But to her surprise, Heimili closed the dining hall before noon.

"The festival is at the main center of town, and everyone brings something to the feast," he explained, stirring the massive pot of soup he'd been working on since dawn. "You and Haz will carry this there."

"Joy," she said.

It was not a joy. She and Haz each gripped one handle of the covered pot, which was easily the size of Heimili's round torso and several pounds heavier, and hauled it into town, Heimili and Amati joining them. The grandmother was, thankfully, strong enough.

Khana asked Heimili to hold onto the threadbare sack she kept her gifts in.

"What's in here?" he asked, poking at the knot she'd tied at the top.

"No peeking!" she scolded between breaths, grateful he had only filled the pot four fifths full. "Those are your presents."

"A new pair of arms?" Haz huffed, toddling behind her. He wore a short pair of antlers on his brow, which would look ridiculous if the rest of town weren't doing the same. The headband attached to the antlers brought some order to his messy black hair that now almost reached his shoulders.

When Khana had asked, he'd explained that they were a symbol of Garmiva, whose summer brought the herds back to their side of the tundra. Khana had politely declined the purchase of a pair for herself.

"You're both soldiers. How are you complaining this much?" Amati demanded. She carried the four big bowls that they'd use throughout the evening.

"It's a skill."

They finally reached the town square. The town hall was open, allowing people in and out. Most people stayed out, clustered around the dozens of mats and blankets on the ground that offered some protection for the food. They found a good spot for the soup between a tower of stacked chuta, a tray of seasoned river fish, and a roasted moose. Khana shook out her hands. The pot hadn't been as heavy as she'd feared, despite Haz's complaints, just big and awkward. Neta's strength training really was divine.

Haz now started poking at Khana's sack with his father, the two of them puppies pawing at a bag of treats. "Can we have our presents now?"

Khana sighed again, more good-natured this time. "Fine. Give it here."

She dug through it until she found what she was looking for. She hadn't wanted to spend any money, but she hadn't wanted to come empty-handed, and supplies for homemade gifts were limited. So, she'd eaten the cost and bought colorful wool cloth and thread, which she then used to sew thick ribbons that could be used for headbands, necklaces, bracelets, or decoration for weapons.

Amati squinted at the birds and flowers Khana had stitched onto her black ribbon, Heimili laughed at the horns of mead and cups of tea on his brown one, and Haz tied his orange ribbon to one of his antlers. The frogs for his – and the other Poison Darts – had been particularly difficult, but after doing nine frogs per ribbon, she'd gotten it down.

Amati tutted. "This is far too nice to wear. You should've gotten me something cheap that I wouldn't feel bad about spilling food on."

Khana recognized it for the oddly-colored praise it was. "Probably. You're welcome anyway."

The old woman carefully folded the ribbon and tucked it away in her pocket before handing out the bowls. "Heimili and I made the same mistake. You'll both find new furs in your rooms. They're moose, not those cheaper, sensible goat and yak pelts."

"Your whole hand will disappear when you touch it," Heimili added. "We might lose Khana completely."

"If it keeps me warm, don't fish me out. Thank you," she said, taking her empty bowl gratefully. She glanced around the festival as more and more people trickled into the square with crowns, headbands, and headdresses. A trio of musicians played flutes and drums nearby, their hats out to accept coins. Farther away she could hear a competing lute.

Haz all but dragged her across the food spread and she pulled him to the musicians, giving them what little coin she could spare as she clapped along with the rest of the crowd. She had every intention of giving her friends their gifts, staying for a few songs, and then disappearing into that new fur blanket back at the inn. Even when she was a child without a care in the world in the desert, she didn't do festivals.

The food, though, was excellent. Someone had made something called *panca*, which Haz explained was meat – usually goat – cooked for hours in an oven with herbs, spices, and vegetables. It looked half-burnt, but that crunchy exterior gave way to an explosion of flavor that had Khana moaning. Haz cackled. "Do you two need a minute alone?"

"Haz! Khana!"

Lueti ran up to join them, a dark pink sash wrapped around her skinny waist. Working tonight, of course. A crown of small, simple, carved-up antlers woven and tied together rested on her gray head. Even though the air was warmer than it had been since last fall, Khana was still amazed at how much skin the woman showed, baring her arms to the lick of spring, the wrinkles hidden by the sheer amount of muscle she'd earned over winter training. Khana herself couldn't leave the house without at least a wool sweater.

"Lueti!" Haz cheered. "Is the rest of the unit here?"

"Heading for the stage. Xopil's wife is competing, remember?"

"In what?" Khana asked.

"She's in group dance, I believe. Then it'll be solo dance, and then music," Lueti explained. "We should go. Come, come!"

She took their hands and pulled them deeper into the crowd. *I'll stay long enough to see Tlastisti and Sava perform,* Khana decided. She did have a present for Sava, after all. Although maybe she shouldn't have? They were friendly with each other, of course, but were they *friends*? She could barely have a conversation with the man before getting so nervous she fled.

They found Xopil holding his toddler, talking to Yxe, Itehua, and Neta. With Xopil's other hand, he scratched a goat behind the ears. Livestock frequently walked the streets of Pahuuda, tied to stakes while their owners visited businesses and homes. She seriously doubted the goat belonged to him, but it made happy bleating sounds as he petted it.

"Found them!" Lueti cheered. Haz immediately started making faces at the toddler, made even more ridiculous by the food spilling out of his mouth. Khana cooed at the goat; it was surprisingly cute, and perfectly docile in Xopil's hands. Like her, most of them went without antlers. Only Neta and Yxe indulged, and he'd squeezed his over his yellow wool cap. Hers was carved with outstanding details of leopards; Khana had a hazy memory of Athicha carving in front of the inn's fireplace, carefully sweeping their debris into the flames.

"Good. I can finally stop carrying these around," Itehua grumbled, pulling a handful of knives and, confusingly, a teapot out of the bag hanging from his shoulder. "I got you all weapons."

Lueti laughed when he gave her the teapot, which was sturdy enough that she could easily kill another would-be child-rapist. Khana handed out her ribbons, all of them different colors and stitched with frogs. To her relief, they all enjoyed them, especially Lueti, who got two: a pink one for work, and a light blue one for time off. She immediately braided the pink one into her antler crown.

From the pack on his back, Haz gave everyone an empty mead horn from the inn, polished to a shine. Neta had splurged on blocks of tea. One brick was enough to last a whole family a year, and from the looks of the others' faces it was an expensive type, too. She'd also gotten the wooden box to give to Athicha to carve. Yxe's gift was wool socks he'd made himself, Xopil's was sweet cornbread, and Lueti's was phallic-shaped stone sculptures that she assured with a wink could be "safely used."

Except for Khana. She didn't get any of Itehua's knives, or Neta's tea, or Haz's horns. Nothing.

She tried to swallow back her disappointment and confusion. Maybe she had been wrong. Maybe she wasn't actually a part of –

"Don't make that face, Khana," Itehua scolded. He nudged Yxe. "Give it to her."

"Give me what?" she asked, still confused.

Lueti's eyes brightened. "We decided to pool our money together to get you one big gift rather than a bunch of little ones. It was Haz's idea."

"Actually Sava's," he admitted as Yxe gave Khana something wrapped in thick wool. "Baba and Mimi pitched in, too."

Intrigued, Khana unwrapped the wool. Her hand froze when she brushed against the familiar strings of a lute.

"You didn't," she gasped, revealing the rest of the instrument. It was gorgeous, the wood painted a midnight black and trimmed with star-silver paint. Given the smell, it was brand new.

"Sava helped me find it. Even contributed to the pot," Yxe admitted, then added under his breath, "Significantly."

Khana couldn't wrap her head around that. Could barely comprehend the reality of holding a lute for the first time in over a year. Had it really been that long since she'd played music?

They'd given this to her. Given her the ability to make music again.

"Oh, please don't cry," Itehua pleaded. "I hate it when women cry."

"I'm not crying," she sobbed, wiping the tears from her face. "Thank you. This is… *thank you.*"

Haz hugged her, sideways so he wouldn't crush the precious instrument. Neta cleared her throat. "I hate to break the mood, but someone's making eyes at Lueti."

The old whore craned her neck. Khana had to peek around Haz to see an old man who lifted his horn of mead with a wink.

"Well, time to make up the money I spent spoiling you darlings," Lueti said, adjusting her outfit and new ribbon. She gathered her gifts, leaning over in a way that presented her bottom directly in her hopeful-client's eyesight, kissed Khana's cheek, and said, "See you around."

"Stay safe," Khana called after her.

"Come on," Haz urged. "Let's go watch Xopil's wife dominate the stage."

The sun disappearing on the horizon heralded the start of the competition. Torches were lit, giving the dancers a warm, eerie glow. Despite the others urging her to dance in the competition, or even test out the lute, Khana refused to get on that stage. Even the lure of a big bag of coins as prize money couldn't get her to join the line of hopeful performers. She'd performed before – private performances with Yamueto never ended well. But public performances for the entire court were always done in a group, where mistakes could be easily covered by those around her. And she was so out of practice.

Those were her excuses, and her friends didn't push. Instead, they watched the competitors perform, first the solo dancers, none of whom Khana knew, then the ensembles. Tlastisti did a rather impressive ribbon dance with a couple of friends. Not court-quality, but enough that she should've landed at least third place rather than fifth, an opinion that Khana grumbled into Haz's ear well into the music competition.

"They even landed a coordinated flag-spin and catch. Do you know how hard that is?" she whisper-ranted.

"No, but I'm sure you'll tell me," Haz muttered. "Oh, look, Sava's next."

Khana – embarrassingly – shut right up and focused on the stage, an elevated stone platform that Pahuuda sometimes used for major speeches. Sava stepped onto the stage to a round of cheers and applause, with his father, too. Thriman held a lute not unlike Khana's new one in his massive hands, and Sava wielded his bone flute. The father and son duo launched into a tune Khana didn't know but was familiar to the other townsfolk, since the crowd immediately began clapping along to the beat. Thriman also sang – very well, with a deep baritone – though Khana could barely pay attention to him. Her eyes were glued to Sava, the way his fingers darted across the flute that whistled like the sweetest songbird.

It was a travesty that they didn't get first place, instead placing second behind a trio of singers. Sava took it well, nodding with the judges' decision, clapping with the rest of the crowd, and even shaking hands and hugging each of the singers. Honestly, how could a man be so humble?

Haz nudged her arm, pulling her attention away. "Baba and Mimi are going home. The rest of us are getting more food, and there's usually some dancing going on, too. You coming?"

"In a minute. I need to thank Sava." She held up the lute. Haz nodded and left with the rest of the unit.

It took a long while to get to the chief's son. It seemed everyone in town wanted to talk to him about his performance or wish him a happy festival or share their life story. Khana eventually managed to wiggle her way through enough to catch his eye. He politely broke off his conversation with one of the judges and made his way to her, brightening as soon as he saw the lute. "You got it!"

The strap had kept the lute safely on her back since she'd received it, a comforting weight against her spine. "It's beautiful. Thank you. You certainly didn't have to…"

He shrugged. His short antlers were so carefully pinned to his dark hair that they looked to be sprouting right from his head. "I know. But you missed being able to play, and I'm always looking to throw money at the instrument makers around here."

"I have something for you, too," Khana said shyly, pulling the last ribbon out of her bag. It felt so insignificant compared to what he'd given her.

She'd considered a wolf design on the ribbon, but that felt trite, despite their symbolic importance. Arrows felt too simple and war-like for such a peaceful soul. So, she'd settled on music, food, and snow, which held their happiest moments – at least to her. Little blue and white musical notes were on the edges; she'd squinted at the sewn flute for hours to make the stitches look like an instrument rather than a rod, and a pair of snowmen danced in the middle with teacups in hand.

Sava laughed when he saw that. "That's adorable!"

She beamed. He carefully folded it up and put it away. She blinked. "You're not going to wear it?"

"It is *far* too nice for me to risk losing. I'll save it for special occasions." He smiled. "Thank you, Khana."

Around them, the crowd seemed to be gravitating back to the food, and Khana could hear more music emerging from down the street. "I thought Garmiva was the goddess of summer, not music."

"Eh. Bunakk is goddess of all things music and art. She's Garmiva's youngest child, so it makes sense for her to be present." He held out his arm. "Join me for a dance?"

I shouldn't. I should get to bed. We'll be marching back into the mountains any day now, is what Khana wanted to say. It was on the tip of her tongue.

But one look at Sava's earnest eyes, and she crumpled, admitting, "I don't know any Ghuran dances."

"They're easy," he promised. "And this isn't a royal court. Most people know even less about dancing than you do."

Khana looped her arm through his and let him lead her into the night.

Chapter Forty

The next morning, when Khana went down for breakfast, Amati wasn't there. "She's not feeling well," Heimili said grimly. "We'll let her rest."

That dampened the mood. Khana nursed some soup as Haz slumped next to her, yawning into his tea. She raised her eyebrows and poked a love-bite on his neck. "That's new."

"Hmm? Oh." He smirked. "The city traders are leaving tomorrow. I merely wished to give him a fond farewell."

Her heart lifted. "And we don't have to feed him to Neta? Or Sava? Or Lueti?"

He snorted. "You are far too protective of me, and no. It was a *really* fun night."

"I'm happy for you." She finished her meal and went about her chores. Lunch was slow, and afterwards she went upstairs to check on Amati, who yawned as Khana poked her head in the room. The old woman was a caterpillar, cocooned in furs and wool blankets, only Khana had no idea what she would turn into. "How's the dining room?" she rasped.

"Haz is cleaning up now. I just wanted to see how you were doing."

The old woman grunted. "If you a have moment, fetch your lute. I'd like to see what my money bought."

Khana was never going to turn down an opportunity to hold her new instrument. She ran to her room and came back, sitting next to Amati's bed. At her insistence, Khana tuned it and did a few warm-up scales, the first she'd done in over a year, then a couple of easier classical songs, letting herself get lost in it.

"Play *Raven-Headed Guide*," Amati said.

Khana paused. That was a Reguallian song usually played at funerals. It was about a soul being guided to the afterlife by Muobra, god of death, lamenting his fate but also celebrating the life he had led.

Khana cleared her throat and began, strumming the notes on her lute and quietly singing the lyrics:

"Would you give me a year,
or even just a day,
for all that I own in this world?
'No,' said he of raven's head.
'I have no need
Of jewels or land or gold.'
Would that I could see
My friends once again
And laugh at their jokes and their tales..."

The song came in multiple formats, many of them shorter for the sake of time. Khana went through every verse she knew. By the time she finished, her fingers felt fuzzy, and her throat was dry.

Amati smiled. "I always hated that song."

She was dead by nightfall.

Chapter Forty-One

The inn was flooded with well-wishers. Many of them, ironically, gave Heimili food rather than the other way around. The Poison Dart Frogs were there the entire time; Neta and Lueti rescued the family several times from over-bearing well-wishers who talked for too long. Sava and Athicha both made an appearance, giving Haz a big hug and staying by his side.

Khana watched mostly from the corner. This wasn't her loss, not really. Amati's death didn't deliver the pang in her chest that Guma and Sita's did. She spent the time watching Haz and Heimili and breathed easier throughout the day as she saw how fiercely everyone cared about them, not letting them be alone.

If only Yamueto was as accommodating. They got the orders to march out the next day.

Khana sat in the dark, shadowy spirit realm. Death approached, and after a beat, sat down across from her. Their multi-colored dress was darker than usual. Somber blues and grays.

"Where did she go?" Khana asked.

"I can't tell you," Death replied apologetically.

"Why not?"

"Because I don't know. There are thousands of different afterlives out there. Damnations, paradises, reincarnations, nothingness... it all depends on the person, and the universe and world in which they lived. I don't decide any of that. I simply take the souls to where they need to go."

Khana wrapped her arms around her middle. "Did she at least... go somewhere good?"

Death's pitch-black eyes were endlessly kind. "I have seen millions of souls like hers. They rarely wind up anywhere bad."

Khana tried to draw some comfort from that thought. "Is it wrong that I... don't miss her?"

"You barely knew her," Death pointed out. "In cases like this, it's not the dead that need to be mourned and looked after, but the living they leave behind."

That was what Khana mourned. Not Amati, though she was sad to see her go and was grateful for all she'd done. But the impact her death was having on Heimili and Haz. They had cried for hours.

Khana had offered to bring her back, but Haz shook his head, reminding her that Amati had expressly forbidden it. They'd burned the body, getting rid of any and all temptation.

"She should've been immortal. Not Yamueto," Khana muttered.

"That was not her choice," Death said. "You can't have life without me. I am the price you pay for your time in the physical world, and your relief from it."

Khana nodded. "I wished for you, back at the palace."

"I know," they said. "And now?"

She shook her head. "I'm not ready."

"Good."

Chapter Forty-Two

It was easier going into the mountains this time. The air was warmer, the ice almost completely gone. Khana gave in to temptation before lunch and pulled out her lute. After some brief tuning, her fingers played a familiar warm-up rhythm, one of the first she'd learned in court.

"Oh, thank the gods, you're actually good," Itehua cried. "I was so worried you wouldn't be."

"So little faith," Khana chided, still playing.

"If you don't play at the inn, Baba is going to be very disappointed," Haz warned. He was still glum with the death of his grandmother, but he carried on with the rest of them. It meant Heimili was left alone, but he'd booted both of them out with bags full of chuta and tea.

"I'm not a professional."

"You're telling me you've never played for an audience at that fancy Reguallian court?"

Khana squirmed. "That was different. Those were group performances. If I'm solo, everyone will know when I make a mistake."

Haz shrugged. "I'll sing along with you. That way you can just blame me."

"I didn't know you sang," she said.

"I don't. That's why it'll be easy for you to blame me."

They marched through the day, Khana fiddling with her lute. Itehua convinced her to play less classical songs, instead switching to melodies she'd heard in taverns, inns, and brothels, which he, Lueti, and Xopil sang to while Haz kept a clapping beat. A couple of other units joined them, one with a flute-player and another with a drum. Khana almost forgot that they were marching off to war.

They made camp for the night. Khana rested her buzzing fingers, wrapping them around a burning bowl of stew as she peered over Yxe's shoulder, Lueti sandwiching him from the other side for their reading lesson. The rest of the unit played dice, Itehua and Neta taking Haz and Xopil's money and trying to topple each other. Their campfires lit up the side of the gray, muddy mountain, and she'd say it looked like the stars if the *actual* stars weren't a hundred times more breathtaking. A few scouts from Blue Battalion made their way over, boots crunching through the thin layer of snow that stubbornly remained despite it being well into spring.

Khana could see the exact moment the scouts noticed her, veering off-course to approach the Poison Dart Frogs. "Heard you playing earlier," one of them said.

"It sounded good, I hope," she replied, not quite at ease. Despite fighting for the same cause, militarily supporting each other, and even grudgingly respecting each other, Blue and Red Battalions tended to stick to their own.

"Surprisingly good, for a frog," the other said. "We heard Sava gave it to you."

"He and my unit." She tipped her head to the others.

Haz raised his hand. "My family, too! Itehua, stop cheating."

"I'm not. You're just really bad at this," Itehua retorted.

"Uh-huh," one of the scouts said skeptically. "You know the chief will never let you have her son, right?"

Khana blinked. "What?"

"He's our pride and joy. And you're a frog bitch from the enemy empire."

"Ex*cuse* you?" Lueti demanded, pulling away from Yxe.

The scout's friend clasped a hand over his shoulder. "What he's *trying* to say," he said soothingly, "is you can't sleep your way to the top, even if you are a witch."

The unit around the campfire was dead silent.

Then half of them burst into laughter. Itehua rolled onto the muddy snow. Yxe went so red under his yellow wool hat Khana thought he would burst into flames.

"Leave," Neta said, her mouth twitching.

The scouts quickly followed her order. Itehua brushed the snow from his armor, still chuckling. "I love how twisted the rumors get sometimes."

"That's an actual rumor?" Khana squeaked.

"Oh, yes," Lueti said, brushing gray bangs from her face. "It exploded last week, after you two danced together."

"*What?*"

"It's just like how me and Tlastisti were when we were courting," Xopil sighed dreamily. "We always danced together at festivals and weddings. Everyone thought we were sleeping together long before we actually were."

"I can't blame the rumors," Haz added. "I was a little surprised he didn't come with you to the inn."

Neta lost her composure enough to gape. "Wait, he didn't?"

"I know!"

"Why would he go to the inn when he lives at his parents' estate?" Yxe asked.

All six of them stared at him.

Yxe turned even redder before he burst into snickers. "Sorry. I couldn't resist."

"You little shit!" Haz cried, throwing a handful of muddy snow at him. "I thought I'd seriously have to explain that to you!"

Khana hunched around her bowl of half-eaten stew that she suddenly didn't want to finish as Haz and Yxe got into a proper scuffle, Itehua and Xopil cheering them on.

Lueti scooted closer. "What's the matter?"

"I wanted to," Khana admitted. "I wanted to at least kiss him, but… Haz was able to find company for the night, but I couldn't do it. I'm not brave."

There had been a moment, at the end of the last dance, where she and Sava had been inches from each other. Her whole body had been humming, flush with music, and she'd thought of kissing him…

But she'd pulled back at the last moment and thanked him for the dance. He'd smiled back at her, but she couldn't help but sense that he was a little disappointed. She certainly had been, later following Lueti's advice on "self-care" in her bedroom and wishing it was Sava's fingers curled inside of her.

"Picking up a man is not brave. That's just a different response to trauma," Lueti stressed. "I've known hundreds of people who have gone through experiences like the two of you, and they all respond differently. Some swear off sex, romance, and anything remotely like it for the rest of their lives. Others fuck anything that moves. And then there's everything in between. None of them are more brave or cowardly than the others. Everyone has their own pace. Regardless of what they've been dreaming."

Khana huffed into her knees. "Probably for the best that mine is so slow. I don't even think he really likes me."

"Oh, he does," Lueti promised. "He's probably just waiting for you to take the first step."

"He's not shy. He's friends with everybody and practically a prince around here."

"Which is precisely why he's waiting for you," she pointed out. "He knows your history and is very aware of the power imbalance between the two of you. And with the drama surrounding Bhayana and Haz? Of course he's not going to push. He's probably scared to even show clearer signs of his interest in case you misinterpret them as an order to get into his bed. He wants to be sure that you're with him because that's what *you* want, which means he's not going to do anything until you do."

Khana pondered that. She *had* told Sava she didn't like to be touched, and he'd followed her desire to the letter since then.

"What if you're wrong?" she whispered.

"I rarely am in these matters," Lueti said. "Neta and Haz know him more personally, so you can ask them if you want. They're quite likely to agree with me."

Khana looked up. Haz had managed to pin Yxe in the snow, although given how hard he was breathing it hadn't been an easy victory. "I heard my name?"

Neta rolled her eyes. "Honestly, I'm a little more concerned about the war and that we may all die tomorrow than Khana's relationship drama."

"Thank you, serji, I'd almost forgotten," he sniped.

"I find this type of drama calming," Xopil said, a wide smile on his face. "Young love is precious. It's one of the things we're fighting for."

"I'm fighting for a bag of coin that I can spend on one of Lueti's trainees," Itehua retorted.

"You're going to need a much bigger bag," the whore deadpanned.

Yxe pulled his head out of the snow. "You can make him work security at your future brothel. Then he'll get a discount."

Itehua pointed at him. "That. I like the sound of that."

Khana chuckled. Everything Lueti had said swam in her mind, making her somehow both more afraid and more interested. Maybe she could make the first move.

Chapter Forty-Three

A horn blew, echoing off the mountain walls and rattling the thick cloth of Khana's tent. She jerked awake, pulled from an old nightmare and straight into a fresh one.

"Ambush!" Neta yelled. "Poison Darts, get your weapons!"

She, Khana, and Lueti scrambled over each other to grab their helmets and weapons and get out of the tent. Luckily everyone slept in their wool armor for warmth, so at least they weren't going into this unprotected. The sun hadn't yet risen, forcing everyone to rely on torches, starlight, and the dying embers of their campfires.

"Not good. We're not in a funnel," Yxe said beside her. He was right. They were in the open, having made camp in one of the mountain's many valleys. The Reguallians must have marched all night to get here.

"Don't we have scouts who are supposed to spot sneak attacks like this?" Haz demanded.

Khana gulped. "Night creatures probably got to them."

"Dammit."

Something whistled in the air, like a thousand dying birds. "Arrows!" Neta cried. "Shields up!"

Several nearby units obeyed, bringing their shields over their heads. Khana winced as the deadly tips smacked and scraped against the reinforced leather. One metal tip poked through right above her arm.

When the wave passed, Khana lowered her shield. A few dozen bodies littered the ground around them.

More horns blew. Orders were shouted and relayed: "They're coming at us from the north! Move!"

They ran to the mountain path leading into the valley. They had to trap the Reguallians there before they spilled into the valley and surrounded the Ghuran forces with their numbers. If the Ghura could bottle them up in a narrow space, they stood a much greater chance of winning.

A nightmare swooped down and snatched a soldier from the ground, ripping her apart with its talons. Another came down on the unit ahead of Khana but was killed by a spear throw. A third was much more successful, snatching a soldier and tossing it to another night creature to eat.

Red units mixed with Blue, but it didn't matter. They reached the lip of the ravine and locked shields with each other. Khana and her unit were back a few rows, so while she couldn't see the foot soldiers coming at them, she could see the shadowy men on top of the two rock walls that formed the narrow ravine. The archers.

How could they fend off the foot soldiers while night creatures and archers attacked from above?

"Target the archers and nightmares!" she heard Sava order. "Fire!"

The Blue Owls Company had lit their arrows on fire, creating streams of flame across the sky that briefly lit up the mountain wall. Half went to the archers while the other half went to various night creatures flying above. Four nightmares hit the ground, bodies burning. Others set Reguallian soldiers on fire. Some fell, screaming or silent all the way to the ground. Others crumpled right where they were, their burning bodies betraying the locations of their fellow archers.

"Shell formation!" Chief Phramanka ordered from somewhere up front.

Everyone behind the front line put their shields over the head of the person in front of them, protecting and being protected by their fellow soldiers. It was a defensive position, making it very difficult to move forward and attack. They were supposed to crouch while they did this, too, making it easier to cover each other. Khana, short as she was, barely ducked down, and only just managed to cover the head of the man in front of her – the serji from Red Frogs Six – as the Reguallian archers released another volley. An arrow pinged off her shield. To her left, a nightmare tried to smash into them, only succeeding in knocking a few Ghura down before it was speared to death.

An instant later, the Reguallian forces crashed into theirs. Or at least, Khana assumed it had, as they were all pushed back. Through the gaps in the shields over her head, Khana could see another volley of Sava's flaming arrows arcing over their heads to the mountain wall.

"Witch!" someone screamed from in front.

For a second, Khana thought they were calling for her. But then the first few rows of the Ghuran troops were shredded by a man glowing blindingly bright.

Chapter Forty-Four

Khana's mind screeched to a halt. *He's here.*

Neta screamed her name, but she couldn't hear it. The first few rows of Ghuran soldiers – at least twenty men and women – were shoved aside like grass to the wind, allowing Khana her first real look at their single attacker. The witch punched through a man's shield, breaking through leather and flesh alike.

He's here. Yamueto is here.

The witch's red-orange-yellow-black-green glow dimmed as he used his âji, and Khana could finally see his face.

It was not Yamueto.

Neta grabbed her by the shoulder and yanked. "Move!"

They all scrambled back in retreat. Haz joined Khana's other side. "Is that–"

"Not the emperor," she breathed. It wasn't Yamueto. She was safe. Well. Saf*er*.

"You have to fight him," Neta ordered. "You're the only one who can."

Fear swamped her again. "I've never fought a witch!"

"Neither has he! He's killing us, Khana! At least hold him off."

The witch grabbed the Red Frogs Six serji's shield and tossed it aside, ripping off the man's arm as he did so. The serji fell to the ground with a gasp.

Their eyes met.

Khana wasn't sure she'd be recognized with her helmet and armor. She was wrong. The witch blinked. "Khana? Shit, it *is* you!"

"Prince Antallo," she breathed, finally matching a name to the face. He wasn't in silk robes, instead wearing proper armor that made speartips and arrowheads ping off him with ease.

The Ghura kept away, shields turned toward him as if that would actually do anything. He didn't even glance at them.

Behind Antallo, Phramanka ordered soldiers to the front, to hold off the incoming footsoldiers. The other Reguallians hadn't reached them yet, but they were close. Antallo must have ordered them back so he could claim more Ghuran lives –more glory – for himself.

Arrogance had always been his biggest flaw.

Phramanka met Khana's eyes and gave her a meaningful look. *Handle that while I handle this.*

This wasn't Yamueto. It was Antallo. A witch, sure. And a threat. But not Yamueto.

Khana nodded and turned her attention back to her target just as his disbelieving face turned into a glare.

"You look ridiculous," he sneered. "A whore playing soldier?"

Her mouth twitched. "You should meet my unit."

He marched toward her. "You're coming with me."

Haz tried to intercept, holding up his spear and shield. "Fuck off."

Warmed though she was by the sentiment, Khana pushed past him, meeting Antallo in two steps, and breathed in.

Some of the excess âji that spilled out of his skin poured into her, and she could feel strength coursing through her. Antallo stuttered to a halt, too shocked that she had the audacity to steal from him, a crime punishable by night creature. He didn't block the spear she drove into his gut, tearing through his armor like it wasn't even there.

The blow forced Antallo back. Khana continued to breathe in his life force. *Don't let him heal, don't let him heal, don't let him –*

Someone shot an arrow in her eye.

The force – the pain – almost sent her to the ground. She staggered back, and with a grunt, grasped the shaft with both hands and yanked it out of her skull.

Her vision went white with pain, then a mix of orange and green as the âji healed the injury. The arrow had knocked the helmet off her head – gods, *again*. Neta was going to be furious. By some miracle, she kept her feet, and when her vision cleared – eyeball completely repaired – she was left in the middle of the field holding a bloodied arrow, barely a glow left to her skin.

Antallo copied her, yanking the spear from his chest. The glow immediately pooled into his belly to heal it, leaving only the rip in his metal armor. But he was surrounded by fresh sources of âji to replenish himself. He grinned, stepping back closer to the wall of Ghuran soldiers.

"No!" Khana cried, running for him.

He breathed in.

The two Ghura directly behind him dropped dead. Those further away swayed with dizziness. Khana ran harder. She had to stop him from –

A spear soared through the air and hit Antallo at the vulnerable base of his neck. He choked on blood.

"Good shot, serji!" Haz cheered.

"Nobody else fire!" Neta ordered. "You could hit a friendly!"

"So, let's get personal," Itehua said, stepping forward.

"Stay a spear's length from him!" Khana shouted, grabbing the end of Neta's spear and dragging Antallo sideways, spinning him away from the line of Ghuran defenders. She breathed in at the same time he did, the two of them fighting for magic, trying to leech off of each other. Khana felt herself get weaker and stronger at the same time.

"Bear-hunting tactics!" Neta ordered, scooping up a fallen spear.

"I never hunted bear!" Yxe cried.

"Get in quick enough for a jab, then run!"

Itehua darted forward and jabbed Antallo's leg with the tip of his spear, then scrambled back before he could pull life from him. "Fucker."

Xopil did the same, jabbing his other side and stepping back.

Haz did it next, then Lueti and Yxe. Everyone in the unit stabbed at Antallo with their spears, none of their wounds enough to be fatal, but certainly enough to distract and keep his âji from increasing his strength. The whole time, Khana continued to breathe in, draining him.

Antallo tried to pull the spear out of his neck, but Khana kept pushing it in. More and more life force went into her with every inhale. Blood poured from Antallo's mouth as his wide eyes sought Khana's. "Please," he gasped.

Khana drove the spear deeper into his neck. "No."

The emperor's son slouched and finally breathed his last.

Khana yanked the spear out before pain shattered through her back. She dropped to her knees, an arrowhead digging into her spine. "Again?!"

"Wall!" Neta ordered. The unit moved behind her, holding up their shields to create a protective wall between her and the archers. The serji knelt behind Khana, hand on the arrow. "Three, two–"

She yanked out the weapon. Khana groaned at her shredded flesh, watching the glow of her skin dim as the injury healed. Every movement hurt. Even breathing.

"We need to stop those archers," Neta said, pointing to the rock walls. "They're picking us apart down here."

"Isn't that Sava's job?" Itehua asked, grimacing as another arrow clanked against his shield.

"He's keeping them busy, but he's at a severe disadvantage. Especially with the nightmares." Neta eyed Khana. "Can you get up there?"

Khana looked at the glow of her hands. So much of what she could have drained from Antallo had disappeared into her wounds. "I've never tried jumping that far," she admitted. "I could maybe toss someone up there…"

"I'll do it," Xopil volunteered. "Just like jumping a slippery stream."

"No, it is not," Haz said.

Neta gripped Khana's shoulder. "But how's your aim?"

Khana peeked around her friends, at the mountain wall. If she didn't throw high enough, Xopil would crash face-first into the rock. Even if she *did* have perfect aim, there was a chance Xopil would get caught by a nightmare. Or be overwhelmed by sheer numbers.

"Not good enough for me to trust it," she admitted. "I'll go."

Alone. No unit, no friends to back her up.

The Reguallian archers fired again. Night creatures shrieked in the sky, picking up victims where they could. The Poison Dart Frogs continued to duck behind their shields, wincing as they saw more Ghura die.

"Then get up there," Neta ordered. "Drain as many as you can, then drop down behind the enemy lines and do what you did last time. We'll squeeze the Reguallians in the middle. Everyone, move forward."

They adjusted their position slightly to make a smaller shell formation: Khana, Yxe, and Lueti in front with shields protecting their chests; Haz, Neta, Itehua and Xopil behind with the shields raised above their heads. They speed-walked to the mountain wall, stepping over fallen bodies. A couple of other units had a similar idea and climbed up the wall, but the archers aimed straight down at their faces, and the nightmares picked off what they could.

Khana concentrated on her breathing. *You can do this. Witches have made similar jumps throughout history. You can do this.*

"Xopil, you'll be the launch pad," Neta said. "Itehua, watch his back. Khana, I'll count you off."

Xopil and Itehua got into position, giving her a good running start. Xopil held his shield up at an angle while Itehua protected his back.

"Are you ready?" Neta asked.

No.

"Yes," she squeaked.

Neta glared at her. "Are you ready?"

Khana cleared her throat and met her serji's gaze. It came out much stronger this time: "Yes."

Haz smacked her in the back and gave a gap-toothed grin. "Hop to it, froggy."

"That was awful."

Neta held up her fingers, redirecting everyone's attention. "Three."

Khana braced her legs.

"Two."

She took a deep breath.

"Go!"

Khana ran.

Chapter Forty-Five

Khana sprinted up to Xopil and jumped on his shield.

He lifted her up – she could feel it. But it didn't matter. The strength of her own legs launched her as if she was a human-sized grasshopper, cracking his shield in the process. She soared through the air, hundreds of feet high.

And it still wasn't high enough.

She smashed into the wall, sliding down the rock until she stopped at a ledge just wide enough to stand on. She dropped her spear to cling to the stone. Coughing up dust, Khana looked up.

All the archers stared down at her.

They aimed their bows.

She held up her shield just in time, cursing herself. She was too far down – ten to twenty feet, at least – to breathe in their âji. She could conceivably climb her way up, but that would leave her exposed the whole way. Since she had used all of her glow just to get here, that would spell her death. Gods, she was such an idiot for thinking she could do this.

I'll have to trade again, she thought. She opened her mouth to say the words…

Fire raced across her vision. Dozens of arrows arched over her head. Rather than going at various targets along both walls like they'd been doing since the battle began, all of them concentrated on the archers attacking Khana. The Reguallian archers stopped firing at her, some ducking for cover, some killed by fire and steel.

Thank you, Sava, Khana thought. She put her shield on her back and climbed.

Sava must have paced out his archers, holding half of them back, because a second volley of fire arched over her head much faster than his company's usual intervals. They all went to the same spot: the ledge

Khana was climbing toward. One arrow smacked into the wall by her ear, making her yelp. The fire flickered on the padded shaft.

Khana froze, realizing just how high up she was. How easy it would be for one of the Ghuran arrows to stray and hit her. She had no magic in her. If she got hit or fell, that was it. She was dead.

"Keep going, froggy!" Haz hollered.

The dumb nickname made her roll her eyes, the fear and adrenaline making her giddy. It got her limbs moving, and she resumed climbing.

Sava unleashed another volley, thankfully without hitting her. A nightmare swung close to her back but was shot down before it could reach her. By the time one of the Reguallian archers approached the ledge to look down at her, Khana was close enough to breathe him in.

The archer pulled back before she could kill him, but she had enough of that beautiful life force to finish the last three feet of the climb in a single jump.

Not her best idea, though. She managed to snatch the top of the rock wall with her fingertips, but there were no footholds. Gravity twisted its fingers around her as her feet scrambled for purchase. Panicked and desperate, she breathed in any life around her.

Light bloomed across her skin. Strength roared through her blood. Using nothing but her fingers, she launched herself up and over the edge, landing awkwardly on her side and rolling.

"Ha!" she cheered. She'd done it. She was up!

The archers were not nearly as happy. At least forty of them stood on this wall alone – three of them already dead at Khana's feet. Arrows notched and aimed right at her.

Khana turned at the last second, almost falling right back off the ledge as dozens of arrows hit the shield on her back. One grazed the side of her head, dragging a line of blood across her temple before disappearing into the night and battle below.

As they reached for their next volley, Khana turned and charged.

Though the front line tried to scramble back, they were too slow. Khana breathed in and watched their bodies drop like grass before a breeze. A few archers closer to the back managed to get a few shots in, some of them even hitting her. The pain made her pause and stagger, and she pulled out the arrows to conserve life force. But she glowed brighter than the moon, and within minutes, every archer on the rock wall was dead at her feet.

Khana smirked.

Then screamed again when another arrow hit her behind the knee.

The archers from the wall across the ravine had noticed her.

She dragged the arrow out of her leg, the agony pulling a punched whimper from her throat. She removed the shield from her back and hid behind it while she caught her breath, too raw to do anything else. The shield had been hit by so many arrows at this point that a few of the shafts managed to stay in the leather, making her look like a porcupine.

Ew. She never wanted to be compared to that animal.

She checked on the battle below. The entire ravine was filled with imperial soldiers, pushing and jostling each other. The front line at the lip of the ravine still contested fiercely; Khana didn't think it'd moved more than a few feet in either direction. There were so many corpses that the Ghura were using them to build a wall to further prevent the Reguallians from entering the valley. Sava had re-directed his archers to concentrate on the night creatures in the sky, and they were much more successful without counter attacks from Reguallian archers.

Her knee finally stopped throbbing. The armor Amati had so kindly given her was covered in holes and soaked in blood, all of it her own. That woman was going to throw a fit in whatever afterlife she'd ended up in.

The archers on the other wall fired another volley at her, trying to get behind or over her shield. *What if I just stayed here?* she wondered. She was drawing the enemy fire, which was what Neta wanted. And the thought of risking another hit, of getting so much as nicked by a blade, made her shudder.

One of the archers turned away from her and shot his arrow at the Ghura below. A second archer followed suit, and another.

I guess not.

She drew her axe from her belt, guaged the distance of the other wall against the glow of her skin, deemed it sufficient, and – as they reached for more arrows – jumped across the chasm.

This time her aim was much better, and she slammed right into an archer. Before he could pick himself off the ground, she'd pulled the life out of him.

One by one the archers fell, either to her magic or her axe. Many dropped their bows and ran. With her shield in front of her this time, she'd even managed to avoid being hit. Soon, the top of the wall was completely clear of life.

She glanced down at the Reguallian foot soldiers again. Many of them focused ahead, trying to push through to the valley, but some had noticed her, staring with wide-eyed fear.

It was... odd. Part of her sympathized; she had worn that very expression for six years in the Reguallian palace. She even wanted them to make it out alive, to just turn around and run away.

The other part relished their terror.

They're here to kill your friends, it said. *Kill them first.*

She dropped into the chasm.

The second her feet touched the ground, the soldiers slunk back. The ones who *could* run, did. Several others tried to rush past her and lost most – if not all – of their life force.

For a moment, she enjoyed it.

Then she heard someone order, "Drop the rocks!" followed by a rumbling.

The rock walls shook. The Reguallian soldiers screamed and pushed even more desperately. Something like thunder sounded from deep in the mountain path.

It's a trap, she realized, and ran.

The doomed Reguallians blocked the way on the ground, but no matter. Remembering Xopil's line game trick, she jumped onto one's shoulder and ran on top of the men, bouncing from shoulder to helmet to rock wall. Like a desperate, glowing frog.

By now she could make out exactly what the Reguallian men were screaming, crying, begging: "Let us out! Let us out!"

She flew over their heads until she was out. She dropped and landed hard behind the Ghuran line, her momentum rolling her forward until she was face-first in the dirt.

She cringed as the screams cut off; the bodies squished under the weight of hundreds of boulders. The Ghura scrambled back, clearing the site of the avalanche. Eventually, the rocks stopped coming, and there was nothing but dust in the air.

Chapter Forty-Six
Sava

Sava glared at Neta. "What were you thinking?"

Dawn had risen on the military camp as they tended to injuries and counted the dead. With the mountain pass blocked, Phramanka had ordered a retreat back to town. Amid all the pre-dawn packing and shuffling, Sava had pulled Neta to the blocked ravine for a private scolding.

"About?" she asked.

"Sending Khana up to fight those archers *alone*!" he hissed. "She was almost killed."

"Those archers were slaughtering us," Neta explained, infuriatingly calm. Her face, armor, and cloak were all covered in dust and blood. "We needed to get rid of them. Khana was our best bet, and she delivered."

"She almost didn't make it up there."

"Yes, we definitely miscalculated the jump," she admitted. "But she recovered, thanks to your help."

"You didn't even have an escape route."

"*None of us* had an escape route," she countered. "We were all ambushed. We *all* almost died. It is only because of Antallo's arrogance, his under-officers' panic, and Khana's witchcraft that we didn't."

Sava hissed, pacing the width of the ravine filled with blood and rocks. A hand stuck out from between two boulders that could've just as easily been Khana's. "Did you force her?"

Neta gave him an incredulous look. "You understand I'm her superior officer, right? You would've given the same order."

"No, I wouldn't have."

"Then you would've died," she said plainly. "We all would have. Good thing for you, Khana volunteered."

That made him pause. "What?"

"She doubted her ability to jump that far, so we considered having her throw one of us up there. But she didn't trust her aim. Probably for the best; I don't think anyone else would have survived the journey."

Given how much difficulty Khana had had getting up there, he couldn't help but agree. Few things had terrified him more than seeing her leap over everyone's heads to smash into the rock wall, and then seeing the enemy archers take aim at her. Once she'd disappeared over the edge, he'd kept an eye on the glow as it moved on top of the rock walls, and almost gotten scooped by a nightmare for it. (Athicha had shot it down just before it could reach him.)

He breathed out, trying to rid himself of the anger. It lingered, transforming into frustration, a sort of helpless rage that was all too familiar.

Neta studied him for a moment, then asked, "Midya Sava, may I speak plainly?"

"Have you not *been* speaking plainly?" he snapped. He hated that she was using his title.

"About Myrta."

He glared at her calm, intensely focused face. "Fine. What do you want to say?"

"Your trauma over her death is affecting your decisions, which is going to result in somebody dying. Quite possibly, us losing this war. Khana is a grown woman–"

"I know," he interrupted.

"Who knows what we are fighting against better than you, me, and everyone else in this town," she continued, barreling over his protest. "And yet, she still volunteered for this. And I have poured *months* into transforming her into as skilled a fighter as anyone else in this army – without relying on magic. The fact that you have so little faith in her and me is an insult to both of us. If you cannot get your head out of your ass, then you need to resign."

He snorted. "Myrta *also* volunteered. And look where that got her."

"If you could do it again, would you take away her choice?" Neta challenged. "Force her to stay? What if she said no? I'm sure Bhayana had several means of keeping *her* partner under control."

"Watch it, serji," he growled.

She held up her hands, silently acknowledging that that was a bit too far. "It was a battle. Plenty of other people were killed alongside Myrta. But she saved Athicha. Who, by the way, is also risking their life, same as me, by fighting in *this* battle. But you don't see either of us throwing a fit."

Sava didn't have an answer to that. Saying *it wasn't worth it* would just be cruel and wrong, especially since he knew that wasn't true.

Neta huffed, and in the growing light of day, she looked tired. She was a few years older than Sava, but in that moment, she carried the weight of centuries. "You seem to be under the assumption that I don't care about the people in my unit–"

"I never assumed that."

"Clearly you did," she snapped, finally letting some frustration crack through. "Clearly, some part of you believes that I would just throw one of the very few people I consider a true friend at the enemy without knowing *damn well* that she can handle herself. Even if she doesn't believe it. I understand that it feels terrible, watching someone you care about fight alone. That it's terrifying. But if you cannot handle that, then you need to remove yourself from this situation. Because it will happen again. There will be another battle where Khana is in danger, where witchcraft is the only solution, and we probably won't be able to help her. So, if you cannot do that, then you should resign. Immediately."

He chuckled darkly. "I am the chief's son. Do you have any idea how that will look?"

"Respectfully, Sava, we can win this war without you. We cannot win it without Khana. Today proved that."

…dammit.

Sava ran a hand over his face. In the cold light of day, he knew that Neta was right. They did need Khana. They needed her in the middle of the bloodshed and horror. But every fiber in his being rebelled against the thought.

Of all the times to realize he was falling in love.

He pulled himself together enough to say, "Thank you for your honesty, serji. You're dismissed."

She gave him a curt nod and left him alone with his thoughts, and his fears.

Chapter Forty-Seven

The march back to town was much more somber. Phramanka had ordered a retreat to regroup with the rest of the militia, now that they didn't know which mountain pass the Reguallians would be using. They also needed to tend to their dead and remaining wounded.

Out of habit, Khana went for her lute. But it wasn't the classical songs or bawdy tunes that had filled the air on their way up. Instead, she turned to the grieving melodies and lullabies that were far more familiar to her. No one told her to stop, so she didn't. Purging her grief this way gave her some relief, as it did several others she caught crying or quietly singing along.

The soldiers returned to Pahuuda with the similar reaction of adoring crowds, but it was muted. More bodies had to be carried to their families than last time.

But over the next few days, the mood gradually brightened. Khana could only marvel at their resilience as the funerals finished and life returned to normal. People shopped. Children played. The inn returned to its busy times. Khana was called to tend to the odd injury or illness, and to her surprise, people were more willing to pay her, even though she still didn't explicitly charge. A few coins, a meat pie, an old but good-quality dress. She even got some smiles.

A little over a week after the battle, Khana braced herself for the dinner rush. It was mid-afternoon and already customers trickled in. The Poison Darts had already claimed their corner.

"Hey, witch!" someone called. "Heard you playing the lute up the mountain. You doing that tonight?"

She didn't recognize the face, but he was probably a Red Frog.

Khana hesitated for a beat. But whether it was the warmth and safety of the inn or the bit of practice she'd had boosting her confidence, she found herself saying, "Let me get it from my room."

She left the dining hall to the sounds of her unit cheering. When she came back down the stairs, Heimili stopped her. He motioned to her instrument. "You play tonight, that's fine. But your tips come from that, not from the inn's pot."

She nodded in agreement. Then found herself standing in the middle of a crowded dining room, holding her lute, every eye on her.

The attention made her squirm. She cleared her throat and shyly asked, "Requests?"

"The Wolf Woman!" someone shouted.

Khana knew that one, but not well. It was usually sung in brothels. "I don't know the lyrics, so Lueti? Care to help?"

The old whore chugged her drink and joined Khana in the middle of the floor with a grin. The minute Khana struck her strings, the inn was filled with one of the filthiest songs she'd ever heard. She was fairly sure Lueti made up some of the lyrics, given the shocked laughter from the patrons. A few people threw coins at them, and Haz slid a bowl across the floor to help Khana collect them.

So it went. When Khana knew the lyrics to a requested song, she sang. But when she wasn't familiar, she snagged a member of her unit or a volunteering customer to be her voice, often paying for their next drink with the accumulating coin.

Eventually she took a brief break to rest, eat, and drink. Her fingers buzzed. Her whole body vibrated. The power and elation almost felt like drinking life force on a battlefield, but it was different. Purer.

Lueti, Itehua, and Yxe bent their heads together, talking about something. Haz was busy with customers. So in between bites of chuta, Khana sat by Xopil and Neta, who had been calmly watching the events of the evening, as she usually did, with a little smile on her face.

"I think you found your calling," the serji commented.

"It's certainly more fun than being shot at," Khana admitted. She hesitated to bring it up because she didn't want to spoil the evening. But she'd seen the way Neta's uncle had barely looked at her, even when returning from the battlefield. Not a "well done" or even a "how are you?" He had glanced at her, then turned away, like she didn't exist.

"How's... the family?" she said lamely.

"My mother's doing great. She's a seamstress, so you can imagine all the rags the soldiers have been giving her to fix up. She's been dancing around a friend of hers worse than you are with Sava, but maybe the festival ended that," she mused.

Khana and Xopil shared a brief look. The big man said plainly, "Your Cituva family are idiots. If I had a child like you – bastard, refugee, or otherwise – I'd be so proud I'd never stop talking about them."

Her smile was fleeting. "I know what you're both doing. Don't worry about it. I came to peace with the fact that most of my relatives will always see me as lesser long ago. And they're wrong. Anytime I find myself forgetting, I have my cloak to remind me. And Athicha. And now, I have my unit."

Xopil nudged her with his elbow. "Good."

"We still worry," Khana admitted.

Neta looked past her. "I'd worry a little more about yourself."

Khana followed her gaze and squeaked. Sava strode into the room, Athicha behind him, scanning the crowd until his eyes landed on her.

She found her voice. "Hello, Sava!"

"'Evening." He sat on Haz's abandoned cushion. Athicha sat with Neta, kissing her cheek. Sava cleared this throat. "Sorry we're late. We got some scout reports from the mountain."

Everyone leaned forward. "And?" Neta demanded.

"The Empire's split its forces. One group's going west, probably looking for the path there. The other has slaves and night creatures digging through the rubble. *Big* night creatures, too. They're guessing elephants and gorillas of some sort."

"Trying to make us divide our smaller force into even smaller chunks," Neta murmured.

"Exactly." His grin was crooked. "But the western trail is treacherous, even to natives. Yellow and Green Battalions will help Mother Mountain take care of them. Blue and Red will continue to go at the main force, and the other battalions are staying in the east to protect the coastal route to the capital."

Khana forced herself to finish her chuta. She couldn't let her stomach turn squeamish now.

"What about the rest of the kingdom?" Neta asked.

"Wreaking havoc on any ships Yamueto sends, from what I hear. Sneaking up on them in the night, stealing supplies, killing the crew, then disappearing. Guerrilla tactics."

Neta nodded in approval.

Sava shook himself. "But enough of that. I heard you playing."

Khana beamed. "I've been getting a lot of practice."

"Hey, witch!" someone called. "You still playing?"

"Yes, yes," she replied, finishing a swig of ale and getting to her feet.

Lueti caught her eye and glanced meaningfully at Sava. *He's waiting for you.*

Khana bit her lip, then held her hand out to the chief's son. "Do you mind?" she asked. "I've found it's a lot easier doing this with someone else."

He smiled warmly and took her hand. "I would be honored."

The next couple of hours passed in a blur of music, dance, and laughter. Unlike Khana, Sava knew how to properly work a crowd, dancing between groups of people while singing or playing his flute, nimbly stepping around drinks and plates. Khana and her unit could rouse a handful of drunken patrons into singing along, but Sava had the entire dining hall joining in with practically no effort. She would've been content hanging back, sticking to the strings, but he pulled her along with him, and she improvised her role in his dance. Everyone got sucked into his whirlpool, and Khana had every intention of drowning in it.

Eventually, as the sun set and the night drew on, customers began to leave. Fewer requests came, and Sava suggested slower, calmer songs to send them off. Haz, Heimili, and the rest of the staff started cleaning, making the motions of closing for the night. Xopil was the first Poison Dart to leave, as usual. Heimili and Haz piled him high with leftovers to bring to his family, and the big man gave Khana a hug on his way out. Yxe was next, slightly tipsy, with Lueti and Itehua making sure he got home safe. Neta and Athicha hugged Sava before they left, saying, "Get plenty of rest. We'll need it."

"Well done," Heimili told her as the last of the customers trickled out. "I know my mother was... stingy with her approval. But she would have loved to see that."

Khana smiled, pressing her hand against Heimili's thick arm. "Thank you. All of you."

By then, Sava was the only customer left. Khana counted the coins in her bowl, pleasantly surprised to see it almost full. Not bad. It was more than she usually made for tips, and she was fairly sure Sava was largely responsible.

"Here," she said, giving him half.

"Ha. No." He pushed them back into her hand. "My family's one of the richest in town. I do this for fun, not money."

She knew it was futile to argue with him, so she pocketed the coin and helped clean up. Quite a few cushions needed to be taken to the back room. Khana piled them into her arms one after another and was just realizing that she'd need to take two trips when Sava scooped up her burden. "I got it."

"Entertaining the crowd *and* cleaning up? Heimili should hire you," she teased, gathering the last of the cushions.

He shrugged. "I don't have anywhere else to be tonight."

He followed her through the back hall, to the laundry room. Khana dropped her burden on the floor and motioned to where Sava should drop his. She bit her lip. "Do you think we're going to win?" she asked quietly. "The war."

Sava crossed his arms and leaned against the stone wall. Outside of his armor, with just a blue wool shirt and trousers, it was the most casual she'd ever seen him. He didn't even have his wolf cloak. She mirrored his stance.

"I think we have a much better chance than any other kingdom," he answered. "The natural terrain is our biggest asset, and we've been a warrior people for centuries."

She hummed, looking down.

"Are you scared?" he asked.

"Every day," she admitted. "You're not?"

Sava's mouth quirked. "Terrified."

"You're much better at hiding it than me."

He shrugged. "Years of practice."

"Why become a soldier in the first place if you're so scared, instead of a bard?"

He blew out a breath, giving the question serious thought. "Lots of reasons. Sense of duty; this is my home, and I want to protect it. I can't do that with a flute. I'm a good archer. People like following me and I like taking care of them... and... I can't stay behind. That – I've done that before."

Khana made a small sound of encouragement. "Your last lover?"

Sava cleared his throat. "Myrta. She went to fight Tlaphar – her and Athicha and Neta. I... decided not to go. My father was sick – a high fever. We didn't know if he was going to make it. Myrta agreed with my decision, said to look after my family, and that she'd be back within a few days."

"She died," Khana finished.

He nodded. "One of the units got pinned down by Tlapharian archers. An arrow got Athicha in the neck..." He motioned across his throat, where the mute soldier's scar was. "The commanders were down, so Myrta and Neta took charge. Neta led a group of soldiers to distract the archers while Myrta's unit fetched Athicha and the other wounded. She helped carry them, slowing her down. They were almost to full cover when she was hit with an arrow through the chest."

She put a hand on his arm. "I'm sorry."

He cleared his throat. "Thank you, though it's no one's fault. I *know* that. I'd have done the exact same thing. But I can't sit back this time. Especially not when people I care about are out fighting, when *you* are jumping onto rock walls to fight a company of archers single-handedly. The dream of being a bard is just going to have to wait for safer times."

Khana swallowed. "What if we're never safe?"

He smiled. It wasn't sad or resigned, but bright and gentle in a way that made her stomach flip. "There are other dreams."

The silence stretched as Khana struggled to think of something to say.

Sava cleared his throat and stepped back. "I should let you get some sleep."

He walked past her to leave the room. Frustration and want mixed in Khana's stomach, finally potent enough to make her to reach out and catch him.

He blinked in surprise when she gripped his arm, pulling him away from the hall. Khana jumped on her toes before she could talk herself out of it and pressed her lips against his.

His beard scratched at her skin, giving way to soft lips that shifted and opened as soon as he got over his shock. Khana gripped the front of his shirt and pulled him closer. Gentle fingers carded through her hair at the nape of her neck.

Gravity pulled Khana back down, her toes cramped. She was ready to ignore it and go again when Sava gripped her waist and lifted her up. She wrapped her legs around him as he pressed her against the wall and, now at an even height, kissed her first.

This was so much better. Her hands explored his cheeks, hair, shoulders, while he nipped at her mouth and neck, his weight pressing her in place. She whimpered when he found a sensitive spot on her jaw just beneath her ear, awakening a near-feral hunger. He groaned when she scratched his scalp.

They stayed in the laundry room for gods knew how long, time blurring as they kissed and petted. Sava pulled back first, stopping Khana from chasing after his mouth with a hand to her cheek. "Wonderful as this is, we should probably move somewhere more private if we want to keep going," he panted.

Khana blinked. It took her squishy, suddenly slow mind a while to comprehend what "keep going" meant. When it did, the thread of panic that unfurled in her spine made her drop her face against his shoulder and groan. "Fuck."

"That doesn't sound like a good fuck," he commented.

"No," she grumbled. "I... argh! I want it. I want *you*. But I know if we 'keep going,' I'm going to panic or start thinking about Yamueto. I'm not – not ready. For that. I'm–"

"Don't you dare apologize," he scolded.

Khana bit her lip, keeping her face on his shoulder. Even when she was finally being brave, she was a coward.

Sava stepped away from the wall and set her gently on her feet, forcing her to look up at him. "If you're not ready, you're not ready. I have two perfectly good hands for that, and they've already had quite a bit of exercise since I met you. A little while longer won't be much of an issue."

"Sava!" she laughed.

"You look *really good* in armor," he said unapologetically. "Better with the lute."

She went back to hiding her face, muffling her laughs. Sava kissed the top of her head. "If you want me to leave, I'll leave," he whispered. "If you want me to stay and do nothing but sleep and cuddle, or more kissing, we'll do that."

He hesitated. Khana peeked up at him.

"And it's not just fucking," he said at length. "If you want to try some gentler bedsports – with you on top, or me – then I can do that, too. Whatever you want. I'm not picky."

Khana thought about that for a moment. She was fairly sure she knew what he was talking about. A couple of concubines had started sleeping with each other at the Reguallian palace. It had been the court's juiciest gossip for a few days, and Yamueto hadn't much cared because it wouldn't result in any pregnancies or problems for him.

She still got a tiny curl of unease in her gut, but not as intense as before.

"Can we start with cuddling and then see how I feel?" she asked.

He beamed. "That sounds like an excellent idea."

Chapter Forty-Eight

The fire in Khana's room had burned out, leaving it dark and chilly. She grumbled in annoyance as she re-lit the bones, Sava chuckling behind her. As light and heat returned, she became self-conscious. Her little bedroom was hardly the height of luxury. It didn't even have any furniture. She carefully set her lute in its case in the corner while Sava tugged off his boots.

"Oooh, moose pelt," he crooned, lying on top of it.

"Heimili and Amati gave it to me. For the festival," she explained. Her face heated as her words stumbled. Why hadn't they continued in the laundry room? This tension and awkwardness had grown as they walked up the stairs, and now it was unbearable.

She shivered. Even this close to the fire, the room was cold. Sava patted the spot next to him. "Come on. You'll feel warmer under the blanket."

She *had* promised cuddles.

She scrambled under the pelt. The two of them hid from the cold under the thick blanket, and with another body in her bed, it got a lot warmer a lot quicker. She was much less hesitant to cuddle up to his chest when he put an arm around her, not caging her, just resting against her back and hip.

Then he started humming. She couldn't quite place the tune, though she was fairly certain it was a love song. She could feel the reverberations through his chest, and it both comforted and thrilled her.

When there was a break in the tune, Khana mumbled, "I think I should warn you that I've never done this before. Not unless you count…"

Sava shrugged. "We all start somewhere. The first time I bedded a girl I was terrified. I wanted it. Badly. But I didn't want to disappoint her and ended up putting far too much pressure on myself. Luckily, she had a better idea of what she was doing. Still made an awkward mess of myself."

Khana smiled, amused by the thought. She couldn't help but tease, "Is talking about the other women you've bedded usually part of your seduction?"

"Well, you're here, aren't you?"

She flicked his bearded chin, his chuckle rumbling through his chest. His gaze was unbearably soft. "Do me a favor?"

"Hm?"

"Help me undo this?" He lifted his braid. "It's gotten rather tight."

Her hands twitched, eager to get into his hair. "Of course. Roll over."

They maneuvered themselves so Sava was on his stomach and Khana on top of him. The room had warmed, but was still chilly, so she kept the blanket over her shoulders like a cape as she carefully undid the braid, being sure not to tug or pull. His hair was soft as silk, a black river in her hands, and about halfway through she realized that she was touching him. Intimately. Willingly.

No panic.

She ran her fingers through his hair, the first few times to make sure there were no tangles, then again for the sheer, quiet joy of it. He hummed contently. Feeling bold, she started scratching his scalp. He stiffened.

She froze. "Sorry. Did I hurt you?"

"No," he laughed. "You've found my weakness. You should stop if you don't want to move beyond cuddling."

Khana considered. That thread of unease was back – had never truly left. But it was easier to tamp it down as heat pooled in her body. Stopping suddenly seemed like a very unattractive choice.

She put both hands in his hair and scratched.

Sava dropped his forehead onto his arms with a groan. She didn't gouge, but she was firm as she explored and experimented. Scratching particularly hard made him moan. Taking a fistful of hair and carefully tugging made him whimper. And scraping a fingernail or kissing the back of his neck made him gasp.

The more she uncovered, the more she wanted. Her voice was breathless when she ordered, "Turn over."

She had to go up on her knees to let him do it without throwing her off. His face was flushed, his pupils the size of grapes. She straddled and kissed him, and he was hungry for it. Licking into her mouth while his arms enveloped her, his hands branding her skin as they moved along her back and sides, though always staying above her dress. She was grateful for it, especially when she felt his bulge through his trousers. His patience kept that constant, annoying unease from blowing up into panic. She could almost ignore it as delicious heat pooled in her belly, her underclothes getting damp.

Sava gentled the kisses, bringing a hand from her waist to curl around her cheek and ear, lightly pushing her away. Not far. They still shared air.

"What do you want?" he whispered.

"Uh... I don't know," she admitted. "It is *very* cruel of you to make me try to think right now."

He grinned, sharp and wolf-like.

"What do *you* want?" she asked.

"Anything."

"That is not helpful."

He gave her a little peck. "At the moment, I'd like to know what you taste like."

Khana's brow furrowed. "Don't you already?"

Sava gave her a patient look and dragged his hand up her thigh, just under the hem of her dress, his thumb dangerously close to...

She blinked. "Really?"

"Only if you want to."

That sounded very odd. She'd heard of people being "good with their tongue" before but had always figured it meant...

She couldn't deny that she was intrigued.

Seizing that thought before it fled, she sat up and removed her dress, her skin prickling in the slight chill now that she was only in her breastband and underclothes. Sava reverently touched her waist before sitting up, gripping her so she wouldn't lose balance, and kissed her again.

She'd thought his touch had been branding before. That was nothing compared to skin on skin. He grazed his knuckles down her spine, sending a shiver through her. A hand on her thigh helped stabilize her, and it was all she could think about even as Sava nibbled on her lip. Another hand massaged her breast, and suddenly her breastband became the most hated piece of clothing in existence.

He turned them both over, pressing Khana's back against the furs, and dove in to suck on that spot on her jaw just beneath her ear. She whimpered, clutching his back and feeling slightly ridiculous for it; they hadn't even gotten to the good part yet.

Being on her back was quite a bit more familiar than being on top, but that was the only similarity tonight had with her past. She had never been treated with such care and reverence, as if every inch of her was a precious new gem to explore. Sava slowly went from her jaw to her neck, kissing her skin and dragging his coarse beard as she whined at the new sensation. He nibbled at her collarbone, following it to her sternum and then down. She stopped him just long enough to remove her breastband, almost tearing the fabric.

His mouth on her nipple was a revelation. She dropped her head back against the blankets, giving herself over to the sensation of his tongue and gentle teeth. She almost didn't notice his fingers trailing up her inner thigh until they reached her underclothes.

She gasped. Sava's fingers pressed against her mound through the thin layer of cloth, sliding up and down, up and down. He gave her nipple one last kiss before raising himself on his other arm, studying her face as he kept stroking her.

She grabbed a fistful of his shirt (*why* was he still wearing clothes?) and dragged him in for another, proper kiss. Those strokes against her most intimate part, even through clothing, wound her up tighter and tighter. He slowed down, breaking away from her mouth to chuckle, "Relax."

She did her best, but that was nearly impossible. Especially when he shifted his hand so that his thumb was right over her nub, moving in a circle as he kissed down her sternum, licking at her other nipple.

Khana took a fistful of inky hair, right by the scalp, and gripped it tight. Sava growled into her skin, hand stumbling in its rhythm. "You're impatient."

"Mm-*hm*," she managed.

He removed his hand, which was not what she'd been aiming for. But she couldn't complain as he slowly slid down her body, showering her stomach with kisses and licking into her bellybutton before going even lower.

She spread her legs wider, giving him room as he settled between them and tugged at her underclothing with his teeth. His hot breath against her inner thighs was the most erotic thing she'd ever felt, and she yearned for more.

He licked her through the fabric, and she had to strangle a moan before it escaped. None of the rooms of this inn had proper doors, only animal skins or wool blankets. If she wasn't careful, *everyone* would hear her.

Sava continued to mouth at her through her underclothes, his tongue and lips teasing her. He finally removed her soaked underclothes – properly and quickly, with his hands – leaving her completely bare beneath him. He settled back between her legs, spreading them just a little wider, and finally slipped his tongue between her folds.

The moan was torn from Khana's chest, muffled only by her own hand. He licked his way inside of her, thrusting his tongue in and out like tasting the inside of a jar of honey.

He pulled away, breath teasing her as he growled, "Delicious," and slipped two fingers inside of her. The way he rubbed the inside of her had her seeing stars, and then he sealed his lips over her nub.

She gripped the blankets in a death grip with her free hand, rocking her hips between Sava's fingers and his tongue. She tangled her hand in his hair as he licked and sucked at her most sensitive parts, fingers thrusting in and out. Liquid heat pooled at the base of her spine, and she found herself stammering, "Don't stop, don't stop, *please* don't stop, oh – OH!"

She tipped over into her climax, crashing into it, and all the while Sava kept stroking and suckling, the pleasure heightening with each beat until it snapped, became too much, and she sloppily pushed him away.

Sava slipped his fingers out and kissed down her thigh, letting her catch her breath and recover. His touches remained soft, undemanding as her body slowly returned from liquid to solid. Everything was soft and hazy yet oversensitive.

When she could finally move, she tugged him back up to kiss him, tasting her own slick on his beard and mouth. Again, he was gentle, even as his restrained bulge brushed against her hip bone.

She flipped them over, Sava giving an *oof* of surprise before she grinned. "Your turn."

Chapter Forty-Nine

Khana gasped awake, sweat coating her skin as she jerked upright. For a moment, all she saw were the wooden walls of the palace, the curtains over Yamueto's bed and the silk sheets–

"Khana? Wha – oh."

Silk sheets. No, she was on furs. And she'd never woken up next to Yamueto; he'd always sent her away when he was done with her.

Sava carefully sat up, not touching her. She had warned him this could happen, muttering about nightmares as they'd drifted off to sleep. He didn't touch, but crouched in front of her, filling her vision. "Breathe," he instructed. "You're not back there. You're in Pahuuda."

Khana sucked in a breath, twisting her hands in the moose fur pelt. Sava got up and added more animal bones to the fire, and she wished she could admire his naked form instead of being swamped by cold sweat and fear.

The night had been going so *well*. Khana had gone to sleep happy and sated and *safe*. Until Yamueto reared his ugly head in her dreams once again. He'd caught one of his other concubines in a relationship with a noble at court – a male noble. Someone who could upend Yamueto's carefully crafted family tree of influence and power. Both had been publicly tortured and transformed into night creatures.

By the time the fire was healthy and hot, Khana had her breathing under control, and she wiped her eyes. Sava glanced back at her, awkward as a horse. "What do you need?"

She gave that a good moment of thought. Eventually, she decided that she wasn't going to let the emperor spoil her night anymore and patted the furs next to her. "Come back to bed?"

Sava slipped in next to her, and she adjusted them so his head was in her lap and she could play with his hair. It was quickly becoming her favorite pastime.

Sava leaned into her touch with a sigh. "Do you want to talk about it?"

"No," she growled. "He doesn't get to intrude on this anymore."

"All right," he said easily. "A little to the left."

She adjusted her fingers, scratching the preferred spot. He made a happy little noise, somewhere between a purr and a moan.

"You're a giant puppy," she stated.

"Mm-hm."

She surprised herself once again that night, going back to sleep after a nightmare, Sava's inky hair twined in her fingers.

Khana drank tea in the kitchen, watching the growing sunlight paint the stone walls pale white, then gold. Despite the nightmare intruding on her sleep, she felt surprisingly well-rested and content. She smirked as she sipped. *Take* that, *Yamueto.*

She'd left Sava in her room. He'd grumbled when she'd accidentally woken him as she wiggled out of bed and kissed him on the temple with a "stay as long as you like, but I need to get ready for work."

Now, he stumbled into the kitchen, yawning, hair mussed up and frizzy around his shoulders. He hovered over her for a second and, as soon as she nodded, slid right behind her, propping his chin on her head, wrapping his arm around her belly, and leaning like she was his favorite piece of furniture.

"Good morning," she greeted, smiling into her cup and leaning into him.

"Hmm."

"Not a morning person, are you?"

"Mm."

She chuckled, but eventually her amusement faded into something more serious. "We should probably talk."

"Mm?"

"Do we... should you... I don't want you to have to slog through any nasty rumors."

Sava snorted and hugged her tighter. "They're already whispering. At least this way I get to say, 'Yes, I *am* sleeping with that terrifying, adorable woman, so you can all shut your jealous mouths.'"

"Aren't you technically my commanding officer? They might think you're ordering me around." She wrinkled her nose. "Assuming they haven't met you."

He kissed her temple. "No officers can order their subordinates in a civilian setting. Furthermore, officers cannot order any soldiers outside of their unit, company, or battalion unless it's the heat of battle or they have permission from said soldiers' commanding officer of equal or higher rank. So, if I wanted to boss you around, I'd have to ask Chaku."

"Might want to ask Neta, too," she offered.

"*You* ask her. She scares me. I tried yelling at her for sending you to fight the archers and it did *not* end well."

Khana laughed.

Sava adjusted his arms around her and buried his nose in her hair. "In all honesty, Khana, I would love to be able to... court you. Properly."

She leaned against his chest, letting him rock her in a gentle sway. "Really?"

"Probably not while we're marching," he admitted. "You have a point that it could get messy. But when we're in town?"

He was asking permission. Khana bit her lip. "I don't know how Ghuran courtships work."

"It's different for each couple. Mostly they just spend time together, doing as they please, and if they don't drive each other mad, go from there. Nothing formal, like I've heard other countries do."

Reguallian courtship was an elaborate dance of gifts and supervised dates and never truly being alone and intimate with each other in any way until after marriage. She'd been too young to learn the customs of the Naatuun Desert.

Khana hummed, thinking. She was still saving up for crossing the tundra. Every time she earned coin, that was the first thing she thought about. But that idea had grown less and less appealing. She found herself wondering if Heimili would find someone else to work at the inn and if they'd remember which customers preferred their tea boiling hot versus a never-ending stream of mead. Who would keep Haz and Itehua out of trouble? What new histories would Yxe uncover? If Lueti would get to own a brothel to train and protect younger workers and how Xopil's son was going to grow up and whether Neta's Cituva relatives would ever appreciate the gem that she was.

And now, this.

"What if I don't know if I'll be staying in Pahuuda?" she whispered.

Sava shrugged. "We're soldiers. Either of us could die any day. I'd like to enjoy whatever time we have."

"Cheery." She looked up and kissed his fuzzy jaw, the only part of his face she could easily reach. "I'd like that."

His whole face lit up, like she'd offered him the world.

"Aw, rats," Haz said, walking in. "If you two had waited a week I'd have won ten coppers."

Khana huffed and turned to their interrupter. "Good morning."

"Not so good now," he grumbled, coming into the kitchen and snagging a loaf of chuta. "That money's going to Lueti, gods dammit."

"You are such a terrible gambler," Sava commented.

Heimili limped in, glanced at her and Sava, and said, "I suppose I won't be charging you for a room anytime soon."

"Don't say that," Haz said, biting into his breakfast. "He'll need to sleep *somewhere* the first time they argue, and he doesn't immediately take her side."

Khana snorted. Sava gave him a wide-eyed look. "I would never be so stupid."

"They all say that," Heimili teased. "Congratulations, but unless you're willing to help with morning chores, you'll have to–"

Something *shrieked* outside.

It wasn't human, and it was no animal Khana had ever heard. Her gut twisted when she realized what that meant.

"Night creatures," she said, tearing out of Sava's arms. In the space of one heartbeat, they were no longer a couple and a pair of teasing interlopers, but three soldiers and a civilian. "Haz, get your shield!"

"I'll call the troops," Sava said, sprinting out of the building. "Meet in town square!"

Swearing, Haz ran after her upstairs. Outside, people screamed. They had no time to get into full armor, not if the Reguallians were already here.

We should've seen this coming, she scolded herself, tugging on her boots and grabbing her shield. She didn't even bother looking for any of her weapons – her witchcraft had proven far more useful.

She and Haz burst outside. They couldn't see Sava, already gone to rally the other soldiers. The few people on the street in the pre-dawn glow took shelter against buildings, looking up.

The shriek sounded again, rattling Khana's eardrums. Like a dozen bats' squeaks and horses' screams and men's yells all in one. A massive, winged beast flew over their heads, soaring over the town, its giant body longer than a whale. She gaped at it, pressing herself against the stone.

Yamueto had always wanted flying creatures that could carry men into battle. Now, it seemed, he had them.

Or rather, one. That was the only blessing Khana could see in this: there were no others in the sky.

She ran down the street, after the monster.

"What the fuck is *that*?" Haz demanded at her heels.

"Night creature. A new one."

"What type of animal could he possibly have gotten that from?"

"I don't know." Some combination of bird and horse, maybe? Or perhaps bird and whale, given that that thing was big enough to hold at least six men.

The streets filled with more and more soldiers in various stages of armed and armored. They followed orders relayed of "Town square!" and "Chief's in the square, go, go!"

The beast circled around the town. It didn't attack, just flew. Squinting through the pre-dawn gray, Khana could make out one rider on its back, wearing ebony and glowing a myriad of colors. A white flag of truce trailed behind him.

Phramanka stood in the middle of the town square, at the foot of the statue of their founding chief. She was in a nightgown and wolf pelt, helmet on her head and spear in hand. Sava and Thriman stood on either side of her; someone had given Sava a bow and quiver. Khana and Haz pushed their way to the front of the crowd. Sava's eyes met hers briefly before he went back to tracking their trespasser.

"Everyone hold," Phramanka ordered. "This is a diplomat."

The beast circled close. Phramanka ordered a spot cleared in the square. The beast landed, close enough that Khana could see that its fur and coloring was similar to a horse, with even a mane trailing down its long neck.

She also recognized the rider.

Every muscle locked up. Her lungs froze. She couldn't breathe, couldn't think, as the rider slid off the beast's back and strode up to Chief Phramanka, not even glancing at the armed men and women around him.

"You have something of mine," said Emperor Yamueto.

Chapter Fifty

"You are in *my* town," Phramanka said curtly. "So unless you're here to surrender, you can climb right back on that behemoth and fly off."

Yamueto stopped when he and Phramanka were two spear lengths apart. Not close enough to use witchcraft. More than close enough to make Khana choke.

"I don't typically let people speak to me like that," he said, in his usual bored tone. He was every inch the emperor in his black silks, hair swept back in a topknot. He glowed with âji, immune to anyone who tried to attack him. There was no question that he was a royal, an immortal, a god among his people.

Phramanka, in her sleep clothes and uncombed hair, replied, "Tough shit."

He didn't respond. Khana's body trembled, muscles locked.

Haz leaned into her ear. "Breathe."

She sucked in a breath, light-headed with the sudden influx of air, then another. Part of her wanted to run. Part of her wanted to stay rooted to the spot. *Don't move, just do as he says. Don't move, don't move, don't –*

"My concubine has taken refuge in this town," Yamueto said, his voice cutting through the still morning air. "A girl named Khana. Dark skin. Black hair. Small. She killed another concubine of mine, and my son."

"Oh, I know. That was a sight to see," Phramanka said.

"Your people have survived for centuries by hiding behind these mountains. An excellent way to block soldiers who *cannot fly*," he continued, as if the chief hadn't even spoken.

Khana swallowed, her throat dry. *He has more of those flying creatures.*

"Give her to me – alive. Surrender the town, and I will spare your lives and livelihoods," Yamueto said. "Not one stone or drop of blood will fall by my hand."

A pit opened in Khana's stomach. A hundred eyes fell on her. She shrank back into Haz, and he put an arm around her shoulders.

Phramanka spat at Yamueto's feet. "I don't trust or obey the word of tyrants."

Khana had seen men die screaming for less.

Yamueto turned his heel, scanning the crowd. His eyes fell on Khana.

She stayed still, trembling. *Say something. Do something. Kill him!*

She couldn't.

Haz tightened his grip, his smile all teeth. "Fuck off, Emperor Asshole!"

The cry went up in the crowd, first by a couple of soldiers, then a handful, until the whole town was jeering: "Fuck off! Fuck off! Fuck off!"

Yamueto silently returned to his beast, saying only, "You have until nightfall," before he flew away. Khana didn't stop shaking.

Chapter Fifty-One
Sava

No one was surprised when Chief Phramanka ordered an emergency meeting of all the Old Family Masters, though Sava did hear some grumbling and cursing when it was not open to the public. Sava was the only non-Master invited, and only to translate for the deaf and elderly Master Mahi Hyrjorna.

As soon as all seven thrones were filled, old Master Pabu Pinnsviri opened his mouth: "We have no chance. With those winged behemoths, we're done."

"The king decides when we're done. Not us," Navana Cila argued. She hadn't had time to grab her eagle headdress, but there was always a loose feather or two clinging to her clothes.

"You just had a child, Navana. You want your babe skewered on a Reguallian spear?"

"I want my son to not grow up ashamed that his people gave up without a fight. You really expect Yamueto to keep his word? He won't. He'll destroy the town whatever we do."

"Agreed," Thulu Bhalu rumbled, bear tooth necklace catching the light. "I don't trust him."

"Do we have a choice?" Pabu demanded. "If we fight, we die."

"Then we retreat. He can't move his *entire* army on those winged beasts. We disappear into the tundra, regroup on the other side."

Sava cleared his throat. "How many does he have?"

"Quiet, boy," Pabu ordered. "You're just here to translate."

"No," Phramanka said, holding up a hand. "It's a good question. How many of those behemoths does he have? Just the one? Two?"

"He's probably making more as we speak."

"We have archers," Navana pointed out. "They're not invincible."

Rivo Phaska barked a laugh, his orange fox fur burning in the sunlight. "Good fucking luck!"

"They're brand new," Phramanka mused. "They and their riders would be untrained..."

Hope filled Sava's chest. They weren't going to turn Khana in.

"We knew this was a long shot," Athor Cituva said, and Sava could see a familiar stubborn intensity in his dark, leopard-like eyes. "Our job, our duty, is to defend the mountains. And we will do it for as long as we can. Evacuate the civilians if we must, but the soldiers stay and fight. We hold for as long as we can to give the rest of Divaajin as much time as possible."

Mahi Hyrjorna nodded, her bharal horns dipping with the movement, and signed, *We swear our spears to Kingdom. We abandon oath, we shame kingdom. Eagle Master correct. We have no chance kill monsters later. Small chance kill them NOW, new and no training.*

Pabu shook his head. "You're all fools."

"And you are outvoted," Phramanka said. "The girl stays. She'll be instrumental in this next fight, I imagine."

Sava's chest tightened.

Phramanka dismissed the other Masters with the Iron Scepter. She waited for them to finish shuffling out of the room before beckoning Sava toward her. "Fear turns people stupid. I don't want anyone in town getting any ideas. Get the girl some protection for the day."

Chapter Fifty-Two

Khana hadn't stopped trembling and Haz hadn't let her go. He half-walked, half-dragged her back to the inn, where he pried the shield from her arms and asked his father for some tea. No one else was in the dining room, and Khana prayed it would stay that way.

They sat in front of the fireplace, burning animal bones for warmth that Khana didn't feel. Out of the cold, away from Yamueto's gaze, touch made her skin crawl, and she pulled away. Haz let her go, putting an inch of space between them.

Heimili made and served the tea, then sat on Khana's other side, grunting as he straightened his prosthetic leg. Despite the fact that Heimili was thicker, broader, with a bushy beard and more gray hairs than his son, the two of them were almost mirror images of each other. Same pensive expression, same facial silhouette, they even sat the same way, one leg folded, the other – flesh or bone – stretched out.

"They won't give you up," Heimili said gruffly. "The chief will make them see sense."

"We can't defend against flying creatures like that," Khana said numbly.

"If he could take us so easily, he wouldn't have bothered with that little show. He'd just do it. People only try to scare other people into doing something when they themselves are afraid."

Her chuckle sounded hollow even to her own ears. "I don't think that man has felt fear in a very long time."

They watched the fire and drank tea. Eventually the trembling subsided, fear giving way to anger. "I should have killed him," Khana growled. "He was right there. Honor be damned, we should have hurled our spears at him."

"I've seen you rip apart an entire company's worth of soldiers with almost no training," Haz pointed out. "I don't think that would've worked on the man who's been doing that for centuries. Especially since he was already glowing."

"And it would've dishonored us, killing a man under a diplomat's flag," Heimili added.

"Well, I should've done *something*! One look at him and I just – I…" Back to trembling. Her tea rattled and splashed in her clay cup. "I should have done something."

At the very least, she could have joined in the call for him to *fuck off*. But she couldn't even do that. She'd taken one look at the man and been utterly helpless. Useless.

Haz glanced at her, then back at the fire. "I'm taller and stronger than Bhayana. Probably have at least half a stone's worth of muscle on her."

Khana blinked at the apparent segue.

"Makes sense that if she, say, came at me with intent to hurt, we'd have a proper fight. I'd probably even get the upper hand, don't you think? I certainly wouldn't *lose* and need to get treated for three broken ribs and a dozen other bruises."

Heimili stiffened on Khana's other side.

"I knew she was going to hurt me," Haz said softly. "Maybe even kill me. And I knew I could've – should have – stopped it. But when she came at me, I just…froze. I couldn't bring myself to hurt her or even raise a hand against her."

The self-anger leaked out of her. Khana leaned against Haz, trying to give and seek comfort. "You loved her."

"That's not what held me back. It was fear, pure and simple."

"You got her eventually," she said. "When she and Sipah's men picked a fight."

"I still froze at first. Wasn't until everyone else started moving that I managed to throw a punch. I couldn't be outdone by *Yxe* of all people."

She laughed. "Gods, he was so drunk and vicious! Didn't he bite a man?"

"He did," Heimili confirmed, relaxing a bit now that his son was done talking about his pain. "Spat out a piece of his clothing; I found it on the floor."

"Ew."

Haz smacked his father on the shoulder. "You should've given it to him as a trophy."

"If I gave trophies for every bar fight I saw, I'd be nothing but the trophy salesman," Heimili argued. "I don't need to encourage anymore fights in my inn."

Chapter Fifty-Three

The orders for the militia went out soon after the chief's decision: defensive positions all night. Civilians were to leave their homes and spend the night in designated bunkers which were more easily defensible than hundreds of smaller buildings. Those bunkers included the town hall, the Old Family estates, and practically every inn and tavern in town. Upon hearing the order, Heimili started making soup and chuta for the night's guests. Sava had arrived at the inn hours earlier with the Poison Darts, something that warmed Khana even as she realized they were protecting her against the rest of the town. Heimili didn't mind; he roped all of them into food prep.

The line to seek refuge at the inn began forming an hour before sundown. Heimili and his workers scooped out bowls of soup, refusing all payment. "We have enough worries. I'll not have empty stomachs be one of them," he said. Most of the guests still left tips, the most Khana had ever seen.

As Khana and her unit left the inn, fully armed and armored this time, she passed dozens of people going into the inn for shelter. After the first nasty look, she kept her eyes down.

Haz draped an arm around her shoulder and loudly said, "Sure glad you're fighting with us tonight, since you're the only person who's been able to stop witches, night creatures, and a whole company of archers. Not like we'll be seeing any of those, of course."

That got a couple of the nasty looks to turn away, one even becoming guilty. Khana poked him in the ribs. "You're not subtle."

"Good. Subtlety doesn't suit me."

Their unit was stationed outside of town, with most others. Yxe explained why: "Many commanders throughout history win by targeting the enemy's food supplies. It's actually a favorite tactic of Emperor Yamueto from his earlier campaigns."

It was late spring. The fields of potatoes and barley were just sprouting. While Neta assured everyone the chief had emergency stores, destroying the food here would still be a major blow.

Archers climbed onto the rooftops of farms and houses, now empty of occupants. Khana scanned their faces, looking for Sava. She couldn't find him anywhere. Disappointed, she followed Neta and the rest of the Red Frogs to their position in the farmland east of the village. They weren't far from the tundra field they'd trained in.

"At least it's a warm night," Xopil said as the sun sank behind them. He was right: their breath didn't even mist, and they sweated in their armor.

"What if we're wrong and he doesn't come for the farms?" she asked.

"The other companies are within the town itself. They'll be the first to know," Neta said. "But Yxe's right: chances are, he'll go for our food. An army that can't eat can't fight."

Khana watched the dying sun paint the sky blood red. Units around her brought out torches, and a few bonfires made of bone got started, the better to see their incoming attackers.

It was during this bustle that Chief Phramanka marched along the companies, a stone-faced Sava beside her. Behind them trailed a man in dark brown servant's wear, leading four yaks that must have been from Phramanka's own farm. They went straight for the Poison Darts.

"Khana," the chief said. "A word?"

She stepped forward, glancing at Sava. He kept side-glaring his mother. "Yes?"

"We need you to act as bait."

Khana's heart stopped. "What?"

"I'm sure there were better ways to say that," Sava said.

"I don't have the patience for blunting any edges," Phramanka retorted. "The emperor's larger goal is to overrun the town, of course. But he seems personally invested in you. We can use that to our advantage. So..."

She motioned to the yaks behind her. "When the fight starts, get glowing. Draw him to the archers. They'll fill him with so many arrows he'll never get the life force needed to heal himself."

Khana couldn't speak. Could barely breathe.

Sava said, "You don't have to–"

"Yes, she does," Phramanka interrupted. "It's not a request, it's an order."

"I–I can't," Khana stammered. "He... I can't."

The chief huffed. "I wouldn't order you to do this if I could do it myself. But this is the best chance we have at ending this now, saving countless lives."

Guilt mingled with the fear choking her. She couldn't go anywhere near Yamueto without freezing up, couldn't even think about him. The only way she could do this was if she was able to hide, blend in with the other soldiers. Not act as bait.

"I can't," she stuttered.

Phramanka gave her a disappointed look. Sava glared at his mother, muttering, "Trauma. I told you–"

"What if it wasn't Khana?"

She jumped, not having heard Neta come up behind her.

"He doesn't care about anyone else," Phramanka said.

"We'll be fighting at night," the serji pointed out. "He'll be high in the air, too far to make out any details in the darkness. He's only going to be looking for the person that glows. And since Khana can give rabala to other people to heal wounds, it makes sense that she'd be able to make them glow, too."

Phramanka raised her eyebrows, considering it.

"We wouldn't even necessarily need *one* person as bait," Sava added, enthusiastically latching onto the idea. "We could get multiple decoys running around, causing confusion. While the enemy tries to figure out who's who, we shoot them down!"

"Divide their forces," Phramanka murmured. "All right, serji, we'll go your way. You and any other volunteers – not you, Sava, you're leading the archers – will lead them on separate chases. Send your volunteers to me and I'll give them a route through town. Sava, go to the other Old Families. Tell them to give us either four yaks or a dozen goats, each. That'll give us a good starting point."

He nodded and ran off. Phramanka went to check on the rest of the soldiers. Khana turned to Neta. "I'm so sorry–"

"Don't," her serji said. "She doesn't get to endanger the life of my soldier without at least considering other options."

"It's not your fight."

Neta's eyes flashed. "The emperor is leading an attack on *my* home, killing *my* people, and endangering *my* family. What part of that isn't my fight?"

Khana said nothing.

Neta nudged her. "Come on. Let's see if we can talk the rest of the unit into this."

The others proved remarkably easy to convince. Neta barely got "absorb life force" out of her mouth before Haz squealed, "We get to be witches? Yes!"

Itehua held up a hand. "What exactly happens when one of those flying monsters snatches us up like the damsel we're pretending to be?"

"You'll survive the fall if you're glowing," Khana assured him. "You just have to get out of the grip."

"Chief Phramanka's going to give each of us a route through town, to lure the imperials to the archers who'll shoot them along the way," Neta added. "We're not fighting together this time: we're splitting up. Divide and conquer."

"We're sure they'll fall for this?" Xopil asked. He stood next to Khana and put a hand just over her head, which barely reached his breast. "We look rather different."

"They won't notice in the chaos until it's too late."

Khana's guilt forced her to speak: "Maybe Xopil should sit this one out. He has a wife and son."

"And some of the fastest legs this side of the mountains," he assured her.

"Yamueto doesn't want you dead," Neta pointed out. "He stressed that he wants you alive. So, pretending to be you is one of the safest things anyone can do tonight."

"Still, we should come up with some sort of order," Itehua said. "Animals have less life force than humans; we might not all be able to do this."

Khana kept her face neutral. She *could* summon more life force beyond whatever animals Phramanka could find for her. But if she did, that would endanger more of her unit, and carve out more pieces of herself.

"Good point," Neta mused. "All right, let's go by height…"

By the time Sava returned with several more animals, the unit had an order of priority: Lueti was first, as the closest to Khana in size and stature, followed by Yxe, Haz, Neta, Itehua, and finally, Xopil.

Neta glanced at Sava and said, "We'll talk to the chief about our routes." And with that very unsubtle announcement, got the rest of the unit to leave him and Khana alone.

"I'm sorry," Sava said. "Ma told me this plan, and I tried to talk her out of it—"

"It's a good plan," Khana assured him. "Even I can see it. I'm just... I can't do it."

"I know. I saw you when he arrived." He jerked his chin at the rest of the unit. "These are the volunteers?"

"They insisted."

"Good." He smirked and leaned closer conspiratorially. "Ma was really impressed by Neta's quick-thinking, and everything else she's done. Don't say anything, but the next time we need to promote a serji to midya, her name is probably going to come up."

For the first time since seeing Yamueto, Khana smiled a real, joyful smile. "That's wonderful! Oh, I can't believe you're making me keep that quiet!"

"We don't want to ruin the surprise, now, do we?"

She huffed. "I hate you."

He reached up to touch her face, but his hand hovered.

She leaned her cheek into his palm, letting it ground her, pretending that that were back at the inn rather than a battlefield. That they were safe, maybe about to sing in the tavern or go to bed.

He kissed her, barely more than a brush against the lips, then stepped back. As soon as his hand left her, Khana felt cold.

"We'll bring him down," Sava promised. "Tonight."

"Tonight," she echoed.

Chapter Fifty-Four

The sky stopped its bleeding, going from red to purple to black of night. The whole town held its breath. Khana and her unit stood by the small herd of animals, eyes to the sky. No clouds obscured the stars or half-moon. She counted constellations. She had not killed the animals yet, waiting for the very last minute to preserve as much life force as possible. They grazed on the short, tough grass. Xopil cooed at them, kept them calm and close together. With how well he fought, it was easy to forget that he'd been a farmer all his life.

Haz broke the silence: "Ten coppers says the emperor was bluffing."

"How are you this bad a gambler?" Lueti laughed.

"Yamueto doesn't bluff," Khana replied gravely.

Haz gave her a breezy smile. "I'll bet that right after he flew off, he realized, 'Ah, shit, I can't attack them tonight. I have something else going on.' And then he got embarrassed, so embarrassed that rather than come back and reschedule with us like an adult, he's just not going to show up."

"Sure, Haz. A three-hundred-year-old emperor cares enough about that shit to get embarrassed," Itehua snorted.

He shrugged. "I see it happen all the time at the inn. People are strange."

"He never expresses emotions, never mind embarrassment," Khana said. "He barely even feels them anymore."

"Maybe that's how he lives forever," Itehua suggested. "Traded emotions for long life to the gods, or something."

Khana bit the inside of her cheek, sharing a look with Haz.

She rubbed the back of her neck, already sore from craning up at the sky. This was going to be a long night. It was an echo of palace life: suspecting that Yamueto would call on her to attend his bed and dreading every moment leading up to it.

"You should've brought your lute," Itehua commented.

"I'm not in the mood to play right now," she said.

"And we're on watch, not being idle," Neta scolded.

Itehua held up his hands. "Just trying to pass the time. Get our mind off things."

Haz grinned. "You know, if you really want to pass the time, the inn has some of that really strong mead–"

"Haz," Neta scolded.

"Kidding! Obviously, a special occasion like this calls for vodka."

"Do you take anything seriously?"

"That is an honor that I only bestow upon people and things that deserve it," Haz said. "Emperor Asshole and his creepy scare tactics don't get that level of respect."

Something shrieked, piercing the night air. Everyone jumped.

"Emperor Asshole's night creatures, on the other hand…"

"Line up!" Neta ordered.

The war horns blew. Khana swallowed, rushing into the middle of the herd of panicking animals. Xopil barely managed to keep them under control, encouraging them to move around Khana. Another animalistic shriek filled the air, followed by another.

She inhaled, pulling âji from every living thing within spear distance. The animals dropped dead around her. The grass shriveled and blackened. Her skin exploded in blue, yellow, orange, and ebony light.

Another shriek, closer this time. Dark wings fluttered just outside the edge of the town's fires. Units around them tightened into protective formations and archers readied their bows.

Lueti stepped up to her. Khana set down her spear, grasped her shoulders, and breathed out, hoping it would work, hoping it wouldn't.

A good chunk of the âji, and Lueti glowed. She grinned and sprinted for town. "Come and get me, you ugly fuckers!"

Yxe quickly stepped up to fill her place, pulling off his yellow wool hat. Khana did the same, and he darted off in the other direction. Neta was next.

Foot soldiers hid under their shields in turtle formations. The smaller winged nightmares joined the shrieking. One smacked into the shields, trying to get at the prey within, and got stabbed with a dozen spears for its efforts. A few others got lucky, able to snatch a soldier, pulling them crying into the sky before tearing them apart or dropping them from fatal heights. The air filled with wings and teeth.

As Khana got Neta glowing, a behemoth shrieked so loud, so close that Khana's ears rang. The massive creature consumed the night sky, charging down at them.

Neta stepped back, flipped her spear, and threw. It soared farther and faster than any normal human strength could throw it. The projectile went straight through a diving behemoth's chest, and it plummeted to the ground.

"Poison Dart Frogs, you bastards!" she cheered.

Its rider – not Yamueto – swore and jumped off as the body slid to a halt on the ground. Half a dozen soldiers slumped dead in the saddle, and where the rider's skin peeked out of his armor, it cast a faint multi-colored glow. He must have absorbed their âji to survive the impact.

Khana charged. The other witch drew a sword and slashed, hitting her shield, but she got close and breathed in. The man choked, tried to reclaim it. But Itehua, Xopil, and Haz backed her up, jabbing him with spears safely out of breath's reach. It took only seconds for him to die.

"Good work," Neta cheered, jogging backwards to her route. Her glow was only half as bright now. "Keep going."

Haz bounced up and down on the balls of his feet. "My turn, my turn!"

Khana had quite a bit more âji now, and she gave the rest of it to the three men in quick succession.

"All right, jerks, get moving," Itehua ordered, jogging to his route, which would take him to the heart of town. Xopil went toward the Pinnsviri estate.

"Be careful," Khana urged as Haz started down his own route, toward the inn, of course.

He grinned. "When have I ever *not* been care–"

A nightmare snatched him, pulling him into the air.

"Haz!" Khana screamed, running after him.

By now at least three other behemoths had landed briefly to deposit their cargoes of soldiers, all carrying flaming torches. The Ghuran foot soldiers, now with an enemy they could reach, attacked with gusto before they could light the fields afire. Sava's father, Thriman, beheaded a man with a single swipe of his massive sword, while Chief Phramanka watched his back with shield and spear. Sipah, the Pinnsviri guard, clashed with another group of Reguallian soldiers, and got speared through the leg, then the gut.

Khana kept her eyes on the nightmare in the sky as she chased it into town.

Haz twisted, making the nightmare scream, almost like a human in pain. It released him, dropping him eight stories down.

He turned in midair and landed on one knee. That would have broken the leg at best, killed him at worst. But the âji seeped into his body on impact, the multi-colored glow vanishing in a poof.

The sudden kidnapping had left him without a spear, but he held a bloodied knife aloft. He grinned as Khana got close. "Not bad for a first-time witch, huh?"

She gave a breathless laugh, checking him for injuries and finding him thankfully intact.

Every rooftop near the farms was covered in Ghuran archers, shooting at nightmares and behemoths in the darkness. More than one got snatched and torn apart. The behemoths swooped down time and again to grab soldiers – three or four at a time in their talons – and cause chaos in the ranks.

Haz looked up and behind her, and the blood drained from his face.

A behemoth came straight at them. It only had one rider.

"Run!" she ordered, grabbing Haz by the armor and pulling him down the street.

But they couldn't outrun a winged creature. As it dove down, Khana pulled them to the nearest building and pressed them against the stone walls. *Fly past, fly past, fly –*

The behemoth landed on the street with a growl, membranous wings scraping against the buildings. Yamueto sat astride its elegant leather saddle and looked right at her. "Idiot girl. Did you really think you could hide?"

Haz gripped her shoulder so tight it'd probably bruise even through the armor. "Oh, go back to your miserable fucking jungle. You don't want to conquer this kingdom – it gets so cold your tiny balls would freeze off!"

"What are you *doing*?" she hissed. Just because Yamueto no longer felt emotion didn't mean that he tolerated disrespect.

"I've had quite enough of your chattering, boy," Yamueto said, tone so level you'd think he was complaining about tea.

Haz pushed Khana to the side and replaced his knife with his axe. "Run," he ordered.

Yamueto urged the behemoth forward. This close, Khana could count the tiny hairs on its long face, and the dagger-sized teeth in its mouth as it snapped at them.

Haz drove his axe into its snout.

Sava – somewhere from the rooftops – shouted, "Fire!"

A dozen arrows hissed through the air. Some hit the behemoth. Three hit Yamueto. He grunted at the impact.

Khana gaped. They'd hit him. They'd *hit* Yamueto.

Snapped out of her stupor, she lurched forward and inhaled, focusing on the behemoth. Yamueto could drain its âji to heal himself, but not if she got there first.

"Fire again!" Sava shouted.

Arrows flew. Two more landed in Yamueto. The behemoth shrieked, deafening Khana, and snapped at the nearest target: Haz.

His shield blocked the attack, the monster's teeth digging into the layers of leather rather than his arm. He struggled with it, and Khana increased her inhalation of the behemoth's life force to weaken it. Haz hacked at the straps of his shield while the behemoth jerked him to and fro, then pulled his arm free of the leather. The shield crunched in the creature's mouth, shredded by its massive teeth.

"Fire!"

More arrows. The behemoth was almost dead, whether by Khana or Sava, she didn't know. And Yamueto had almost ten arrows sticking out of him. Khana almost laughed. They could do this. *They could kill him!*

The creature moaned one last time and died. Yamueto slid out of the saddle, knees on the ground.

Haz started to approach, but Khana grabbed his arm. "Don't get too close!"

"Right. The life force," he said.

They watched the emperor's chest rise and fall. "Is he dead?" Sava asked from the rooftop.

Despite her own advice, Khana crept closer. Close enough, barely, to hear Yamueto mutter, "Vigerion, I wish to trade."

Oh, no.

She grabbed Haz and yanked him back before Yamueto exploded in multi-colored light, so bright it blinded her.

Dammit, Death! Why are you trading with him?

Khana and Haz scrambled away as Yamueto rolled to his feet, now unbothered by the arrows sticking out of his chest. The two took shelter behind the behemoth's corpse as Sava's units unleashed another volley; Khana couldn't tell how many of them hit.

Stupid, stupid, stupid. Of course he was going to trade!

"Only *you're* allowed to cheat like that," Haz complained. Something caught his eye behind her. "Reinforcements."

He was right: another behemoth flew for them.

"He's coming to you!" Sava shouted.

Khana grabbed Haz's hand and ran. They couldn't fight Yamueto. He was too powerful. There was nothing they could do but run.

Haz stopped with a yelp, hand ripping from hers. She staggered forward a few feet, carried by her momentum, before she managed to turn around.

Yamueto had Haz by the back of the neck.

He tried to escape the way Neta had taught them – swing at the elbow to break the hold, then swing at their face to break the nose. But Yamueto barely flinched when his inner elbow was attacked, still glowing far too bright to have anything less than the strength of twenty men. Haz tried striking him in the face with his axe, but Yamueto blocked it with his hand.

"You are such a *cheater*," he wheezed.

"Haz!" Khana cried.

Yamueto tsked. "Consequences, dear." And he inhaled.

It barely took longer than a second. Haz stiffened, then went completely limp.

No.

Khana stared, too shocked and terrified to move.

No, I can revive him. I know how. I can do it.

Yamueto stepped toward her, and Khana scrambled back.

An arrow shot him through the eye. He grunted at the impact, stopped in his tracks. The other behemoth landed, its rider calling, "We can't break through! We need more men, more behemoths!"

The emperor pulled the arrow out of his head only for two more to hit his chest. His eye healed, and still he glowed, but only just, as the archers continued to fire at him, the new behemoth, and its armored rider. At this rate, Yamueto would need to make another deal with Death or drain this new behemoth to survive. Khana continued moving away.

How much does he have left to trade for? she wondered, eyes still on Haz's limp form. *Most of his army is still stuck on the other side of the mountains. Is it worth it for him to continue the attack?*

Apparently not.

Yamueto tossed the body – Haz's body – over his shoulder like a sack of potatoes and jumped right into the behemoth's saddle behind the rider, covering a distance of ten feet as easily as a child hopping over a pebble.

"Until next time," he promised. The behemoth snapped its wings, sending wind and dust across the street, and shot into the sky, leaving Khana alone.

Chapter Fifty-Five

They saved the crops.

Khana got a perfect view of the near-untouched farms as they piled their dead onto pyres of animal bone. Over thirty warriors had been killed, some of them identifiable only by their clothes or trinkets, their heads separated from their bodies by the nightmares' rampage. They also gathered the bodies of the Reguallian soldiers that had fallen, piling them onto a separate pyre to burn. Their ashes would be gathered and presented to the empire at the next opportunity.

But they didn't have a body for Heimili to burn. For some reason, that thought made her feel guiltier than watching Haz die; Yamueto had not only killed him but *stolen* him, right in front of her.

Neta had been the one to break the news to Heimili. She'd been stone-faced when she'd found Khana in the middle of that street. Khana was in shock, numb, unable to breathe life into the words. Athicha and Sava had come down from the rooftops and explained.

The rest of the night was a blur. Khana remembered sitting in the inn, nursing a cup of tea while Heimili cried and Neta spoke, the tightening around her eyes the only sign of the grief she kept leashed. She remembered removing her armor, replacing it with a dress and cloak. Somewhere in there, Sava had hugged her, whispering apologies as his own eyes watered.

Heimili stood with her, with the rest of the town, watching the bodies go onto the pyres. They covered about a quarter of the training field. The rest of the unit stood by them, looking grim. Xopil kept wiping his eyes, and Yxe's chin wobbled.

"We send these souls to Tsermayu's starry realm, that she may reward them for their bravery and courage," Chief Phramanka said, her voice carrying out over the field. She still wore her armor, but she'd cleaned off the blood. "They fought nobly, so that the rest of us may have a chance to live in peace and freedom. We will not forget their sacrifice."

They lit the pyres. Khana wondered how many more bodies would go up in flames before this was over. Which other members of her unit would she lose? Yxe? Neta? Sava?

They returned to town. Khana was surrounded by her unit, but they were all silent. She kept expecting to hear Haz's voice, cracking a joke or spiraling into a ridiculous story just to break the tension. There was nothing.

"Did you hear? Bhayana Pinnsviri is missing," said someone across the street.

"Missing, or they just didn't find a body?" their companion replied.

"Probably the latter. Her guard Sipah is definitely dead. I heard she got snatched by one of the nightmares right after he went down."

"Ah. That'll do it."

"Maybe we should've given up the death-bringer," someone else muttered, cutting Khana like a knife.

"Don't be an idiot," their friend scolded. "Those bastards would've come for us even if we'd delivered her on a platter."

Neta tugged her away, leading the unit farther from the rumors. They all kept their pace slow to keep up with Heimili's limp. "We'll get him next time," she promised.

"How?" Khana asked dully.

"We'll find a way."

Which Khana interpreted to mean *I have no idea.*

"Serji, we should probably talk about our chances," Itehua said. "We were doing fine until they figured out how to fly. With a few more of those monsters, we're done."

"We might have to retreat," she admitted. "But one thing that will *never* help is losing hope and causing panic."

"I'm not panicking, I'm just trying to find a way for the rest of us to survive."

"I don't want to retreat," Xopil said. "Crossing the tundra takes weeks. People die."

"And no one dies from war?"

"Tlastisti is pregnant."

Everyone stared at him. Xopil gave a tight smile. "She can't cross the tundra. Neither can Ponti. It'd be too dangerous for them. Their best chance is to stay in town, even if the emperor wins."

Khana could see the logic in that. Yamueto didn't like burning towns or cities if he could use them, and Pahuuda was a very useful point of contact between the empire and the kingdom it was trying to conquer. He'd want this town to tend to the armies he sent through the mountain pass, possibly even grow it into a city.

But what type of life would that be for Tlastisti? What kind of world would Ponti, and his baby sibling grow up in? The empire didn't let its people choose their leaders or protect them if those leaders turned sour.

Itehua clasped Xopil on the shoulder, and Yxe managed a somewhat cheerful, "Congratulations!"

Heimili visibly shook himself, despite his wet eyes. "Best to celebrate new life while we can. Come on."

Xopil shook his head. "Heimili, you don't have to–"

"You know my son would be all over this, making ridiculous faces at your baby and flirting with your wife. He'd drag you all to our dining hall by the ear so we could host the announcement. So." He poked a thick finger at the bigger man's chest. "Go fetch your wife and son. Tell her she's not cooking tonight and to be at the inn so we can feed her and the babies dinner."

A last meal, Khana realized. Any of them could be next.

Chapter Fifty-Six
Sava

The Seven Masters met privately after the mass funeral. Few of them were in their fine clothes. Thulu Bhalu was still in his blood-splattered armor from the night before, his bear cloak torn in two. Navana Cila had a nasty scratch on her cheek that had been hastily stitched up, and the chief herself had sprained her wrist in the fighting. Pabu Pinnsviri looked every one of his years, and Sava almost felt sorry for him. Bhayana's corpse hadn't been recovered, but as she hadn't been present for roll call, hers was probably among the shredded body parts or even eaten.

"So..." Athor Cituva said, breaking the silence that had descended upon the throne room. "We should probably discuss giving up the witch."

From behind Phramanka's throne, Sava bristled. So did Mahi Hyrjorna. *We give up witch, we give up our honor.*

"She's not even a citizen."

She soldier. OUR soldier.

"I don't expect the emperor to spare us at this point, anyway," Thulu grumbled in agreement. "He has us cornered and he knows it. What use does he have for such a deal?"

Athor huffed, glancing at Pabu. He gave a weak snort. "It's worth the chance."

We. Swear. Oath, Mahi signed sharply. Navana Cila nodded in agreement.

Athor turned to Rivo Phaska pleadingly. "What about you? You accused her of being a spy not too long ago."

Rivo gave him an incredulous look. "Not since she killed the Reguallian prince. And if she was spying on us, she would've disappeared during any of the three battles she's fought to talk to the other side and give them whatever information they wanted. She could've easily faked her own death last night and disappeared. She didn't."

Athor grumbled in frustration. Sava tried not to look smug.

Rivo turned to Phramanka. "I do think we should talk about evacuation, though."

Navana agreed. Some of the smaller eagle feathers from her headdress had got caught in her hair. "For the civilians, at least."

Phramanka glanced up at Sava. "Any word on the reinforcements from our kin?"

Sava grimaced. The messenger had arrived that morning. "The coast is being bombarded, so Black, Purple, and Green Battalions are needed there. Yellow and Orange are two weeks out, and the city forces in the south have just now gathered on the other side of the tundra."

Athor swore. "It'll take them weeks to get here! And they'll lose a good chunk of their forces to the elements. Phramanka, the trade would at least buy us time."

The chief glared at him. A dark chuckle bubbled out of Sava's chest.

"What's so funny, boy?"

Nothing. There was absolutely nothing funny about any of this. He didn't know why he laughed when all he felt was despair. First Pinnsviri, now Cituva. His mother had been the one to use Khana as bait in the first place, not caring whether she survived. How long before she swallowed her pride and surrendered her to Yamueto? How long before the other Masters stopped fighting her on it?

He didn't say any of that. He looked at Athor and, still smiling, said, "Here I was thinking Neta got her courage from *your* side of the family."

Athor's face turned brick red as he stood from his throne. "What did you say, you son of a–"

Phramanka intercepted him with the Iron Scepter. "Sit down, Athor. Try to scrape together some dignity. You–" She pointed the scepter at Sava. "If you can't be civil, you can leave."

Sava left, colder than he'd ever been in a blizzard. He headed straight for his house and walked into his parents' bedroom. He felt numb as he shifted a loose stone in the floor by Thriman's side of the bed, revealing a chest filled with gold and jewelry accumulated over decades. Of course, it was locked. He was trying to remember where the key was when someone cleared their throat.

He winced, looking up at his father.

Thriman leaned against the door frame. "I remember when you were six years old. Napha was making ginger cookies, but you thought the dough tasted better raw. You got your pudgy hands around a solid handful before I caught you, cheeks puffing, all wide-eyed with terror..."

"Where's the key?" Sava asked.

"Why? Trying to make a purchase?"

"Khana needs to get out of here. She's not safe."

"None of us are."

Sava glared at him.

Thriman let out a gusty sigh. "They're talking about giving her up, aren't they?"

"Pinnsviri and Cituva. And Ma used her as bait last night–"

"During a *battle*," he pointed out. "Phramanka's not going to give her up to the emperor. She'll kill her first, quick and clean, just like Khana asked."

Sava shook his head. "Better for her to get out of here, instead. She has a chance at a happy life, for the first time."

Thriman visibly considered that. "She's also, arguably, the only true weapon we have against the empire."

"That was before they had the flying advantage. She can't be everywhere at once." Sava sat back, leaning against the pelt-covered wall. Thriman came over and joined him, grunting with age as he did. For a moment, neither of them spoke.

"You're going to hate me for this," Thriman said. "I was glad when I was sick, during that skirmish, and you stayed behind."

Sava paused, caught off-guard. That had not been what he expected to hear.

"I know you wanted to go to war," he continued. "Not because you like war. You don't like being a soldier, I know that. You just wanted to be with Myrta. It's the same reason I'm right there with your mother whenever she fights. But I was so relieved when you stayed. And when word got back that Myrta had died, and what she'd died *doing*... that would've been you. I know it in my bones. Given the choice, I'd pick you to survive, no matter how it hurts. Every time."

Sava rested his head against the wall. "I can't hate you for that. I'm sure Heimili's thinking something very similar right now."

"You still love Myrta?"

He didn't know how to even answer that question. "I think so? It still hurts, just not as often. Athicha and Haz helped me out of it, and now..."

Thriman took his hand and squeezed it. "Losing a friend can be just as painful as losing a lover."

Sava squeezed back. "It really is. And I hate it. I don't want to go through it again."

Thriman shifted to give him a half-hug. Sava hadn't realized he'd started crying until he tried to take another breath and hiccupped. He wiped his eyes. "I didn't even realize I was falling for Khana. It snuck up on me. It wasn't until she enlisted and started fighting that I... I didn't *want* to fall for her. Especially not *now*. But she's been so ridiculously brave, and that – that just rubs off on you. And with her powers, I started thinking that maybe she was safe to love. She's walked off injuries that would've killed anyone else."

"Against any other enemy, you'd be right," Thriman said, clutching Sava's shoulders.

He sniffed, straightening and meeting his father's eyes. "We still have time to get her out. To give her a head start. I'd never see her again, but at least... at least she'd be safe."

Thriman gave a grim smile and pulled a corded necklace out from under his shirt. The chest's key dangled from it. "Normally, your mother carries this."

Sava didn't reach for it. "Why isn't she doing that today?"

Thriman's smile turned into a smirk. "She said if *you* weren't going to get the girl out of here, I was to do it for you."

Chapter Fifty-Seven

Khana knew she should offer to help Heimili, but the idea of being with other people made her skin crawl. She wanted to hide from the world, so that's what she did. While Heimili, Tlastisti, and the unit had a subdued celebration, she went upstairs to her room, took off her boots, and sat on her bed, leaning against the wall.

Her hands found the lute resting against the furs. She plucked a few strings, listening to the sound swirl within the stone walls. A melody formed, slow and mournful, grieving everything she'd lost and was about to lose. Because Yamueto would return. He would win. And she'd be back in his clutches. If she asked Phramanka or Heimili to burn her body and then killed herself, would they honor her wishes? Neta probably would, though she'd be disappointed.

She was still thinking it over when Sava poked his head into her room. "Hi."

"Hi."

"Can I come in?"

She shifted down the bed. Sava joined her, brushing against her shoulder.

They sat in silence for a while, the only sound Khana's mournful lute melody. Sava let out a shaky breath, his eyes red. "He told me once that he wanted to be a soldier not for glory or respect, but so his life would have meaning. I wish I had found a way to tell him that it already did. That even if he'd never put on a uniform, losing him would be like losing a lung."

"I think Bhayana put those thoughts there," Khana said. "Or at least made them worse."

"He looked so scared and angry, when…" Sava shook his head. "Why did the emperor take his body?"

She swallowed. "Because… I know how to bring back the dead."

Sava blinked. "What?"

The words spilled out of her: "You make a deal with Death, but you have to sacrifice a part of yourself. A significant part. When I tried to revive Sita, Death told me they'd need something like my conscience or emotions. Giving them my memories is how I get extra âji without draining anyone. But that's not enough to bring back a human soul. Or immortality, or the ability to create night creatures, which is what Yamueto got when he traded his compassion. But I *can't* be like Yamueto, Sava. I can't!"

He stared at her, slack-jawed. She stared back.

"Have you told anyone else this?" he asked.

"Heimili knows. Amati knew. And Haz...."

"Keep it that way. We wouldn't want..." He let out a breath. "That's a power that would be too easy to abuse."

She slumped back against the wall, sliding so she was against his shoulder. "Thank you. For understanding."

"Don't thank me yet." He pulled something out of his cloak. "Here."

A coin purse bulged in his hand. Khana frowned, taking it. "What?"

"It's from our emergency stash. We have plenty more," he said. "I know a tundra guide. He's agreed to escort you to the city."

Khana hadn't known her heart could break any further. "You're sending me away?"

"Ma's not declaring evacuation yet," he said. "She thinks there's a chance we can still win if we hold out for reinforcements. But when it comes to you, I don't know if we can–" He stopped, biting the inside of his cheek. His eyes were wet. "I don't know if this town will protect you," he admitted. "The Pinnsviris still want to offer you as a bargaining chip, and now the Cituvas agree."

Distantly, Khana thought that Neta was going to have words with her relatives when she heard about that. But now, the coin purse weighed a thousand pounds in her hand, and Sava wasn't looking at her. "You... don't want me here?"

"Of course I want you here!" he burst. "But that doesn't matter. Not when that means..." He huffed and turned so he was facing her completely. He took her face in his hands and rubbed her cheek with his thumb. "I want you to stay with me. To explore what we have. Watching you make a place for yourself here, building up your courage and community, I can't even put that into words. You've helped me heal, helped me find my courage again, and I wish..."

She leaned into his hands, vision blurring. He brushed her tears away with his thumb, hardly seeming to notice the ones falling down his own cheeks.

"I don't know what Yamueto has in store for you," he said. "But I know it's bad enough that you begged us to kill you rather than send you back. I'll be damned before I let that happen. So please: take the money, take the guide – take your whole damn unit if you want – and get out of here. As far as you can."

She dropped the coin purse and lute, curling her hands around his wrists. "Come with me," she begged. "You and me, and your parents, and our friends…"

He shook his head. "This is our home. We won't leave until we have to. And probably not even then."

Khana opened her mouth, but no words came out. She wanted to scream but couldn't make a sound.

Sava rested his forehead against hers. "Haz told me you enlisted to look after him, and that he felt guilty for it. That's why he kept looking after you, especially in fights. He didn't want you getting killed for his sake, and I refuse to let you be killed for ours."

"Yamueto will kill you," she croaked. "You can't stop it."

"No, but we can slow him down. Long enough for you to get to the coast, at least."

He kissed her. It was all salt and no grace. It was good-bye.

Sava pulled away, visibly steeling himself, and stood. "Leave before nightfall," he said. "We'll hold him off as long as we can."

Chapter Fifty-Eight

Khana packed her things. She hadn't accumulated much: her lute, her spare clothes, the moose-fur blanket Heimili and Amati had given her. She considered her armor and weapons but decided to leave them. The armor was Amati's, a family heirloom – not that Heimili had much of a family left. The shield, spear, axe, and knife belonged to Pahuuda. They'd need it.

Within minutes, her room was as bare and impersonal as when she'd first arrived almost a year ago. She took a trembling breath. *Better get used to this*, she thought. She should've left this place months ago. Should have just stolen what she needed and been on her way, until she reached the coast. Or until she found a boat to take her to another land. Or until she got to the other coast of that land.

This would be her life now. Always moving. Always alone. Always chased by a monster.

She told herself this was the right thing to do. The smart thing. She'd always planned on running. Half of these people didn't even like her.

She tightened her grip on her lute case. Could she even justify bringing it with her? Her friends had given it to her out of kindness, and here she was abandoning them to their fate.

She set the lute by the shield, biting her lip to keep from crying. Musician and soldier. If she could leave her witchcraft behind, she'd do that, too. Those powers had brought her nothing but trouble.

She removed the necklace of her tokens of war, running her fingers over the nightmare tooth, an arrowhead from the battle with Antallo that Neta had gotten for her, and obsidian frog, no longer a Ghuran soldier.

She'd never liked killing people. Had barely enjoyed using her magic. But her unit had always been there, watched her back, teased and encouraged her to pursue Sava, made her feel a little less scared.

And Yamueto was going to kill them all. If she ever made more friends down the road, he'd kill them, too. On and on until he was stopped.

No one would be able to stop him. No one else had a chance.

She clutched her necklace so hard the tooth cut through her skin. A drop of blood hit the stone floor.

Fuck Yamueto.

He'd taken one home from her. He wasn't going to take another.

She put her necklace back on and ran out of the inn, almost running over Heimili.

"Khana?" he asked.

"Back later!" she hollered, boots hitting the muddy streets.

A few people gave her odd looks as she ran but she darted past them, almost leaped up the stone steps of the town hall, and latched onto the first person she recognized.

Sava was talking to another midya in the hall. He jumped when he saw her. "Khana! What are you–"

She grabbed his wolf cloak. "Where's your mother?"

"You should be–"

"*Where*?"

He pointed down the hall. "Throne room. She's still in a meeting with the other Families."

She kissed his cheek – needing to get up on her toes – and ran down the hall. Sava hurried after her. "Khana, you want to tell me what's going on?"

She said the words when she reached the doorway, in sight of the seven thrones and heads of families: "I know how to beat Yamueto."

All talking in the room stopped.

"Or at least, I know our best chance," she amended.

Chief Phramanka raised an eyebrow and beckoned her forward. "This should be good."

"We need to give me up," Khana said.

"What?" Sava demanded.

Master Pinnsviri pointed to her with a gnarled finger. "See? Even she agrees!"

"You really think he'll spare the town and the rest of the kingdom for one girl?" Master Bhalu asked dubiously.

"Oh, not at all," Khana said, before anyone else could. "Not for more than a fortnight. But I can get close enough to cut off his head. Not even magic will heal that."

Sava sucked in a breath. Phramanka's mouth flattened into a line. "You want to use yourself as bait. You?"

Khana swallowed, her fingers brushing against the arrowhead on her necklace. "Their rock trap would have worked much better if they'd lured us into that crevasse with a fake retreat. If they had done that, instead of catering to Prince Antallo's ego, all of us would've been crushed. That's what I'm suggesting: a fake defeat."

Master Phaska grinned, looking like a true fox. "I like it."

Master Hyrjorna shook her head, signing. Sava translated: "Witch or not, she's one person."

"And a frog," Master Cituva grumbled. "She could join him."

"He'll be more interested in torturing me than recruiting me," Khana corrected. "I've caused him too much trouble."

He grunted, clearly doubting it.

Sava ran a hand down his face. "Assuming this works and you kill him, how do you plan on getting out of there?"

She hadn't thought that far ahead. "Drain whoever I can and walk?"

"Seriously?"

"That's how I got here the first time."

"What if there are other witches?" he demanded.

"There will be. His descendants are his generals, and the illegitimate ones are his bodyguards."

"Yamueto made life force from *nothing*. He has centuries of battle experience. How can you possibly–"

"Sava!" she snapped. "I can't run from him anymore. I just... I can't do it."

He shut his mouth with a *snap*.

Chief Phramanka broke the silence: "So you understand that you're essentially undertaking a suicide mission."

The fear that was a constant presence in Khana's life was still there. But it was squashed down by a calm, cold rage. A love for this town and the community she'd built for herself here, and a determination to keep it. Or die defending it.

"Yes, chief," she said.

Phramanka quietly sighed, suddenly a decade older. "All in favor?"

There was a beat. Then all other Old Families raised their hands.

Chapter Fifty-Nine

They sent a messenger into the mountains with a red flag, so he'd be easy to spot. Phramanka dismissed the meeting, watching the other six Masters leave. "There are several ways this could go wrong for you."

Khana swallowed, the fear creeping back. "I'm aware."

"I hate this," Sava muttered.

"We noticed," Phramanka said, standing. "Be sure to return the gold you took."

He sputtered. "I didn't take it. Baba *gave* it to me!"

"And I'm certain you had no plans to break open that chest yourself if he hadn't been there."

Sava scratched the back of his neck and stayed suspiciously silent. Khana bit back a giggle and handed the chief the bag of coins.

"I'll let you know when we hear back from the emperor," Phramanka said. "Tell your unit what's going on. If there's a way to get you in with backup, it should be them."

Khana grimaced. "I'd rather not endanger them."

"Neither would I. But that's how war works," Phramanka said, not unkindly, before leaving the room.

Sava pointed after her. "See, that's why I could never be chief."

"You'd be better than a Pinnsviri," Khana offered.

"So would a goat."

They chuckled. Khana stepped into Sava's chest and hugged him. "Thank you, for trying to look after me."

He tightened his arms around her. "I'm glad you're staying, but..."

"You hate this?" she giggled.

"Very much."

She rested her forehead against his collarbone. "I am so tired."

"Need a nap?"

"Not that type of tired." She squeezed her eyes shut. "I just want this to be over."

Sava didn't say anything to that. Just held her, humming a little tune, until she felt ready enough to leave.

The two of them found her unit – plus Heimili, Athicha, Tlastisti, and Ponti – at the inn, doing the world's most subdued celebration of pregnancy Khana had ever seen.

Neta took one look at them and set down her horn. "What happened?"

"Khana came up with a terrible plan to take down the emperor," Sava said, turning to her.

"Oh, you're going to make *me* say it," she muttered, and told her unit the details.

Heimili was shaking his head before she even finished speaking, flour falling from his beard with the movement. "You'll die. Or worse."

"Probably," she said, pouring herself a cup of tea. Her hands, surprisingly, did not shake.

"You... are remarkably calm about this," Neta commented.

"Can you come up with a better idea?"

Her lips pursed. "No."

"Maybe we should rough you up," Itehua commented. "Give you some bruises."

"Itehua!" Lueti scolded.

"What? It'd sell the bit."

Sava skipped over the tea and helped himself to a horn of mead. "I didn't think I could hate this plan more, but now I do."

"Wouldn't she just use life force to heal?" Tlastisti asked, holding a sleeping Ponti.

"If I got âji to heal bruises, I'd have it to escape," Khana mused. "That's not the worst idea, Itehua..."

"Well, hold on, let's make sure Yamueto wouldn't see through that before we start punching," Neta said.

"So, congratulations again on your pregnancy," Yxe said to Tlastisti, face turning red at her laughter. Ponti shuffled and whined.

"If we were *really* going to give Khana up, we'd probably do it at spear point," Itehua said.

"Unless she was going willingly," Neta pointed out.

"If I were Yamueto and she came willingly, I'd be suspicious."

Khana hummed. "I was thinking he'd believe that he broke my spirit, or I felt so guilty my conscience made me give myself up."

Itehua shook his head. "If you were doing it to save the town, then you'd be willing to attack Yamueto to protect it. But if you were doing this because *we* forced you, then you'd have no loyalty to us. You'd have nowhere to go, no path to victory or even survival at that point."

"Wouldn't that make her more desperate?" Yxe asked.

They went around the room, talking about the best way to go about it. By the time the messenger returned, half of the group looked deeply uncomfortable, while the other half seemed calmly willing or at least resigned to beating Khana up. Khana herself... well, she wasn't looking forward to it, but she'd gone through much worse pain for much less noble reasons.

"We got a response," the messenger said. "One of the people riding a behemoth saw my flag and flew down to pick me up."

Were Haz here, he'd be peppering the boy with questions about flying on a night creature. As it was, Neta said, "And?"

"Emperor Yamueto will send one of his behemoths to accept Khana on the northern end of town at sunset tonight."

Sava cursed. "So he's flying her there. No chance of sending you with backup."

"Maybe," Neta mused. "Those things can carry multiple people. Khana, how did you want to do this?"

She drained her horn of mead, stood, and said, "Punch me in the face."

The inn went silent.

"I hate this," Sava muttered into his horn.

Neta stood, towering over Khana. "Are you sure?"

"I've taken an arrow to the eye, serji," she dryly replied. "Just don't make me so injured I can't fight."

"Obviously." Neta backhanded her.

Khana's teeth cut into her lip as she reeled from the blow. She wiped the blood with her thumb. "Good start. More."

"Oh, gods, I can't look," Heimili grumbled, closing his eyes and covering his ears.

Neta smacked her across the other cheek, likely leaving an excellent bruise. But it wasn't enough. Khana huffed. "Want me to make this easier?"

"How?" Neta asked.

Khana punched her.

It was the first – and probably last – time Khana had ever gotten the drop on Neta like that, enough to actually land a hit. Itehua laughed as

Neta stumbled back. The serji growled and palm-struck Khana's nose. Pain exploded on her face, and her eyes watered. Blood drooled down her lips and chin.

She checked the injury. Bloody, but not broken. And once the watering in her eyes went away, it wouldn't impair her vision.

"And that's enough of that," Lueti decided. "Honestly, you girls are worse than drunken whores fighting over coin."

"That's a lie," Itehua accused. "Those girls pull hair and bite."

Lueti gave Khana a kerchief to wipe up the blood. The blow she'd landed on Neta barely bruised. The poor messenger who'd watched the whole thing shakily asked, "So... shall I tell the chief?"

"Please," Khana replied.

Chapter Sixty
Sava

Phramanka pinched the bridge of her nose. "When I said I wanted the girl to go in with backup, I didn't want *you* in that group."

Sava counted his arrows, sliding them into one of his two quivers. "Sounds like you should've thought of that sooner."

"It's a suicide mission."

"So you've said."

"Maybe the two of us can go with him?" Thriman suggested. "Sell the lie."

She shook her head. "No. The more people we have there, the antsier they'll be. And Yamueto might send another attack on us while Khana's in his camp. But that doesn't mean Sava has to be there!"

He looked up from his weapons. "Ma, I really don't want to start this night by disobeying a direct order." She narrowed her eyes at him. He held her gaze. "I'm not losing another person I care about by standing back and doing nothing. Hate me if you want, I don't care."

He finished with his weapons and went to move past his parents into the stone hall. Phramanka stopped him with a hand on his shoulder.

He sighed. "Ma, can we not..."

"Shush." She went over his armor, checking the thickness of the joints and other weak points. "Unbelievable. The only Bvamso who can inherit our family title and estate. And he's going to provide backup to a woman who can instantaneously heal an arrow shot through her eye."

"You're the one who suggested she have back-up!"

"Shush! She's already got that Cituva girl with her, and the entire rest of her unit. All of those Reguallians who can better blend in with the enemy and not get themselves stabbed."

"I'm fluent."

"Yes, you're very easily mistaken for Reguallian. Don't stand out among them at all," Thriman drawled.

Sava glared at his father. Phramanka finished her inspection with a huff. "I suppose it's our own fault. Should've raised you to be a coward. Or at least kept you out of the military. What happened to being a bard?"

He could count on one hand all the times he'd seen his mother cry. Given how misty her eyes were, that count might go up.

He chuckled. "How dare you give me morals and a backbone. That's every parent's nightmare."

She hugged him. Thriman joined them. Sava tried very hard to believe that it would not be the last time.

Chapter Sixty-One
Neta

Neta really didn't want to tell another parent of their child's death. Or in this case, their probable, eventual death. But she wasn't going to leave her mother in the dark, so as she packed some extra food in her bag, she told Varisa, "Khana's got a plan to take out the emperor in his camp."

Varisa paused. She'd been weaving at her loom, and now turned around. Despite being mother and daughter, they looked nothing alike, Varisa tall and willowy with almost blond hair. "Tell me you're not going with her."

"Of course I'm going with her."

Before Varisa could protest, Neta added, "We can't beat them in an open field. This is our only chance to win."

"Who's ordering this?"

"The chief approved it, but no one ordered it. Like I said, it's Khana's plan."

"So I don't have to butcher your uncle for trying to get you killed?"

Neta paused. "Ma, you wouldn't be able to... Well, maybe. If you snuck past his wife and sons."

"Don't underestimate me."

"Wouldn't dare," she promised.

Varisa left her loom and packed a bit more food into Neta's bag. "You're going through the mountains?"

"Most likely. I doubt we'll be able to steal a behemoth on the way back."

Varisa took a deep breath. Neta pretended not to notice how shaky it was. "Don't let yourself become one of those night creatures. I chose to settle and have children here specifically so they wouldn't become slaves of the empire."

It was a bad idea to make any sort of promise in war, but Neta couldn't deny her this one. "I won't let that happen, Ma."

They hugged. Neta tried to convince herself she'd be back. She had every faith that she and her unit would bring down Yamueto. Whether they would survive was another matter entirely.

"They may attack the village again tonight," she warned, pulling away. "Stay close to Rasku."

"Is that your way of giving me your blessing?" Varisa asked, wiping an eye. Rasku was the hunter/soldier Varisa had been flirting with for *months*.

"Has he hurt you beyond my sight?"

"Not at all."

"Does he make you happy?"

"Almost as much as you do."

Neta smiled. "Then, yes, I suppose that's my blessing."

"Good," Varisa said. "You never asked for it, but Athicha's a good one, too. I always love having them here. They'd be a good parent."

"They have a vagina, Ma."

"I suppose you could find a third, once you get back."

"Ma!"

"Or you can adopt. I'm not picky," she corrected. She gripped Neta's arms. "Be careful."

Neta was halfway to the meeting point when she spotted Athicha coming down the other street, also packed, with bow and quiver on their back.

"I thought I'd find you at your house," she called.

Athicha shook their head, signing, *Singing Wolf's unit fight with him.*

Neta's stomach sank. *We probably not come back,* she warned.

I know, they retorted. *That why I come.*

"I swear, if you're about to say you're doing this 'for me'..." Neta warned.

Again, Athicha shook their head. *For you. For Singing Wolf. For Pahuuda. For Smile.*

Haz's sign.

Neta deflated. She kissed them, soft and quick. "Let's get killed together."

Chapter Sixty-Two

The sun set, bathing the mountains in red light and black shadows. Lueti had tied ropes around Khana's wrists to secure her hands, on top of her clothes rather than letting the hemp dig into her skin. Itehua, Xopil, Lueti, and Yxe pointed spears at Khana, staying carefully out of breath's range. Neta stood a little apart, and everyone else was hidden in the mountain, in little caves and under boulders, invisible even to the trained eye.

Even in a thick dress and boots, Khana felt naked. No armor, hands bound, only one little knife hidden in her boot. The dried blood on her nose itched, and her cheeks ached. She reached up and touched her necklace, fingers finding the obsidian frog. It steadied her breathing. Small, inconspicuous, and deadly to the touch. That was what she was going to be.

It ends today. One way or another, I'm ending it today.

"Incoming," Itehua warned, sharp eyes on the sky.

The shriek of a behemoth over the mountains made everyone jump. The group tightened the grips on their spears.

The behemoth landed, dust sweeping up under its wings. Khana swallowed. *Please let this work.*

A man in full metal armor slid off, followed by eight bodyguards. Khana bit back a smile, instead trying to look scared and beaten.

"You're Reguallian," the man said to Neta.

There had been some debate over who should lead these negotiations. Sava was technically the correct choice, being the highest ranked Ghuran. But they'd decided he was best as an archer, which required being hidden, so Neta took the lead.

"Half," she said. "I'm Serji Neta."

"Prince Chanido." His helmet allowed them to only see his eyes, but

Khana could vaguely recall his face. One of Yamueto's younger grandsons, or maybe great-grandson. His armor was thick and all-encompassing; it would be almost impossible to get a blade into his flesh without magical strength.

"Chief Phramanka sent me to ensure the terms of our agreement," Neta said.

"As far as I'm aware, the terms are we take the traitor concubine, and in exchange give you and your town a grace period of one fortnight."

Neta nodded toward Khana. "Be careful with her. She almost killed my soldiers."

Chanido grunted and held up a vial. "Have her drink this. It'll knock her out."

Uh-oh.

"For how long?" Neta asked.

"What do you care?"

"If she wakes up halfway through and causes trouble, I don't want your emperor to blame us."

Chanido gave a condescending sigh. "We have the greatest alchemists in the world, girl. She'll be down for at least an hour. Probably more, given her size."

Yxe shifted. Khana glanced at him, sharing a quick panicked look.

"You're a witch?" Neta asked.

"Obviously," he said.

She stepped aside. "Then you give it to her. Boy."

The prince glared at her. Neta did not back down.

Chanido approached Khana, keeping half an eye on Neta. She stepped aside so she was not directly behind him, instead closer to his bodyguards.

Chanido stayed just outside of spear range of Khana. He held up the vial. "You're going to drink this, and not cause any trouble," he said, like he was speaking to a child.

Khana shrank into herself, glancing at Neta, now within arm's reach of the bodyguards who all watched Khana. Neta tightened her grip on her spear and gave Khana a tiny nod.

She obediently opened her mouth.

The prince sighed, stepping forward and uncapping the vial. "Would that you were this obedient in the palace," he muttered.

Khana waited until the glass was almost to her lips before grabbing Chanido's wrist. She flipped him over her shoulder, knocking him into

Lueti's spear. The metal shrieked against his armor. Khana inhaled, taking advantage of the chaos to steal as much of Chanido's âji as she could.

Arrows sprang from bows. Bodies hit the ground. She could hear Neta fighting two others, and Itehua snapped, "Xopil, help her!"

Chanido inhaled, taking some of his life force back as he grappled with Khana. Her tied hands made it difficult for her to grab him, so instead she pulled the knife out of her boot and went for the visor in his helmet.

He grabbed her arms before she could stab him, keeping the blade an inch from his eye. They each continued to try to absorb the others' âji, magic swirling from one to the other. Khana readjusted her grip on the knife and pushed down harder, but the blade barely moved. Itehua and Lueti tried to use bear tactics, but their spears couldn't puncture his armor.

"Yxe, don't–"

Someone touched Khana's back, and she pulled in their life force, enough that she was finally able to overpower Chanido and drive the knife into his brain.

Yxe crashed to the ground beside her.

Khana froze. She glowed with extra âji, and it wasn't just Chanido's. Yxe must have… did she…?

Lueti rolled him over, ripped off her helmet, and put her ear to his chest. She sighed in relief. "He's alive."

Khana put her hand on Yxe and returned all the âji. He coughed. "Oh, that made me dizzy."

"What were you *thinking*?" she demanded.

"You needed the help, and you absorb faster with touch than breath."

They helped Yxe sit upright, Itehua and Lueti muttering about him being an idiot. Sava quickly joined them, with his previously hidden unit of archers coming out of the rocks, and Khana checked on the other fight. All eight bodyguards were dead, peppered with arrows and spears. Neta and the archers stripped them of their armor while Xopil cautiously approached the behemoth.

Khana hissed. "Xopil, be careful…"

"I am," he soothed, reaching a hand out for the creature to sniff. This close, Khana could see thin scars on its face and neck, pink and white skin cutting through the shaggy dark fur. "What do you eat, hm? I imagine it's meat. Did they feed you before bringing you out here? Carrying so many big humans all this way, you deserve a treat, don't you?"

The behemoth sniffed his hand, then licked it with a tongue big enough to be a baby blanket.

Athicha gaped, turning to the others for an explanation. Itehua shrugged helplessly.

Neta huffed down at the bodies. "Well... it'd be a shame to waste them."

"Right," Neta said, looking at the nine suits of metal armor. Eight were green, and one was Chanido's silver. They'd cleaned up the blood as best they could, hoping that any spots they missed were hidden by the night. "Seems we're all going to be able to go."

Itehua glanced at the behemoth. "I'm not sure we can fly on that thing."

"Think you can control it, darling?" Lueti asked.

Xopil interrupted his cooing to beam. "He's almost as sweet as my goats! It'll be fine."

The behemoth snatched the last Reguallian body and chomped, breaking bones with a single bite and swallowing.

Lueti paled. "All right then..."

Athicha held up their hands, backing away.

"So, the real question is, who passes as Prince Chanido?" Neta mused.

"As soon as someone asks them to remove their helmet..." Sava pointed out.

"We'll just have to risk it." She scooped up one of the bodyguards' green helmets. "Chanido's helmet is the only one that covers the face, and you and Athicha are the only ones who can't pass as a full-blood Reguallian."

"You *are* technically a prince, Sava," Khana teased.

He grimaced. Athicha snorted a silent laugh.

Everyone got busy. While they worked, Khana noticed a familiar bit of cloth wrapped around Neta's wrist. It was the ribbon she'd given the serji for the festival, the nine little frogs hopping over the red wool.

Now that she was looking, she noticed they were *all* wearing them: Itehua and Yxe wore theirs like a necklace while Xopil had his tied behind his shield and Sava had his braided in his hair.

Lueti noticed her gaping and lifted her helmet, enough that Khana could see the pale blue ribbon braided there. "Presents given during the Festival of Garmiva are good luck charms."

"Really?"

"Probably. We're also wearing Yxe's socks, and they brought Itehua's knives, but I couldn't fit the teapot in my armor."

Khana giggled.

By the time all was said and done, the Poison Dart Frogs looked very convincingly like imperial soldiers. Sava was almost unrecognizable in Prince Chanido's armor, even with the helmet at his feet. Khana bit her lip. She wished they could at least send Xopil back to town – he had a family. Or maybe Yxe, being so young. Or Neta and Athicha. They all had lives to live.

Athicha wrapped bows and quivers in blankets so they could better smuggle them. The remaining archers took all the Poison Darts' possessions. Neta carefully folded her snow leopard cloak and glared at the archer who came to take it. "If I find a *thread* out of place on this, I'll become your worst nightmare. You hear?"

"Yes, serji," he said, carefully taking the cloak like it would explode.

It took some work getting on the behemoth. Xopil mounted first, muttering soothing words to the surprisingly docile creature. The rest followed, some better at hiding their unease than others, before helping Khana and Sava climb up. The saddle had straps that could clip to a person's belt in case they fell. They all strapped in.

"How do we get this thing flying?" Itehua asked.

Xopil tsked. "Well, when they attacked the town, the riders would…" He gathered up the reins and snapped them with an, "Up!"

The behemoth walked in a circle, jostling the riders. Then, with a mighty flap of its wings, it launched itself into the air, leaving the remaining archers and the town of Pahuuda a speck in the distance.

Chapter Sixty-Three

Khana was certain that the only person having fun on the behemoth was Xopil. He whooped and cheered as they flew. She gripped the back of Athicha's armor with white knuckles, closing her eyes so she wouldn't have to see the ground shrinking below them. Sava was stoic behind her but would likely leave bruises on Khana's waist. Given Itehua's swearing and Yxe's hurling, they weren't having a good time, either.

"Where are we going, serji?" Xopil shouted over the wind.

"Pelete, just over the mountains," Neta called back. "Scouts say that's the emperor's military base."

That was the town where Khana had found her mountain guide to get her to Pahuuda.

It was *cold* up here, and while her dress and cloak were enough for the late spring weather on the ground, the wind cut through it like a knife. She hunched down, trying to protect herself with Athicha's bulk.

She still hadn't opened her eyes when Itehua casually noted: "So, we're over the fucking clouds."

She cracked open one eye, and gasped. They were above the mountains. Stone and snow and wisps of clouds spread out below their feet. Above them, the stars stretched, as untouchable as ever. If Khana leaned her head back, it was like she was swimming in the sky.

There was a beat of silence, eventually broken by Itehua: "Serji, Sava, I was thinking, why stop at the emperor?"

"What?" Neta asked.

"When I was a crime lord, I got into a turf war with a neighboring ring. We tried killing that ring's boss a few times, but it never worked. Instead, we found where he kept his most valuable assets and burned them. He never stepped on my toes again. Maybe we can do the same here?"

Neta tapped her fingers against her thigh. Sava whispered in Khana's ear, "Did he just say he was a crime lord?"

Khana nodded as Neta decided: "Killing Yamueto is top priority. But if we get the chance, we'll do it your way."

Itehua quietly cheered. Yxe pointed off the left of the behemoth. "We're here!"

They all peered over the side. The wing disallowed complete sight, but Khana could still see most of the lights of the town. After so long in Pahuuda, it was strange to see so many trees. The black forest and the distressingly huge number of tents that spread out from it swallowed the town. Rows and rows of fire pits cut endless lines through the darkness.

"I almost wish we were doing this in the day," Sava muttered. "I'd love to see it when it's all green."

"Where do we land?" Xopil asked.

"*How* do we land?" Itehua demanded.

Neta squinted at the ground. Khana bit her lip, trying to figure out where she would put the monster stables if she were running the camp. The lines of fire sparkled next to a handful of shadows moving in the...

"Northwest corner," Neta decided. "That's where the other behemoths are."

Xopil shifted his weight, and the behemoth responded, going just a little bit lower. Khana stayed very still, hoping to avoid confusing the beast. Xopil shifted further, but that only brought them a few feet lower. Sava's grip on Khana's waist tightened, and she couldn't tell which one of them whimpered as her stomach was left somewhere above.

"Everyone lean forward," Xopil ordered.

They did. And the creature immediately dove down, charging.

"Lean back! Lean back!"

They moved again. The behemoth stopped its charge, pulling up a couple hundred feet off the ground. Xopil used the reigns to figure out how to get it to land the rest of the way. Athicha twisted to catch Khana's eye, making a sign even she recognized as *sleep*.

Right. Chanido would have given her the potion. She closed her eyes and went limp, leaning against Sava.

They hit the ground hard. Someone around them swore. Sava undid her own and Khana's safety lines, leaned her against Athicha, and slid off.

"Damn, Your Highness. You never land one of these before?" came a voice.

He grunted in the same low pitch as Prince Chanido. "We got the traitor."

"I see that. The emperor's expecting her," a guard said.

"Where?"

A puzzling pause. "The lord's house, of course. Did you think he moved?"

Another grunt. "Thought this would be public."

"I'm glad it won't be."

Itehua's hands had the faintest shake as he helped Sava slide Khana off the saddle. Khana kept herself limp as Sava carried her bridal-style, but she took a small peek at her surroundings. It was hard to see, with it being night, but there were a lot of soldiers on patrol, or laughing and drinking in the streets. A handful of civilians mingled with them, and she couldn't tell if their laughter was forced or true. After so long in stone homes, she'd almost forgotten that buildings could be made of wood. Now, it just seemed like a fire hazard.

The imperial soldiers took the reins and led the behemoth away. When it didn't move fast enough, one of them took a whip and lashed at its face. "Move, you idiot!"

The behemoth growled. The man whipped it again, and it hunched in on itself, giving a pitiful whine.

Xopil stopped. Khana gritted her teeth. "Come on, darling, there's nothing you can do," Lueti muttered.

Itehua smacked his shoulder and pushed him forward. "They'll get what's theirs."

They got a couple of stares – either because of the presence of a fully-armored prince or because of Khana, she didn't know – so she quickly closed her eyes again, feigning unconsciousness. *Stay still. Don't move.*

The sound of footsteps changed, going from dirt to wood, the cool night air replaced by the warmth of a hearth. Sava quietly asked someone where the emperor was. They walked some more. Then a bored, awfully familiar voice said, "Excellent work, Antallo. Set her down there."

Ah, Yamueto. You never could remember anyone's name.

Sava set her on the wooden floor, against the wall. He hovered.

Liquid was poured. Wine?

"You're dismissed," Yamueto said.

Khana's heart skipped a beat. She cracked open one eye.

Neta moved first, slamming her fist into Yamueto's throat. He staggered back, and everyone else pounced.

Lueti, Yxe, and Itehua drew their swords and swung wildly, slashing at the emperor and his guards – two were with him, fighting back and doing their best to protect him. More guards from the hall burst in, drawn to the fighting, and ran right into Xopil, Athicha, and Sava's blades. Khana jumped to her feet, grabbing the knife from her boot and running for Yamueto, hidden in the mass of bodies. She had to make sure he was dead, that he stayed down –

"Lueti!" Neta shouted.

Khana looked back. Lueti had dropped. And one of the Reguallian guards glowed.

Witch bodyguards, Khana realized, changing course. Lueti couldn't be dead. She couldn't.

Neta dropped to a knee, the witch nearest to her starting to glow. Khana barreled into him, stabbing him in the gut again and again with her knife and breathing in his life force.

Sava took his sword and lopped off his head, staggering against the wall as soon as he did, weak and faint.

More people poured into the room, clashing with Khana, Neta, Athicha, and Sava, or pushing past them entirely. Khana breathed in as much âji as she could, but the witches fought her for it. She managed to bring another one down, slitting his throat and draining him the whole way, when Neta hit the floor and did not get up.

"Serji!" She surged forward, trying to reach her. One of the witch-guards snatched her, twisting her arm behind her back and bringing her down. Her hand spasmed, dropping the knife.

Sava brought his sword down on the man's head, splitting it vertically from forehead to neck. Khana shoved the corpse off her, only to be tackled again while another witch slammed Sava into the wall.

Athicha managed to cut off a guard's leg before a second disarmed them. Hissing, they lunged, scratching and punching before the soldier bashed them into the floor, sucking out their life force.

"Enough!"

Everyone froze at Yamueto's yell.

Khana's heart dropped as she finally got a good look at the carnage. Yamueto stood, his clothing bloodied and torn, but he was alive and whole. The half dozen witch guards around him were no longer glowing – all extra âji clearly funneled into him.

A handful of guards and all Poison Darts lay still at their feet.

Sava was pinned to the wall. Yamueto removed his helmet and studied his face. "You are not Chanido."

"*Now* you know his name?" Sava sneered.

Yamueto shrugged, then looked down at Khana. She gritted her teeth, holding back her tears even with the corpses of her friends surrounding her. They'd failed. They'd all failed. But Yamueto wasn't getting anymore of her tears.

"Death, I wish to–"

Quick as a snake, the guard pinning her to the floor covered her mouth, gagging her. No matter how much she struggled, she couldn't get free enough to speak.

Yamueto was still alive. Would remain alive. Was... now laughing.

Khana blinked, shifting her head as much as the other witch would allow to check that she wasn't hearing things. The soulless emperor gave a big-bellied laugh that almost tipped him over. She had never heard him laugh before. It terrified her.

"Oh, Khana," he giggled. "Every time I think I have you figured out, you surprise me once again."

"Are you all right, Your Excellency?" one of the witches asked, clearly as unnerved by this as Khana was.

He waved a hand. "I'm quite fine. Are these invaders still breathing?"

"Most of them are," someone said.

Khana stilled. There was a chance.

Yamueto smirked. "Bring me my new toy."

One of the guards left. Khana looked around the room, trying to find a new way out. The space was small, barely containing the near-twenty people within it. There was only one door, and the windows were mere slits, too small to squeeze through. It might have once been an office, or a bedroom, but was left almost completely bare, with one small table in the corner that held the wine pitcher and goblet, miraculously untouched by the scuffle.

The guard eventually returned with something – some*one*.

She had expected some sort of torture device. Maybe a potion that alchemists claimed to be a truth serum. But the man who squeezed into the room carried nothing. And her heart jumped to her throat.

"Haz?" Sava breathed.

He wore the Ghuran armor he'd died in. Not a scratch on him. They'd cleaned him up; even his normally messy hair was neat and combed out. But he stood perfectly still, perfectly silent, and his eyes were pure white.

Khana's insides froze.

"You turned him into a night creature?" Sava said frostily.

"These two seemed so close," Yamueto replied mildly, motioning to Haz and Khana. "I wanted to see why. Let her up but keep her restrained. If she says a word, kill one of her companions. If she speaks again, kill another."

The two witch guards hauled her to her feet, keeping her pinned in place between them. Khana clenched her jaw but didn't speak.

Sava was escorted out, needing to lean on his two guards while their companions carried out the unconscious Athicha and Poison Dart Frogs.

Yamueto was last to leave, stopping to put a knife in Haz's hands. "Hurt her for as long as she's conscious, but don't kill her."

The night creature wearing Haz's face nodded.

"You two." He pointed to the two witches holding Khana. "You'll report how much she struggles. If she makes it difficult, I'll turn one of her other friends into a night creature and have them take their turn, starting with the youngest."

"Yessir."

Khana gulped. The door closed and locked behind the emperor.

Chapter Sixty-Four
Sava

Sava had never been as tired as he was in that moment. The witch had drained all life and vivacity from him.

Yet he'd never been so angry.

The witch walking in front of him had Athicha slung over his shoulder, their arms and beaded hair dangling down his back.

"Athicha," he whispered. *"Athicha."*

One of the witches smacked him. "No talking."

Sava gritted his teeth. He was on his own.

The guards took them outside, into the warm night air. They had walked through the whole town to get to the flimsy wooden building at the foot of the mountains, the entire rest of the town/military camp stretched below.

"Don't we have a dungeon?" one of the witches complained.

"No, the emperor doesn't keep prisoners long enough. But we've got chains and stakes."

The ones carrying the unconscious Poison Darts set them down on the grass and went to get what they needed. Xopil still had Sava's bow and quivers in the bag on his back, just a few feet away.

Sava's two guards set him down and glared at him. Much as he wanted to face his fate on his own two feet, he couldn't. He could barely sit upright.

"What were you thinking?" one of them demanded. "The emperor is descended from the gods of death! You can't win."

His friend frowned. "I thought he was *chosen* by the gods."

"They chose him because he's descended from them."

"No, I heard he'd proven himself in battle, so they chose him to be immortal."

He rolled his eyes. "He was born immortal, you idiot. Because he's descended from immortals."

"If gods slept with mortals, there'd be a bunch of immortals running around!"

"They don't sleep with just *any* mortal."

"Who's his mother then?"

"I don't know! Some pretty face."

"What does it matter?" Sava grumbled. "He's a monster."

One of the soldiers punched him, sending him sprawling on the grass. "Shut your mouth."

Blinking the pain from his eyes, Sava turned and spat out a mouthful of blood. A plan formed in his mind. "You want to talk about gods? Khana sees and talks to one of them. The goddess of death."

One guard snorted, but the other looked intrigued.

"She used a deal with a goddess of death to escape your emperor the last time," he continued. "She'll do it again."

"You're lying."

"No, no, let him talk," the other insisted.

Sava shook his head, letting his eyes fall closed. The grass was a very odd, somehow soft and spiky cushion for his head. "Said she knew how to kill the emperor…"

"What? How?"

He didn't respond, pretending to drift to sleep. It wasn't hard.

Someone slapped him. He moved with it but didn't open his eyes.

"He's not going to wake up. We took too much saviza."

"He said she knew how to kill the emperor."

"He was bluffing!"

"How do you know? If he's telling the truth, then we need to know about it."

"Ugh. Fine. Get him on his feet, and we'll question him."

"With what, *my* life force?"

"You're the one who wants to hear what he has to say."

"Can't we use one of the servants? Or infantry? You! Get over here."

Footsteps hurried closer, whispering on the grass. Sava bottled up his frustration. If he was careful, he could take all three of them.

"Yes sir?"

"I need some of your life force."

"Sir, please, I have another six hours in my shift…"

He was cut off as the witch inhaled sharply. Then suddenly a jolt of energy rushed through Sava. He jumped, opening his eyes.

The witch – no longer glowing – snapped his fingers. "You back with us?"

Sava groaned, testing himself. He wasn't completely recovered, rather feeling like he had run a few miles in a blizzard. But he could work with it.

The two witches loomed over him, their armor thicker and more intricate than the poor foot soldier they'd stolen from.

"What?" he grumbled, rubbing his eyes. The handle of a knife winked at him from the witch's belt.

"You were talking about the traitor. How you planned to kill the emperor?"

"Right, right... it's..." He went into mumbling, letting his eyes drift closed.

"What?" The witch leaned closer, almost touching their foreheads.

"Wait, I think he's—"

Sava snatched the knife and drove it into the witch's neck.

He rolled through a waterfall of blood as the witch fell. His friend yelled, drawing a sword. Sava got up to a crouch and threw the knife straight through the witch's eye.

As neither witch glowed, they both succumbed to their injuries, and did not get back up again. The infantryman gaped at the carnage, terrified, before Sava tackled him. There couldn't be any witnesses.

They rolled and scrambled along the ground, bumping against Itehua as they scratched at each other's faces and necks. Sava had the extra protection and weight of the prince's ridiculous metal armor, rendering his opponent's attacks useless. He managed to get on top and get his hands around the man's throat. The soldier beat against Sava's arms, but it didn't even leave a bruise. Eventually, he stopped struggling.

Sava kept squeezing for another moment before letting go, making sure the soldier was dead. He dragged himself to his feet, collecting his bow and quivers from Xopil's unconscious form.

He checked everyone's pulse, starting with Athicha, breathing a sigh of relief as one after the other proved alive. Yamueto's witches had immaculate control...

Except for one.

Lueti wasn't breathing, and she didn't have a pulse.

He shoved that problem aside for now, focusing on the much bigger issue. He was alone in enemy territory, and he needed help.

"How do I get you all up?" he muttered. He needed Khana. He *wanted* Khana. She was being tortured by a puppet with Haz's face. He had to get her out of that hell immediately –

He wouldn't be able to get to her. Not without the surviving Poison Darts on their feet. But the corpses he'd just made complicated things, and there was no way he could convince any of the empire's witches to revive *all* of them...

I can get one, he thought.

He put the helmet over his head, silently apologized to the others, and started for Athicha.

He paused. His best friend was an excellent soldier, but what he needed was a strategist.

He changed course and hauled Neta over his shoulders, along with her stolen sword. He'd noticed a few people marked by elite witch armor at the behemoths' stables. Hopefully they hadn't heard about him being an imposter yet.

Sava got a few odd looks as he speed-walked to the behemoth stables. The quicker he did this, the sooner he got Khana back. He was breathing hard when he found someone in the right armor and pointed to them. "You! You a witch?"

"Uh, yes, Your Highness," he stammered.

The power of confidence and the right uniform was a wonderful thing.

"Good," Sava said. "Get some saviza and come with me."

The witch turned to a few random people on the street: two soldiers and a civilian. "You three. On me."

Sava went into the nearest building, which turned out to be a bakery connected to a small house. The family was asleep until he barged down the door. He tried not to feel guilty as the children immediately cowered and their father – unshaven and bulky – got between him and them, bowing his head. "Sir prince?"

"Out. All of you."

They obeyed.

Sava laid Neta on one of the beds – really just blankets on the wooden floor – as the witch returned glowing brighter than the stars. "Revive her," Save ordered, quietly pulling a knife.

The witch pressed a hand to Neta's chest, and the glow transferred from him to her. She jerked awake, and Sava shoved the knife into the witch's neck, stabbing him repeatedly until he went down and stayed down.

"That didn't go well," Neta grumbled, sitting up. "Where are we?"

He told her everything that had happened, stressing that Athicha was alive (which made her relax a bit), Haz was a night creature (which made her swear), and that Lueti was dead (another swear).

She huffed. "We can't go back there. The two of us will get slaughtered."

"Maybe you didn't hear me," he gritted out. "Khana is being tortured. By Haz."

"And there's nothing we can do about it," she snapped back. "Not alone."

"Then what *can* we do?"

She glanced out the door, then smirked. "What Itehua suggested. Start burning shit down."

Chapter Sixty-Five

It was Neta's endless hours of self-defense training that saved her.

After Yamueto left the room, and Haz approached her, Khana slammed down on one of the guard's feet with all of her weight and might, breaking the arch. As he screamed, she inhaled his âji. The other witch tried to take it, but she pushed his companion into him. They clashed, dropped, and hauled Khana down with them.

She wiggled out of their grip just as Haz tackled her to the floor. The knife sliced through her arm, scraping against her bone and punching all the air out of her lungs. It stayed in her bicep, hilt-deep.

"Get her pinned," one of the guards ordered. "You all right?"

"My foot is *broken*. How the fuck did she do that?"

"She's stronger than she looks."

Khana gritted her teeth, her arm on fire, Haz impassively staring down at her.

It's not him. It's just a husk.

She inhaled, sucking out all of Haz's âji until he dropped on top of her. Not breathing.

Sorry, Haz.

She pushed away his corpse and pulled the knife out of her arm with a cry.

"Hey!"

The uninjured witch cursed and glowed, his friend weakly looking up as his life force was stolen.

"Wait–"

The uninjured witch punched his friend and inhaled the last of his âji. She couldn't tell if the drain killed him or simply rendered him unconscious, but he didn't move from the floor.

Khana's arm had completely healed, absorbing Haz's âji, leaving her with barely a glow. She'd have to be quick.

The remaining guard unsheathed his sword and charged.

Khana parried, pivoted, and sliced at his chest. Her knife shrieked against the metal armor. He turned and swung at her. She ducked, the force of his blow creating a hole in the wall and sending splinters into her hair and face.

She scrambled back, devising her next attack. His head and torso were fully armored, she wasn't. And she wouldn't be able to steal his âji until he was distracted or injured.

The armor doesn't extend to the legs, she realized, just as he came at her again. She dropped to the floor and rolled, slicing at his calf as soon as she was behind him.

He roared in pain, then shoved his sword into her back. The tip came out of her chest. She gasped, every movement sending fire pulsing through her.

He hauled her up by her dress. "Listen to me. This'll go a lot easier if you just do as you're told. I'm not about to get turned into a night creature because you decided to be a bitch!"

Khana gritted her teeth, blood pooling in her mouth. Raising her arms took herculean effort, but she gripped her knife tightly and stabbed him in the neck.

He wheezed, stumbling to his knees. Khana clung on to him, pulling the knife out and stabbing him again as he healed. She stabbed once more immediately after, knowing how impossible it was to breathe with such a neck wound. And again, and again, until he stopped glowing, until he stopped moving. By the time she was done, they were both soaked in blood, and his entire neck and face were annihilated.

Sword still in her chest, Khana stumbled away from the corpse, dragging herself to the table with the pitcher, all but collapsing against it, her hands glowing. The pitcher wobbled and fell off, shattering on the floor. Khana angled herself so the tip of the sword was against the table and pressed forward, pushing the sword out slowly and painfully.

The sword's tip disappeared within her ribs, then the weight of the handle and blade finally made it drop, leaving her body entirely with a clatter. Khana wheezed, spitting out blood as the âji she'd stolen knitted her wound back together. She stopped glowing after a few seconds.

She checked herself, grimacing when she saw a weeping wound still on her chest – and probably her back, too, not that she could reach it. Entry and exit. But they were shallow, nothing that a few stitches couldn't fix.

She huffed and went to Haz's side, dropping to her knees next to him.

"Death, I wish to trade."

Khana blinked, and she was no longer in the building.

Well, she *was*. She could see the wooden walls and the broken pitcher and even the shade of Haz. But it was dark and muted. As if all the light had been sucked out, including her own body. No matter how many times she came here, it was always bizarre.

"You, again."

Death appeared in front of her, their robes a multi-colored swirl that Khana saw even when she closed her eyes.

Khana gritted her teeth, anger erasing desperation. "Why did you accept that trade with Yamueto? We almost had him!"

"He summoned me and offered a deal. I obliged."

"But *why*? All of this suffering, everything he's done, it's because you let him!"

"I do not discriminate," Death said evenly. "I come for everyone, and thus, I trade with everyone. When they have something to trade."

Khana glared.

"Is there a reason you called, or was it just to yell?"

She took a deep, steadying breath. "I need my friend back. Hasyamin. I'm next to him now."

Death prowled around Khana, getting a closer look at their darkened bodies. They tipped their head at Haz. "This young man? Fiercely loyal? Hides his own suffering with poor humor?"

As Death talked, they changed their form again, until it was an exact copy of Haz crouching before her. "He called me a killjoy when I collected him," they said.

Khana blinked back tears. "Yes. That's him."

"Great. What are you willing to give?"

Khana let out a shaky breath. "Would memories work?"

"Not for a soul," Death said gently. "Not unless you have at least his lifetime's worth of memories. You're close enough in ages that I could make it work, but you would have complete amnesia."

She shook her head. If they were safely back in Pahuuda, then she may have gone for it. But in their current situation, that was a recipe for disaster.

"What about your witchcraft?" they asked.

Oh, to give *that* away. She almost said yes immediately. Even if she failed tonight, if Yamueto lived for centuries more, he'd have no more use for Khana. He might even give her a clean death.

But...

She groaned. "I hate it. But I don't have a chance of killing Yamueto without it. And if one of my friends gets hurt, I'll need to be able to heal them."

"Ah, the hazards of war," Death mused. "That means we need to get a little more existential. We'll need a significant piece of your soul."

Khana ran through a mental inventory of herself, trying to figure out what she could give that wouldn't render this moot. Or worse, turn her into the same type of monster she was trying to kill.

"You said Yamueto gave up all of his passions for the ability to create night creatures," she said at length. "What about just one passion?"

Death grinned Haz's gap-toothed smile. "It will have to be a significant passion. Something you truly love."

Khana swallowed, mind going straight to one thing. She remembered the joy she felt at receiving her lute. Channeling her rage and grief to get through the Reguallian nights. Dancing and singing with Sava.

"Music," she said quietly.

Death stepped forward and raised their hand to touch her. She jerked back. Death waited.

Khana forced a breath – did she even have air and physical lungs in this strange place? – and let Death touch her forehead. After a few seconds, they nodded. "From you? That'll work."

No more dancing at festivals. No more singing songs in Heimili's inn. No more playing for her unit.

She looked at Death's face. Haz's face.

It wasn't an easy choice, but it was the one she knew in her bones was right.

Still... "It can't be that easy."

"No?" Death asked.

"Doesn't reviving the dead run counter to your very being?"

They laughed. Haz's voice, but a different rhythm and cadence. Not unpleasant. "Dear, I am *death*. This is just a loan. Everyone returns to me eventually."

They sobered, face gentling. "You only get one life, and I hate taking spirits so young, almost as much as suicides. So why not give him a second chance? Maybe this one will have a happier ending."

She smiled. "If I survive tonight, I'm going to make you wait a long time for that."

"Good." They held out their hand. "Last chance."

Khana didn't hesitate this time. She took it.

Chapter Sixty-Six

Khana gasped, returning to her body as if suddenly waking from a vivid dream. It took a few seconds to remember where she was, why every inch of her hurt, why she was kneeling over Haz's body with her hand on his back.

He was tense and silent beneath her. She couldn't see his face.

She gulped, unable to speak. Had it worked, or had it all just been a vivid hallucination?

Then Haz spoke: "All right, whoever's pinning me down, I've got an itch on my right butt cheek I need you to scratch. That's the *right*, not the left–"

Khana pushed him away. "Haz?"

He blinked. His eyes were back to their deep brown, no longer soulless white. "Khana? Why were you smushing me against a floor worth more than our lives?"

"What's the last thing you remember?" she demanded, pressing her hand against his forehead, like she could check the status of his soul the way she'd check for a fever.

"Um... you and I ran from a behemoth, Sava shot Emperor Jackass full of arrows, you said something about a deal with death, then..." His eyes widened. "Did that prick *kill* me?"

She pulled him into a hug. Haz settled his arms around her, nose brushing against the crook of her neck. It was the best feeling in the world. She couldn't believe that he was breathing, talking, right in front of her.

"He stole your âji and brought you back as a night creature," she explained, pulling back.

"Why would he do that?" The instant the words were out of his mouth, Haz's eyes trailed down her. "Whose blood is that?"

She motioned to the two dead guards. "Theirs."

"Riiight. That's why your dress has holes in it."

"*Mostly* theirs."

Haz looked her over, blood quickly staining his palms. "How much of this did I do?"

"*You* did nothing," she snapped. "Your soul was gone, you had no control. It was Yamueto, not you. Besides, it's nothing I couldn't heal."

"Right, yeah," he said with a shaky breath.

"If it makes you feel any better, I killed you right away."

His jaw dropped.

"I needed the life force," she said defensively.

"So, you cheated?"

She sputtered. "Cheated? It was three against one! Two of them witches!"

"Cheeeeateeeeer," he laughed.

Khana couldn't help it; she giggled right along with him, only slightly hysterical.

"I need you to know that I am *never* going to let you forget that," he chuckled. "Where are we, anyway?"

She explained the mission she'd made for herself and how poorly it was going. She glossed over the deal she'd made to bring him back, hoping he wouldn't remember what she'd told him of that aspect of witchcraft.

She didn't feel any different. Shouldn't losing a more significant piece of her soul feel more traumatic? Of course, she hadn't tried playing her lute or dancing yet.

He seemed to accept her answer, asking only, "And Baba?"

"Coping the best he can. He'll be beyond happy to see you." She poked his nose. "Don't you make me bring you back again."

He grinned. "I'm sure you were terrifying enough that Death wouldn't dare come back for me."

She snorted.

"We should probably get to the others," Haz said. "Neta will know what to do."

"No, we should get to Yamueto," Khana said darkly.

He stood and checked the door, smashing his shoulder against it. He swore. "You'd think something as flimsy as wood would be easy to break, but they must have some sort of lock on the other side."

"Probably a deadbolt."

Haz put a hand against the door, then studied the windows across the room.

"Those are definitely too small," Khana said, amused.

"Yes, but, a strengthened witch could probably break it down."

"Haz, no," she hissed. "I just got you back!"

"I'm not saying kill me! Just take enough to get going, and then return it."

"I'll make another deal with Death," she offered.

He studied her. "What did you give up?"

"What?"

"To bring me back. A deal goes both ways, so what did you give up?"

She grimaced. "Music."

He went white. "K-Khana, that's... you *love* music."

"Which is why it worked. But âji isn't like that. It's not nearly as valuable. It only costs a single memory. You know that!"

He put his hands on her shoulders. "Khana, you've given enough of yourself for today. Please, just take some of mine. And do it quickly. As soon as the Reguallians get everything under control, Sava and the others are dead or worse. You know that."

He was right, damn it. Sava was the only one of their friends still conscious. Everyone else was knocked out, completely helpless and unable to escape, never mind fight back.

Khana huffed and pulled herself to her feet. "All right."

Luckily there was already a hole in the wall from her fight and, even better, it showed that the other side of the wall was *outside*. She'd aim for that.

Haz waited. "Well?"

"Are you sure about this?" She didn't want to be like the dead witches at their feet, stealing âji from each other to save their own skins.

"Just take it."

It was much easier now that they weren't trying to punch each other. He slumped against the table as she drank enough to get her skin glowing. He yawned. "Did you do it yet, because I don't feel anything."

"You're a menace," she said, then ran at the wall at top speed.

The wall splintered but didn't break. She had to run at it again, and this time it shattered completely, wooden splinters spraying everywhere.

This wasn't like Pahuuda's town hall. This had been a minor lord's or gentry's estate, isolated from the rest of the town with gardens instead of gargoyles. She stumbled into some shrubs, disrupting a cloud of bugs.

The estate was a little elevated from the rest of the town – what was it with rich people always needing to physically lift themselves over everyone else? – and so she had a perfect view of the black, shadowed town. Though it looked like someone had started a big bonfire near the stables.

She had just gotten her feet under her when a pair of guards rushed around the corner, investigating the sound.

She charged them and inhaled. One immediately dropped at her feet.

"The prisoner's out!" the other shouted, comingat her with a spear. Khana pivoted out of his thrust and drank him dry, then ran back to Haz.

"Oh, you're back," he groaned, having braced both forearms against the table. "You can go on ahead; I'm just going to nap."

"No, you won't." She gave him all the excess âji, lighting him like an orange-yellow-black star.

Haz jolted. "Whoa, that's more effective than a bucket of ice!"

"Good. We need to lure Yamueto to me."

He looked her up and down. "Then why aren't *you* glowing?"

"I will be soon," she said dryly.

They ran out of the hole, Haz twirling his knife. They ran around the building and went back inside the front door. Someone had alerted a couple more guards, and they were waiting for them, blocking the hallway. Both glowed faintly.

"Line game!" Haz cheered.

Khana reached them first, and the struggle for âji began, all of them trying to steal it from each other. Haz barreled into one and stabbed him in the weak spots of the armor beneath the armpit, killing before he could take his life force. The other went for Haz, but Khana kicked him in the leg, trying to bring him down. He went to draw his sword, but she grabbed his arm and put all of her weight against it. They battled for life force and the sword, at a standstill until Haz got behind him and stabbed him in the back. It wasn't a clean kill but allowed Khana to drain him herself.

Haz huffed, kicking at their weapons. "Why aren't these men using spears, like sensible people?"

"Rich people use swords."

"Blech."

She didn't get it, either. She'd learned the spear the quickest and appreciated its reach.

They walked through the large house, looking for more targets. It had bigger, wider rooms than what she was used to in Pahuuda, the air not getting as cold and thus requiring less heat conservation. A servant, or more likely a slave, pressed herself against the corner of a richly decorated audience chamber when they poked their heads into the room, eyes wide with fear. Khana spoke softly: "We have no quarrel with you. We're looking for Emperor Yamueto and his commanders."

"The – The emperor went out. I don't know where. Most of his commanders are gone, too, looking for him. Only his guest is here."

"His guest?"

The servant shrugged. "I don't know anything. Just that she's here. And rude."

Khana and Haz shared a confused look. "Thank you. Stay hidden; they'll likely try to steal your life force to strengthen themselves when they come back."

The servant nodded and hunkered down further in her corner.

They left the room and went up the stairs, hunting for more âji that wouldn't come from an innocent.

They reached the second floor, the stairs leading to a long hallway with multiple doors on both sides. Khana tested a doorknob. It was locked. Something shuffled on the other side. Haz grinned, grabbed the handle, and yanked it out – along with the lock and a fair bit of the doorframe.

He froze.

Khana came in behind him, almost barreling into his back.

Bhayana sat in a cushioned chair, a piece of cake halfway to her mouth. Someone had given her a Tlapharian-style linen dress, which she wore under her porcupine cloak.

She sighed, setting the dessert down. "I liked you better as a night creature."

"What?" Khana said hotly.

"What are *you* doing here?" Haz demanded.

Bhayana gestured to the room. "Diplomacy. I'm trying to negotiate with the emperor so that he doesn't slaughter us all. What are *you* doing?"

"We thought you died during the attack on the town," Khana said. "Chief Phramanka didn't say anything about sending you here."

"Better to ask for forgiveness than permission."

"You traitor."

She gave them a flat look. "Negotiating for the lives of our people is betrayal? He's going to win. I'm simply making sure we survive."

"And that he kills whoever you don't like," Khana snapped. "You tell him who to execute, and in exchange he spares the Pinnsviris and packs the council with a new set of Families that suits your needs. Is that your plan?"

She crossed her arms. "Is the idea of the town being run by us so abhorrent that you'd rather see it burn?"

Khana lunged.

Bhayana dove from her chair and threw a knife. It struck true, burying itself in Khana's chest. She coughed, hitting the floor.

Haz charged, swinging with his knife. Bhayana pulled another blade from her belt and blocked, steel shrieking against steel as they crashed into furniture. Khana pulled the blade out of her chest, letting her âji from the fight downstairs heal her while she tried to breathe through a storm of needles.

Bhayana disarmed Haz and slit his throat.

He staggered for a beat, the glow around him softening as the injury healed itself. Bhayana snarled and stabbed him twice more in quick succession before pinning him, no longer glowing, to the wall. He blocked her knife hand with his arm, keeping her from dealing a fatal wound. They hovered there for a moment, breathing hard, trying to find a weakness.

Khana pulled herself to her feet, silent against the carpeted floor.

"It's been a while since we were this close," Bhayana purred. "Emperor Yamueto and I both enjoy having you as a pet. That doesn't have to change just because you're no longer a night creature."

"Fuck off," Haz wheezed.

Khana drew herself up behind Bhayana and stabbed her through the back of the head, at the base of her skull.

The woman gurgled around blood and steel. Haz pushed her stiffening form away. They let her drop to the floor, watching the blood leak out of her mouth.

"Are you all right?" Khana asked him.

He studied his dead ex-lover, then shrugged. "Ask me again some other time."

Chapter Sixty-Seven

They cleared out the rest of the house, sucking âji from three imperial officers and handful of witch bodyguards. By the time she and Haz went back downstairs, they both glowed like twin moons.

"Where would Yamueto keep the rest of the unit?" Haz asked.

"I don't know," she admitted. Keeping them unconscious would be Yamueto's safest option, but maybe he'd gotten a head start on transforming them into night creatures. Did she have any other passions to trade away?

"Is the town supposed to be on fire?"

She paused, looking back at him. He'd stopped by a window, from which came an odd, warm glow.

She joined him at the window and gaped. At least two buildings – three? – and a good chunk of the surrounding forest were engulfed in separate infernos. Shadows flew in the sky; behemoths. It was too dark for her to count them.

"I'm going to guess... Itehua?" Haz said.

"He was unconscious. Everyone was, except for Sava."

One fire she could dismiss as a fluke. A lazy or careless soldier not watching the flames of his camp. Two? In separate areas of town, no less?

Haz whistled. "Where can I find *me* a man like that?"

She pushed him. Normally, while glowing as bright as she was, he'd have gone through the wall. But he barely budged.

They rushed to the front door when an achingly familiar voice said, "Ah, I guess she escaped."

"Yes, I see that, Sava. Where did she escape *to*?" Neta demanded from the room that had served as Khana's prison cell.

Khana and Haz shared a grin.

She removed the wooden bar from the door and opened it. Neta and

Sava both whipped around, him with bow and arrow, and she with a spear and shield. Several spears, in fact, resting in the holder on her back.

"Khana!" Sava cheered, blinking. "Very bright!"

"You're all right!" Khana cheered. "We were worried!"

"We?" Neta echoed.

Haz poked his head in. "*I* had every confidence in Neta's ability to stay alive."

They gaped at him. Sava dropped his bow, letting it clatter to the ground. He rushed over and dragged Haz into a rough, desperate hug. Thankfully he'd gotten rid of Chanido's armor at some point, or that would've left bruises. "You ass!"

Neta refrained, still staring, eyes suspiciously misty. She turned to Khana. "I thought you couldn't bring back the dead."

She winced. "I lied."

The serji raised an eyebrow.

Sava looked up. "You made a deal. What did you trade?"

"My passion for music," she said, trying not to feel guilty. It had been one of the things that had brought the two of them together.

He let out a breath. Haz grimaced. "Yeah, I told her that was a bad idea..."

"What about the emperor? Did he hurt you? Are you all right?" He left Haz to look her over.

"I'm fine. He barely did anything," she promised, stilling his hands on her cheeks. "Most of this blood is from the guards. And Bhayana."

"Bhayana?"

"She came to make a deal with Yamueto, pledging herself and probably her family to his service."

Sava opened and closed his mouth, then shook his head and turned to Haz. "Are you all right?"

He shrugged. "At least she won't torment me anymore, right?"

Neta gave a sharp sigh. "We lost one of the Poison Darts."

Her stomach dropped. "Oh, gods. Who?"

"Lueti."

Khana covered her mouth. Haz hissed.

"Possibly more. Sava checked them a little over twenty minutes ago."

"They sent guards to tend to the fires and behemoths. We set them free," Sava said. "We were trying to figure out how to get you so you could revive the others. They're chained out in the yard."

* * *

Athicha, Xopil, Lueti, Itehua, and Yxe all lay on the grass, manacles attached to their wrists leading to stakes in the ground. Four witch-guards stood nearby, anxiously watching the growing fires creep closer.

It was almost impossible to hide Khana and Haz with how much they glowed, so they didn't bother. They strode right out to meet them.

The witches all stiffened when they approached. They stopped several spear-lengths away.

"Gentlemen!" Haz cheered. "Crazy night, huh?"

"We will give you one chance to surrender peacefully," Khana declared. The witches all glared at her, and she held their gaze. "I'd rather limit the number of people I kill today."

The witches considered. One of them said, "Drain the prisoners–"

An arrow shot out of the darkness and into his throat.

While the witches reeled in shock, a spear followed. Neta's aim was excellent, hitting the witch in the thigh just under the armor. Khana charged, grabbing that spear and jamming it up, digging until she found the artery. The guard's screams tapered into whimpers and then shock.

Sava shot the third through the eye, as the fourth went for the unconscious Poison Darts –

Only for Haz to tackle him to the ground and drag him away. The witch tried to drain Haz's life force, until Khana took the spear and drove it into his neck, right above the armor.

"Did they get any of the unit?" Neta asked, coming out of the shadows.

"No," Khana said, handing over the spear. She checked the witches' bodies, ensuring they were all dead.

Sava walked out of the bushes he'd been concealed in, shaking leaves from his hair and clothes with a grimace.

Khana revived Xopil, first, who woke as if he'd just been sleeping. "'Morning, Khana," he yawned. Then scrambled upright. "Khana! The emperor! What–"

"It's fine. I'll explain soon," she promised, moving on to Yxe. He squeaked, then relaxed when he saw her and Neta. The serji had found the keys and was undoing their manacles.

Itehua came to swinging, punching Khana in the mouth. "Ow!"

"Oh, shit! Sorry, Khana."

"Id's bine," she gurgled, waving him off. Her excess life force quickly healed the swelling, but after three revivals her blinding glow had dimmed considerably. "Haz, I might need some of your âji."

Itehua blinked at her. "Uh, how hard did I hit you? You just called for–"

Haz put a hand on her shoulder, grinning down at Itehua. "I'm too stubborn to die."

Itehua stared, slack-jawed, as Khana took some of Haz's excess and revived Athicha.

Finally, she moved on to Lueti. She'd hoped that Sava had been mistaken, that he was too drained, too exhausted to assess properly. But he wasn't. The elderly woman was dead.

The group's joy at Haz being alive immediately soured.

"Wait, so you brought him back, can't you do the same to *her*? Is she not worth as much or something?" Itehua asked.

"Itehua…" Neta warned.

"What can I give up?" Khana whispered.

"What?" Itehua demanded.

Sava and Neta stepped in to explain. Athicha whistled lowly.

"So you *can* bring someone back, but it'll hurt," Xopil realized.

"And… the more deals you make, the more you lose yourself," Itehua added, nodding with understanding. Face still pained with loss.

Khana hugged her knees. It wasn't helplessness that gripped her but being trapped. Caught between two terrible outcomes.

Haz shook his head. "Look, Khana, as the person who *has* been revived… I'm glad to be alive. Thrilled, even. But if you give up anything else, you're basically turning into Yamueto."

"She wouldn't want that," Yxe agreed, wiping his eyes.

"No," Itehua conceded. "She wouldn't."

Khana shook her head, vision blurry. "Maybe there's something else, something that I'm not seeing–"

"Khana!" Neta barked. Her tone gentled. "You'll hate me for saying this, but we need you whole more than we need Lueti."

Her temper flared, and she strode up to the serji's face. "How can you say that? Lueti's our friend!"

Neta didn't flinch. "But she's not a witch. And that's who we need to bring down the emperor and save Pahuuda. She knew the risks. We all did. We all went into this believing we could die, thinking it was impossible for you to bring us back at all."

Sava put a hand on Khana's shoulder. "If you still feel strongly about this, then it's your decision. But for now, Neta's right. This mission must come first. I'm sorry."

Khana's rage simmered into helpless grief.

Xopil sniffled. "I'll carry her."

"That'll slow us down," Neta argued.

"We can't leave her here for some other witch to turn her into a night creature."

Neta visibly paused, tipping her head, eyes on Khana.

Khana knew exactly what she was thinking. "No."

"Carrying her corpse is too big a risk," Neta countered.

"Absolutely not."

"And we could use the extra fighter."

"Neta–"

"There's no one else she would trust with this!" Neta stressed. "If I was the one on the ground right now, I would want you to turn me. Because then I could still fight and I would be under *your* control, not the emperor's. After that, then I'd be able to rest."

Silence.

"Agreed," Itehua said at length. "If I go down, bring me back up to finish the job."

"Yeah, being an undead abomination was fun. I'm up for doing it again," Haz drawled.

Khana ran her hands down her face, hysterical laughter and tears bubbling out of her. "I thought the whole point of me not bringing Lueti back was to avoid me becoming like Yamueto."

"This doesn't make you like him," Neta stressed. "We're simply being practical and protecting our friend from being used by others."

Protection seemed like a strong word for it.

But as Khana thought more about it, she realized the truth. If they left her here, Lueti would likely be raised by one of Yamueto's witches, and she knew her friend would find that unacceptable. Short of burning the body here and now, this was the only way to be sure.

Wiping her cheeks and muttering apologies, Khana pressed the remaining life force into Lueti.

Within moments, Lueti opened milky, soulless eyes.

"Rise," Khana ordered.

Lueti obeyed, her movements perfectly healthy and coordinated, but unnatural. It wasn't how Lueti moved at all.

"Your primary task is ensuring the safety of the people you see before you," Khana stressed. "Your secondary task is helping us kill Emperor Yamueto. Do you understand?"

Night Creature Lueti nodded.

Yxe cautiously poked her. She stared at him, unmoving. Not blinking. He shivered.

"Right," Itehua said, giving the night creature an unsettled look. "What's the plan?"

"Sava and I burned down the behemoth stables, the granary, and at least one barracks. We stole these while we were at it." Neta handed out the extra spears she'd carried on her back, while Athicha reclaimed their bow and quiver. "And we released the behemoths, which should slow them down if we fail."

"Why not kill them?"

Xopil made a noise of protest while Neta said, "Not enough time."

"Whatever," Itehua said. "Let's find the emperor and—"

"Get our asses kicked again?" Sava interrupted. "We surprised him the last time, and it didn't work."

"What else are we supposed to do? We're never going to get a better chance!"

Athicha clapped to draw attention, then signed. Sava translated: "'I think our mistake was that he was surrounded by bodyguards. We have to pull him away from them.' Athicha's right, but what if he makes another deal with Death?"

"He has to run out of things to trade eventually," Khana pointed out.

Neta pondered for a moment. "Haz is still glowing a little. Khana, does he have enough to share with the rest of us? Give us a little extra strength? Or at least a buffer against other witches trying to drain us."

She considered. "For all of us? No, I don't think so. But there's a lot of people and livestock between us and the emperor."

Catching a small group of soldiers was easy. A quarter of a mile from the lord's house, a dozen foot soldiers surrounded a well, filling buckets to deal with the burning granary. As distracted and frantic as they were, it was easy for Khana to slip in alone and drain them – just to unconsciousness. When the others joined her, she gave each of them enough so that they all glowed like a star cluster, including Lueti.

Khana led the march into town. Neta wanted to wait at the noble's house for Yamueto to come to them, allowing the unit to set up the battlefield a little better to suit them. But when Khana pointed out how Yamueto didn't hesitate to draw âji from slaves, servants, or any of his other citizens, and how much he could accumulate before reaching them, she relented.

So, they were going to him.

The townsfolk thankfully stayed well out of their way. Most soldiers who spotted them either ran off or ignored them, likely believing them witches. A small handful of soldiers did approach, probably fooled by the Reguallian armor worn by most of the Poison Darts. But by the time they got close enough to realize their mistake, Khana drained them to unconsciousness, dividing the âji among her friends.

She swallowed, looking away from Lueti's walking corpse to her feet. "I'm sorry I couldn't get Yamueto earlier. I've dragged you all into this mess."

Athicha snorted.

Sava wrapped an arm around her. "You're not dragging anyone anywhere we don't want to go."

"Yeah," Haz piped up. "I, for one, would love to punch that jackass in the face before going home. And I *need* to steal at least one of those behemoths for a ride."

"It was fun," Xopil said, grinning.

Yxe hiccupped. "Right. Fun."

Neta nudged her. "Soldiers don't fight alone. This emperor has hurt all of us. We do this together."

Athicha signed something. They must've asked what the plan was, because Neta explained, "Khana gets up close for the kill. The rest of us: bear tactics. Don't get within breathing distance."

"And for those of us who don't have spears?" Haz asked, twirling his knife.

"Find one."

They reached the night creature barracks. The building was still on fire, and Khana couldn't hear any animalistic shrieking. She didn't see any bodies outside, but she smelled roasting flesh.

Yamueto stood in front of the burning stables, tapping his foot as he watched his men pour buckets of water and dirt onto the flames. He finally noticed them when some of the soldiers stopped momentarily to stare, then jolted back into action.

The emperor turned slowly on his heel to face them. He raised an eyebrow at Khana, first, then at Haz. "Really? You could've bargained for anything, and you asked for him back?"

"I'm irresistible," Haz deadpanned. He brushed shoulders with Khana, offering his strength and courage as always.

And she... didn't need it. Not anymore. Yamueto stood backlit by the fire, dressed in black silks making him look ten feet tall, as immovable and untouchable as ever. But she didn't see the unstoppable emperor she always cowered from. She wasn't sure what had changed. Maybe it was his sheer disbelief at why she'd choose to save her friend above all else. But she decided that what she saw in front of her was a pathetic person who had sold himself for scraps of power. Power that he would now lose.

Yamueto's eyes drifted to Lueti. "At least you have the sense to not trade more than you need to."

"Haz," Yxe called. He'd broken off from the group to collect one of the spears that the soldiers had dropped in favor of buckets. He tossed it to him.

Yamueto's mouth twitched the barest imitation of a smile. "Well. I need to kill some time before this fire burns down, anyway."

He pointed to a group of soldiers. "You three. On me, now."

"Don't do it!" Khana warned as they stepped forward. "He's going to kill you."

She didn't know why she expected them to hate him as much as she did. One of them sneered at her. "We would gladly give ourselves for the emperor."

Sava fired an arrow, hitting Yamueto in the shoulder. Khana charged before the soldiers could get to him, intent on taking him out first. The soldiers ran to intercept, triggering her unit to intercept *them*, and it dissolved from there.

Khana tackled Yamueto to the ground and fell into the familiar rhythm of trying to steal his life force while he tried to steal hers. Yxe flipped a soldier over his shoulder and onto Itehua's spear while Xopil picked up and threw a man into the burning building. Neta, Lueti, and Haz helped establish a perimeter around Khana and Yamueto so no one could get in to help, and Sava and Athicha shot anyone who got close.

Yamueto's hand wrapped around Khana's throat, choking her, preventing her from breathing. Âji poured into him from her, more quickly than any other witch she'd dealt with, and his enhanced fingers began crushing her windpipe.

She grabbed the arrow in his shoulder and twisted, digging into his flesh. He hissed, the drain of life force slowing as his pain grew. She twisted harder.

He kicked out her legs and brought her down, choking her on the ground. Khana tried to throw him off, but he wouldn't budge. Her skin had almost completely stopped glowing.

The tip of a spearhead poked out of Yamueto's chest, splattering Khana's face with blood. He gasped in pain, loosening his grip on Khana's neck.

She gulped in air, dizzy and lightheaded. Neta twisted the spear before pulling it out and dancing away.

Yamueto's âji healed the wound immediately, and he whipped around to go after the serji. Khana grabbed his ankle and tripped him, breathing in hard. Neta jabbed him again, this time in the other shoulder.

He snatched her spear away and broke it. Swearing, Neta drew an axe from her belt, stepping away from the emperor, closer to the soldier she couldn't see sneaking up behind her.

Khana pulled Yamueto back at the same time Itehua called: "Serji, behind!"

Neta spun around and blocked the soldier's sword with her axe in the nick of time. Lueti came to help her, docile as a lamb but vicious as a snake as she sliced open the back of his ankles.

"Watch Khana! I have no spear!" the serji ordered.

Yamueto kicked Khana in the face. Her nose crunched under his boot but healed quickly before her head hit the ground again.

Towering above her, Yamueto made a great target for Haz and Lueti, who threw their spears at the emperor's chest. One missed, but the other went through at least one lung and stayed there. He spat and coughed blood, wrapping his hands around the weapon.

Khana scrambled to her feet. A soldier rushed Haz, but he caught the man's arm with glowing hands. Even with the chaos of the fire and the shouting and Khana's own ragged breathing, she could hear the snap of the unfortunate soldier's bones.

Yamueto pulled out the spear, coughing up more blood even as the wound healed, only to be hit with an arrow. Athicha notched a new one, changing tact quickly to fire at a soldier racing toward them and Sava.

Yamueto yanked the arrow out of his gut with a growl, dropping the shaft as the wound healed. Khana found and scooped up an abandoned knife. *Not great, but better than nothing.*

He lunged at her with the spear. Khana pivoted and stepped inwards, trying to get within striking range. Yamueto flicked his wrists, and the spear darted to the side, nicking her in the arm. She grabbed it just under the tip with a hiss, trying to wrestle it away from him. This far apart, they couldn't get each other's life force.

"Why would you want this?" she asked. "I never wanted a fight. I don't want revenge. All you had to do was leave. Me. Alone."

Yamueto pulled at the spear. Khana kept it in her grip, refusing to let go. "You, this world, *everything* is mine." He said, like he was stating the fact about gravity.

"Not anymore."

Xopil screamed.

Khana looked up. The man had taken a hit to the side and dropped to a knee. The injury healed, but he stopped glowing. The soldier who stabbed him raised his sword again, and Xopil was barely able to get his spear up in time, almost crumbling under the blow.

Haz was busy with another soldier; Itehua and Yxe were back-to-back, swarmed by foes. Neta's glow was almost out, yet she still battled two soldiers with her axe. Lueti was closest, but unarmed and busy stopping another soldier attacking the serji. Sava tried to shoot an arrow, only for a soldier to swing a sword at him. The bowstring snapped, rendering it useless. Athicha fired off a shot to help Xopil, just as another soldier tackled them to the ground, sending the arrow flying off-target.

None of them would be able to get to Xopil in time.

Yamueto studied her. "Decisions, decisions."

Khana still had her knife in hand, but she'd never been good at throwing them.

So, she chose the easier target. She threw the blade at Yamueto, startling him enough that he loosened the grip on his spear even as he was only hit by the handle, not the blade. Khana yanked the spear out of his hands, twirled it, and threw it at Xopil's attacker.

She went too low, only grazing the man's thigh. It still made him yelp and pull back, giving Xopil enough time to surge up and bury his spear in his gut.

Yamueto slammed into Khana, and white-hot agony exploded in her chest. He had hold of her knife and twisted it between her ribs.

"Khana!" Sava screamed.

It was a surreal moment of numbness, pain, and clarity, as Khana realized that they weren't going to win. The âji she'd given her friends had almost vanished, Yxe and Sava the only ones still visibly glowing. They'd racked up several Reguallian bodies, but already reinforcements pooled in from town, their armored bodies swarming the streets like beetles.

Yamueto put a hand on her shoulder, pressing her down. She dropped to her knees. He knelt next to her. "This has been fun," he said coolly. "But I've killed hundreds of people more skilled than you, with far more gumption."

Haz brought down his attacker with a kick to the gut and sprinted to them.

Khana's breath rattled weakly as her lungs filled with blood. Haz's fingers brushed against her shoulder. "Death…"

Yamueto's eyes widened. "Vigerion–"

"I wish to trade."

Chapter Sixty-Eight
Neta

This isn't going well, Neta thought, getting to her feet. She could see Yamueto and Khana entangled out of the corner of her eye, but if she ran in without a spear, she would be drained completely.

Athicha – barely glowing – rolled on the ground with a Reguallian soldier, unarmed and gritting their teeth. Neta dashed over to help, burying her axe in the back of the soldier's head. Athicha rolled the corpse off them and jumped back to their feet.

"Khana!" Sava screamed.

Neta twisted. The emperor had shoved a knife in Khana's chest and dropped her to her knees.

Neta readied her axe for a throw, only for something cold to pierce through the weak point in her armor, just under the armpit.

The cold turned to agony as the soldier twisted the spear he'd shoved into her chest.

Furious – at herself, at the emperor, at this *fucking soldier* – Neta grabbed the spear with her other hand and, ignoring the pain, turned so she could drive her axe right into the soldier's face.

The blade cut through bone and flesh. The handle slipped from her hands as the corpse dropped, and she fell with it.

Athicha caught her, the whole thing happening so fast. Neta wheezed, unable to draw a full breath, the pain fading out into numbness.

Right in the heart, she realized. *Not bad, for a grunt.*

Athicha shook their head, eyes wet, but Neta couldn't say or sign anything before she breathed her last.

Chapter Sixty-Nine

Everything around them froze and darkened.

The pain vanished. Khana stepped out of her body, grimacing at the blood she could just barely see drench her shadowy chest. Suspended in time, she took a second to look over her friends. Athicha huddled over the still, bloody form of Neta.

Please just be injured, Khana prayed.

"You'll all be dead in two minutes."

Khana startled. She and Yamueto had called upon Death at the exact same time, and his spirit stood next to hers, watching over the fight as she did.

But what was more shocking was how his spirit looked. While Khana herself was a swirl of vibrant and muted colors in the spirit world, Yamueto was little more than shades of gray.

"You should have kept that life force to yourself," he said. "You could have punched right through my ranks."

"Then all my friends would be dead, and you probably would've killed me, anyway," she countered.

"So?"

She shook her head.

"Uh... where are we?" Haz's spirit stood in the middle of the darkened spirit world, looking around wide-eyed. He was a blur of color, more so than Khana.

Yamueto gave a tired sigh. "You touched her as she entered the spirit world, so you got pulled along."

Haz glanced down at their darkened bodies, the shadow of the burning building and battle raging around them, and smirked. "Charming. Do you think we can build a summer home here?"

Movement caught her eye. Death, appearing as the old man Vigerion, raised their lantern high. They looked between the three of them, flickered into Tsermayu, then morphed into wearing their multi-colored robe. "Well. This is awkward."

"I demand life force," Yamueto said. "Enough to finish this impudent creature off once and for all."

"Demand, hm? My, have you gotten arrogant in your old age." Death turned to Khana and Haz. "And you two. Back so soon?"

She gave a sheepish smile. "I was wondering if you could kill the emperor for me?"

Yamueto raised an eyebrow.

"Unfortunately, no," they said. "I *am* death, but I don't *cause* death."

Shoot. Khana scrambled to think of a backup plan, which was made more difficult by the fact that she hadn't had an original plan in the first place.

"Life force," Yamueto demanded.

Haz glared at him. "That's *Death*. Or Tsermayu, or whatever they prefer to be called. Maybe be a little more polite?"

"When I'm done with my disobedient concubine, I'll kill you again. *Slowly.*"

"What could you possibly have left to trade, Yameuto?" Death asked, more curious than anything else.

"I have centuries worth of memories."

The deity touched Yamueto's forehead with a pale finger and tsked. "*Weak* memories, all blurring together with no emotion and barely any life to them. You gave up the memories of your favorite concubine for that last piece of life force, and that was the best you had to offer."

Khana's hand went to her trophy necklace. "How much âji would my memory of glass diving give me?" she asked.

Death moved past Yamueto and touched her forehead. "More than enough to heal the hole in your chest. A little extra to fight some more."

She squashed down the feeling of guilt and tried not to look at Haz. That was the day the Poison Darts had truly become a unit. The day she'd begun to realize that she could trust these people. It was the start of their friendship. And she was giving up that memory.

Emperor Yamueto sputtered. "You would give her the gift of saviza for something so – so plebeian?"

"Plebeian to you, perhaps," Death said. "But from her, it's very significant."

"Hardly the only one," Khana agreed. It was a precious memory, despite how terrifying it'd been at the time. She was giving up a prized jewel, of course. But she had a whole chest full of others, with the promise of several more to come.

"No god will be agreeing with *you* over *me*," Yamueto insisted. "I am an emperor. Immortal. Divine! You're nothing but desert scum. A minor, insignificant noble. *Barely* a royal. *Blessed* with the opportunity to live in my court."

Khana stared at him. Not because of what he said, but because he had shown more emotion in the last minute than she had ever seen from him or heard of him displaying. Haz gave a low whistle.

Death nudged her. "This happens so many times with rich, powerful mortals. All those years with people kissing their feet, they forget that they're no more special or important than the next bag of meat and bones. It's really quite fascinating."

"Then we have a deal?" Khana asked.

"No!" Yamueto snapped, and shoved Death away.

Death exploded in blinding light and colors, sounds and smells. Khana grabbed Haz, the two of them covering each other as she squeezed her eyes shut against the blood reds and pus yellows and black depths. She still heard everything: the earth shattering, bringing down buildings atop of screaming civilians; soldiers clashing and yelling and killing each other; a sigh of relief from a weathered, old throat accompanying a broken, sickly whisper of, "Finally." The stench of blood and dirt, smoke and sugar, piss and medicine assaulted her nostrils.

When silence and sterility finally returned, after the three of them had experienced hundreds of deaths in the span of seconds, Khana cracked open an eye.

Death stood in their usual form, arms crossed, giving a visibly shaken Yamueto a disappointed look. The emperor trembled.

Death beamed at Khana. "To answer your question: yes, we have a deal."

Haz had Khana in a vice grip. He let go with one hand to hold up a finger, squeaking, "Question: is it possible for you to take one of *my* memories instead, while still giving that rabala to Khana?"

"No," Yamueto said, voice cracking. He cleared his throat, and managed to look a little smug, "No, that won't work. I tried it myself."

"No, you *ordered* them to trade parts of themselves for your own benefit," Death corrected. "These deals must be made freely, with informed consent. Haz is quite willing, and Khana will receive the amount of life force that equals the intensity of the memory."

"You don't have to do this," Khana warned him.

"Pretty sure that's the point," Haz said with a grin. "You've given up enough. Too much, actually. It's only fair. And you know if any of the other Poison Darts were here, they'd make the same deal. Because we need *you* to save *all* of our asses."

Yamueto scoffed.

Haz ignored him. "Would you be mad at me if I gave up the memory of when you first told off Bhayana?"

"Not at all," she promised.

"He's not even a witch," Yamueto argued. "Deals with Death are performed by witches."

"Only traditionally," Death pointed out, shrugging.

"Exactly. Tradition is just pressure from dead people," Haz added. Then he paused, turning to Death. "Oh. Wait."

Khana looked around Haz's shoulder at Yamueto. Really looked. "Why are you even doing this?"

"I am emperor," he insisted. "I am the first witch in a thousand years to contact Death and bend it to my will–"

Death barked a laugh.

"– and this world will bow to my whim."

"Right," Khana said slowly. "But why? You already gave up your best memories. Your compassion, passions, and everything else that makes life worth living. Yes, you're immortal, but I want you to honestly tell me: what is the point?"

Yamueto opened his mouth. Closed it.

"I knew you were going to kill me that day," Haz interjected. "And while I wasn't thrilled about it, I still fought you because I care about my friends and family and town. They're what make life worth living. So why would I get rid of the part of me that cares about them to put off dealing with *this*," – he waved his hand at Death – "for a little while longer?"

"I have remade history," Yamueto growled. "I have reshaped the world. I am above such petty, tiny insignificances like yourself and your pathetic life."

Khana shook her head. "Yamueto, you live the most pathetic life I have ever seen."

"And it ends today," Haz said gleefully.

"Better men have tried and failed," Yamueto promised. "Entire *armies* have tried and failed."

"But not poison dart frogs!"

Yamueto blinked. "What?"

"You'll see." Haz held out his hand to Death. "We have a deal?"

Smirking, Death took his hand.

Khana blinked, and the world exploded back into color, sound, and pain. The knife was still in her chest, tearing her lung and filling it with blood. Her breaths were wet and ragged. Xopil's shrill whistle cut through the howls of dying men and cackle of burning buildings. Yxe punched a glowing fist clean through a soldier's chest. Sava called Khana's name. Yamueto knelt next to her on her right, Haz's hand fully hitting her shoulder on her left.

Âji flooded through her veins, more than she'd ever carried at once.

Yamueto still held the knife's handle. He tried to drive it sideways along her chest, to more vital areas, and breathed in.

But he suddenly hit the ground, tackled sideways by Sava, who rolled off and out of breath's reach.

"Back off! She has it!" Haz ordered, stepping away.

Khana plucked the knife free from her chest, letting the wound close and the blade drop. Before Yamueto could stand, she bent down, grabbed his throat, and squeezed, cutting off his air and magic.

"You," she said, tightening her grip on his neck, "are nothing."

His eyes bulged. He struck at her arms, but it was like getting hit by a fly.

Gripping his neck with one hand, she drove her nails into the flesh just below his chin. Blood rained down her arms as her fingers pierced through skin, sinew, and bone. With a *snap*, she tore his head from his body and watched the torso slump into the bloody grass

The Immortal Emperor was dead.

Chapter Seventy

A strange sense of numbness settled over Khana as Yamueto's blood soaked the ground. The fighting gradually stopped as everyone realized what had happened. The unit carefully stepped away from the Reguallians, circling around Khana. Except Sava, who went forward to a huddled Athicha. His face blanched when he saw who his friend cradled.

"He'll come back," a Reguallian declared, breaking the silence. "The emperor will return."

"He's descended of the gods," another agreed.

Khana laughed, feeling light and airy. Because it didn't matter that Lueti and Neta were dead. She had a workaround. "Death doesn't care."

Xopil whistled again, like one would for a horse.

Khana hauled herself to her feet, exhausted, but knowing that they weren't out of danger yet. If they didn't leave now...

A behemoth roared, flying over their heads and landing a little way from the fire. *Their* behemoth. Xopil whooped and rushed over, petting the night creature's scarred pelt with a coo. "Good boy. Oh, you're such a sweetheart! You came when I called!"

Haz choked. "Right. Sweetheart."

"Poison Darts, we're leaving," Sava ordered. "Athicha, come on, you can carry her..."

With the behemoth and witch, the Reguallians shied away, keeping wary eyes on all of them. Yamueto's head dangled from Khana's fingers. She held it up for them to see. "For anyone wondering, Haz and I struck a deal with Death – Vigerion, Muobra, Tsermayu, whatever you want to call them. They gave me the power, knowing what I'd do with it. Yamueto will never return."

The unit mounted their flying steed, thankfully still saddled. Khana lingered last, daring the soldiers to attack. None did.

"He'll come back," was all one of them said.

She bared her teeth. "Then we'll just kill him again."

Yxe lost whatever had remained in his stomach over the side of the poor beast as they flew. Khana could see Haz smiling, right behind her, but his joy was dimmed. Lueti was still a night creature, and Athicha had Neta's bloodied body laid over their legs.

They reached Pahuuda just as the sun rose. By then, Khana was ready to fall asleep in the saddle, despite the multiple layers of blood dried into a crusty shell over her skin and clothes. She roused herself as the behemoth circled the town, causing everyone below to come out and ready their weapons.

Sava whistled, some complicated pattern that turned all the military coordination into cheering. "All right, Xopil, put us down."

He did, with about as much grace as the last time, on his own farm. The sudden landing almost threw them from the saddle.

Tlastisti gaped at them from her door. "What on earth?"

"Honey, we got a new pet!" Xopil cheered.

"No!"

"Yes!"

"Xopil!"

"He's a sweetheart!"

Tlastisti buried her face in her hands. The rest of the town poured out of their homes, running to the fields to see. Chief Phramanka and Thriman pushed their way through the crowd, as did several other Old Families. The chief's face melted with relief when she saw Sava.

As the unit stumbled off the behemoth, Khana hollered, "I need the families and loved ones of Neta Cituva and Lueti, right now!"

"Why?" Phramanka asked.

"Because they're dead, and I need to bring them back."

That caused a spur of whispers and shouts. Sava and Haz also protested while Athicha looked hopeful. Khana silenced them all by throwing Yamueto's head at the chief's feet. "The emperor is finished, and I know how to revive the dead. Fully. But there is a cost, and it's one I cannot bear alone."

She explained her deals with Death to the crowd. By the time she was done, the townsfolk had grown considerably. She was interrupted once by a woman screaming and running to Neta – her mother. Athicha and Sava let her cradle her daughter but calmed her down enough to let Khana finish what she was saying. Heimili also made his way through the crowd, latching onto Haz as soon as he saw him. She doubted he heard a word she said, but that was fine.

"...accepted *Haz's* sacrifice instead of mine," she concluded. "Which means I can bring someone back. But I cannot slice off parts of my own soul anymore. I will need someone else to make a sacrifice."

Varisa wiped her face. "What do you need from me?"

"Either a great passion, or however many years of memories Neta's been alive..."

"Do it."

Athicha snapped their fingers, stopping Khana in her tracks. They signed something, and Haz's jaw dropped. "Oh, shit, yeah. They might let us do that!"

"Do what?" Khana asked.

"Athicha's asking if we can spread the deal. So instead of *one* person taking the whole brunt of it, we have a bunch of people take smaller hits," he said. "I mean, you brought me in there with you. Why not more?"

"That's definitely worth a try," Phramanka declared, her first words since Khana began her explanation. "We'll start with Neta, then your other fallen comrade."

Unsurprisingly, all the Poison Darts volunteered, as did Athicha, Sava, Varisa, and Heimili.

A few people glanced at Athor Cituva. He shook his head. "I'm not meddling in Tsermayu's affairs. That's not natural."

"Coward," Heimili accused.

"I'm not!"

Any other protest was quelled when Phramanka herself joined the pile. Thriman then squeezed his way through the mini crowd to join his wife and son. "So, we just touch Khana, and she drags us to this shadow realm?" he asked.

"Theoretically, yes," she said.

It was awkward and crowded. Several people had to crouch or even lie on the cold, muddy ground to get to her. All four limbs, the front and back of her torso, and the top of her head were covered in hands.

Closing her eyes, she whispered, "Death, we wish to trade."

Chapter Seventy-One
Sava

Sava was gob-smocked when the world plunged into gray darkness while everyone around him exploded in light.

Haz whooped. Everyone who had been lying or kneeling stood, unnerved as they left their own bodies.

Sava had lived in Pahuuda his whole life, had seen it in glittering daylight and the darkest of nights. But he'd never seen it like this, in muted shadows while everyone's bodies were reduced to frozen shades. He waved a glowing pale blue hand over his own darkened face.

This is what I'll see when I die, he realized.

"You get used to it," Khana assured him.

Phramanka snorted, poking her own body. "Really?"

"No."

A woman crooned, "Well. I haven't had to deal with something like this in quite a while."

Everyone stilled. Khana had described Death as a shapeshifter who usually came to her in a multi-colored dress. But now, they appeared as Tsermayu, an ink-skinned woman whose dress was the night sky, a crown of stars, fish, and coral floating around her indigo head. She seemed to float, her dress and hair billowing around her as if she was underwater.

The Ghura did not kneel or bow. But that was what one did for a goddess, right?

Sava and everyone else stood half-frozen, staring at the goddess in awe and trepidation, trying to figure out what to do.

Khana strode forward with casual confidence. "We have a proposition."

Athicha anxiously tapped their foot. Sava gripped their arm, hoping that their all-too-familiar agony would end in just a few moments.

Khana explained their idea. Tsermayu pondered it. She tipped her head to the others. "They aren't witches, which means there's not much wiggle room I can squeeze through. Whatever collective total they offer must equal a full human soul, not a part of it like you did with Haz. Who are we bringing back?"

"Neta Cituva," Khana said. "And I'll also need the life force to heal her injuries."

Tsermayu paced, disappearing briefly from Sava's view with Khana blocking them. When she came out, she looked *exactly* like Neta, down to the leopard cloak. Except her eyes were all black and had only a fraction of her intensity. "This one?"

"That's it."

"She specifically told me that you were not to trade any part of yourself for her. That if you did, she would refuse to return. I must honor that."

Damn it, Neta, Sava thought.

Varisa choked, but Khana smiled. "All right. *I* won't trade anything."

Tsermayu grinned with Neta'a face. "I love it when you humans find loopholes. All right, then. What are we trading?"

There was a long, awkward pause as Sava and everyone else realized that they hadn't actually thought this far ahead.

Khana dropped her face in her hand, muttering about how they should've planned this better. Tsermayu chuckled. "No rush. Time is frozen here."

"Memories or passions, goddess?" Phramanka prodded. "The more intense and emotional, the better?"

"I also accept emotions themselves, although taking one usually means taking its opposite. You can't have joy without sorrow, after all."

Sava wracked his brain. He knew he had several options: all of his memories of Myrta, his passion for music, his love of Pahuuda… but parting with any of them sent a lance through his chest. Next to him, Heimili ran a hand down his face, scratching his beard in thought.

"Fuck. This is *hard*," Itehua muttered.

It shouldn't have been, right? Logically, the choice was easy. But being forced to pick which parts he could slice off and still be *himself*…

Sava looked at Khana, her soul slightly dimmer than the rest of them. Missing pieces of herself for their sake. How did she do this so often?

"Maybe I can give my love of animals," Xopil suggested.

Itehua snorted. "Now that we have a behemoth in town that only you can keep in check?"

"Oh. Right…"

"It's too much of a part of you," Tlastisti agreed.

"When I traded a memory, Khana agreed to tell me what I gave up," Haz offered. "So, if you're going that route, I'd recommend something that someone else can tell you about."

Not a bad idea...

Yxe tugged on his wool hat, then went up to Tsermayu and muttered something to her. Khana, nearby, hissed. "You don't want to give up fear, Yxe. That keeps you alive."

"Not all of it!" he squeaked, then ducked his head when he realized he had a lot more people's attention. "Just... uh... public speaking? Please, goddess, ma'am?"

Tsermayu raised a finger and touched Yxe's forehead. She chuckled. "Yes, from you that would be quite the offer."

Sava straightened. "We can give emotions about a *specific thing*?"

Tsermayu looked at him with Neta's face. "Yes, if it's intense enough."

"And... we won't lose our *memories* of it?"

"Not unless you want to."

Well, that made this *much* easier, even if it made him feel guilty.

Sava replaced Yxe. "I still have feelings for a dead woman. Will they be acceptable?"

"Sava, no," Khana protested. "That type of thing makes you who you are."

His chest warmed at her concern. "I have to bury her eventually, Khana."

Tsermayu tapped his forehead, frowning. "You already are. There's only about another couple of years of life left in them. Less."

"Are they acceptable?"

She nodded. "You'll remember Myrta but feel nothing for her."

Athicha pulled him away, signing, *You certain?*

Sava thought about Myrta's wide smile, the way her singing voice would go wobbly and off-tune when she got drunk, their first kiss in a snowbank. His next breath was shaky. "You know she'd want this. She's gone. And if she knew her ghost was keeping us from living our lives, then she'd find some way to come back with or without a witch just to kick our asses."

Athicha's eyes watered. They pulled Sava into a hug.

"Thank you."

Sava almost jumped at hearing his friend's voice. He shouldn't have been surprised, though. This was a spirit realm. Physical scars, even those that stole a person's voice, would mean nothing here.

One by one everyone else came to their decision. Most of the Poison Darts agreed on some combination of memories: Itehua's first fight with Neta the day they met Haz's first battle. He waffled between that and his whole experience with Bhayana but elected to keep those memories of abuse "so I know what to look out for next time."

Phramanka and Thriman, after a bit of discussion, swapped memories: she giving up their first few weeks of their courtship and he giving up the bumbling weeks of flirting leading *up* to that. Tlastisti gave up a two-year period where Xopil took care of an aging tortoise (it was apparently the first time he'd cared for an animal and it left an impression), while Xopil offered the day he got stabbed and accidentally revealed Khana's witchcraft.

Athicha offered their passion for carving. *Not* snow-sculpting, but carving solid materials such as wood, bone, and ivory. Heimili gave up his hatred of Bhayana, after confirming with Haz that she was dead.

Sava drifted to Khana and squeezed her in a hug. "I'm sorry. I hope you never have to make another decision like this again."

She snorted, and he knew that hope was futile. But for now, with what they were all doing here, they could push that day off further.

Varisa was last. She asked, "What's left?"

The goddess thought for a moment, and Neta's form shifted and flared with dozens of colors and lights before settling back down. "I'll need either five years' worth of strong memories or a very intense passion or emotion. Especially if you want the life force Khana needs to heal your daughter's injuries. They were extensive."

The businesswoman pondered those. "I've started a romance with a hunter named Rasku, but I wouldn't categorize it as a 'very intense passion or emotion…'"

Tsermayu poked her forehead and shook her head. "No. It has the potential for it, though."

"Then my time in the empire, before escaping the man my parents tried to sell me off to. However many years you need."

Tsermayu smiled. "That is more than enough."

Chapter Seventy-Two
Neta

Neta gasped awake, choking on blood and pain. A swirl of color blinded her, and as her wet breaths came easier she heard the chief's sharp order of, "Get back! Give her some air!"

It took a moment for the pain to end, her breathing to come easy, and for the colors to disappear. When they did, she saw Khana beaming down at her.

A second later, memories of dying in Athicha's arms slammed into her, and she scowled. "I *told* that bitch you weren't allowed to give up – oof!"

She was dogpiled by her mother, Athicha, Sava, and half of her unit, all while Khana laughed and protested, "I didn't! I didn't give up anything! They did! I swear."

Neta managed to claw herself free from the pile, though Varisa and Athicha didn't fully let go of her. She got up on a knee, getting her bearings. They were back in Pahuuda? And it was just past dawn. The behemoth Xopil had tamed napped on the field a few paces behind her.

"What do you mean?" she demanded.

"Athicha and Haz found a loophole," Khana said, grinning. "I off-set the cost to all those who volunteered to bring you back."

That… was a lot. Neta knew if she stopped to think about that for the time it deserved, she'd break down in tears, in public, so she pushed that aside for now.

"The emperor?" she asked.

"Dead. And not ever returning."

"Lueti?"

"We're reviving her next." Khana stood and held out a hand. "Want to help?"

Chapter Seventy-Three

Khana jerked awake, sweat and tears staining her fur and wool blankets, the ghost of hands on her skin.

"Really?" she snapped.

Next to her, Sava yawned and pushed himself onto an elbow. "Nightmares again?"

She grumbled swears. Apparently, she could kill Yamueto, but she couldn't kill her dreams.

"Sorry," she said, wiping her face with a sleeve. "Go back to sleep."

"Do you want–"

"No." She ran her fingers through his hair. "I just need a minute. Sleep."

He grumbled, lying back down.

It'd been two days since the battle. The first night, they'd slept in their own homes. She'd asked Sava to spend the second night with her. She didn't regret it, especially when it meant falling asleep in Sava's arms. But it did mean she had to grope for her clothes in the dying embers of the fire.

She found her dress by the lute case leaning against the wall. The joy and gratitude she used to feel whenever she saw it wasn't there anymore. Yesterday, she'd tried to play. The skills were still there; she could do the scales and play the most complex of songs. But that burning love, that need to express herself in the audio art, was gone. All that was left was apathy.

Modesty covered, she crept out of the room and shuffled downstairs. Dawn was still hours away, but she wasn't getting back to sleep tonight. She wanted tea and maybe some light to work on a bit of sewing.

She expected the kitchen to be dead at this hour, but a soft light came from the oven that led her through the dining hall.

"Haz?" she yawned.

He looked up from his teacup. "Couldn't sleep?"

She shook her head. She didn't bother asking him if he'd tried getting any rest. His rumpled sleep clothes and messy hair told her the attempt had failed.

"Was it Sava's snoring?" he teased, pouring her a cup of tea and sliding it across the counter.

"If he snores, it's quiet enough for me to sleep through it," she said, sitting on the stool next to him. "How insulted do you think everyone will be if I sell the lute and return their money?"

"Well, they get to see my charming face every day, so it all evens out," he said with a grin that quickly vanished. "I'm sorry. I still think you shouldn't have given that up."

She sipped her tea, letting the sharp flavors sink into her tongue. "It was hard. Music is what got me through Yamueto. It's one of the few things that kept me going, that gave me some bit of joy in my life. But while I think I'll always miss it, I don't need it anymore. Not since I came here."

He smiled. "I'm glad."

They drank tea, warming themselves by the fire.

"Why are you up?" Khana asked.

"Eh. Still thinking about the fact that I was dead for a while and then had to kill the woman I once loved," he said with faux casualness. "Also, I was pulled into a spirit realm I didn't even know existed to broker a deal with the entity of Death itself while telling off an emperor for making several bad life choices. Three times in a single day. And we just won a war. And my grandmother died this month. You?"

She shivered. "Nightmares. I thought that when I killed Yamueto, they'd be gone. But... apparently he never will leave me alone."

Haz slowly opened one arm, and when she nodded, gave her a half-hug. "Even after Bhayana and I broke up, I still woke up scared that I did something that would make her punish me. It takes a while to remind myself that that's not going to happen."

She rested her head against his shoulder. "Does it ever end?"

"I'll let you know if it does."

The town came to life as Khana prepared the dining room for lunch. A few customers waved to her, calling out greetings. A couple called out a friendly *good morning, witch* or even her name. Others avoided her altogether.

Well. You can't win them all.

It proved to be a slow day. Which was good, because the Poison Darts trickled in, Lueti being first. Her eyes were back to normal and sparkling with far too much energy for such a slow day. "Good morning, darling! Sleep well?"

"Well enough," Khana said, getting the tea.

"Did you hear? Pabu Pinnsviri finally passed away. They say the shock of his granddaughter's betrayal did him in."

Khana tried to scrounge up a bit of sympathy, but could only muster a trite, "May he rest in peace."

Lueti snorted. While the Poison Dart Frogs had, of course, all dived back into the spirit realm to negotiate with Death for her soul, they'd almost been unnecessary. Lueti had been in Pahuuda long enough that she had befriended and offered help to almost every whore – former and current – in town, and they'd been eager to pay her back.

Xopil came in next, face flushed red. "I figured out how to land without almost crashing!"

"Proud of you," Haz said drolly from the kitchen.

He had managed to convince Tlastisti – and the entire rest of the town – to keep the behemoth. Or at least make sure it didn't eat anything and any*one* that it shouldn't. Khana had scraped together what she remembered about predatory night creatures and guessed how much it needed to eat (a truly obscene amount every week), and Xopil took the beast out to hunt over the tundra, picking off elk and moose. The behemoth itself stayed in a cave in the mountains, about a two-hour hike from the town. Hunters had once used it as a rest stop, though that probably wouldn't happen anymore.

Sometimes Khana wished she had used her deals with Death to relieve herself of her memories in the imperial palace. But times like this reminded her why that was a bad idea. She was the closest thing to an expert on night creatures, Reguallian politics, and witchcraft that Pahuuda had. If the cost of that was a few nightmares and having to tell Haz how she'd first met Bhayana by playing the dumb immigrant girl, so be it. Those terrors were gradually dying, anyway.

Neta came next, with Athicha, Itehua, and Yxe, and finally Sava. Heimili waved Khana and Haz off as the Poison Darts (and honorary members) claimed their usual corner. Khana sat with a grateful sigh, leaning back on Sava.

"What are you going to do?" Lueti asked her. "Now that you don't have music?"

"I don't know," she admitted. Without the emperor on her heels, she no longer had to steal moments of joy while constantly running. Didn't have to run at all. It was bizarre.

"I was thinking of finding someone to teach me how to do tapestries," she said.

"Bo-ring," Itehua scolded.

"They are not! They're beautiful! And *someone* has to record everything that's happened." She was already trying to figure out how to accurately portray all the different colors of Death's dress. Or perhaps she should go with the Tsermayu depiction?

Sava tightened his grip around her. "Ma will tell you she's not the best at tapestries, but she can definitely get you in touch with people who are."

Pleased, Khana burrowed deeper into his chest. "Would you all be mad at me if I gave away the lute?"

"Not at all," Lueti promised. "In fact, one of the boys who offered to work for me knows how to play."

"One of the boys?" she echoed.

Lueti, Itehua, and Yxe grinned.

"We figured it out!" Yxe cheered. "There's a building for sale downtown. If the three of us pool our money together, we can buy it and turn it into our own business. We've already talked to the owner, and he's agreed!"

Khana squealed and hugged all three of them. Athicha gave a polite clap while Haz whooped.

"So you're all running it?" Neta clarified.

"*Lueti's* running it," Itehua corrected. "I'm security. Yxe's our treasurer."

"Does your mother know you'll be working in a brothel?"

"I'm a veteran soldier. I can handle a brothel," Yxe said, though his face turned pink. Apparently losing his fear of public speaking did not mean losing his sense of embarrassment.

The serji grinned. "They're going to eat you alive, boy."

"No, they won't! I can already say cock and vagina without blushing."

"Baby steps," Sava encouraged. "Are you doing anything with your money, Haz?"

He motioned to the inn. "Just giving it to my baba. We might get a few more wooden doors installed." He snapped his fingers. "That's what we should've done: we should've taken a bunch of wood from that town."

"Haz. We were fighting for our lives and assassinating an emperor," Khana retorted.

"And most of our fighting was in a *wooden* building!"

"You're welcome to go back there."

"Xopil? Care to fly me?"

The big man barked a laugh. "Not a chance."

"What about you, serji?" Lueti asked, getting everyone back on track.

Neta took a long draw from her horn of mead, letting the tension build. She smirked. "They're promoting me to midya."

All of them burst into cheers. Xopil hugged her, almost knocking her and Athicha over. "First Reguallian midya in Pahuuda! In all the mountains!"

Khana grinned. The Ghuran military wouldn't know what hit it.

"You're getting transferred back to Yellow Battalion next week," Sava promised.

"Why not stay with Red?" Khana asked.

"Blue and Yellow are the only full-time battalions. All others are made up of reserves and are disbanded during peacetime."

"And we all know Blue has the best soldiers," Haz complained. "So why isn't she with them?"

Sava grimaced. "Because the Old Family Masters threw a fit. Said all the Blue midya positions had already been held or promised to 'proper' Ghuran soldiers and there was no room for her."

Khana didn't know the sign Athicha made, but she would bet her boots that it was either *stupid* or *idiot*.

Neta held up a hand before Haz could get going. "I seem to recall that none of you were considered 'proper' Ghuran soldiers when we met."

That quelled them.

"I don't know who to pity more: the folks about to go through your training, or the other midyas when they realize you're going to gut them," Itehua commented.

"Pity my commanders, when I become *their* commander."

"Those assholes deserve no pity."

They continued to chat. Khana leaned against Sava and watched the unit celebrate, sipping her tea. Well, everyone but Neta, Xopil, Sava, and Athicha had been discharged, so she supposed they weren't a unit anymore. But they were her friends, practically her family at this point.

Watching all of them get excited about the future, she realized that she herself had a future she could look forward to. There was a place for her here. People who cared about her and who she cared about in turn. A future of joy and contentment and maybe some tragedy, but also healing and love.

She was home.

Fancy some more fantasy?
Check out
The Last Phi Hunter by Salinee Goldenberg

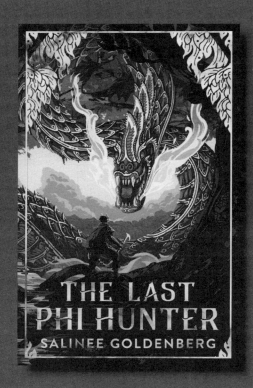

Read the first chapter here...

Chapter One
The Hunter

No two phi were ever alike, but every Hungry Ghost and demon in old Suyoram shared one thing in common – they had all been human once. And that made them more dangerous than any other creature, dead or alive.

Perched on a high branch of a chamchuri tree, Ex watched the kongkoi and prayed to the devas it would take the bait. The young phi hunter scarcely breathed, every muscle tensed, dark eyes steady beneath his fearsome khon mask, his body as still as the tree itself.

The Hungry Ghost took two tentative hops forward on his one foot, cat-ears flicking, owl-neck head twisting every which way. The pale grey-green flesh of its skin coiled and unwound around its throat in tandem with its nervous twitches.

Patience. Ex could almost hear his masters now. *Patience is one of our greatest weapons.*

But the second the phi entered Ex's range, it took every ounce of patience he had not to drop down and stab it with a real weapon. He'd been after this bastard for three days and nights, with no food or sleep, and about half of that time was spent here, in the Everpresent – the realm of spirits and magic that simmered between the threads of the physical world and the deva's.

For hunters, it was second nature to walk in the Everpresent. In there, colors were bright enough to taste – reds spicy, blues soothing, yellows sweet as sunbeams. Scents were read in history and motion – a trail one can follow, the age of spilled blood. Sounds were sharper. Ex could hear the sticky smack of spit in the phi's mouth, and the low, distorted hum of dark energy from his hiding spot.

Still, dipping in and out of the Everpresent like a starved koi fish took a toll on Ex's nerves. He ached for a hot meal and a warm bed, but most of all, he needed the coin to pay his dues. He'd be back to the guild soon and feared the wrath of the masters if he came up short. Again.

His fist tightened on the hilt of his chainblade as the kongkoi neared a pile of meat that had once been the fattest macaque in the forest. The phi bent down, its tubular snout twitching. Its tongue snaked out and flicked over the carcass. Sniffing again, the creature then jerked up, neck spinning all the way backward for whatever had alerted it. Ex rolled his eyes with a soft exhale and grit his teeth.

A moment later, the phi returned to the corpse, clearly deciding that whatever it heard wasn't worth giving up a fresh meal. The hairs on its ears relaxed, and with a satisfied grumble, it tore in, teeth first. This was the hunter's chance.

Ex leaned forward, bracing his feet against the branch.

A rustle in the canopy, then a quick movement caught the corner of Ex's eye. A troupe of monkeys were warily approaching, led by one as fat as the dead one below it. They stared at the slurping kongkoi, muttering amongst themselves. Then, the biggest, burliest female stared at the hunter, anger glinting in her dark eyes. Ex shook his head ever so slightly in a lame attempt to communicate that no, he was not the man who murdered her husband, but he was very sorry for her loss–

She screeched a high-pitched monkey scream, and they all scattered in a flurry of fur and squealing. The kongkoi's head snapped up. Mortal animals were of no threat to a Hungry Ghost, but then its gleaming yellow eyes locked onto the hunter's.

The phi screamed its namesake out loud. "Koi!" And Ex pounced.

Half a second late.

He missed the head but flattened the body. The pair wrestled together as the kongkoi's pathetic, twig-like arms slapped at him. Its arms were withered and useless, but the fact it had them at all meant there might be more things inside its body. Valuable things. A second skull? A parasite full of eyes and claws? A heart encased in ice?

As the kongkoi's hypothetical value increased, so did Ex's intrusive thoughts of shrimp bami noodles, spicy chili-basil fried fish, fermented quail eggs and rice, huanglai curry...

The phi gnashed its jaws, spewing chunks of its own disgusting meal on Ex's full-face mask. Its teeth caught the armored part of his forearm, near his elbow. One of the fastenings cracked, which excited the phi. It excited

Ex, too. Those teeth were decently sized, and phi teeth were always in demand.

Sensing blood, the kongkoi giggled and tried to rip the rest of the hunter's arm off. But Ex raised his other arm, the one holding his blade, and stabbed.

The sickly greying flesh of its thigh split open. It screeched in dismay, pressing its face against Ex's mask. But then it reared back as if it had been burned when it recognized the design, one that showed this human wasn't the average woodsman.

Hunter! The kongkoi's voiceless words surged through the Everpresent, fear crashing in icy waves. *Wait! This dead thing was not my doing–*

You know why I'm here, Ex returned.

Ex shoved his forearm further into the phi's mouth and against the ground, pressing all his weight down.

Hunter, it wasn't me! You are making a mistake! I will bring you to the real killer, let me go!

First rule of phi hunting – never make deals with a phi. They always lie.

Ex leaned in, snapping its jaw in half. The phi twitched once, then laid still.

Watching the glow leave its eyes, the second rule came to mind – Phi are deadliest after they die, make sure they bleed.

Most only died once, and some didn't bleed at all, but it was best practice to be patient. Hunters often waited hours, or even days during their hunts, so what was a few more minutes?

Ex figured it was less of a rule and more of a mantra, to remind them that these ghosts were once humans whose life choices led them into this karmic fate. It was okay to be brutal.

A yawn interrupted Ex's thoughts. Well, it had its chance to revive, and must have decided getting murdered over and over by a pissed off, ravenous phi hunter wasn't how it wanted to spend the rest of its miserable existence.

After a quick appraisal of its body parts, Ex concluded the real money resided in its foot, specifically the gnarled, yellow toenails that flaked when he tapped them. The village elder's reward for killing the ghost was fine too, but half of that would go to the guild. Any money he made from selling body parts went straight into his pockets.

"Koi!"

The sneaky phi kicked Ex with his over-sized foot and sent him flying. He smashed against a tree and flopped to the ground, covered in splintered bark. Delayed revival tactic. Not a bad move. Then it took off running like a one-footed jackrabbit.

Seeing that his blade was still sunk into its thigh, Ex rolled over in time to snatch the attached chain. The kongkoi zipped into the brush with an awkward gliding hop, dragging Ex along with it. Thick bushes with spindly branches whipped at him, and rocks scraped against his body. But the hunter held on, bouncing over muddy, mossy roots, scattering any nocturnal animals in their way.

Wrapping the chain around his hand, Ex pulled and inched himself towards the phi, cursing it with every pull.

Accept your fate, asshole.

Its head turned backward to stare at Ex in disbelief, broken jaw lopping around like a rooster's neck.

Please, hunter! The fear rose to terror, now piercing sharp like an icy breeze. *I vow I will never kill again! Spare me and I promise, I'll–*

Everyone's gotta eat.

They burst out of the thicket, and the kongkoi collided face-first into the iron-hard bark of a great teak tree, the corded trunk at least ten arm spans around. The momentum whipped Ex forward and he smashed into both tree and ghost.

If blades wouldn't kill it, magic would have to do.

The kongkoi squirmed like a trapped worm and gnawed at him, but it was pointless to bite with a broken jaw. Ex swiftly backhanded it, then pinned its leg to the ground.

Uttering in the voiceless tongue, words imperceptible to human or phi ears alike, he called upon the Smoking Palm of Anewan.

The edges of his fingers lit up like embers. With a blaze of dark red light, molten magic dripped down the kongkoi's leg and seared canyons into flesh and bone. The kongkoi wailed as Ex squeezed the spell, raising the intensity. The phi's kneecap melted and its leg severed into two, both pieces thrashing. Bright white blood poured out in one long rush that finally ended with a trickle, like an emptied bladder.

After catching his breath, Ex returned to the ordinary plane of awareness and the vivid Everpresent dissipated, leaving him in the dark. He cringed at the sudden roar of insects, and the tasteless air. It was always a bitter shock, returning to the ceaseless, mortal world, or what some hunters called the World of Men, the Long Day, the Veil, or his favorite, the Blinds.

After a quick chant of gratitude to the First Hunter for a bountiful harvest, Ex hummed as he went about his work, popping each of the kongkoi's eyes into a sack, coiling up the tongue into a jar, yanking each tooth from the gums, then shearing away skin and muscle in search of anything else of value.

Sadly, nothing much. He set aside the kongkoi's major organs and tossed the rest of the remains into a pile for the Hound – Ex's occasional hunting companion. He would appreciate the flayed skin, spindly bones, and noodles of sinew once he followed his nose to the kill.

Ex saved the kongkoi's bulging stomach for last, his good cheer withering. With a slow breath, his carving knife sunk into the swollen gut, carefully gliding around the edges. He peeled back the skin. And met the half-digested face of its last victim.

A small boy. Small enough for the kongkoi to swallow most of his head whole.

Gooey gut fluid pasted the boy's short hair to his pale forehead, his eyelids remaining closed in what could be mistaken as peace. The rest of the missing villagers stewed together in a confused jumble of splintered bones, mottled flesh, and twisted hair. Loose fingers grasped for nothing, teeth glittered like gems amidst the viscera. They were hardly recognizable as human, though he found bits of jewelry that might be used to identify some of them. Ex knew their loved ones would appreciate the closure.

As he parsed these small tokens from the mess, his chest boiled over with anger. How terrified that little boy must have felt when this monster cornered and chased him into the dark. All the residual terror of the victims soured the coagulated blood with the stench of fear, cold and heavy under his palms.

The third rule of phi hunting – exploit their fear. Hunters and phi are closer to one another than they are to the rest of the living world. These moments reminded him why, despite their monstrous habits, the phi did have fears. Most of all, they feared people like him.

Ex placed the child's head into a separate sack, then tossed the rest of the villagers' unrecognizable remains into the discard pile.

Maybe phi hunters mirrored their prey with their powers and spirit magic, but Ex had to believe he was still human in every other way. Even if others vehemently disagreed.